THE BULLET

Also by Iris Johansen
(in order of publication)

EVE DUNCAN SERIES

The Face of Deception
The Killing Game★
The Search
Body of Lies
Blind Alley★
Countdown★
Stalemate
Quicksand
Blood Game★
Eight Days to Live★
Chasing the Night
Eve
Quinn
Bonnie
Sleep No More
Taking Eve+
Hunting Eve+
Silencing Eve★+
Shadow Play+
Hide Away+
Night and Day
Mind Game★
Shattered Mirror
Dark Tribute
Smokescreen
The Persuasion★
★Starring Jane MacGuire
+Featuring Margaret Douglas

CATHERINE LING SERIES

Chasing the Night
What Doesn't Kill You
Live to See Tomorrow
Your Next Breath

KENDRA MICHAELS SERIES

(written with Roy Johansen)
"With Open Eyes" (short story)
Close Your Eyes
Sight Unseen
The Naked Eye
Night Watch
Look Behind You
Double Blind
Hindsight
Blink of an Eye

STANDALONES

The Ugly Duckling
Long After Midnight
And Then You Die
Final Target
No One to Trust
Dead Aim
Fatal Tide
Firestorm
On the Run
Killer Dreams
Pandora's Daughter
Silent Thunder (Iris & Roy Johansen)
Dark Summer
Deadlock
Storm Cycle (Iris & Roy Johansen)
Shadow Zone (Iris & Roy Johansen)
The Perfect Witness
No Easy Target (featuring Margaret Douglas)
Vendetta
Chaos

THE BULLET

IRIS JOHANSEN

GRAND CENTRAL PUBLISHING

NEW YORK BOSTON

Grand Central Publishing

Hachette Book Group

1290 Avenue of the Americas, New York, NY 10104

grandcentralpublishing.com

twitter.com/grandcentralpub

First Edition: June 2021

Grand Central Publishing is a division of Hachette Book Group, Inc. The Grand Central Publishing name and logo is a trademark of Hachette Book Group, Inc.

The publisher is not responsible for websites (or their content) that are not owned by the publisher.

The Hachette Speakers Bureau provides a wide range of authors for speaking events. To find out more, go to www.hachettespeakersbureau.com or call (866) 376-6591.

Library of Congress Cataloging-in-Publication Data has been applied for.

ISBNs: 978-1-5387-1319-8 (hardcover), 978-1-5387-0607-7 (large print), 978-1-5387-1317-4 (ebook), 978-1-5387-0666-4 (Canadian trade)

Printed in the United States of America

TR

10 9 8 7 6 5 4 3 2 1

THE BULLET

CHAPTER 1

NALAM PHARMACEUTICAL WAREHOUSE
MANILA, THE PHILIPPINES

Craaak!

The bullet came within an inch of Diane Connors's head before it buried itself in the crate beside her.

Shit! She had to get out of here.

Those bastards had taken her completely unaware. No warning. The two security guards were supposed to be gone another five minutes while they completed their rounds of the warehouse. She would have been gone if they'd just kept to their damn schedule.

She tucked her camera into her jacket, then grabbed a handful of manila files out of the file drawer before she bolted toward the steps leading to the back entrance, where the driver of the truck was waiting for her.

Another shot! This one hit the railing of the steps beside her and ricocheted into the wall ahead of her.

The guards were shouting now, and she heard them cursing and the sound of their boots on the wood floor behind her.

"Stop! I'll blow your head off!"

Why stop? He'd probably do it anyway, she thought desperately.

The Nalam security guards were notorious for not thinking twice about firing on anyone breaking into the property. She'd known that when she'd made the decision.

And they were gaining on her!

She ran faster. Her heart was pounding, threatening to jump out of her chest. The door for the parking lot was just ahead, beyond a row of cardboard cartons.

Two more shots!

She was at the door, jerking it open. The truck was outside in the lot several feet below her, but she didn't bother running down the metal steps.

No time.

She braced herself and then launched her body into the bed of the vehicle. She hit hard.

Pain!

Her shoulder...

"Go, Manos!" she shouted to the driver. "Get the hell out of here!"

Another bullet hit the metal cab of the truck.

She saw two uniformed guards standing at the spot from which she'd just leaped. They were aiming at her again.

But Manos had almost reached the gates.

Then they were through and on their way toward the pier!

There might be pursuit, but Manos had arranged to have a boat waiting for her. With luck, she'd be on the high seas by the time those guards reached the pier.

And so far, luck had been with her. Her hand slipped into her jacket pocket to make certain she still had her camera, then tightened on the manila folders she'd taken from the file cabinet. She'd gotten what she'd come for tonight. She hadn't been shot. She might have a broken or sprained shoulder, but she'd gladly accept that in exchange for making it to the boat.

Yes, luck was definitely with her, and she'd soon be on her way to Alon and the island...

HAKALI ISLAND
SOUTH SEAS

"Your shoulder's not broken," Alon said curtly. "Just a bad sprain. Better than you deserve. How did it happen?"

Diane flinched as he finished bandaging her shoulder. It just showed how angry he was that he wasn't being gentle with her. Alon Hakali was never anything but kind to her or anyone else with whom he came in contact. "The way you warned me it might happen. I got caught trying to steal the file on Kai."

Alon swore softly but his touch was suddenly no longer rough. "You're an idiot, Diane. You've come so far, and yet you'd risk everything to get those damn records? I told you to forget about them. They might not tell me anything."

"And they might tell you everything. You told me yourself that they were the only evidence left that might give you a hint of where Nalam stashed Kai. They were important." She tried to keep her tone light. "Because I knew it was only a matter of time before you went after those records yourself. They were sitting there in that office like bait for the tiger. Which probably is exactly what it was. Well, they didn't get you and they didn't get me. But there was no way I could forget them."

"And so you broke into that warehouse and tried to steal them. You could have gotten yourself killed. Those contractors who guard Nalam's properties don't hesitate to shoot first and ask questions later."

"I'd heard that, and I found out it was true," she said wryly. "But I'd already taken photos of the document and was on my way out of the warehouse when they started to shoot. They only managed to force me to duck a couple of bullets and then brace myself as I jumped into the back of the truck I had waiting." She smiled. "You would've been proud of me, Alon."

"No, I would've been terrified," he said soberly. "Nalam is a monster, and no one knows that better than I do. You might not have gotten shot, but that doesn't mean there won't be ramifications. They saw you tonight. That means I might be safer, but you won't. You knew that would happen, didn't you?"

"I thought there would be a possibility." She shrugged. "I hired Leo Manos to get me out of Manila. He's a professional, but someone might track him down. And there are so many super-duper surveillance gadgets these days, and Nalam certainly has the money to afford them in all his warehouses. I tried to avoid the cameras and disguise myself as much as possible. But one of his cameras might have caught me, and I'm not that good at disguises. Then there's trace evidence..." She made a face. "Yeah, I made a choice. But you shouldn't be so rude as to ignore what's important here." She reached into her backpack and pulled out her camera. "I brought you a gift." She handed it to him. "Now say, 'Thank you, Diane.'"

"Thank you, Diane." He cleared his throat. "Even though it's much more important to keep you safe than it is me. The first thing Nalam is going to do is find out what's missing and then figure out why and who might have done it. No one knew anything about you, but that will change, Diane. We both know that you shouldn't have done this. It was neither wise nor safe."

She chuckled. "Since when did my decisions ever reflect either one of those qualities? Now stop being so serious. I wanted to do it and it's done. I didn't take the file itself. I took photos of it and then took a handful of other files so he wouldn't know what I was after. It will be a while before the results catch up with me, so I'll have time to find a way to take the next step and maybe protect myself along the way." She got to her feet. "But not too much time. Consider it a goodbye gift. I'll be leaving your island tonight. It's not safe for you or your people if I don't." She stood looking at him. She had always thought him the most handsome man she had ever met. He was everything that was tall and strong and golden. He was of Polynesian descent, but that golden glow wasn't only genetic. It came from the soul within. She held out her hand to him. "Come and take a walk with me on the beach, Alon. I'm not sure when I'll be able to come back here, and I'll miss it."

"It's only a place, Diane." He took her hand and walked with her toward the veranda. "I thought I'd taught you that people are much more important than places."

"Oh, I might miss you, too." Her voice was unsteady as she added, "Remember that you're the best friend I've ever had, the mentor who taught me, perhaps even the father who was never there for me. But neither of us are that sentimental, are we?"

"You certainly try not to be. But actions speak louder than words." He smiled at her. "However, it would probably be less emotional for you if you told me where you plan on going after you leave here tonight. You do have a plan, I hope?"

"Of course, as much a one as I could throw together on the way here to the island. I'm even planning on asking someone to help me . . . if I can talk him into it."

"That sounds like you. Brilliant on research and creativity, not so good on keeping your head above water. Who are you planning on trying to persuade?"

She looked away from him into the scarlet of the sunset. It was beautiful and peaceful here, and soon there would be no peace in her life. She was leaving Alon, who had been her bedrock since the bad days, and going where no certainty existed. "You've heard me talk about him, but you've never met him. I'm going to Hong Kong." She didn't take her gaze from the sunset, which now seemed to be exploding with all the color and fire that her life held. "I'm going to see Hu Chang."

LAKE COTTAGE
ATLANTA, GEORGIA

"I'm glad to be back home," Eve murmured as she cuddled closer to Joe on the porch swing. Her gaze turned to the moon shining down on the lake, the trees of the forest surrounding it like dark protective bastions. Yes, that's how she'd always thought of the cottage. A serene bastion, a place to come back to and recover from all the battles of life. A place of healing, home, love, family. She felt as if she could reach out and touch it all at this moment. They'd only arrived here this afternoon and had been so busy settling in after the long trip that this was the first time she'd had the opportunity to really appreciate the fact that they were here at last. She glanced up at Joe. "We were gone too long. Africa was too far away. I know that job in Maldara was entirely my fault, and I can't be sorry that I accepted the chance to bring those poor kids back home to their families. But will you promise to remind me how I feel right now if I ever tell you I want to go any farther than to Michael's school for one of his soccer games?"

"You bet I will." He lifted her chin and kissed her. "Not that it will probably do me any good. We live in the real world, not some far-off planet. It's big and sometimes scary and you've never dodged facing it even when I've begged you to turn your back."

She frowned. "You've never begged me."

"Haven't I? Maldara came pretty close." He shrugged. "And I think you've forgotten a few of the other times because I let you forget. Maybe I couldn't bear to make you choose."

"What?" She sat up and looked at him. "What's this about? You'd always come first. You know that, Joe. After all the years we've been together, you'd better know that."

"But it wasn't always like that and perhaps I have a few lingering memories..." He suddenly threw back his head and laughed as he saw her expression. "Just thought I'd make this a moment to remember for both of us. I like the idea of you never wanting to leave here again."

"What lingering memories?"

He shook his head. "I was joking. I'm not going to go in that direction when you're so happy at being home. The only lingering memories I have are good ones that tell me what a lucky guy I am to have you and Michael back here again."

She settled down against him again. "Damn you. But it's funny you came up with that nonsense just now. Did something upset you? You haven't said practically anything since you and Michael got back from checking out the boathouse after dinner. Did you find something wrong there?"

He shook his head. "Just as we left it. I didn't expect anything else since I had the guys at the precinct check it out once a week from the time we left. Michael can't wait to get out on the water again. I told him we'd go right after breakfast tomorrow. Are you coming?"

"Probably not. I have several texts to answer that I put off while I was in Maldara." She wrinkled her nose. "The last one I received was a little pushy, so I imagine I'll be receiving a skull to reconstruct by FedEx sometime this week. I probably can't put it off."

"You'd be bored out of your mind if you didn't have something to work on. We both know it." He tilted his head. "But I don't like that it was pushy. Don't they realize you're probably the foremost forensic sculptor in the world and they should treat you with respect?" His lips tightened. "Maybe you'd like me to tell them?"

"It might not send the right signal if I sic the cops on them. Particularly not *my* cop." Her eyes were twinkling. "It might create an international incident. We keep having immigration disputes with Mexico." She added gravely, "And I wouldn't want to have to fly down there to make my apologies. My Spanish isn't that good."

"Mexico?" he asked warily.

She was chuckling. "And no, the job is not in Mexico. The government is just requesting my help with a reconstruction of the skull of a citizen found buried out in Nevada."

"Nevada." He made a weighing motion. "Mexico. I thought I might have to invoke the promise I made you. But I might be able to accept the wide-open spaces of Nevada."

"I don't know if I can. I'll probably just have them send the skull here and make my report." She threw her hand out in an expansive gesture that included the lake, the forest, and everything else in view. "Like I said, I've missed this, Joe."

"So have I." He was silent a moment. "I got a call from my captain when I was down at the boathouse with Michael. He's had a request from Quantico to lend me to them on a special service detail."

"That's happened before." But her smile was fading. "You have connections everywhere. You were FBI before you became a detective with ATLPD. Everyone knows how sharp you are, Joe."

"This sounded . . . different. I didn't get the impression it was a routine request." He grimaced. "And the last thing I want is to become involved with something that's going to take me away from you and Michael right now."

"Then tell them no," she said. "After all, I gave up Mexico for you. You can tell the FBI to get someone else, can't you?"

He nodded slowly.

Of course he could, Eve thought. But Joe was a former SEAL besides being ex-FBI and probably the most patriotic man she knew. It would never be easy for him to say no if his country needed him. He was as bound by his duty and code as she was by her own. "Okay, let's compromise. You talk to the FBI, and unless some sleazebag is going to blow up something irreplaceable, you stay home with Michael and me. Is it a deal?"

He grinned. "It's a deal."

"Good." She kissed him and got to her feet. "Then I'm going to go say good night to Michael. You go to bed and wait for me."

"Delighted." His brows rose quizzically. "Any particular reason?"

"I've got to make sure your judgment isn't clouded when you make that decision. I don't mind losing out to some scumbag terrorist if it's a fair fight." She headed for the porch door. "But I guarantee before this night is over, *all night*, you'll know you've been in a battle. You'll make sure that whatever the FBI wants you to do is worth it."

She heard him laugh as she closed the door behind her.

There was a lingering smile on Eve's own lips as she crossed the living room and started down the hall toward Michael's room. Laughter, love, family: The concepts existed wherever they were, but here there were also memories and that was precious. "Time for bed. Did you take your shower, Michael?" she called. "I heard you on the computer talking to Tomas before I went out on the porch. You have to remember there's a five-hour time difference from his hospital in Scotland."

"I took my shower before I got on the phone." He was sitting on his bed with legs crossed, dressed in his blue striped pajamas. She noticed that he was starting to outgrow them. He was only ten years old, but he'd had a growth spurt since she'd bought them four months ago. His mahogany-colored hair was slightly mussed, and he was grinning at her. "I didn't know how long it would take to get Tomas used to Skype. Neither he nor his mother have ever used computers before. But I thought it important they start right away. Isn't that right? They're going to be lonely now that we can't visit them for a while." He put his computer on his bedside table. "I told Tomas that Dad and I were going out in the boat tomorrow and that when he came to visit, we'd take him and his mom on the lake."

"That won't be soon," she reminded him quietly. "The doctors said it might take several surgeries before they'd release Tomas from the hospital." The reminder wasn't really necessary, she knew. It had been Michael who had been instrumental in helping to save that little boy after he'd been savagely tortured by the monster who had fathered him. "He'll get well eventually, but it might take longer than we'd like."

"That's why I have to make certain he knows it will happen someday," he said simply. "I know you and Dad and Jane are taking care of everything you can with all those doctors and therapists, but he has to know what's waiting for him when it's over."

"Hope?" she asked gently.

"Sure." His expression was sober. "That's what you do, Mom. Whenever you do a reconstruction on a skull and bring that person back to the people who love them, you're giving them hope."

"Am I?"

"You know you are." His forehead was wrinkled in thought. "You're giving them back the memories they had. You're giving them the hope that there might be something beyond those memories if they look hard enough. If they *try* hard enough."

"Really?" She had to clear her throat. "You've evidently thought this through. And do you think there is something out there beyond those memories?"

"Of course. We both know that." He met her eyes. "Bonnie is there, and so much more."

Bonnie, Eve's daughter who had died when she was seven years old. He had mentioned her to Eve before, but that had been a long time ago. She had known from the day he was born that Michael was very special and had psychic gifts no one else possessed. It had proved to be both a difficulty and a blessing the older he became. Yet she would never give up one iota of what made him who he was. "Yes, so much more . . . " She reached over and turned off his lamp. "Good night, Michael." She gave him a hug and a kiss on the forehead. "I'll see you for a late breakfast when you and your dad get back tomorrow morning."

"That's right." He yawned before he cuddled down under his covers. "You've got that Mexican guy, who's not really . . ."

"What?"

"Never mind. It doesn't matter right now . . ."

"Be sure and tell me when it does matter," she said dryly as she got to her feet. She wasn't going to worry about it right now. Michael had probably mentally picked up on what she'd told Joe about Mexico and Nevada. It wasn't the first time and wouldn't be the last. "And we'll call Tomas's doctor tomorrow and see how he's doing."

"Good." He nestled into his pillow. "But I think he's okay. I'll keep checking on him . . . "

She knew he would, she thought as she closed the door. Tomas was designated as both Michael's friend and a mission, and he would never be forgotten while the boy needed him. How lucky she was to have a son like Michael.

"The kid okay?" Joe was lying in bed as she came into the room.

His arms were beneath his head and he was smiling. "I believe it's a yes. You've got that mushy look on your face."

"Maybe it's for you." She pulled her nightshirt over her head and threw it aside. "Let's see if it is." She slipped in bed and crawled over to him. "I think it might be." She could feel her heart start to race as she stared down at him. Lord, he was gorgeous. Even after all these years together she never got tired of looking at him. The same mahogany hair Michael possessed, the amber-tea-colored eyes, the muscular chest, and the tension that she knew would explode the instant they came together. Along with everything else between them, that wild attraction had always been there almost from the beginning. "No, it's not mushy, it's pure erotic sex. If you decide that's okay with you."

"It just might be okay." He pulled her down on top of him. "Since you got me so hot, I practically ran back here when you made me that promise." He was sinking deep inside her. "All night?"

She couldn't breathe. Deep. So deep. She already wanted to scream. "All night..."

ATLANTA AIRPORT
11:40 P.M.

"You must be Catherine Ling? I'm Diane Connors. Thank you for coming to meet me." The woman coming down the gateway toward Catherine smiled wryly. "Though you probably didn't have a choice. Hu Chang can be very determined. Were you able to obtain the information Hu Chang asked you to get for me?"

"Yes, Eve's at the Lake Cottage," Catherine said curtly. "But it wasn't so much a request for information as an order, wasn't it?" She led Diane Connors down the escalator toward the baggage claim. "Eve, Joe, and their son arrived back there this afternoon. According to Joe's captain, it's supposed to be an extended stay unless Quinn agrees to go to Quantico as requested. Is that what you wanted to know?"

"That's what I wanted to know...for now." Diane Connors smiled. "Thank you. I know you didn't want to give me any more information than you had to. I thought for a minute that you might refuse entirely. Why didn't you?"

"I was tempted. I don't like *this*." Catherine's tone was cold. "I'm doing what I promised to do, but I'm not going to wait until you walk out of this airport before I learn what's happening. You're traveling under an assumed name, and your ID must also be bogus. And when I called to get that information from Langley you wanted, I could tell it was sending up red flags."

Diane Connors's gaze flew to Catherine's face. "What kind of red flags?"

"Mild, but significant. You tell me. I could see that the only reason that I wasn't transferred to be questioned more thoroughly is that I'm down as a close friend of Eve's family, and all I was asking was where they were presently located. I'll probably hear more about it later. I'm CIA, and although they told me what I wanted to know, I was ordered to cooperate with both the FBI and the ATLPD if they requested my services or information regarding Eve's family." She added coolly, "It's obvious whatever you're doing might involve Eve in a major criminal case category."

"It would seem so, wouldn't it?" She was frowning. Then she shook her head. "But I don't believe that was a red flag, merely an alert to keep an eye on Eve because she might turn into a key player. I think it's still safe for me to see her."

"Really? Since I don't know what the hell is happening, I'm not about to accept the judgment of a woman who might be a criminal herself."

"I can see why you're suspicious, and I'll try to tell you as much as is safe." Then Diane shook her head. "First, I'm not a criminal. I'm what you might call a person of interest." She suddenly chuckled. "I can see how frustrated you are and I'm sorry that I had to bring you into my particular nightmare. I'm sure you'd have promptly called your CIA gurus and squealed on me when you got that red flag if it hadn't been Hu Chang who had called you and requested you give me what I wanted. Was he very insistent?"

"No, he's never insistent. He's just Hu Chang."

"I appreciate the distinction. I gathered that he was your mentor while you were a child growing up on the streets of Hong Kong until you were hired by the CIA when you were a teenager. That must have been a strong tie."

"He told you?" She stared intently at Diane's face. "That's not like Hu Chang."

"And you think I might be lying? I'm not, Catherine. In a way, I was also taught by Hu Chang. I'm an MD, but I've a passion for botany and medicinal and herbal research. You probably know what exotic plants and herbs Hu Chang has gathered from every country in Asia and Europe. I've worked in his labs in Hong Kong and also Northern California. He taught me more than anyone I've ever known." She made a face. "Believe me, I needed teaching. I've made a lot of mistakes in my life. I'm still making them. Just call Hu Chang and ask him."

"He wouldn't tell me. He'd keep it confidential. No one respects personal privacy more than Hu Chang. That's why I wonder why he told you about me."

"He trusts you." She paused. "And he thought I might need you."

"That answer's not good enough. Why? Because I'm CIA?"

"Maybe. Partly." She shook her head. "Not really. I told you, all those damn mistakes. He knows how impulsive I can be. If I get cornered, he's afraid I might make another one." She hesitated and then sighed. "Oh, hell, I think Hu Chang is probably all wrong about this. There's no real proof that anyone knows anything about me being here. But it seems there are people out there who very much want to capture or kill me. And I absolutely agree with Hu Chang: It's essential that I stay alive. So you can see there may be a problem."

"I understand why you might think that for any number of reasons," she said dryly. *What have you gotten me into, Hu Chang?* Catherine wondered in exasperation. He'd told her practically nothing when he'd called and asked her to pick up this woman at Atlanta Airport. Only that he'd appreciate her cooperating and protecting Diane, and that he'd be in touch later. "But he didn't mention the possibility of me becoming intimately involved in your problem on a long-term basis. And it's too coincidental that he sent you here on the same day that I got notice that there's something very troublesome stirring with both Quantico and the CIA." She added, "Now, over the years I've known him, Hu Chang has been involved in all kinds of less-than-legal, even deadly, enterprises whenever it suited him. He's always marched to his own drummer. But we're friends, and I could have sworn he'd never send anyone to me without telling me exactly what I might run into." Her lips tightened. "He didn't do that this time. Just some vague request for me to cooperate. Not like Hu Chang at all."

"Exactly like Hu Chang," Diane said quietly. "I told him my problem had to remain completely confidential. I didn't want a bodyguard, but I did agree I needed help. If he could get you to give me that help, I'd accept it." She smiled crookedly. "So Hu Chang got his foot in the door and will probably be on the phone later to try to persuade you that you should extend that help to whichever direction he intends it to go."

"You do know him well," Catherine said slowly. That was exactly how Hu Chang would have handled such a difficult situation. "But if there is a real threat to you, he must have told you that I'm very good at my job and it would be smarter if you'd take his advice."

"He said you're excellent, but excellent agents tend to want their own way. I can't have that, Catherine. It has to be my way or I walk." She added quietly, "If I'm going to make any more mistakes, they're going to be purely my own. Do you understand?"

What Catherine was beginning to understand was that in spite of Diane's frankness, she might be a force to be reckoned with. She had sensed from the moment she saw her walking down the gateway that she seemed to be the complete package. She was elegant, sleekly blond, mature, and totally stunning in an Angelina Jolie kind of way. She also gave the impression of being smart, quick-witted, and completely controlled, with a dry sense of humor. But that didn't mean she might not be as dangerous and deadly as some of Hu Chang's other associates. She definitely hadn't liked that first request Diane Connors had asked Hu Chang to pass on to her. "I can understand that you want your own way, but it could be the biggest problem of all for me. I don't want to get killed because you're doing something stupid. You clearly know Hu Chang and probably have an idea that I'd do almost anything he asked me to do." She paused. "Almost. Sometimes Hu Chang's goals and motives can be enigmatic, and his philosophies suspect, and I have to question them. You might be one of those exceptions."

"I probably am, but still, he sent me to you. He could have chosen someone else, but he trusts you." She hesitated and then confessed, "Along with the fact that I told him I might have to use Eve Duncan—and you know her."

Catherine stiffened. "Not only do I know her, but we've been friends for years, and she did me one of the greatest favors a person can do for another. You're crazy if you think I'd let you use her."

"And yet you used her yourself when you were trying to find your son years ago." Diane stared her deliberately in the eyes. "You used her and almost got her killed. Because that was the only thing important to you at the time. Sometimes we're all willing to do anything to get the job done, no matter what the cost."

Catherine gazed at her, shocked. "Did Hu Chang tell you that?"

"No, I knew I was going to have difficulty if I had to bring Eve Duncan into it, so I did my own research." They had reached the exit doors leading to the parking lot, and Diane stopped and turned to face her. "I realize how close the two of you are, so I know that I have to be honest with you and make sure you know I'm not trying to manipulate her in any way. I have a favor to ask Eve. It will be purely her choice if she agrees to help me." She made a face. "And it may be a hard choice for her to make and she might tell me to hit the road. I probably deserve it. But I've got to try because she's probably the only one who can do what I need."

"But you're still using me to get to Eve?"

"Yes. I thought it might help to have a neutral in my corner when I face her."

"I'm not neutral. I know nothing about you." She added bitterly, "Except that you invaded my privacy to find out about my relationship with Eve."

"And that Hu Chang thinks it worthwhile to keep me alive." She added coaxingly, "If Eve does me this favor, it might help with that."

"But I'd never trade Eve's life for yours."

"I'm not asking that. I agree that her life appears to have a good deal more value, but then she's always had so much more going for her in the morals department. All those mistakes again." She shrugged and then asked bluntly, "Yes or no? I promised Hu Chang I'd try to work with you, but I don't want to offend any of those scruples you seem to have developed... since you got your son back."

The jab was obvious, but Catherine thought it was more teasing than vindictive. "I'll take you to meet her, but I won't give you any recommendations. You'll be on your own."

"I don't want recommendations. I'm sure Eve would laugh if you tried to tell her what a wonderful, caring person I am. I just want to have you there to tell her that Hu Chang and maybe a few other people believe I'm worth keeping around." She shrugged. "And that sometimes leopards can change their spots."

"You don't want guarantees?"

"No." She turned and opened the door. "Tonight I want you to take me to a hotel, and tomorrow we'll go to see Eve and have a discussion. You'll do your part to make Hu Chang happy by keeping me alive so that I can at least talk to her. After I get an answer, I'll make my next decision. Is that okay with you?"

Catherine hesitated. "I don't see why not. You're not asking a great deal. I don't promise not to call Hu Chang tonight and ask him a few more questions."

Diane lifted her shoulder in a half shrug. "He expected it, didn't he?"

Catherine nodded. "And I'll have to contact Jonathan Terrell, my superior at the CIA, and tell him that I'll be in touch with Eve Duncan. Though that shouldn't be a problem. The messages we were receiving were primarily about Joe Quinn and whether or not he was going to go to that meeting at Quantico. Nothing about Eve."

"There would have been. It's only a matter of time," Diane said grimly. "Do what you like, but you might get some interference and questions you might not want to answer. Who knows? I might be wrong about no one being aware I'm here. If I am, they'd make contact, set up, and then go in for the first strike. Those messages probably weren't really about Joe Quinn at all. They were all about Eve."

She frowned. "That doesn't make sense."

"Believe me, it does." Diane's voice was slightly mocking. "Anything that involves Joe is connected to Eve. No one knows that better than I do."

"Of course it does. It's natural with couples." Her gaze narrowed on Diane's face. "But that isn't what you meant, is it?"

She shook her head. "No way. But thinking about Eve might have led me down a path that brought back a few memories." Her lips twisted cynically. "And I thought I'd put all that behind me."

"Put what behind you?"

"Eve. Joe." She gestured impatiently. "One of my more idiotic mistakes. Perhaps the worst one of all."

"What are you talking about?"

"I'll say it once and then I'm through with it. Don't ask me any questions because I won't answer them. You'll probably hear details from everyone else, but it won't be from me." Her voice was stilted. "But you should know one of the reasons that I might have trouble getting Eve to help me is that we have a history."

Catherine repeated slowly, "History."

"If you can call it that. The triangle was always confusing. I never really knew what it was between us from the moment I met him." She turned and strode across the street toward the parking lot. "Even though I was Joe Quinn's wife long before he married Eve."

CHAPTER 2

I take it all is well with Diane?" Hu Chang asked when he picked up Catherine's call an hour later. "Since I didn't hear from her, I assume that you came to an amicable agreement?"

"More an agreement not to agree for the most part," Catherine said dryly. "Until I could call you and get answers that she wasn't about to give me. What the hell is this all about?"

"I'm sure she told you the principal problem was the one I asked you to deal with." He paused. "You have her safe?"

"I checked her into the Renaissance Hotel with me. She's in the adjoining room. I left the door cracked and I'll hear if she so much as sneezes during the night." She paused. "How careful should I be, Hu Chang? How much danger is Diane Connors in?"

"How much do you think?" he asked quietly. "I sent her to you for protection. I would never have done that if I hadn't needed someone who would give everything in their heart and soul to keep her alive and away from the dragons waiting for her out there."

"What dragons? You let me go into this blind."

"Because that's the way she wanted it, and I had to handle the situation carefully. Diane is an exceptional woman but she's very emotional in this instance."

"What dragons?" she repeated.

"You want a name? Hmm. I fear there are many who would like to destroy her. I believe the most likely and current is Joshua Nalam, but that doesn't mean another might not pop up tomorrow or the next day."

At least she had a name. "Why?"

"She'll have to tell you the details. I tried to convince her she should trust you, but she has little faith in law-enforcement organizations."

"Even though she told me she was once married to Joe Quinn?"

"I thought that would have to come out. It might cause her a good deal of trouble. But the key word in their relationship is *once*. Divorce seldom leaves behind a bountiful amount of faith."

"I didn't even know Joe was married before. It's just always been Joe and Eve. Are we sure it's true?"

"It's true." His voice was totally indifferent. "Diane mentioned it to me years ago when she was working with me in Hong Kong, but I didn't feel it was important. Neither did she. Diane was totally involved in her research at the time. I got the impression they were at opposite ends of the world in geography as well as philosophy. That appeared to be the way Diane liked it. Which is more sensible than she is about a good many other things."

She could see how Hu Chang might have felt a past relationship was unimportant. Total acceptance. No curiosity. He probably wouldn't have mentioned it to anyone unless something pertinent like this had come to the forefront. How many secrets did Hu Chang know that he didn't consider relevant? "You're not being very helpful."

"I promised her, and you'll have to get most of it from Diane." He was silent an instant. "But I've been thinking about it, and sometimes a situation demands more than just a nudge to get it to come out the way it should. This might be one of those times. I do not want this to go badly for Diane Connors. I would find the result most distasteful. So I'll give you all the help I can within those limits."

That was a huge commitment for Hu Chang, she realized. Whatever was happening with Diane must have huge ramifications as far as he was concerned. "You wouldn't consider just giving me the story and letting me start out ahead of the game?"

"A promise," he said quietly.

"Okay. Twenty questions? Tell me about Diane Connors. She said she's a person of interest, not a criminal. Is that true?"

"It's true. She's very honest, sometimes emotional and stubborn, but no real criminal tendencies past or present."

"She said she worked with you in your lab, that you taught her. What did she do?"

"I did teach her." He paused. "And she taught me. She was brilliant and innovative. She worked with homeopathic healing herbs she found in the jungle and rain forest and experimented with creating different treatments."

"She's a chemist?"

"And a doctor."

"Evidently not a very good one. She told me she's made a lot of mistakes."

"But they weren't in the medical field. Yes, she does make mistakes on occasion, and the fact that she's impulsive tends to make them more serious. She isn't perfect. But then who is perfect?" He added slyly, "Except me, of course. I come very close."

"What does she want with Eve?"

He didn't answer.

"Does this Joshua Nalam have anything to do with Joe and Eve or why Quantico wants Joe to go to Washington?"

"I have no idea." He chuckled. "No more, Catherine. I've probably told you enough that you can figure some of it out for yourself. Why else did I choose you?"

"Because I'm the only one who would put up with this nonsense you make me go through to help you?" She paused. "This means something to you, doesn't it? She's your friend?"

"She is my friend. Not like you, Catherine. She does not let anyone get that close. But I've watched her over the years, and I've seen how she's gradually changed and transformed herself without even knowing she was doing it. I would go out of my way to make certain that no one destroys the unique person she's become."

"That's saying a good deal," she said slowly. "You don't use the word *unique* lightly."

"No, I don't. It's reserved for people like you, Catherine." He paused. "And for the man whom I was considering calling to take care of this matter before I decided to ask you instead."

She could sense a hidden meaning in those last words and instinctively tensed. "What are you talking about?"

"I just feel it's only fair that I let you know that you're not the only one who would put up with my eccentricities if he thought it was worth his while. I thought long and hard before I called you. It was tempting... all that power. I might still have to bring him aboard if I deem it necessary."

Now she thought she knew where this was going and couldn't believe he'd do this. "Bring who aboard?" she asked curtly.

"Richard Cameron," he said simply. "I know your relationship with him is complicated, but you can see that he would have the ability to keep Diane hidden indefinitely if he chose."

"Cameron!" She swore softly. "Or maybe persuade her to join his army of malcontents, and suddenly another brilliant scientist would just disappear from view. He's like a damn Pied Piper."

"It's not as if he kidnaps them," Hu Chang said mildly. "He gives them a choice. A good many people have lost faith in the direction our world leaders and politicians are taking us. They evidently think that it's not a bad idea to prepare in case we need a Shangri-La to come back to after some idiot sets off the big one. He just provides them with a place and protection so that they can do their work in peace."

"And away from government interference."

"Their choice," Hu Chang repeated. "And I've never heard of any of the people who have chosen to go with Cameron deciding to come back."

"Pied Piper," she repeated. "He's brilliant, psychic, and he can talk the birds out of the trees."

"So why doesn't the CIA or FBI know what a threat he is to all of us?" he asked mockingly. "Why haven't you launched a hunt for him, Catherine?"

"It's not as if I can prove that he's some kind of terrorist or revolutionary. There have been rumors about him, but that's all they've been. Rumors."

"And?"

"He's not a monster." She added grudgingly, "And he can be useful on occasion."

"My point exactly."

"But he's *wrong*. He shouldn't do things like that. He should try to make life better, not just get ready to clean up after all the megalomaniacs."

"A matter of opinion. You and Cameron have never agreed... about that."

"What do you think?" she demanded.

"I really don't care. I'll cope with whatever comes my way. I just wanted you to know that I might have to call on him if I see difficulties."

She remembered something else he'd said. "You said if he thought she was worth his while. Do you think he would?"

"I haven't discussed Diane with him yet. But I think there's every chance he would think her worth it." He paused. "Still, sometimes one doesn't have to tell Cameron when someone appears on the scene that would interest him. He has his ear constantly to the ground, and his organization knows what he's looking for."

Catherine knew that from past experience. Cameron's network appeared to be everywhere, and he showed up when she least expected to see him. "She's that good a scientist?"

"Totally remarkable. But you needn't worry yet. You may be able to handle Diane's problem without assistance." His voice was suddenly gentle. "I will try not to involve him. I realize your attitude toward Cameron is . . . conflicted."

"I'm *not* conflicted. Of course I'll be able to handle this by myself," she said impatiently. "And the last thing I want is to have to deal with Cameron and try to keep him from persuading Diane that she should run away to never-never land. She seems to be confused enough about what's happening to her."

"Yes and no," Hu Chang said. "However, if she chose never-never land, she would make a good thing of it. But I will not have her forced to do that if there is another way. You agree to keep her safe for me?"

"You know I will. I agree to do everything I can. But you gave me practically no information. And I'll probably end up balancing my job with the CIA against whatever Diane is going to demand Eve do tomorrow. You're not making it easy for me."

He chuckled. "Very true. But when did you ever want anything easy? From the time I first met you in that shop in Hong Kong, I could see what you were and what you were going to become. It is all very simple. You will get what information you need from Diane and I will keep my promise. You've balanced your duties with the CIA before and will again because they realize that you're an expert operative and they value you. As for Eve, you knew you had to go with Diane to see her so that you could judge whether you had to protect your friend as well."

"Yes, all very simple."

"And I thank you for doing me this favor. I believe that after it is all over, you will agree it was interesting and valuable enough to be beneficial." He paused. "I will keep you informed if I hear word of any problems. Call on me if you need me."

"Believe me, I will," she said dryly. "Good night, Hu Chang." She pressed the button to disconnect.

She leaned back against the headboard with a sigh of exasperation. Not simple at all. Hu Chang had been his usual enigmatic and complex self, but it had been clear Diane was important to him—so important that he'd considered using Cameron. In fact, for an instant Catherine had wondered if he'd mentioned the possibility to make sure her instant rejection would reinforce her own decision to stay with Diane. Anything was possible with Hu Chang.

And even though she'd denied it, he knew that *conflicted* was hardly the word for her relationship with Cameron over the years. From the day they'd met in Tibet, she'd found him stormy, erotic, passionate, and completely fascinating. It hadn't mattered that she'd disagreed with his philosophy or that they were often on different sides. The attraction was there and the only sensible thing was not to see him, which she'd been trying to do. Though it would have been easier if Cameron would stop dropping in on her unexpectedly whenever he found she was in the same city.

Don't think of him. At least she wasn't going to have to deal with Cameron in full attack mode, since Hu Chang wasn't going to turn him loose on Diane Connors. But that meant Diane was definitely in Catherine's court, and she would have to do her best for the woman no matter how difficult. To do her job she had to know her, how she thought, what was important to her, just as she did with any subject she was investigating.

Information. Find out everything she could about Diane that Hu Chang had been so chary about telling her. She might as well start right now; she was too charged from Hu Chang launching the threat of Cameron showing up on the scene to sleep anyway. Everyone had secrets, but by tomorrow she wanted to know as much as she could about Diane Connors's past, her present, and everything that made her tick.

She took out her computer and got to work.

Diane and Catherine had eaten breakfast and were on the road by nine the next morning.

"You're very quiet." Diane gave Catherine a sly smile. "Have a bad night?"

"You might say that," Catherine said. "I had a few things to sort out. But I got through them."

"Did Hu Chang help?"

"Not much. He gave me his version of support, which mostly added to the confusion. So I decided I had to clear it up for myself." She glanced at Diane. "You're almost as much an enigma to me as Hu Chang. I can only accept one at a time since I'm such a simple person. So I did a little research and got to know Diane Connors a little better."

"Really?" She tilted her head curiously. "Did you find me interesting? How far back did you go?"

"I didn't find your early years very interesting at all, so I skipped through them. You were just a rich kid, and your parents seemed to have spoiled you rotten because they didn't want to deal with your tantrums. Though you were very intelligent and your grades in college were exceptional when you were interested enough in a subject to put out the effort." She paused. "Which wasn't often. Then Joe Quinn appeared in your life and something changed. Actually, he'd been around for a while. Your families had known each other for years. But he was nothing like you. Night and day. Which didn't seem to matter, because you married him within six months."

"Yes, I did," Diane said coolly. "But I believe I told you that any conversation about Joe Quinn was out of bounds. I meant it, Catherine."

"That's all right. I wasn't going to probe; you didn't stay married to him that long." She shrugged. "And I admit you only became intriguing to me after you divorced him. That's when you left Atlanta for L.A. and disappeared from view. You went back to college and then to medical school and earned a doctorate in medicine and several associate degrees. Within five years you were working with a unit of One World Medical in the South Seas and the Amazon jungle in South America. Quite an unselfish decision and accomplishment considering your rather self-indulgent background. Quinn's influence?"

"You're thinking he saved my soul?" She grimaced. "Be for real. Joe had nothing to do with it. I liked the idea of healing people, particularly kids. I've always been fascinated with medicine and finding and developing new drugs. I needed a change after that last horrendous mistake of a marriage, and I went out and worked until I erased it from my mind."

"Erased? Yet evidently you seem to have remembered Eve quite clearly."

"She's essential. I always remember anyone that's necessary to me. I'm sure you do, too."

"Yes." She paused. "And I agree Eve is essential. She always will be to me, Diane."

"You don't have to warn me. I'm not going to force an issue. It's either yes or no."

"I just wanted you to be—"

"I hear you," she said jerkily. "Look, we're almost at the cottage. It's the turn ahead. Do you want to go in and tell Eve of the treat she has in store for her? I can wait in the car."

"I called her before we left the hotel to be sure that we'd be able to talk to her in privacy. I didn't mention you by name, so I'll just run in and explain." She was suddenly frowning. "How did you know we're almost at the cottage?"

"Evidently you didn't do that good a job of investigating my marriage with Joe." She made a face. "He had this house when we were still married. We never spent any time here. I was planning on renovating it."

"Shit."

She nodded her head. "I know. Some things change, some things don't. I wasn't sure I'd remember the way, but it came back to me." The cottage was suddenly in sight and she stiffened. "I see Eve agreed with me, they've done some building. It's much larger than it was the last time I saw it."

"Eve and Joe's place always looked just cozy to me," Catherine said. "And it's hard for me to think of anyone living there but them."

"And you resent it."

Catherine nodded. "I think I do."

"I can see how you would. She's your friend, and it must seem as if I'm stepping on her turf." She shrugged. "I guarantee I won't bring it up when I'm talking to Eve."

"You'd better not. You're the interloper here." She pulled up into the driveway. "I won't have her upset."

"Don't worry," Diane said wearily. "I've been an interloper too often to forget my place in the scheme of things. I don't promise not to upset her, but it won't be intentional."

And Catherine believed her. Diane would do her best not to create any more havoc than was needed to protect herself. In this moment, she appeared very vulnerable. Catherine's first impression of a stunning woman who had all the confidence in the world was fading the more time she spent with Diane. Yes, she might be able to hold her own, but Catherine had no real idea what the odds were that had brought her here and made Hu Chang so concerned. "Eve is very strong. She can take care of herself." She got out of the car and headed for the porch steps. "I'll be right back."

"Diane Connors?" Eve's eyes widened in shock. "What the hell, Catherine? I haven't heard from her in years. I haven't even thought of her since I heard she and Joe had filed for divorce years ago. I wasn't here when it happened. She just disappeared, and Joe said something about her going to California."

"She did go to California and quite a few other places," Catherine said. "She's a doctor now and has somehow managed to get herself into a situation where even Hu Chang is concerned about her." She paused. "And didn't you think it unusual that she would just disappear?"

"Of course it was unusual." She grimaced. "I suppose I just didn't want to think about her after she divorced Joe. I didn't know her that well, and he never talked about her. At the time we weren't romantically involved; we were just friends. I guess I thought she'd made him unhappy and I didn't want to rub salt into a wound." She rubbed her temple. "I don't know what I thought. It doesn't matter now, does it? You say she wants to talk to me, not Joe?"

"That's what she said. I believe she wants to ask a favor." She added quickly, "But you don't have to do it. I told her that I'd bring her here, but I wouldn't recommend you help her. I wouldn't have even gone that far if Hu Chang hadn't been putting pressure on me. He's been giving me a guilt trip."

"What does she want me to do?"

Catherine shook her head. "She won't tell me, and I don't know if I really want to be clued in. I'd just as soon keep my distance and not influence you in any way. She just said you were the only one who could help her."

"I'm as confused as hell and I wouldn't mind a little outside influence at the moment." Eve shook her head. That was an understatement, she thought. Diane Connors was a complete stranger to her these days, and she preferred to keep it that way. What she remembered about Joe's ex was very sketchy, and the few times they'd met, they'd had nothing in common. She could vaguely recall stilted conversations and finding excuses to leave. "The whole situation makes me uneasy. And why would Hu Chang be involved with her?"

"Who knows why Hu Chang does anything?" Catherine asked curtly. "I only know he cared enough to pull me into the mess and ask me to take care of her. So do I go out and bring her in?"

"Of course you do." Eve knew she was being foolish to feel this sense of panic. "You just caught me off guard. I only hope that I'll be able to get rid of her before Joe and Michael get home. We've never spoken to Michael about Diane. It might be . . . awkward."

"I think Michael can handle it." Catherine turned toward the door. "I'm sure that many of his school friends have parents who are divorced."

"Yes, but that's not us. We'd have to... prepare him." She had a sudden memory. "Take care of her? Why would you have to do that? What do you mean?"

"Hu Chang appears to think that Diane is in some kind of danger. She said he sent her to me because he wants to keep her alive."

"Now I know I don't like this," Eve said. "Is she involved in drugs?"

Catherine held up her hand to stop the questions. "I don't know. Ask her yourself. Hu Chang wouldn't tell me anything else." The next moment she was out the door and running down the porch steps.

Eve followed her out onto the porch and stood watching as Catherine opened the car door and spoke to the woman in the passenger seat. Then Diane Connors got out of the car and was starting toward the steps.

She was as beautiful as Eve remembered, and it came as a shock. Perhaps more beautiful... Slim, graceful, and yet there was a strength and vitality that hadn't been there when she was younger. Her face was thinner, and that made her high cheekbones even more interesting.

Then she looked up and met Eve's eyes. She stopped short, then smiled and nodded before starting up the steps. Confidence, boldness, yet also a kind of wry acceptance were all there in that smile. Eve took an involuntary step back as she approached. She wasn't feeling either confidence or boldness herself in this moment.

"It will be okay, Eve," Diane said quietly, studying her as she climbed the rest of the steps. "Don't be nervous. You're the one in control."

"I'm not nervous," Eve lied. "It's just an unusual situation and I've no idea what you want from me. Let's get this over." She held out her hand as Diane reached the porch. "You're looking well. Would you like to come in?"

Diane shook her hand. "Please." She hesitated, her gaze on Eve's face. "But you *are* nervous." She turned and called down to Catherine: "Come and join us. She'll feel better if you do."

Catherine shrugged and started up the stairs.

"I told you I wasn't nervous," Eve said. "And I don't need Catherine to chaperone us." She forced a smile. "I can handle you."

"She won't interfere," Diane said. "But she's your friend and she'll be your support team. If I'm going to have my chance of getting what I want, I'd prefer you to be in the best possible mood."

"Have it your way." Eve headed back inside the house. She gestured to the couch. "Sit down. You'll excuse me if I don't offer either one of you coffee? I take it this isn't going to be a social occasion. I prefer to have the discussion over before my son and Joe return."

"Your son..." Diane repeated. "Michael." She looked at a photo on the wall of Joe and Michael dressed in T-shirts, hair mussed, grinning at each other as they worked on a jeep. "He looks like a fine boy."

"Extraordinary," Eve said. "You have no idea."

"I believe I do. It's all in that wonderful expression. And he looks like Joe."

"He looks like both of us. Yes, he does have Joe's eyes." She dropped down in an easy chair. "But you didn't come here to talk about Michael."

"No, I didn't. I'm sure Catherine has told you I need a favor."

Eve nodded. "And you should know that I don't feel any duty to oblige you. I barely knew you when you were married to Joe. We were practically strangers. I just tried to be polite to you because Joe was a friend with whom I worked, and I didn't want to offend him."

"Yes, I remember how polite you were." Diane smiled wryly. "So polite at times, it was difficult for me to keep from slugging you. You didn't realize that, did you?"

Eve blinked. "No, you were always very courteous."

"That was because I was also smart enough to realize what side my bread was buttered on. I knew better than to antagonize you in any way. It would have been a mistake. But it still rankled." She made a face. "And it seems I didn't learn anything, because here I am doing just that after all these years. I guess I couldn't resist. I must have been holding it in some deep, secret place waiting for it to break free."

Catherine cleared her throat before saying sharply, "Knock it off, Diane. I didn't bring you here to upset Eve. Do what you came to do or I'm going to leave."

"I'm not upsetting her." Diane's gaze switched to Eve. "Am I? You're very tough these days. Though I guess you always were. Everyone was so sad you'd lost your little girl, Bonnie, that they treated you with kid gloves. But the steel was always there."

"Is this going somewhere, Diane?" Eve asked sharply.

"As far as you'll let it. But I decided that I need to be as honest with you as I can, and I wasn't back then. I didn't learn about honesty until I found out how to balance it against a very selfish nature that no one had seen fit to curb." She added quietly, "Not even Joe, and I suppose I cared more about him than anyone else. Though it was hard to tell until I learned what that really meant." She looked her directly in the eyes. "I did learn eventually, and if we make a deal, you'll find I keep my word these days. I won't hurt you; I won't cheat you or anyone who matters to you. And if you help me, you'll be doing something that Hu Chang regards as extraordinary." She grimaced. "I believe that, too, or I wouldn't be here. But all I can think about now is getting what I need from you. I'm obviously still pretty selfish. Right?"

"One would assume that's true." Eve was getting impatient, but she was also curious. "I won't know until you stop this sales pitch and let me know what the hell you're talking about. What do you want me to do, Diane? Tell me."

"Amen," Catherine murmured.

Diane shrugged. "I want you to perform a reconstruction on the skull of a man who is supposed to be buried somewhere in the Rocky Mountains of Nevada and help me identify him."

"Somewhere? That's a little vague."

"I might be able to pin it down. But I have to locate the grave first. The area was supposed to be a virtual killing field. Legend has it that there are graves all over the mountain."

"Legend?"

"For the last five years, there was cartel drug running and immigrant trafficking from Mexico through Nevada to Central California. The cartels brought the migrant workers in by the truckload and sold them to the richest farmers in the area. If they couldn't get rid of them fast enough or there was trouble with the border patrol, the migrants were sometimes left locked in the trucks on the side of the roads until they starved. They were buried later but there was doubt if all of them were ever found."

Eve shivered. "Monsters."

Diane nodded. "But the authorities have located a good many of the victims. And the cartels are very careful about their disposal these days."

"How charming," Eve said. "And this reconstruction you want me to do was of one of those poor Mexican victims brought across the border by the cartels?"

She nodded. "Jose Morales was having family problems with his elder brother and thought it would be best to flee from both his brother and the family entirely. He paid the Ramez cartel to smuggle him across the border into Nevada to start a new life. But once there he completely disappeared from view."

"Then why would you believe he was one of the people buried in that killing field? He could have run away, gone to another state."

"Yes, he could. But I received information from one of Hu Chang's sources that he left the group, went on the run, and was killed in cold blood by one of the cartel's gunmen." She shook her head. "Maybe not-so-cold blood—evidently they were very thorough. When they found him, he'd been butchered and his remains scattered over the mountain. They located what they thought was his skull, but it had been burned and almost completely destroyed."

"And I'm supposed to put Humpty Dumpty back together again?" Eve asked. "Your best bet is to find the body and skull and then bring in a DNA expert."

"There might not be enough left to gather DNA," Diane said bitterly. "I said they were thorough. They were common thugs, but they'd clearly been given orders and carried them out. It was almost as if they'd tried to avoid leaving even a hint of DNA."

"Why?"

"Perhaps the same reason that Morales fled Mexico," Diane said.

"Perhaps?" Eve's eyes narrowed. "But you're not going to tell me?"

"Not at this time. It would only be a guess and I don't want to speculate." She paused. "I recall that you prefer the truth and nothing but the truth when it comes to your work. You were like that years ago when I was with Joe, and according to what I've learned about your reputation since then, you're still a stickler."

"I'm a professional," Eve said. "But that doesn't mean I don't speculate. As a forensic sculptor, that sometimes comes as part of the territory." She added, "However, I've no intention of playing guessing games on this project. It would be a waste of my time."

Diane nodded. "I wouldn't want to do that. I realize you want to spend that time with Joe and Michael. I'll just finish up and let you make your decision." She leaned forward. "Hu Chang's source swore that the background info I was given was accurate and also that he could supply the location of the area where Morales's remains were scattered. As you can see, that portion of the situation isn't as hopeless as you might think. If I can deliver the skull to you, then all you'd have to do is the reconstruction."

"Simple. Providing I choose to do it." She stared her in the eye. "And I'm supposed to trust you? Hu Chang has always been an enigma in spite of Catherine's closeness to him. Now she tells me that you've been working with him? You could be a smuggler or a thief or drug dealer. Anything or anyone."

"True." She nodded at Catherine. "That's why Hu Chang brought her into the mix. You do trust her, and you know she'd never let you be hurt by some scam artist. Isn't that right?"

Eve nodded reluctantly. "But she still doesn't know why you're asking me to do this. I want answers or I'm waving you goodbye."

"I knew it would come down to this." She hesitated. "It's because I made a bargain with the Morales family in Mexico to have him found and identified."

"What?"

"His parents suspected that his brother was responsible for them losing their son, but they wanted to know for certain what happened to Jose. If it was a Cain-and-Abel situation." She shrugged. "And I desperately needed some information from them I couldn't get anywhere else. We struck a deal."

"And used me as a pawn? I don't think so. Whatever made you believe I'd consider it?"

"I told you, I was desperate." Her voice was suddenly shaking. "No way on earth would I want to go begging to you. It took me too long to get over what you and Joe did to me. But I knew you had the skill to do this and I had to try. If you wouldn't do it, I'd just find another way. He's worth it."

Eve went still. "We did nothing to you. You talk as if I was the other woman in your divorce. Joe and I didn't get together until you were long gone."

"Really? It didn't appear like that to me. It seemed as if you were always together. Though I admit I did some things that weren't exactly honorable, too." She waved her hand. "It doesn't matter. I was determined to be civilized and I'm blowing it." She closed her eyes for an instant and drew a breath. Then she opened her eyes. "Look, if you help me get this done, I'll pay you back in ways that most people would consider to be fantastic. You were always different, but you love your son and Joe and the gift I give you would also be for them. I promise you won't be sorry."

"You're trying to bribe me?" Eve asked in disbelief.

"You're damn right. Any way that I can," she said recklessly. "Hu Chang says that I'm to do anything I can to stay alive, but I'm not the only one I have to worry about. If I don't come through for the Morales family, then the bargain will be broken. The idea scares the hell out of me. That can't happen." Her hands clenched into fists. "I can probably get my hands on any amount of money you want as a down payment. Just trust me and give me a little time. But we should move forward right away if you'll please do this for me."

"I probably will not," Eve said. "I can't see any reason why I should. What you're asking, if not illegal, is likely dangerous. Besides, I just got back from Maldara, Africa, and I want family time here. Joe and I promised each other that we'd stay home for a while."

"How cozy." Diane's tone contained equal amounts of wistfulness and bitterness. "Promise you'll consider it. I should take a flight out of here tomorrow night, but I don't want to. Think about your son. You have no idea what I'm offering you."

"No, I don't," she said dryly. "You haven't been very explanatory, and Joe and I would probably turn it down anyway. We have enough to live quite well without taking bribes."

"I can see that. You don't need anything. But promise you'll consider it." She got to her feet. "I'll give you anything you want. Catherine will contact me if you change your mind." She headed for the porch door. "Thank you for allowing me to see you, Eve. I know I disturbed you." She glanced at Catherine. "Are you ready to go?"

Catherine nodded and got to her feet. "After I apologize to Eve. You *did* disturb her."

"Right." Diane nodded grimly as she went out the door. "I'll wait in the car."

Catherine turned to Eve as the door slammed behind Diane. "Sorry. I didn't think there would be that much emotional angst involved when I asked you to meet with her. She gave me the impression of being very sharp and in control of herself and everything around her since I met her at the airport."

"She was always sharp," Eve said jerkily. "And I believe she was trying to be in control today. But whatever was bothering her kind of blew that to hell and back. She really wanted me to do that reconstruction."

"She really did. Very intense." Catherine's eyes narrowed thoughtfully. "Maybe too intense. I think you were so preoccupied with her remarks about you and Joe that you missed that last sentence when she said, 'He's worth it.'" She frowned. "'He'? Who was she talking about?"

"You're right, I did miss that." Eve shook her head wearily. "Who knows? The rest of what she was saying was all too bizarre for me. After just coming back from doing the reconstructions on those twenty-seven schoolchildren in Africa, I found her story of murder and drug trafficking and killing fields a little over the top. Particularly since I had no idea whether she was telling the truth."

"And if she was?"

"Then I'd refer her to someone else. I'm not the only forensic sculptor in the world."

"Only the best." She held up her hand. "I'm not trying to persuade you. It's your decision. I just promised Hu Chang that I'd be there for Diane if she needed me. If that doesn't include your services, then I'll find some other way to help her." She smiled as she headed for the door. "If you change your mind, contact me."

"Don't expect it," Eve said dryly as she followed her out onto the porch.

"I got that impression." She glanced back as she started down the porch steps. "If it means anything, I do believe there's a good chance she might be telling the truth as she knows it." Then she added wearily, "Or maybe not. She's a complicated woman."

"I don't remember that about her. She always seemed basic and straightforward. Almost . . . blunt."

"But then maybe she's not the same woman you knew back then." Catherine stopped on the steps, looking out at the lake where a boat was pulling up at the pier. "Dammit, there's Joe and Michael. I know you didn't want to have to make any explanations. I'll get Diane out of here."

"Too late." Eve was watching Michael jump out of the boat onto the pier and waving at her. She waved back and saw his eager gaze turn curiously to Catherine's rental car in the driveway. "It's not as if I was trying to hide anything from him. It just seemed awkward right now." Her eyes shifted to Joe, who was now beside Michael on the pier. He was grinning down at him, strong, loving, vibrant, everything she had ever wanted. Memories were suddenly bombarding her. He was so very much her own, she thought fiercely. Anything else was wrong and didn't make sense. And that woman who had been sitting in their home only moments ago and staring critically at that photograph of Joe and her son was very, very *wrong*. She suddenly wanted to strike out with all her strength. She mustn't give in to it. This wasn't who she was. She drew a deep breath, tensed, and tried to shake off the rage. "Don't worry. I'll handle it. You don't have to run away." She forced a smile. "No big deal, Catherine."

"No?" Catherine was gazing skeptically at her with raised brows. "I believe I'll still pull Diane out of the line of fire." She was hurrying down the steps. "I'll whisk her away and then you can do whatever you like..."

But Joe and Michael were already walking up the driveway, and Michael had seen Catherine. He ran eagerly toward her. "Hi, Catherine. Mom didn't tell me that you were coming. Did you bring Luke?"

"No, Luke's still away at school in Boston. He told me to tell you the next time I saw you what a great time he's having learning how to sail." She gave him a quick hug. "This was just a chance for me to drop in and say hello to your mom. You okay? I have to leave now, but I want you to tell me about all your adventures the next time I come."

"I will." He was glancing curiously at Diane sitting in the passenger seat, and Eve knew it would only be a minute or two before he asked Catherine about her. "But it's good to be home. I missed everyone." He turned to Joe. "Catherine's here, Dad. But she can't stay. She just wanted to say hi to Mom."

"Now, that's rude, Catherine." He embraced her and called up to Eve on the porch. "What's the idea of keeping her to yourself?"

"There were reasons," Eve said quietly. "It was kind of a surprise visit in more ways than one."

He went still, his eyes studying her. "Really? Intriguing."

"Oh, for pity's sake." Diane abruptly got out of the car on her passenger side and walked toward Joe and Michael. "I can't take this anymore. I'm not going to hide in corners or fade into the background to avoid problems. I haven't done that for a long time, and I *won't* go back." She was standing in front of Joe now, chin up and shoulders squared. "Hello, Joe. I won't say I'm glad to see you, but I want you to know that I'm not here to cause any more disturbance than I can help."

Shock.

Eve could see Joe's sudden stiffening and then the wariness as his eyes focused and recognized the woman in front of him. "Diane?"

Diane nodded jerkily. "How nice of you to remember. But this isn't what Eve wants so I'm going to get out of here." She tore her gaze away from him and looked down at Michael. "Hello, I'm Diane." She smiled at him as she took his hand and shook it. "I'm very glad to meet you. I know this must be confusing, but your mom and dad will explain everything, and you'll realize that I'm not important enough to worry about."

"Hello, Diane." His eyes were fastened intently on her face; then he suddenly took a step closer to her, his hand tightening on hers. "You shouldn't be sad. And I think you're very important."

Eve stiffened in shock. She had no idea what Michael was thinking or feeling. It could be one of his psychic flashes, or he might just be responding to the charm Diane was now exerting. Whichever it was, she was experiencing a twinge of sheer pain as she stared down at Joe, Diane, and Michael together.

Joe must have sensed it, for he glanced up at Eve. "Suppose we go into the house and discuss—"

Diane was shaking her head. "Eve and I have already had our discussion. Catherine and I were about to leave." She moved quickly around the car. "Goodbye, Joe. Be happy, Michael."

Catherine was already slipping into the driver's seat. "She's right. We've got to leave. I'm sure I'll be talking to you later, Joe."

"I imagine you will," he said dryly as he watched her pull out of the driveway. "I'm wondering why I was left out before." Then his hand closed on Michael's shoulder and nudged him toward the staircase. "Come on, let's go up and see your mom and tell her all about our morning."

Michael nodded absently as he looked back over his shoulder at the car that was now headed down the road. "It was fun, wasn't it? It would have been better if Mom had been there, but I guess she had to be here to see Diane..." He took the last steps two at a time and rushed into Eve's arms. "Hi, everything was great. We saw four big bass jumping. I took some photos to show Tomas."

"Good." Eve held him close for an instant before releasing him. "Why don't you text them to him right now? Go inside and do it and then wash up while I see about making lunch."

"Okay." He started for the door and then stopped. "Who is Alon?"

Eve frowned. "What?"

"Never mind. I thought you might know, since you were talking to Diane. She kept thinking about him..." The door slammed behind him.

Joe was instantly beside her. "What the hell, Eve?"

"Shut up." She went into his arms. "Just hold me. This hasn't been a good morning and those last few minutes watching you down there with Diane made it twice as bad. I felt *alone*, dammit."

"Then you're crazy. Why?"

"Because I had no idea I was insecure, but it turns out I am. I'd forgotten how damn beautiful she is, and she hasn't changed." Her voice was muffled as she nestled her cheek on his chest. "How dare she do that? It's totally unfair."

"I didn't notice."

"Liar. You're very, very masculine. You would have noticed."

"Then it didn't matter." He pushed her away and looked down at her. "What did matter is that she was here at all. And the second thing was that I didn't know you were going to see her. Why didn't you tell me?"

"I told you, her visit was a surprise in more ways than one. This morning, Catherine showed up with Diane in tow." She rubbed her temple. "And chaos promptly ensued. It wasn't my finest hour. I don't believe it was hers, either. What was I supposed to do? Phone you and have you run home to rescue me?"

"Maybe. Why was she here?"

"I'm going to tell you about it." She pulled him toward the door. "And it has to be right away before Michael decides to ask me any more questions I can't answer. He *liked* her, Joe. I could see that he was sensing...something. The last thing I wanted was to have that psychic voodoo stuff flare up in connection with her."

"There's no way of controlling it, Eve," Joe said quietly.

"I might have managed it if he hadn't met her." She grimaced. "I guess I could say the same about you, Joe. But I didn't get a lucky break in either case, so we'll just have to handle it." She rubbed her temple again. "Along with the nightmare of a problem she tried to drop in my lap." She went behind the kitchen bar and started to make them both a cup of coffee. "I'll go through the entire story but I'm going to need a caffeine fix to do it."

CHAPTER 3

Well, I wouldn't say that went well." Catherine glanced at Diane as they made their way toward the freeway. "No one can call you in the least consistent. You went from diplomatic to aggressive with every other breath. I'd have tossed you out, too. It's a wonder Eve had the patience to put up with you as long as she did."

"But you're not Eve. Neither am I," she said bitterly. "We're both warriors who go for the jugular. Eve always thought long and deep and agonized before making decisions."

"So you felt safe?"

"Hell, no. I was nervous and half the time I didn't know what I was going to say next. The words just flowed out whether I wanted them to or not." She was looking out the window. "I realize I screwed up. Was I as bad as I thought I was?"

"Probably. It didn't help when you jumped out of the car to confront Joe. It probably put her on the defensive."

"I couldn't just sit there. You were all talking around me." Her lips were tight. "I told the truth; I can't be that person anymore. I didn't cause a scene. I only put an end to it as quickly as possible."

"No, you didn't cause a scene. Though it was close. And thank heavens you were kind and polite to Michael."

"Why wouldn't I be? I like kids, and Michael seemed... special."

"No doubt about that. He seemed to like you, too."

"Yeah, I guess he did." She was silent a moment. "Though he made me feel a little uncomfortable when he said that about me being sad. Kids aren't supposed to see below the surface."

"Most kids aren't Michael. And Eve and Joe have done a terrific job of raising him and keeping him steady."

"But then Eve would have made sure of that after she lost her little girl." Diane was still staring out the window. "And Joe is Joe. Everyone knows he's the perfect man every woman would want to father her child. He'd give everything, do anything, to make certain Eve was happy."

"You're damn right. But it's always a team effort with them." Catherine glanced at her. "And you might have antagonized Joe by insisting on seeing Eve alone today."

"Maybe. I'm not perfect. I thought it might be better not to have him there and on the defensive." She smiled crookedly. "And I still managed to do it anyway by going on the attack."

"That's a fair assessment," Catherine agreed. "Now what do you do?"

"I go back to the hotel, make a few phone calls, and wait and see if the pot I brought to a boil erupts. Perhaps she'll change her mind. Or if she doesn't, I'll find another way to get what I want." She added bitterly, "I'm very good at that and I've had a lot of practice. Ask Joe."

"And Eve?"

"No, not Eve. Joe made certain I didn't get anything I wanted when Eve was around." She gave a half shrug. "But that might change now. We'll see."

"Yes, I guess we will." Diane's attempt to persuade Eve had obviously been a complete disaster, but Catherine found she was feeling sorry for her. "Do you have any alternative plans?"

"I'll think of something."

She hesitated and then asked, "You said something in there about 'He's worth it.' Who were you talking about?"

Diane's gaze shifted guardedly to her face, suddenly wary. "Did I say that? I don't remember. It just goes to show you how nervous I was."

"But you wouldn't tell me anyway."

She nodded. "It would take too long. Stop probing. Perhaps another time." She was looking straight ahead again. "All that's really important is the conversation that Eve and Joe are probably having right now..."

LAKE COTTAGE

"I can't believe Catherine would involve you in a mess like this," Joe swore beneath his breath when Eve had finished. "Or maybe I can. She'd do anything for Hu Chang."

Eve nodded. "And there might not have been any danger for me in doing the reconstruction." She wrinkled her nose. "Though Catherine said that Hu Chang told her it could be life or death for Diane. That doesn't sound promising for anyone standing too close to her."

"You're damn right it doesn't." Joe put his cup down on the coffee table with a decided click. "Which is my point. She should never have agreed to take on anything to do with Diane. I can't believe she did it."

He was angry. Joe was always protective, but Eve was surprised the anger was aimed almost exclusively at Catherine. "It wasn't as if she forced me to see Diane. She gave me a choice. She even defended me when she thought Diane was stepping out of line."

"How kind of her." His lips tightened. "And you didn't mention that Diane had stepped out of line with you. Just how ugly did she get?"

"Not that bad. I think she just got overemotional and lost it a couple times. We were both pretty worked up before she left. Between the shock of seeing her, and what she was asking of me, I was barely able to think."

"And she shouldn't have put you through that," he said sharply. "She's out of our lives. She should have stayed there."

"Evidently she thinks differently. According to Catherine, her situation might be desperate. Desperation tends to block out everything but the main objectives."

"Of which she told you little or nothing."

She grimaced. "Though she did offer me any amount I wanted to do the job."

He stared at her in disbelief. "You're not thinking of doing it?"

"No, of course not. I'm just trying to—" She stopped, frowning. "I think I'm trying to defend her from you. Why are you so angry?"

"Because she's trying to take advantage of you. Just as I knew she would. I could see it coming."

"See what coming? We haven't had anything to do with Diane for years." She had a sudden thought. "Unless you've seen her sometime that I didn't know about. Have you?"

"No way," he said harshly. "I haven't seen or heard from her since we filed for divorce. But I knew how she felt about you and I was always on guard."

"And how did she feel about me?" Eve asked slowly. "I didn't have any idea there was any animosity until she dropped a few remarks today. You and I were just good friends and coworkers during the time you were married to her."

He was silent.

"Joe?"

"The only reason we were just good friends is that I thought that I probably could never be anything else to you," he said quietly. "That was the time after you lost Bonnie, and the only use you had for me was to help find her body and the man who had killed her. I'd given up hope of being anything else." He paused. "It was a bad time for me, Eve. I was frustrated and reckless and I needed something to hold on to."

"Diane," she whispered.

"It was in no way a love match," he said harshly. "Our families were in the same social set and we'd known each other for years. She actually proposed to me. She was just out of college but couldn't claim her trust fund until she was married to someone her father approved of. She was fairly wild at the time, and he thought a detective like me would be stable enough to keep her from going completely off the tracks." He shrugged. "It seemed to work out for a while. There was passion and convenience and maybe a way to still keep you near me without hurting anyone. I wasn't thinking straight. I didn't take into consideration that people change and sometimes aren't what you think they are."

"Diane changed." Of course she changed, Eve thought. Even the shallow, selfish girl she'd been at the time would have been influenced by Joe. Diane might have even been in love with him before she proposed that marriage. At any rate, she'd probably liked the idea of staying married to Joe and building a life with him. It seemed Eve had been the only one blind during that time to the qualities that had made Joe Quinn so unique. "She started to resent me?"

"I didn't realize it at the time. I never spoke of you as anything but a good friend, but Diane is very clever."

"Yes, she is. What led to the divorce?"

He was silent a moment. "You remember the time I was shot and in the hospital for weeks?"

"How could I forget? You almost died. I was scared to death."

"But you never came to visit me. Everyone else did, but not you."

"I tried. There was some mix-up at the hospital."

"Yes, quite a mix-up," he said harshly. "I found out that Diane had told the hospital not to let you see me. As my wife, she had the right to restrict visitors."

"What?" Her eyes widened in shock. "I had no idea. You didn't tell me."

"You were the last person I could tell at that point. I'd realized what a thoughtless ass I'd been and knew I had to get myself out of the mess I'd made before I hurt anyone else." His lips twisted. "On top of everything else I was feeling guilty as hell. I'd been just as selfish as Diane from the minute I agreed to that marriage. So I had a talk with her and told her we needed to file for divorce. She wasn't pleased, but I persuaded her not to talk to you or upset you."

"That was... generous of her." She was stunned. It seemed incredible that she had been so blind. "Since I really was the other woman in the breakup."

"Bullshit. You were the only one totally innocent."

She shook her head. "I didn't ask any questions about your divorce. I told myself that I was being sensitive, but I probably realized even then that I loved you and was glad that she was gone. I didn't admit it to you or myself until much later, but that doesn't make me less culpable." She moistened her lower lip. "It makes me the center of all that pain and confusion anyway."

"Don't be ridiculous. I made a mistake and so did Diane. You had nothing to do with it." He looked her in the eye. "And I'm not going to let her show up and make you do something you don't want to do because we screwed up all those years ago."

"I'm not taking the entire blame. There's plenty of that to share. You were an idiot, and Diane was obviously a selfish woman who didn't care who she manipulated as long as she got her own way." Her hand was shaking a little as she brushed her hair back from her temple. "All I'm saying is that somehow we were all in this together and maybe something we did caused a bad domino effect that put Diane Connors in the mess she's in now."

He stared at her in exasperation. "How can you—" Then he started to chuckle. "Only you. Didn't anyone ever tell you that you should be seething with resentment in a situation like this?"

"I'll think about that later. Right now, all I can see is that because I was hurting so badly back then, I was blind and managed to hurt you, too." She swallowed to ease the tightness of her throat. "And that somehow out of all that hellish misery and misunderstanding, I came out of it with all these years of happiness with you and Michael. I've been incredibly lucky."

His smile had faded, and he was coming toward her. "Eve, I never thought that—"

"No." She held up her hand to ward him off. "This isn't the time. I know what you're going to say because I know *you*. I know what we are together." She nodded at the hall. "But Michael is going to burst in here any minute, and we've got to deal with explaining to him about Diane and what she was to you."

"I'll take care of it. It's my responsibility." His smile held a hint of mischief. "Since you politely pointed out what an idiot I was."

"We'll probably both end up handling it, but you can go first." She paused. "And I meant it when I said that there's another responsibility we might have to face with Diane. But we can wait to talk about her after we deal with Michael."

"If he doesn't beat us to the punch. She had an unusual effect on him."

"I noticed."

"Did it bother you?" He was walking toward her again, and this time she didn't stop him. She'd been entirely too reasonable, and she needed him. "I won't have her hurting you in any way." She was in his arms now. "She's nothing to us." He kissed her slowly, with exquisite gentleness. "And you're everything. You know that."

Her arms tightened around him. So dear, so strong, everything she needed and wanted. "You bet I do," she said fiercely as she buried her face in his shoulder. "And that's the way it's going to stay."

"Are you okay?" Catherine's gaze was focused on Diane's face as she unlocked the door of her room. "I have to call Hu Chang, but would you like to order room service in an hour or two? You didn't have much breakfast."

"Maybe later. I have a call or two to make myself." Diane forced a smile. "You're being very protective. I wish you'd stop. I'm really not accustomed to it."

"Hu Chang sent you to me, and I made a promise to him. Until you give up on Eve and walk away, I have to keep it." She tilted her head. "Any chance of that?"

"Not yet. I'll let you know." She entered her room and closed the door. She leaned back against it and closed her eyes as she whispered, "I think I really screwed up, Alon. I meant to be so cool and show them how much I'd changed, but I didn't do it. I can just see you shaking your head at me. But it was harder than I thought..." She opened her eyes in self-disgust. Yeah, that was the way to behave. Put Alon in danger and then whine about it later. But Alon wouldn't have been shaking his head; he would have smiled sadly and tried to understand. As he always did.

Diane pushed away from the door and turned on the lamp. She reached for her phone as she sat down in the easy chair beside the bed. Now wasn't the time to imagine how Alon would react to her failure today. She had to phone him as she'd promised and give him a progress report that would keep him from doing something she wouldn't be able to bear. No, she had to tell him the exact truth. He could always see right through her. She quickly dialed his number and started speaking the moment he picked up: "I had my meeting with Eve and I completely blew it. I said all the wrong things. But that was because I was nervous and scared. At least I got my foot in the door, and this was just the beginning. I can give her tonight and then—"

"Hush, Diane." Alon's voice was very gentle. "I know you did the best you could, and it's okay that it didn't work out. I always knew that there was a chance it wouldn't. I told you that when you spoke to me about going to see her."

"But it will work out. I just have to try harder. Stop being so philosophical, dammit."

He chuckled. "I know you've always hated it when I react with reason instead of emotion, but I can't help it. It's my nature." He was silent. "If you want emotion, I'll tell you that I'm quite overcome with gratitude that you'd do this for me. It means everything to me. Now will you stop crying?"

"I'm not crying . . . yet."

"Then don't start. And don't blame yourself. This was always my fight and not yours. You just pushed your way in, and I was too selfish to shove you away. It's time to bow out gracefully."

"Shut up." The tears were running down her cheeks. "This sounds like goodbye and I'm not going to listen to it. You promised me a week and I'm holding you to it. I'll do better tomorrow and everything will be fine."

"Except you might try a little too hard, and that could be fatal. Let me end this now."

"The hell I will. You gave me a week. Say it."

He sighed. "A week. Satisfied?"

"Yes. No." She drew a shaky breath. "Are you on the island?"

"For the time being."

That sounded too temporary, and it frightened her. "I want you to stay there until the week is up. Will you do that?"

"Why?"

"Whenever I think of you, I want to know you're safe and there where you belong. Will you do that?"

"I should make preparations, Diane."

"Will you do it?"

"I'll do it. You're a difficult woman, but then I always knew that. However, I thought my sterling example might have had some small effect to temper it."

"How wrong can you be? I changed you as much as you changed me. Are you on the beach now?"

"Yes, why?"

"I'm going to hang up, and I don't want to quite leave you yet. Goodbye, Alon. I meant it, tomorrow I'll get what we need." She cut the connection.

She closed her eyes and let the memory of Alon and the island ease the pain and crushing disappointment she was feeling. It was one of the techniques Alon had taught her. Blue skies. White sands. Sun glittering on turquoise seas. Alon walking barefoot beside her, smiling, talking…

She would rest for an hour and then call Catherine and try to persuade her to intercede for her again with Eve tomorrow. If not, then she would go and confront her again by herself. She'd failed today, but there was no way she could ever give up.

For now, though, she would cling to memory and hope and Alon...

"You were right, Nalam," Ralph Daniels said as soon as Joshua Nalam picked up his call. "Diane Connors did show up on Eve Duncan's doorstep today. I was staking out the cottage when I caught sight of Connors and another woman walking into the place. I wasn't sure what you'd want me to do so I just maintained surveillance. She stayed and talked to Duncan for an hour or so and then left. That's what you wanted me to do, right?"

Joshua Nalam swore beneath his breath. "No, you idiot. I also want to know what they were talking about. You were there for a full day and didn't bug the cottage?"

"I'm not an idiot," Daniels said with deadly softness. "You might be able to talk to those goons who work for you like that, but not me. You hired me because you knew my reputation and that I could get you anything you wanted. I'm a professional, and that's a lot different from those yes-men you have at your beck and call. I couldn't bug that cottage because the security there is top-notch. What else could you expect when it belongs to Detective Joe Quinn? You know his reputation. So I observed and waited, and when Connors and that other woman left the cottage, I followed them. I'm now standing in the lobby of the Renaissance Hotel, and I've found out that the other woman is Catherine Ling, who registered two hotel rooms in her name. I haven't been able to get the room numbers yet, but I should manage that within the next hour. The question is, What do you want me to do to Connors after I break into her room?"

Nalam smothered his rage. He wasn't accustomed to having underlings talk to him like this, but he had no intention of losing Daniels. He was too excited about moving forward; besides, he could handle the bastard. It had cost him a fortune to locate this man with his lethal qualifications and willingness to use them in any way ordered. He had brought in an outsider because he'd wanted to make sure that what he was planning now could never be traced to him. "Perhaps I was a little short," he muttered curtly. "You appear to have the situation well in hand."

"Of course I do." Daniels's voice was icy. "And I'd be happy to eliminate Connors tonight if you like. I just have to have my orders."

The son of a bitch was trying to manipulate him, Nalam thought. He probably just wanted the job over with. Didn't he realize who he was talking to? Not to mention Nalam's power and money and ability to bend governments and companies to his will. *Be patient.* Daniels would learn soon enough to appreciate him. If not, he would disappear, just like anyone else who got in his way. "There are other people involved now. I'll have to explore the consequences of taking any action. And there's the question of any information she could be privy to. Interrogation might be better."

"I can do that, too."

"I know you can. Your dossier was quite . . . interesting."

"Yes or no?"

"Don't push me." He hesitated. "Let me think about it. She stole from me and thought she could cheat me of something I wanted. She's probably trying to do the same thing here. She has to be punished. I just have to figure out how. I'll call you back with a final decision. For the time being, surveillance only and as soon as possible bug her room. No violence yet. You understand?"

"I understand. But I still think you should go for the kill." He cut the connection.

Homicidal bastard. Nalam drew a deep breath as he leaned back in his leather chair. He understood the thrill of a death hunt. He was feeling it himself. But he was struggling between fierce satisfaction at locating Diane Connors at last and rage at the disrespect Daniels had just shown him. He was tempted to pick up the phone and call Galman and tell him to get rid of Daniels for him. The satisfaction won; he'd have that Connors bitch soon enough. All he'd have to do was decide whether torture or death was the way to go. He was leaning toward torture. She was definitely the one who had stolen those documents in Manila, which almost certainly meant she knew where he could find Alon Hakali. Torture would make her tell him everything she knew. But what if it didn't? The satisfaction he might get from her death would not be worth finally ridding himself of Hakali after these years of searching. So, keep Daniels on the leash and make the required decision?

On the other hand, death was clean and efficient, and he had need of that efficiency at this particular time.

And after all, there was something to be said for having a homicidal bastard like Daniels eager to obey his every command.

LAKE COTTAGE
9:20 P.M.

Michael looked up from his computer when Joe came into his bedroom that night. "Hi, Dad. I was just emailing Tomas about our trip on the lake today. He's really going to like the photos I sent him. I told him that you said we'd probably go out again tomorrow. Is that still on?"

"Sure, why shouldn't it be?" He dropped down on the chair beside Michael's bed. "We need to check the entire property over before we get too busy. You'll be starting back to school next month."

"Yep, and you and Mom might get busy, too." He shut his computer. "Now that Diane is here."

Joe went still. "Why do you think that would make a difference?" Michael hadn't spoken about anything to do with Diane or Catherine all day. Joe had been waiting for the questions to begin, but Michael had remained silent. He'd just chattered about the trip on the lake and Tomas and what he was going to do when he went back to school. "What does Diane have to do with our schedule?"

"Nothing right now. But sometimes things change." Michael propped himself higher on his pillow. "Isn't that what you came in here to tell me?"

"Maybe. In a manner of speaking." Joe leaned back in his chair. "But possibly not in the way you think. What did you mean, Michael?"

He shrugged. "Diane came here to see Mom, and it upset her. I know Diane didn't mean to do it, but I think sometimes she can't help herself. I was going to ask about it, but you and Mom got all quiet and I decided you'd tell me when you were ready. Was it about Alon?"

Joe shook his head. "We don't know anything about this Alon. What do you know about him?"

Michael shook his head. "Only that Diane is worried about him and wants to protect him. It's all she can think about. She'd do anything for him."

"Really? She didn't mention him to your mom."

"She will. She probably doesn't know how good Mom is at taking care of everyone. Did she just meet her?"

"No, but it's true that perhaps she and Diane don't know each other as well as they might." He grimaced. "My fault. Though I'm beginning to believe I might not know Diane that well myself. That's what I came in here to tell you." He braced himself and then went for it. "A long time ago, I was married to Diane Connors. Long before your mom and I were married."

"Wow." Michael's eyes widened. "Why would you do that? It doesn't make sense."

"There were times back then that evidently I didn't have much sense. And Diane seems to have been equally impaired. We made a huge mistake. But then we were divorced and haven't seen each other in a very long time. During which time I'm certain we both changed enormously."

Michael shook his head. "Not you. You never change, Dad. You're like a rock for Mom and me."

"That might have been my problem with Diane," Joe said gently. "I could only be a rock for your mom and then you. It was probably my fault a mistake was made."

"No!" Michael launched himself into Joe's arms. "I didn't mean that. You don't make mistakes. You're perfect. Diane just misunderstood." His arms tightened around him. "Don't worry, we'll make it right. Do you want me to talk to Mom for you?"

"I believe we've settled everything between us," Joe said huskily. He was so very lucky. "But thank you for the thought." He kissed his forehead. "Anyway, that's why Diane came here. Not to cause trouble, but to ask your mother a favor."

"Is Mom going to do it?"

"I don't know. The favor is your mom's to give. I don't have the right to interfere."

Michael frowned. "But Mom always talks to you about stuff."

"This is kind of a delicate situation. I'm being careful of her feelings."

Michael shook his head. "Why? She knows she always comes first with us."

"Absolutely. But Diane's visit came as a shock. I'm letting your mom become accustomed to the idea that she's suddenly appeared again." He released him and got to his feet. "And now I think I'd better go and tell her that we've had this discussion. Anything else you want me to tell her?"

"No." His face was suddenly sober. "Maybe. You said that you wanted Mom to become accustomed to having Diane here. Why did you say that if you're going to let her make up her own mind about doing that favor?"

"A slip of the tongue? It really is entirely up to her. Why would you think anything else?"

"I don't know." He was gnawing at his lower lip. "I guess because I want Diane to get what she's wanting from Mom. I think she's hurting and I'm worried about her. There's . . . darkness all around her."

"That's not up to you, either, Michael."

"I know that, but it seems like it is. Don't you think I should help her?"

"No," Joe said sharply. "Your mom would definitely not like that. She wouldn't want you involved."

"But Diane is hurting and she needs . . . someone."

"We're not certain about that. If she's in trouble, we'll get someone to help her." He bent and brushed a kiss on Michael's nose. "Are you going to go back to working on your computer or should I turn out the light?"

"Turn out the light. I want to lie here and think for a while."

That's what he was afraid of, Joe thought. He didn't like the idea of Michael lying there and going over ways and means to help Diane. He was grateful that the boy had accepted his previous marriage to Diane calmly—that had been his primary objective. Yet he knew how intensely Michael could become obsessed with any kind of thought or situation that intrigued him. But it was probably wiser to let him go through that process and then come to him about it. "Whatever. Good night, Michael."

"Dad."

He looked back at him. "Yes?"

"Diane's really afraid, Dad," he said soberly. "Not for herself, but for this Alon. But she should be afraid for herself. That darkness..."

How was Joe supposed to answer that? "Sometimes things aren't as they seem. Suppose we both sleep on it? Good night, Michael."

"'Night, Dad."

Joe paused for a moment outside the door. Son of a bitch, that last thought from Michael wasn't what he wanted to take back to Eve from this discussion. Well, it was what it was. They'd find a way to work it out.

He turned and headed for the porch where Eve was waiting.

CHAPTER 4

It seems to have gone very well, considering," Eve said. "You're still his hero and I didn't come out badly, either." She nestled closer to him on the swing. "You did good, Joe."

"I'm not so sure. I think the only one he's rooting for right now is Diane. That's not what I wanted, Eve."

"But it's pure Michael." She was silent a moment. "And there's a chance he saw something in her that you didn't." She wrinkled her nose. "Something that I never even tried to notice. As I was sitting here waiting for you, I was doing my best to remember that time when you were married to her. But it was all a blur. I believe it might be because I didn't want her to be there; I mentally ignored her existence."

He shook his head. "That doesn't sound like you."

"Why not? I'm far from perfect. You're not the only one who was going through a hell of an emotional trauma then. Yes, I was confused about how I felt about you. But you'd *married* her, Joe. I knew I cared about you, that you were a big part of my life. It would have been natural that I'd subconsciously resent her." She lifted her head to look at him. "Just as I resented her when I saw you and Michael with her today. I didn't want you near her."

"Shit." He pressed her head back on his shoulder. "I really did screw up, didn't I? God, I feel guilty. She's nothing to me. You're everything." His voice was raw, hoarse. "Tonight Michael said you always came first, but it's more. I couldn't live without you."

"Don't be ridiculous. Yes, you could. Because you have Michael and all the rest of our family and friends who love and need you." She sat up again. "And I didn't mean to be melodramatic. I just want you to understand that my feelings toward Diane are far from angelic. I'm feeling very human. But I think we have to face that we can't wish Diane out of existence. She was part of our lives that we somehow left behind." She smiled ruefully. "I have a hunch that Michael's already made that decision. We'd better catch up."

"And do what?"

"I'll call Catherine tomorrow and tell her that we both want to see Diane. I won't make any promises. We'll just listen. Is that okay?"

"No." He kissed her. "I'd rather talk to her on my own and see if I can handle the problem myself. After all, I'm the one who screwed up. But that's not going to happen, is it?"

"You've got it." She suddenly grinned. "You weren't listening. I told you I didn't want you near her. I'm reluctantly allowing you to be present during the discussion."

"Interesting." He was smiling back at her. "I believe I'm flattered. Are you really that jealous?"

"No, I'm really that possessive of someone I value very highly." She pulled him to his feet. "And now I want to go to bed and hold you and let you convince me that I'm doing the right thing in allowing that gorgeous, intelligent woman back into our lives."

His arm slid around her waist as he led her toward the door. "I'll try, but my heart won't be in it. I don't think I can concentrate on any woman but you tonight..."

RENAISSANCE HOTEL

"It didn't work out, Hu Chang," Catherine told him when he picked up her call. "Diane's not the most diplomatic person in the world. The way she described Morales and the situation was not comforting. Though it would have taken someone a hell of a lot more persuasive than her to talk Eve into leaving Joe and Michael behind right now."

"I was afraid that Diane would prove less than convincing." Hu Chang sighed. "But if she won't give up, you mustn't, either, Catherine. I'm counting on you to keep her safe."

"You made that clear," she said dryly. "It would help if you could spell out exactly *who* and *what* I'm supposed to keep her safe from. You were completely lacking in those details. Diane wasn't much better."

"Yet you managed to learn about the basics of Diane's problem, didn't you?"

"Vaguely, with gaps as huge as an abyss."

"But you'll still be there to help her cross that abyss?"

She didn't answer. "You mentioned Joshua Nalam," she said instead. "I researched him last night. What the hell does she have to do with someone like that? He's a billionaire with greedy fingers in every pharmaceutical conglomerate in the world. Besides being a personal friend of the president. As far as I could tell, Diane had no connection with him in the past. Why would he be a danger to her?"

"Sometimes things aren't what they seem. There are connections, and then there are connections. This one might not be direct. Queries were made concerning her, but he's made no attempt to contact her as far as I know. You wanted a name and I always try to please." He paused. "As you do, Catherine. What about that abyss?"

He wasn't about to give up. She hesitated. "I told her I'd call Eve again tomorrow and see if I could persuade her to let Diane come to the cottage again. I don't know how much good it will do."

"Excellent."

"I'm glad I've pleased you," she said sarcastically. "But I didn't do it to make you happy. Diane's difficult and tough, and there are moments when I want to sock her. Though I still like her." She was nibbling at her lower lip. "And I feel sorry for her."

"Don't feel too sorry for her. She's quite capable of taking care of herself in most cases."

"Yet you sent her to me. You can't have it both ways," she said. "And that's why I'm lying in this bed and looking across the room at her door cracked open again tonight. I'm going to hang up now that I've given you my report. I'll let you know if she manages to talk Eve into changing her mind. Good night, Hu Chang."

"Wait. Perhaps there's something I should tell you." He added, "Though you won't be pleased."

She stiffened. "Tell me."

"I received a call from Richard Cameron today."

"Received a call or phoned him yourself?"

"I did *not* call him. I knew that would displease you, and there was no reason. You were doing what I needed." He paused. "I told you he would probably find out about Diane Connors on his own, given time. He knew more than I thought he would, but he still asked me for more details. I refused to give them to him."

She muttered a curse. "And he took no for an answer?"

"I did not say that. He asked me another question."

"What?"

"He asked how you were, Catherine."

She closed her eyes. "He *knows*, Hu Chang."

"Not from any information I gave him. But it's entirely possible. However, I will make certain not to divulge anything regarding you. If you wish to avoid contact with him, it would be wise if you could persuade Eve to take the job Diane is offering with all due speed."

"I can only do what I can. It's between Diane and Eve." She opened her eyes. "I'm not going to worry about it. But my fingers will be crossed. It must have been tempting when Cameron asked you to let him take over. Thank you for trusting me to do the job."

"You were my first choice. You are always my first choice. Good night, Catherine."

She lay there for minutes after he had cut the connection. She was shaking. *Stop it.* Cameron might not know as much as Hu Chang believed. Besides, he was always busy and Diane might not be a top priority yet. But Catherine was definitely a top priority to him. He had shown her that in a dozen cities, in a thousand intimate ways.

Block it out. Go to sleep. Tomorrow would come soon enough, and she would do her best to bring Eve and Diane together if it seemed best. Perhaps she could avoid Cameron entirely. She turned out the light.

Darkness. Embrace it.

Forget Cameron . . .

Something was *wrong*.

Catherine went from asleep to wide awake in the space of a heartbeat.

She had heard something . . .

No, that wasn't right. She had *felt* something.

Her wristwatch was vibrating.

She looked down and saw the band of light on the watch face.

Which meant the motion sensor she'd placed on Diane's mini-bar pointed at the door to the corridor was signaling entry. Catherine had locked that door herself before she'd gone to her own room.

But that door was now opening. It might be perfectly innocent. Diane might have just gotten out of bed to go to the bathroom and set off the sensor...

Or someone might be trying to open her door—or already be in the room!

Either way, Catherine wasn't going to take a chance. Her hand moved to the bedside table and she quickly, quietly grabbed her gun she'd set out in readiness.

Then she was out of bed and gliding silently toward the adjoining door.

Listen.

Watch.

Nothing to watch. Diane's room was as dark as Catherine's had been. She could barely see Diane's shape huddled in the bed across the room.

But she could hear something... breathing.

Not the sound of steady breathing that Diane would make while sleeping. This sound was harsher and close to the door leading to the corridor. Someone was standing beside that door!

And he wasn't staying there; now he was moving toward Diane's bed. She couldn't tell if he had a weapon. Better not run the risk, just take him out. Ask questions later.

"Stop right there," she hissed as she ducked to one side of the adjoining door. "One more step and I'll—"

A bullet whistled by her head, grazing the side of her neck! Well, that answered her question about the weapon, she thought grimly. She couldn't return the fire and risk him using that gun on Diane. She flew across the room and launched herself in a low tackle.

"*Bitch!*" It was a man, strong and powerful, and he was beating her around the head and shoulders with the butt of his pistol as she brought him to the floor.

Pain.

Dizzy...

"Catherine!" It was Diane's voice. "What's happening?"

"Get out of here, Diane." She was trying to lift her gun again as she fought the man off her. He was cursing and so strong... "Now!"

"Don't be stupid. I can't leave you." She jumped out of bed, jerking the bedside lamp out by the cord. The next instant the lamp came crashing down on the head of the man struggling with Catherine. He staggered but didn't fall. "Who the hell is he?"

"Go!" Catherine aimed her gun blindly at the attacker and pressed the trigger.

He cried out, but the butt of his gun came down with even greater viciousness on her head one more time. "Whore. I'll *kill* you!"

The pain in her temple was so great, Catherine wasn't sure he hadn't already done that. Then she was dazedly aware that he was tearing himself away from her and hobbling across the room toward the door to the corridor. She caught the briefest glimpse of him silhouetted against the light of the hall; then he was gone.

More lights.

Diane had turned on the overhead lights and was kneeling beside Catherine on the floor. "Crazy." Tears were streaming down her face. "You're crazy. You just barge into my room and let some weirdo beat you up. All this blood...But I think that's just the one cut on your throat. Still, I shouldn't have listened to Hu Chang. He said you were so wonderful, but this isn't wonderful."

"Stop . . . yelling at me. I couldn't fire my gun. He was standing right over you at the bed. I might have caused him to fire at you."

"I wasn't yelling at you. Or maybe I was. I was scared. But I'm okay now. Be quiet while I get something to take care of all those bruises and cuts. I'm a little worried about that bruise on your temple."

"You do that," Catherine whispered. Her vision was straining, blurring, fading. "I promise to be quiet, but I'm not sure I'm going to be able to stick around . . . until you find a way to patch . . . me together. I'm having trouble seeing you . . ."

Michael was screaming!

"Shit." Eve sat up straight in bed and then swung her feet to the floor. "What the hell is wrong with him?"

"Nightmare?" Joe raised himself on one elbow, shaking his head to clear it.

"You know he swears he never has nightmares. He just *sees* things." She grabbed her robe and headed for the door. "Maybe something frightened him."

"Or maybe there's a first time for everything." But he was throwing the sheet aside even as he spoke.

Eve wasn't waiting for him. She was already halfway down the hall toward Michael's room. An instant later she threw open his door. "Hey, why were you screaming? Did you want to scare your dad and me—" She broke off as she saw his face. It was pale, tears were running down his cheeks, and he was frantically putting tennis shoes on his bare feet. "What happened?" Then she was sitting on the bed beside him. "Talk to me, Michael."

"She's hurt!" He flew into her arms. "Blood. Not as much blood as Diane said but she was hurting, and now I can't reach her anymore.

We have to go, Mom." He tore away from her and was trying to tie his shoes again. "He was hitting her and she was bleeding."

"A dream?" Eve asked. "You dreamed Diane was hurt."

"Not Diane." He frowned. "Catherine was the one who was hurt. And it wasn't a dream. I was in the dark with her and she was afraid for Diane. She could hear him breathing and she had to keep him away from the bed."

"Catherine." Eve felt a bolt of terror. Catherine was his friend. The idea of her being hurt or killed was infinitely more frightening than if it had been a stranger. Not only to him but also to Eve. Don't think about herself. Soothe him. "It must only have been a dream. You know how tough she is, Michael. She's been CIA since she was a teenager."

"He had a gun and he was hitting her with it. We have to go help her."

"We will." Joe was standing in the doorway. "But don't you think that it would be better to call Catherine and Diane and make certain you've got the facts right?" He pulled his phone out of the pocket of his robe. "I'll try Catherine first. Why don't you change out of those pajamas while I do that? Your tennis shoes don't really make that good a statement with them." He glanced at Eve. "Renaissance Hotel?"

She nodded. She was profoundly grateful that Joe was here and handling the situation with his usual cool professionalism while keeping Michael calm. "That's what Catherine said." She turned back to Michael. "Come on, let's wash your face and then get you dressed."

"But we'll go?" He was wiping his eyes on the sleeve of his pajama top. "She needs us, Mom."

"If she needs us, we'll be there for her." She gave him a nudge. "Come on, kid."

Joe came to stand in the doorway of the bathroom a few minutes later. "No answer in Catherine's room." He held up his hand as he saw Michael's alarmed expression. "I'm calling Diane's room. You said that was where she was?"

He nodded. "It was Diane's bed. He was going toward—"

"Diane?" He made a shushing gesture to Michael. "Joe Quinn. Michael's had a disturbing dream and wanted to speak to Catherine. Is she there?"

"Did you think I wouldn't recognize your voice, Joe?" Diane asked, her voice shaking. "For once I'm glad as hell to hear it. Catherine's here right now, but she won't be for long. They're wheeling her out of my room now. Someone broke into my room and she went after him. He got away, and by the time I got security up here, he was long gone. I called an ambulance to take Catherine to the hospital. I did the initial exam and bandaging but I decided to get her in for testing. My luck hasn't been good lately and she deserves the best."

"How is she?"

"Pretty beat up. I think she'll be okay, but I want her to have all the usual scans and X-rays. I don't like the fact that she's still unconscious."

"Neither do I. Where are they taking her?"

"The EMT said Northside Hospital." They heard conversation in the background, then Diane came back on the phone. "I've got to hang up. I'm going in the ambulance with her."

"Stay with the EMTs and hospital personnel. We'll be there as soon as we can."

Diane hesitated. "'We'?"

Eve took the phone from him. "We," she repeated. "Catherine's my friend and you almost got her killed. Don't you dare let anyone shoot you or do anything that will make what she did meaningless. Do you hear me?"

There was silence. "I do feel terrible about Catherine, Eve. And I'll try my very best to obey you. Though evidently, I'm not so good where self-preservation is concerned. I'll see you at the hospital." She cut the connection.

OUTSIDE THE ER
NORTHSIDE HOSPITAL

"How's Catherine?" Eve asked as she strode toward Diane across the waiting room. "Is she still unconscious?"

"No, she regained consciousness in the ambulance coming here." Diane made a face. "But she's been in and out while they've been examining her. Other than that, she's not in too bad shape. A few cuts and bruises on her face and shoulders, and a deep scratch on her neck where that son of a bitch's bullet skimmed entirely too close. They've got several tests scheduled that will probably take a few hours and then, if all goes well, I think they'll release her."

"But you're not sure."

"What do you want me to say? It's in their hands now. But if the tests go well, I'd feel safe in releasing her." She stared her in the eye. "And I'm a damn good doctor these days, Eve. You can rely on my judgment."

"Can I? I'm having problems relying on anything about you. Catherine wouldn't be in that ER if she hadn't been trying to protect you."

"I know that," Diane said wearily. "I was hoping that Hu Chang was wrong about the risk when he sent me to her. But he wasn't, was he?" She shook her head bitterly. "Or maybe I would have just told myself it was safe to do it anyway. I desperately wanted her help persuading you. And then we've already established that I'm not a very nice person."

"I don't know if you are or not," Eve said. "I didn't know you all that well when you were married to Joe. And I can't say I'm impressed with what I've seen since you showed up here. I certainly don't like you putting my friend in danger." She paused, then said reluctantly, "But I don't believe you had any intention of deliberately letting that happen to Catherine. I watched the two of you together. I think I'm a good enough judge of character to realize that there was no antipathy between you." She added, "And Catherine didn't seem troubled by you, only the situation..."

"Because Hu Chang had hijacked her into doing something she didn't want to do," Diane said bluntly. "And I helped him. It was partly my fault."

"Perhaps," Eve said dryly. "But I find I'm hesitant about blaming you when you're so eager to blame yourself. It gives me a sense of—"

"Is Catherine okay?" Michael was running across the waiting room toward Eve. "I think she has to be. I would have known if she—"

"She's better, Michael." Eve put her arm around him and held him close. "We just have to get the final report from the doctors." She looked beyond him at the elevator. "Where's your dad?"

"After we dropped you off at the front, we parked, and then Dad needed to stop at security for a minute to get permission to talk to Catherine about what happened to her." His gaze shifted to Diane. "Hello, Diane. I'm glad you're not hurt."

"So am I." She was trying to smile. "You shouldn't be here, Michael."

"Yes, I should. I had to make sure about Catherine. She's my friend." His gaze was searching her face. "Don't be sad. She won't blame you."

"I'm not sure about that."

"I am," he said gravely. "Catherine is CIA, that means she's kind of a policewoman, sort of like my dad. It's their job to catch the bad guys and take care of everyone. They don't blame us for getting into trouble."

"That's very generous." She glanced at Eve. "I hope he's right."

"He usually is," Eve said. "Sit down, Michael. I don't think they're going to let you go in to see her."

He sighed. "Because I'm a kid." He took his computer out of his backpack, but he didn't open it. "Dad didn't think so, either. He made me bring my computer. But Catherine would want me here. She'd know I'd never bother her."

"Yes, she would. But doctors have to be careful." She glanced at Diane. "Don't they, Diane?"

"Yes." Then she suddenly smiled. "But you should do as I say, not as I do, Michael. I've been known to be a little reckless on occasion."

"But not if it meant Catherine getting hurt," he said quietly. "You wouldn't want that."

"You're very sure." Diane's smile faded and she glanced at Eve. "No, I'd never want that to happen. These days when I'm reckless, I'm usually the only one at risk. I try to keep it that way."

"But that didn't work out for you this time, did it?" Eve asked. "You brought Catherine into it."

She flinched. "I was careless. I wanted it too much. And I didn't believe I'd been followed. I wasn't sure that anyone knew I might be a danger."

"A lack of knowledge that might have been fatal for Catherine," Eve said. "I can't tell you how angry that would have made me. I barely know you, but she's my friend. You'd do well to get yourself—" She broke off as she saw Joe getting off the elevator and coming toward them. "We'll discuss this later. I have to know who did this. I want the entire truth, Diane." She got to her feet as Joe reached them. "Diane said that Catherine was doing better. Are they going to let you question her?"

He nodded curtly. "They've given me twenty minutes to get as much of a statement as I can while she rests before they take her up to radiology for X-rays and more testing. Do you want to go in with me?"

"Of course." She looked at Diane. "I'll let you know how she's doing when I come out."

Diane nodded. "I don't imagine she's going to want to see me any time soon. I'll stay here with your son. But will you let her know I'd like to apologize to her as soon as they allow visitors?" She gazed at Joe and said defensively, "I did do my best for her."

"I know you did," he said as he took Eve's arm and turned her toward the ER. "The EMTs reported you did a good job before they got her here to the hospital."

She nodded. "Damn right. But I don't think you'll learn anything from her. It was all darkness and chaos, and I'll bet she won't be able to tell you who was on the attack."

"Well, then I might have to come back and talk to you. Right?" He was nudging Eve across the room. "You'd better have answers, Diane."

"Darkness and chaos," Diane repeated. "I can't pull answers out of nowhere, Joe."

"But it might not be nowhere to you. I have no idea who you've been with or what you've been experiencing all these years." He added harshly, "We'll have to explore that possibility if Catherine can't help us." The doors of the ER closed behind them.

Diane muttered a curse beneath her breath as she tore her gaze away from the door leading to the ER. It was no surprise to her that Joe was going to insist on asking her questions. Not only was it his job, but the victim had been a friend of both Eve and him. Victim? No, it was Diane who was meant to be the victim. All the more reason for Joe to go on the hunt for a reason that Catherine had been caught in the crossfire.

The questions would come and she would not be able to satisfy them. Any answer would invariably lead to Alon, and she could not involve him. It would probably be better if she disappeared before Joe finished taking Catherine's statement.

But she couldn't leave before she was sure that Catherine was going to be all right. She'd accepted Hu Chang's offer to have Catherine help her, and Catherine might have died in that hotel room tonight.

"Who is Alon?"

Diane stiffened, stunned, her gaze flying to Michael in the chair next to her. "What?"

"I'm sorry." He was frowning uneasily at her. "I know I'm not supposed to ask questions about private stuff, but it's not as if you're a stranger. You were married to Dad, and that's kind of like family."

"Not necessarily. It entirely depends on how people think about each other. That was a long time ago, Michael. You should talk to them about it." The words were tumbling out and she barely knew what she was saying. What he'd just asked her had almost thrown her into shock. "Why did you ask me about Alon?"

"Because you kept thinking about him," he said simply. "It was running through everything that you thought and felt. Even at the cottage, I could feel him there." He was frowning. "You're worried about him. Worried and sad and I think it's all mixed up with what happened to Catherine. Is it?"

"Maybe." Okay, Diane had seen signs ever since she'd met Michael that he was a little strange—maybe more than strange. During her time in the rain forests and jungles with One World Medical, she had run across tribal members who claimed mystical skills: mind readers, clairvoyants, even a few boasting to be witch doctors. In dealing with them, she had come to accept that extrasensory skills sometimes did exist. She was willing to bet that Michael was psychic. At any rate, since the boy appeared to take his own ability for granted, she decided to do the same. "Alon is my friend. But there's a reason why your parents told you that you shouldn't eavesdrop on private stuff. There are times when it not only seems rude, but is difficult to explain."

"I was only wondering if I could help," he said soberly. "Sometimes I can, Diane."

She was touched. He meant it. Those clear, amber eyes that were so like Joe's were gazing at her with a troubled look. "Thank you. But you can only help me by being my friend and not mentioning Alon again. He wouldn't like it. He's a very private person, Michael. Okay?"

He nodded. "Whatever you say." He opened his computer. "But if Mom and Dad knew you were this worried, they'd try to help you."

"Because I'm 'family'?" Her lips indented at the corners. He clearly had not paid any attention to what she'd said regarding relationships.

"Yes, you should really have another talk with them..."

"Look, Joe, I told you everything that happened. I don't know anything more," Catherine said jerkily. "All I knew was that someone was after Diane and I had to stop him. I only caught the faintest glimpse of him as he ducked into the hall. The only thing I can be sure about is that he knew what he was doing. I locked that door, but he got it open. Do you think I haven't tried to remember any possible clue or description of him?" She grimaced. "Though that would pretty much be a lost cause even if I wasn't in this shape. It was too dark."

"Darkness and chaos, Diane said." Eve's hand tightened on her arm. "He could have killed you. Why did you do it, Catherine?"

"Diane was my job and I had to take care of her." She tried to shake her head and then flinched with pain. "I'd do it again. Hu Chang said she was worth it."

"His opinion. That's debatable," Joe said. "You said that you knew very little about her."

"That's going to change," she said. "As soon as I get out of here, I'm going to have a long discussion with Hu Chang. I've earned it."

"We'd do better to have that discussion with Diane," Joe said grimly. "She's the one who almost got you killed. I was only waiting until I made sure you were all right before I had a talk with her."

"No," Catherine said sharply. "The last thing I want is to have you grilling her, Joe. Let me handle it. I'll talk to her as soon as I'm better. She's on edge. If you scare her, she might take off, and then I'd have to go after her."

"I believe it would take a lot to scare her these days," Joe said dryly. "And it's my job to interrogate her after what happened tonight."

"Then wait until I can do it with you. Please, Joe." She made a face. "Though you're right about her not being scared. You should have seen how she jumped on that asshole and hit him with a lamp. That's what made him finally let me go and run away."

"The fact that you shot him might have had something to do with it. You shouldn't worry about me hurting her tender feelings."

"Please, Joe," she repeated. "Hu Chang wouldn't have sent me if there hadn't been good reason. Diane could have died tonight. She might still be tracked down and killed if she bolts because you're pressuring her."

He didn't speak for a minute. "I'll wait," he finally said gruffly. "I'll assign an officer to keep watch over you until we get you out of here. But I won't wait long, and I'll be keeping an eye on Diane." He turned to Eve. "We'd better get out of here and let them take her up to radiology."

Eve nodded and leaned forward to brush a kiss on Catherine's cheek. "Diane wanted to come in and apologize. It's up to you. You don't have to do it. Is it okay?"

"Yes." She closed her eyes. "Send her in right away. I do want to talk to her..."

"I didn't want you to be hurt."

Catherine opened her eyes to see Diane standing beside the bed. "I know you didn't. But whatever you're mixed up in made it happen. I figure you owe me."

"Maybe," Diane said warily.

"No, positively. Now be quiet and let me get this out. My head is aching, and those nurses are going to stream in here in a couple of minutes and whisk me up to take all kinds of tests that probably won't be pleasant. When that's over, I don't want to hear that you ran out on me." She met her eyes. "Because we're in this together for the long haul. If you run, I'll be coming after you. Do you understand?"

Diane smiled faintly. "You're being very clear."

"Good. When I can manage to think, we can get down to making sense of this craziness you've entangled me in." She waved her hand.

"Now get out of here." She closed her eyes. "And don't upset Eve or Joe while they're so worried about me. You seem to be able to do that without even trying. There's every chance we're going to need them."

"I'll be very good," Diane said shakily. "Am I allowed to say thank you for saving my life?"

"No, waste of time. Just do what I told you. Everything will be fine..."

"It will be fine, Nalam. Don't worry about it," Daniels said through set teeth. "I just wasn't expecting that other bitch to come bursting into the Connors woman's room. Things went haywire from there. But as soon as I get back on my feet, I'll take care of it."

"You bet you will." Nalam's voice was vicious. "She actually shot you? What kind of weakling are you?"

"A flesh wound, it's nothing," Daniel said. "And never call me a weakling again. I'll take care of Connors and I'll cut the heart out of that CIA bitch, Ling. I just need a little time. I'll be on my way to that hospital where they took her as soon as I finish bandaging my leg."

"You'll do no such thing. You've raised enough hell for one night. I won't chance you causing more trouble at that hospital. Be patient and wait for the right moment. After Ling's been released, you can go after both of them. Connors was never the main target anyway. She was always just a way I could get to Hakali. It just seemed too coincidental that she was heading for Atlanta, the same place where Duncan does her work. I thought I'd have you take her out before she could do anything that might spoil my plans for luring Hakali into a trap."

"I want Ling *now*," Daniels said coldly. "She'll be vulnerable at the hospital."

"Do what I tell you. You can tend to her later. Move on to the next target."

"I'll do it after I finish off Ling."

Nalam swore. "You'll do what I pay you to do. You're lucky I don't tell you to go screw yourself. If I didn't want this job to remain confidential, I wouldn't put up with this. I'm being very tolerant with you."

Tolerant? Daniels's hand clenched on his phone. He was the one who had been shot. All Nalam could think about was that the job hadn't gone off perfectly. Didn't the asshole realize that he would never forgive these insults? Well, he'd know soon enough. After this job was over and he got his money, he'd go after the big man himself. "Yes, I'm very lucky. I'll do whatever you say."

"That's what I like to hear. Now find out what's going on at the hospital and we'll make plans."

"I already have a few plans of my own. I'm on my way. I'll call you." He hung up and looked down at the blood trickling from the wound in his calf. First blood, he thought. Ling had drawn first blood.

Rage was tearing through him. She had made him look like a fool in front of Nalam.

But both of them would see that would never happen again. He would bind up this damn wound and head for the hospital.

And if he felt like it, he would stop waiting patiently for the right moment. It was stupid to waste this time while Ling was lying helpless and vulnerable.

He'd cut the bitch's throat and watch her choke on her own blood.

CHAPTER 5

CATHERINE'S HOSPITAL ROOM
ONE DAY LATER

The scent of him...

Lord, how well she knew that scent. Clean and spicy and somehow distinctly his own. How often had she lay beneath him with it surrounding her while his hands—

"Open your eyes, Catherine," Cameron said grimly. "Yes, it's me, and I'm tired of waiting around for you to regain consciousness. Having to sit here and look at those wounds on your face and throat is really pissing me off." His hand covered hers on the bed. Warm, strong, vibrant. "I'm annoyed with a lot of things that have been going on with you lately, so don't try my patience."

Her eyes flew open. He was looking down at her, those brilliant blue eyes glittering, but his lips were tight. For an instant she was swept away by the sheer magnetism of everything he was. Power. Electricity. Grace. Intense sexuality. Cameron... It took her a few seconds to come to full consciousness and realize she should resent what he'd said, and what he'd done... "I don't give a damn what you're annoyed about, Cameron." She jerked her hand away. "And you were *reading* me. You promised you'd never do that again."

"That was before you decided to go out and get yourself half killed." He covered her hand again. "And then let me find out from Slade, the man I had watching you. Why didn't you at least tell Hu Chang to call me?"

"Because he didn't know I was here. And because I'm not any of your business." She didn't try to push him away again. She was not going to involve herself in a physical altercation with him. That never turned out well. "And how did you get in here anyway? Joe has one of his men from the precinct guarding me."

"And I compliment him on his choice. The officer was very competent. But I managed to convince him he needed to take a break while I sat with you."

Of course he did, she thought in frustration. Cameron could persuade anyone to do anything if he chose. It was one of his psychic gifts that she found annoying as well as dangerous. "And why would you have any of your people watch me? I told you the last time we met that it should be the last time."

"You did say that. I don't remember agreeing. I always know where you are. And as it happens, I had a specific reason to determine your exact location this time. But I didn't expect to find you in a hospital. I just told my friend Slade to track down Eve Duncan and you'd probably be close." He added wryly, "Lo and behold, by following Eve he found you'd been brought here by Diane Connors, in whom we both evidently have a very active interest. What a coincidence. Needless to say, I was most unhappy to hear you'd been hurt because Hu Chang had sent her to you."

"Too bad. Here I am." She shrugged. "Now call off this Slade and get out of my life. You and I really have nothing in common, and I have enough disturbances without you being on the scene."

"I'm a very great disturbance, aren't I, Catherine?" he asked softly. "But you're wrong about us having nothing in common. We have a difference in philosophy and the way to accomplish a common aim, but our desires couldn't be more similar." He smiled. "And there's nothing ordinary about them; they tend toward the unusual and erotic. Remember?"

He knew very well she remembered. She wasn't at all sure he wasn't still reading her. Even if he wasn't, the electricity between them was causing her heart to pound and her breasts to tauten and swell. His thumb was now gently rubbing the inside of her wrist, and she could feel the muscles tense, the pulse leap. "Stop it, Cameron."

He immediately stopped. "You're right, I shouldn't try to seduce you at the moment. I'm still annoyed with you. It's just damn tempting to ignore it and go for the sure thing."

She stiffened. "It is not a sure thing."

"Yes, it is. It's the one thing that *is* certain between us. But it's not fair to use it and risk spoiling it because you're making things difficult for me." He released her hand and leaned back in his chair. "So we'll talk and try to get this straight. I talked to your doctor and he said that you could have gone home when all the tests came back clear. You chose to stay here overnight. Why?"

"Why not? I was hurt, maybe I needed the rest."

"You never pamper yourself. You're one tough cookie. If you stayed, you must have had a reason." He gazed thoughtfully at her face. "Tell me. I don't want to have to read you again. I'm trying to keep my word, but I was damn impatient." He grimaced. "And a little worried. Even though they said you were okay, I had to bring you back to me. Did they give you sedation?"

"One shot," she admitted ruefully. "It was clear not wanting to leave the hospital was looked upon as a threatening sign."

"My thought exactly." He tilted his head. "Why?"

She didn't answer.

"There was no reason unless I'm not looking deep enough. Is that it? You're very smart. One of the CIA's best. What did you want to accomplish?" He added, "Maybe we should be talking about Diane Connors. Everything appears to lead in that direction."

She stiffened.

He nodded slowly. "I realized she would be a challenge, but I was hoping she wouldn't be a danger to you. It seemed I was wrong. I knew Hu Chang would probably tell you what I said when I spoke to him the other day. Did you panic when you thought I was getting close?"

"I don't panic."

"I didn't mean to insult you. But you might have suffered a degree or two of alarm."

"Perhaps."

"You knew I'd come after her. She's too valuable to leave out there to be scooped up by the bad guys." He added quietly, "What I heard about her was amazing. Can't we work together on this, Catherine?"

"Together? You never cooperate. You just take. Well, I won't let you take Diane Connors. Hu Chang asked me to protect her, and as far as I'm concerned, that includes you." She shook her head bitterly. "And you probably know more than I do about all this. You usually do. Diane didn't give me more than the sketchiest outline of what she wanted from Eve."

He gave a low whistle. "And you still went in and risked your life trying to save her."

"It was my job. I promised Hu Chang."

"Such devotion," he murmured. "I really must persuade you to come and work for me."

"Not a chance."

"Someday. When you see how right I am." He looked at her speculatively. "And this might be the way to lure you away from all the warmongers out there. I'll have to think about it."

She frowned. "By using Diane?"

He nodded. "It's really an exceptional opportunity. You'll see what I mean when you get her to open up for you." He paused, still staring at her curiously. "Why did you stay the extra day? I'm not going to tattle on you."

She shrugged. "Don't be ridiculous." Oh, well, why not tell him? "The situation with Eve and Joe was extremely difficult for Diane to handle. When I regained consciousness after the tests, Eve, Joe, and Diane were all here. All of them concerned about me and totally absorbed in getting the man who was trying to kill Diane." She paused. "And because they seemed to be getting along much better than any other time since I'd brought them together, I thought it might be an opportunity for Diane to bond with Eve." She added, "So I decided staying the night wouldn't hurt to keep the goodwill flowing."

He chuckled. "Quite true. And brought you one more step closer to accomplishing the mission Hu Chang assigned you. Lord, I have missed you, Catherine."

She found herself smiling back at him in spite of herself. And she had missed him, she thought as she looked up at him. He was probably the most dangerous man that she would ever encounter, but she hadn't been able to fight what she felt for him since the moment they'd met. She kept her voice steady. "I promised Hu Chang. Go away, Cameron."

"I can't do that," he said gently. "Diane Connors is too great a risk, and I have to control her." He got to his feet and bent down; his hand stroked her long dark hair with exquisite gentleness. "Beautiful, everything about you is beautiful. You're all shimmering ebony and silky gold, and I can't tell you how much I missed touching you like this." He kissed her forehead. Then his lips moved down and gently brushed across the place on her throat where the bullet from the assassin's gun had skimmed the flesh. "But they've already hurt you, and I can't permit that to happen again."

"Permit?" Catherine was abruptly jarred out of the haze that he was weaving around her. "Go to hell, Cameron."

"Someday, perhaps." He laughed again and kissed her on the lips before straightening. "But you'd probably follow and try to save me from myself." He tucked her sheet higher. "In the meantime, you'll just have to become accustomed to the idea that you're not getting rid of me for some time to come. It appears that the game is on. I won't get in your way, but I do have people who will keep an eye on you."

"So you said." She tried to remember the name. "Slade? I've never heard you mention him. Someone new in your group?"

He nodded. "James Slade. New and very talented. If he works out, he'll probably end up my second in command someday. He's an ex-marine who's done everything from special services to hunting down terrorists in Afghanistan. He spent his entire life in the military trying to save the planet before he became disillusioned." He reached in his pocket for his phone. "Take a good look at him. I don't want you to be alarmed if you catch a glimpse of him."

"I won't be alarmed." She barely glanced at the tall, slim man in the photo. He appeared to be somewhere in his forties with crew-cut graying hair and tan, weathered skin. The primary impression she received was of power and watchfulness. "I'm sure he's very competent. But you'd better warn him not to get in my way or I'll take him down."

"I'll be certain to advise him of that," Cameron said solemnly, though his eyes were twinkling. "But he's valuable, so I'd appreciate you going easy on him." He turned and headed for the door. "Take care, Catherine. I don't want to hear about you ending up like this again. It would cause me to indulge in actions that I prefer to delay if possible."

"And I don't want you to give me—" But he was already gone, she realized in frustration. Give his damn orders and then leave her and go about his business. What else could she expect from Richard Cameron, who was looked upon practically as a prince by his followers all over the world? The answer was that she could expect courtesy and respect, and she would demand it from the arrogant bastard the next time she saw him. Whenever that might be, she thought. Yet it would probably be soon based on those last remarks he had made.

Well, then she'd better get out of this bed and get to work. She felt a sudden surge of exhilaration as she threw the sheet aside and her feet hit the floor. No time for gentle persuasion with Eve and Joe. No time for patience with Diane's silence.

Cameron was on the scene.

And the game was on.

"Is she all right?" James Slade straightened away from the wall in the corridor where he'd been waiting outside Catherine's hospital room. "You were a long time, Cameron. I was wondering if I should come in and check."

"I'm glad you didn't." He grimaced. "Catherine doesn't appreciate surveillance and she wasn't in the best humor. She threatened to put you down if you got in her way."

"I imagine I could take care of myself," Slade said dryly. "She might be CIA, but I have a good deal of experience. You wouldn't have assigned me to find her if you hadn't trusted me. Everyone knows she's special to you." He saw the flicker of expression cross Cameron's face. "Was that out of line? No one ever accused me of tact. I call it the way I see it. Get someone else if you want me to ignore all the scuttlebutt I've been hearing since I signed on with you."

"I might do that," Cameron said. "If I didn't believe that you're being overdefensive." His gaze searched Slade's face, which had no more expression than the craggy side of a mountain. "I admit I was a bit rough on you when I heard about Catherine being hurt."

"You tore me a new one," Slade said bluntly. "And that was okay because I respect you more than anyone I've ever met. I wouldn't have joined you otherwise. But it bothered me that I wanted to do well for you and hadn't. I'd failed to protect her. It won't happen again."

"No, it won't," Cameron said quietly. "It can't happen again or I'll have to step in. I don't give a damn about any scuttlebutt you've heard, but Catherine Ling *is* special. Nothing must hurt her in any way. Do you understand?"

Slade nodded jerkily. "I told you I did."

"Good. And it seems she's involved herself with someone else who is going to become important to me and a good many other people. Diane Connors. So make certain I know everything I should about her also."

"Is that all?"

"Not quite. I've had reports that Nalam Pharmaceuticals has been hiring additional personnel to search for this Diane Connors. I want to know how close any of those men might have come to what happened in that hotel room. Other than that, you're on your own." He smiled. "One thing will lead to another. You have great instincts. You'll know when it's time to move to the next phase. I respect you, too, Slade. That's why I gave you this assignment." He looked back at Catherine's room as he punched the button for the elevator. "She'll be on the move now. You should probably get back to her and be on high alert. Contact Corbett if you need any resources. Keep me informed."

"You're leaving?"

"I assure you that she won't want to see me again anytime soon." He smiled wryly. "And I have a few calls to make and my own agenda to take care of in preparation for when she does." He got on the elevator. "One must always be prepared for Catherine."

"So I'm here," Diane said warily as she came into Catherine's hospital room an hour later. "You command, I obey. What's wrong?"

"Probably more than I want to know about," Catherine said grimly. "But I have no choice. I'm not going to be blindsided again like I was when I walked into your hotel room the other night. I was hired to take care of you, but I won't do it without knowing what I'm up against." She gestured to the one chair in the room. "Sit down. We're going to have a discussion." She sat down on the edge of the bed. "No more stalling. I'm going to have to talk to Eve and Joe, and I have no intention of lying to either of them. You used me to get to Eve. And for Pete's sake, I had to persuade Joe to let me talk you into giving facts in an attempted murder case." She looked her directly in the eye. "Time's up, Diane. I want the truth."

"And I don't have to give it to you." Diane slowly sat down. "I could walk away." She smiled crookedly. "I probably *should* walk away. I'm feeling very guilty about almost getting you killed the other night. I don't want it to happen again."

"Neither do I," Catherine said dryly. "And I intend to prevent it at all costs. But Hu Chang said that you were worth saving, and I promised him that I'd do it. Not with my hands tied behind my back, though. Not any longer." She shrugged. "And who knows? Maybe

I won't agree with Hu Chang that you're important enough to risk my neck. I won't be able to judge until I hear what you have to say. Perhaps you'll get your way and I'll just tell you to hit the road."

Diane chuckled. "Don't insult me. We both know Hu Chang is an excellent judge of value." Her smile faded. "I don't want to do this. As long as you have no real knowledge, you're much safer. That's why I told Hu Chang you weren't to know."

"It didn't seem to keep me from ending up here in the hospital. I don't care whether you want to do it or not. Just do it."

"You're very pushy, Catherine." She lifted her chin and said recklessly, "You will remember I tried to save you from yourself, won't you?" She paused. "Okay, what do you want to know?"

"You could start with that man who tried to kill you. Do you have any idea who he was?"

"I told all of you the truth. I only caught that one glimpse of him at the door, and I didn't recognize him." She shrugged. "But that didn't mean anything. Hu Chang said that I should expect hired goons coming after me and not to trust anyone."

"Hired by whom?"

"I don't know for sure. My guess is it could be Joshua Nalam. He owns Nalam Pharmaceuticals and half a dozen other multibillion-dollar companies."

"Nalam." Catherine nodded. "Hu Chang mentioned the name when I called him that first night—when you were being so uncooperative. I was going to follow up on it, but Hu Chang was being vague. Why on earth would some billionaire businessman want to have you killed? What did you do to him?"

"Nothing yet." She raised her shoulder in a half shrug. "Perhaps he's scared of what I might do to him in the future. There's every chance I might get in his way."

"In what manner?"

"Everyone is afraid of losing something. Nalam is a rich, powerful man who might be afraid I could take away both the riches and the power." She made an impatient gesture. "But it may not even be Nalam. We thought it likely because Hu Chang heard that he was asking a lot of questions about something that was taken from his office in a warehouse in Manila. He might have found out that I was the one who did it."

"You *stole* something from him?"

"It wasn't like that," she said. "I had to do it. It was important."

"Stop right there." Catherine held up her hand. "Let's go back to why Hu Chang believes you're worth saving. I'm sure it wasn't because you're such a competent thief."

"Actually, when I told him about it, he said I'd been very clumsy." Diane made a face. "He was right. But he also said I made up for it with the bullet. He said that everyone would agree that I could be forgiven almost anything for discovering the bullet."

"Bullet?" Catherine frowned. "What the hell are you talking about? What bullet?"

Diane was silent a moment. Then she sighed and said quietly, "Okay, here goes. Sometimes it's known as the silver bullet. It has several names, but everyone agrees that it could be tremendously important. I was terribly excited myself when I realized what I might have found."

"Silver bullet," Catherine repeated. Then she made the connection. "Do you mean—"

"Panacea," Diane said. "The ultimate remedy."

"Which doesn't exist. It's only a myth. Impossible. And you're claiming you discovered this universal cure-all?"

"I believe I have." Her voice was firm and completely confident. "I've been working on it for the past five years. I've had incredible results. For the last two years I've not had one failure, even in cases that were declared hopeless. I showed Hu Chang my findings, and even he was impressed."

"I admit that's saying something. If it's true." Catherine continued to shake her head. "But it's still too much of a fairy tale for me to accept."

"When I first started working on it, I thought the same thing. It was only an experiment." She leaned back in the chair. "I'd been sent to a village in the rain forest on Salkara Island in the South Seas with a team from One World Medical. There had been a terrible fire that had almost destroyed the entire village. It was followed by a new strain of flu that was killing the villagers who were still alive." She shuddered. "It was terrible. The children . . . It seemed to attack them the hardest. We had to work day and night to keep them alive. But we finally got to a point where we were able to turn the patients over to the people in the village to care for." She added bitterly, "Those that were still alive. It was then that I managed to get my breath and began to notice what else was happening around me. I found myself watching three villagers who . . . intrigued me. They were members of the Hakali family, Lono Hakali and his two daughters Malie and Akela. The flu had been debilitating and deadly, yet they appeared to be impervious to any symptoms and showed an amazing defensive ability to fight off the disease itself. Even though they'd been helping us night and day with the patients in the quarantine area and had been exposed to several of the victims. They were . . . unusual. Not like the other inhabitants of the island. The islanders were all principally of Polynesian descent, but the Hakali family were positively magnificent looking. They were taller, with large bones and wonderful features. They had amazing stamina and they were *glowing* with health and strength. How could I not be tempted to explore a bit deeper?"

"There are always cases that prove the rule in any situation. You know that, Diane."

"I can't blame you for scoffing. But if you could have seen the contrast...I told you, at first I was just curious and decided to explore why they might have escaped that flu virus."

"And what did you find out?"

"I didn't find out anything from that Hakali family. The minute I started to ask questions, they backed away and shook their heads. The next night they didn't show up at the quarantine tents. So I started to ask around the village, and it appeared that immunity to the disease might be transferred down through this one particular family. A bit unusual, but flus always have their own agenda. The other villagers told me that as long as they could remember, the members of the Hakali family seemed to have inherited not only robust good health but longevity. That's all they could tell me other than that they seemed to be restless and unhappy on Salkara Island. Someone in the Hakali family was always leaving the village and traveling to other islands, and even as far as China to settle."

"Why?"

She shrugged. "Perhaps the other villagers were jealous and resentful? As I said, when One World Medical arrived, there had been thirty-two flu deaths already, and it took us weeks to bring it under control. Principally because most of the villagers were in very poor basic condition to begin with. The island was beautiful but very undeveloped. There were no medical facilities on the island and few of the children had even been vaccinated, which meant preventable diseases had run rampant. It must have been tragically discouraging for those poor people to have to rub elbows with the Hakalis, who were virtually blooming with health. When I started questioning them, I could tell there was an obvious coolness. The Hakalis were definitely the outsiders." She grimaced. "I couldn't let it matter. All I wanted to know was if the medical anomaly I'd noted was caused by inheritance or environment. I went looking for my answer. It wasn't easy. The only information I had was that the Hakalis didn't live in the village itself but on the outskirts, near the rain forest, and the area had been completely destroyed by the fire. Which left me with no one to question and only smoking rubble where their homes had been. But by going back and questioning the villagers again, I did find out that they didn't plant crops or raise chickens or other domestic animals to eat. Instead, their diet seemed to be principally vegetarian. They often scavenged in the rain forest for berries, roots, and plants."

"Now, that's interesting. What kind of plants?"

"Some I'd never seen before. One was compounded of several different roots I couldn't identify. I wasn't able to find it on the Internet or in any reference book. That's not totally uncommon in the jungle and rain forest. I'd run across it before when I was researching in the Amazon. That's why so many scientists are always trekking through the jungles trying to find the next breakthrough medication."

"And you were one of them?"

"Of course. Every chance I got. It was a passion with me. But those roots on Salkara Island were unusual enough for me to examine them thoroughly and run tests." She made a face. "Though it was pretty difficult for me to gather enough to do it. The fire had burned a good deal of the rain forest, too, and the earth was scorched. But I found a small pocket that held enough to work with." She leaned forward. "I even began to make up a few potions and experiment on local wild animals to see if the plants could be the reason for the Hakali family's great condition."

"With what results?"

"Promising." Her cheeks were suddenly flushed, her eyes glittering. "No negatives, and increased energy and strength in every animal that was given the formula. It encouraged me to keep on with the work."

"I don't doubt it. *No* negatives?"

Diane shook her head. "The animals seemed to be getting healthier and more energetic with every dose. Particularly the monkeys. I was pretty excited. It's not every day a doctor comes close to something that rare and special."

"That's why there are laws about restricting experimentation to animals and not humans." Catherine's gaze was fixed intently on Diane's face. She wasn't certain she liked where this was going. "You said you were excited. Were you able to obey those laws?"

"At first," Diane said unsteadily. "I tried very hard, Catherine. I wasn't about to become some kind of Frankenstein monster. I was even grateful that I had to leave the island when One World Medical pulled the unit after another two months and sent us back to South America. I knew I was getting too excited. After that, for the next three years all I could do was research, work on the formula, and study how to improve it. It became an obsession, because I ran out of the original tri-roots six months after I left the island. But by that time I'd analyzed every bit of the composition and chemicals of that plant, and I started to try to synthesize it."

"What?"

"I know," Diane said impatiently. "It was crazy, and I shouldn't have been able to do it. But I wanted it so much. I tried everything under the sun. I worked for months and months. I didn't eat. I didn't sleep. But then it began to come together. It wasn't perfect; it wasn't even the same composition any longer. But somehow when I started running the experiments, it appeared to have the same properties and effects as the tri-root."

"You actually did it?" Catherine asked. "It wasn't a fluke?"

"It wasn't a fluke. And because I'd virtually re-created it, I was able to work with it, improve it. It was *mine*. Every day I was taking a new step. The process was getting more complex and yet smoother, like a bullet zeroing in on a target. That's how I came to think of it. The bullet... I was getting closer and closer. Yet I was still learning so much..."

Catherine was staring at her in fascination. Diane seemed to be lit from within. Glowing, reliving those moments of creation and dedication. *This* was the real Diane Connors. "Learning enough to play with the lives of actual human beings?"

"There was no play about it," Diane said desperately. "I told you, at first I was just curious, but all that changed. I'm a doctor, I *care* about the people I treat. Sometimes it's pure agony to see a child I realize is going to die and not be able to do anything about it." Her voice lowered to a whisper. "Only now I *could* do something if I just reached out my hand and tried."

"That sounds like a God complex. You couldn't be sure you wouldn't do harm."

"That's what I decided." Her voice was becoming unsteady. "I had to make certain I would do no harm." She added quickly, "So I spent six months giving myself injections of the medications I'd created."

Catherine's jaw dropped. "What? You could have killed yourself."

"I thought a long time about it. I *had* to be the guinea pig. I couldn't run the risk of giving it to anyone else until I knew it was safe." Her hands clenched on the arms of the chair. "Because I realized that the next time I ran across one of those lost ones I knew I could save, I was going to do it."

Catherine just stared at her. She didn't know what to say.

Diane drew a deep breath. "Speechless? I expected it. But maybe it's not as bad as you're thinking. The injections I administered to myself were an unqualified success. The bullet caused absolutely no damage. I'm healthier than I've ever been in my life. After six months, I checked into one of the local hospitals and ran an entire gamut of tests. I'm absolutely perfect."

"For how long? What if something changes?"

"I can't promise that it won't. That's why I've never medicated anyone else who wasn't at death's door."

Catherine stiffened. "You *did* it?"

"Nine people in the last year." Diane met her eyes. "Five children who had terminal cancer and are now in remission. Four adults. Two formerly with AIDS, two who had Ebola. All now doing well."

"And you'd do it again?"

"You bet I would," she said. "Though it could turn into a nightmare. I was only able to administer the medication because the conditions were primitive, with no formal hospital supervision. Otherwise, I'd probably have been arrested and prosecuted."

"But you'd have a chance of being exonerated once it was realized you'd saved lives, not taken them."

Diane shook her head. "You mentioned the laws regarding experimentation on human beings to me yourself. They're good laws, Catherine. I'd want to throw anyone in jail myself for violating them." She added bitterly, "If it didn't mean losing something so precious that there's no way the world could afford to do it."

Catherine's gaze was searching her face. "You believe in it that much?"

"Absolutely." She hesitated. "I told you, I'd made improvements. One of them was to combine the bullet with several other chemical elements with which I'd been experimenting so that I can inject them into the body to create a constant system of cell renewal."

Catherine had to think about it to realize what that meant. "You're saying it heals itself?"

She nodded. "A panacea."

Catherine closed her eyes for a moment. "Shit." Then her eyes flicked open. "You'd better be right about this. If you're not, it's going to cause a hell of a lot of trouble."

"I'm right. I didn't do in-depth testing on any of those patients after I determined that they were definitely cured of their diseases. I didn't want to bring attention to any obvious anomalies. I'm going to go back later and do that check after all the hoopla about their miracle cures is over." She smiled faintly. "But when I went begging help from our mutual friend, Hu Chang, I knew he wouldn't put up with not having every bit of information at his disposal. So I told him that I'd go through the most extensive examinations possible and let him judge for himself what I'd done to my body during those six months of injections. Hell, that's what I wanted, too, and I knew Hu Chang could bring to the table experts who would be completely discreet."

"No doubt about that. He has international contacts in the medical professions on both sides of the law," Catherine said. "And what did they tell him?"

"That I'd found the silver bullet." Diane paused before adding quietly, "And that my cellular structure had changed and wasn't operating like any other they'd ever run across. Renewal, Catherine. They were very excited."

"I imagine they were. And that means exactly what?"

"Presumably my body can fight off anything that attacks it," she replied, "perhaps even old age. Though it might take a long time to determine the boundaries." She shook her head. "And I don't even want to think about dealing with those complications. I'm having enough problems trying to figure out the first part of this puzzle. We're only at the beginning of this mess and I already almost got you killed."

"Mess," Catherine repeated. "Strange synonym for a miracle."

"Not strange at all. Until I figure out how to keep this 'miracle' from smothering me." She sat up straight in the chair. "So there you are. Believe it or not. It's the truth. But you can understand why there might be a good many people out there who don't want me alive. Among them is anyone connected to the pharmaceutical companies that make their living providing expensive medicines to the masses. And that may only be the beginning of the fallout." She got to her feet, and her voice was shaky as she headed for the door. "Now I've got to get out of here and give myself a little time away from you. I'm not accustomed to baring my soul to anyone these days." She glanced over her shoulder. "And you need to decide whether you believe me or not. You can't go any further with me until you do. I'll phone you later today. Call Hu Chang and talk to him. You know he won't lie to you."

Catherine shook her head in confusion. For some reason she didn't want to let Diane go yet. These last moments had been overflowing with emotion and stunning revelations, and she wanted to make sure she understood and could accept it. "I don't think you're lying to me, Diane."

"But you're not sure. Or maybe you believe I'm just a little nuts. That's okay, it's a wild tale and I don't have great credentials. Call Hu Chang." The door closed behind her.

"You say Diane told you everything, Catherine?" Hu Chang asked. "I'd be surprised if I hadn't received a call a short time ago from Cameron informing me that you were in the hospital and I should contact you." His voice was distinctly cool. "I don't have to tell you how displeased I was that you didn't tell me yourself. Would you care to tell me why?"

Damn Cameron. "It wasn't necessary. I would have let you know eventually. I wasn't badly hurt, but Eve and Joe were upset, and I had to figure out what my next step was going to be. What I *didn't* want was for you to use what happened as an excuse to have Cameron interfere."

"I never make excuses, only decisions," Hu Chang said. "And I don't like the idea of being closed out when I should have known what was happening to you. It tends to keep me from making the correct decision. If Cameron had not assured me that you weren't seriously injured, I would have been most angry with you."

"You weren't the only one who was closed out," Catherine said curtly. "You wouldn't tell me what was going on with Diane, and you were keeping Cameron in the wings as a threat. Not fair."

He was silent. "It was a delicate situation. Since she's confided in you at last, you can see why she didn't want me to trust anyone if it wasn't necessary. Her life could well have been on the line. I had to leave it up to her."

"Her life *was* on the line. And I was blindsided. I don't like that, Hu Chang. I can't let it happen again."

"It won't happen again. I will not permit it." He paused. "You are truly well?"

"Fine. Except for the fact that I have no idea if what Diane was telling me was the truth or a figment of her imagination. She told me to ask you. That's what I'm doing. I know how careful you'd be. Were the results of all those tests you made her take as groundbreaking as she said?"

"Probably more impressive. Those experts who conducted the tests were stunned. I insisted they make certain that their conclusions were unanimous or I'd discard the results entirely. There was no problem, the doctors were in unanimous agreement. The results of Diane's tests are now locked in a box in my bank vault in Hong Kong."

"What?"

"A necessity," he said softly. "And those eight doctors who conducted the tests are occupying suites in a wonderful château on a lake in Canada on the pretext of attending a conference. It's a very well-guarded place, and they all agreed that they'd be better off there for the foreseeable future. They're very clever, and they realize it could be exceptionally dangerous for them to be involved in any way with Diane Connors."

"They regard her as that much of a hazard?"

"It's not only the fact that she could topple a financial empire or two with what she's taught herself to do during these last years. Just by injecting herself with those medications and changing the way her own body processes work, she automatically became a threat. She's an incredibly efficient machine these days, and those doctors signed their names and bore witness that it was possible to make that happen."

"Which would also make them a target."

"We're watching them very closely, Catherine. I knew when I brought them to my lab to do the testing that I'd have to protect them afterward."

"And were you also going to pack me off to some wonderful château if you decided I'd need protection after I'd done my duty?" she asked caustically.

"If I could, but you're very difficult. However, I'd already started to consider my options."

"Forget it," she said flatly.

"I find that hard to do where you're concerned. I already have a plan or two in mind. But I will listen to what you say."

"No, you won't. I'll discuss my own plans when I have them. I'll get back with you then." She hesitated and then asked, "It's deadly serious? Everything she said is true and bad news?"

"Bad news? It depends on how one looks at it," he said gently. "It could go either way. But yes, the choices are deadly serious."

"That's all I wanted you to tell me. I'll let you know when I've made a decision. Goodbye, Hu Chang." She ended the call and sat there a moment, thinking.

There it was in a nutshell. If she trusted Hu Chang, then this wild improbable story Diane had thrown at her would have to be dealt with. And she had trusted her old friend from the moment they had come together when she was only fourteen in that shop in Hong Kong. She trusted him now.

So lean back, relax, and make a decision regarding what to do about Diane Connors that might keep them both alive. No, not only Diane and her, there was also Eve to consider...

CHAPTER 6

HOSPITAL CAFETERIA
5:40 P.M.

Diane stopped abruptly in the cafeteria doorway, her gaze on the corner table where Catherine and Eve were sitting. She took a deep breath, her grip tightening on the briefcase she was carrying, and then strode toward them. "You didn't tell me Eve was going to join us," she said to Catherine as she pulled out a chair, sat down, and set her briefcase on the floor by her feet. "Is this an ambush?"

"No, it's hopefully a solution," Catherine said. "If an ambush was involved, it was aimed at Eve. You told me you wanted to have another meeting with her, and I'm obliging you." She added deliberately, "But I wasn't going to do that without making sure that she knew what she was getting herself into. So I allowed time for the two of us to discuss why you appear to have half the world out to assassinate you."

"You told her?" Diane's gaze flew to Eve's face. "Of course she told you. I was going to do it myself after Catherine was hurt but I kept putting it off." She grimaced. "As usual, I was trying to find a way to get what I wanted, and I was scared that I'd blow it." She braced herself. "Did I do it?"

"I'm too stunned to make up my mind," Eve said. "Catherine took my breath away and I haven't gotten it back yet." She was telling the truth. Whatever she'd expected when Catherine had asked her to meet her today, it had not been the story of Diane's journey from the person Eve had barely been able to tolerate who had been married to Joe, to this selfless woman who had risked both her career and her life to change the world. "Give me a little time to become accustomed to the idea of this new and different Diane and I'll let you know."

"Nah, don't bother. I've tried, but I haven't really changed." She shrugged. "Maybe I've learned a few lessons. But doesn't everyone? Heaven knows, I've burned enough bridges. You can't go through life in a vacuum."

"That's true." Eve found herself smiling. "But the lessons you've learned might have a far-reaching effect. And I believe the choices you've made aren't entirely without merit."

"Tell that to Joe or any other cop," Diane said. "They'd tell you my choices probably sucked." She lifted her chin. "But they were *my* choices, and nine people are living because I made them."

"We both know Joe isn't like any other cop," Eve said quietly. "He's totally unique. I don't know what his opinion would be. We'll have to ask him."

"I can hardly wait," she said caustically. "He's been so warm and supportive to me since I showed up on your doorstep. Where is he, by the way?"

"At home with Michael," Eve said. "We try to take turns or he'd be here, too." She paused. "Joe may not be supportive, but he's very aware that you both made mistakes. He'd never put the entire blame on you. As far as being warm, I'm afraid Joe can be very protective of me."

"No one knows that more than me," Diane said. "Our entire

marriage was dedicated to my walking on eggs to avoid upsetting you. That's why I wanted to approach you by yourself this time."

Eve frowned. "It was that bad?"

"I knew he was in love with you. He never talked about it, but it was always there. At first, it didn't matter." She added, "But things changed later."

When she'd fallen in love with him, Eve thought.

Diane nodded as she met her eyes. "But it's okay now. I found that I was very resilient. I have a career that I'm passionate about. I've had any number of lovers to amuse me. I bounced back very nicely, thank you."

"I'm sure we're all glad to hear that." Catherine pushed back her chair and got to her feet. "But this is getting a little too intimate for me. I believe I'll go to that Starbucks counter over there and pick us up some coffee while you straighten out the more important reasons why I brought you together. I'll give you fifteen minutes."

Eve smiled as she watched her move across the cafeteria. "She wasn't really embarrassed. She's just impatient and wanted us to get down to business."

"Then why don't we do it?" Diane asked bluntly. "Did she convince you that I'm not a criminal and that I might even be doing something worthwhile? Will you help me? Is it going to be yes or no?"

"You're jumping the gun," Eve said. "You only gave Catherine the bare bones of what this is all about. Fascinating, but you left out the one basic bit of info that would be most important to me." She was no longer smiling. "Not that she didn't catch it. She just wanted to discuss it with me before we confronted you. That's why she made her exit as soon as possible."

"You want to know if I lied to you about the reconstruction I asked you to do," Diane said. "I did lie. Or rather I twisted the truth around a little so that I wouldn't have to dive in and tell you the whole story right away. Hu Chang thought it wasn't safe for me to tell you anything that concerned myself, so I'm afraid I got a little inventive. Jose Morales doesn't exist. He's not the man I want you to do the reconstruction on. I thought you'd be more likely to do the job if you didn't have to swallow it all down in one gulp."

"Like a bad medicine?" Eve asked grimly. "Who is the man you want reconstructed?"

"It might be Kai Hakali, Alon's brother. I'm not sure. That's why I need you."

"Alon," Eve repeated. "Back up. Michael is very interested in this Alon."

"So was I. Particularly when I started to investigate the history of the Hakali family. After I was forced to leave Salkara Island with the team, I had nothing to do but research those plants and discover if there was any special connection between them and the Hakali family. So when I wasn't working, I was on the phone and computer constantly with a few contacts I'd made with the villagers on Salkara."

"Alon." Eve brought her back on target.

"I'm getting there. From what I was told, Alon Hakali was the head of the family and very brilliant. He also loved his family and his home. He had ideas how he wanted to improve the island that had to do with the tri-roots, and he tried to convince the family to listen and go along with him. He'd been watching members of his family drifting away from Salkara for decades and couldn't convince them to stay and make the island better instead of abandoning it."

"From the way you described the place to Catherine, one could hardly blame them."

"Alon didn't see it that way. It was his home." She shook her head. "And he didn't get a chance to persuade them. That week there was that terrible fire that burned his home and half the rain forest to the ground. There were tremendous losses, not only in the village but among practically everyone he knew and loved. He lost his mother and his brother, Kai. He almost died himself. He was unconscious when they found him in the jungle, and they had to take him to the nearest island that had basic medical facilities. He had a bad concussion and wasn't able to return to the island for weeks. By that time the flu had struck the village and my unit had come and gone."

"So you didn't get to do an interview with him?"

"Oh, I did. But not until almost three years later when I went back to Salkara. Though I'd heard that Alon Hakali had left the island again, I still wanted to try to find some more of the tri-roots to examine. Besides, I figured it wouldn't hurt to make another attempt at questioning Lono Hakali and his two daughters who had been so edgy about talking to me before." She shrugged. "But when I arrived, I found that Lono and his girls had packed up their belongings and left Salkara the year before, so I had to mark them off my list. That left the tri-roots."

"You found some?"

She shook her head. "I camped out in that rain forest for two weeks searching, and every trace of the plant had disappeared. I was disappointed, but mostly I just thought I was lucky to have found the small amount I'd stumbled on." Her lips curled bitterly. "Until I ran across the cave about two miles into the rain forest and then I realized just how lucky I'd been to find even those few samples of plant life. There were empty gasoline cans, footprints of boots in the mud inside the caves, and other signs that the fire had been deliberately set."

Eve sat up straight. "What?"

"That was my reaction," Diane said. "Why deliberately set a fire that would destroy innocent villagers and acres of rain forest? The Hakali family were almost all killed and so were many other villagers. No one suspected that it was anything but some bizarre accident. Maybe a lightning strike from a freak storm."

"And it could have been."

"Do you think I don't know that? What I found in that cave wasn't cast-iron proof. But it was weird, and it shouldn't have been there." She added, "And I couldn't get it out of my mind. Because one of the other weird signs that the fire had been set was four metal drums full of plants. The insides of the containers were scorched, and it was clear that the plants had been dug up and thrown in the drums to be burned. It was difficult to tell but I was so familiar with the shape that I knew at least a few of those burnt plants were tri-roots." She paused and then said harshly, "Probably all of them. And that didn't make sense, either. Why make a concerted effort to destroy the tri-roots? If they recognized that the plant had value, then why not gather it and experiment as I did?"

"Because not everyone is Diane Connors," Eve said quietly. "I believe you must have figured that out when you were working the puzzle. What else, Diane?"

"The flu," Diane said jerkily. "But that didn't occur to me until later. I told you that it was an unknown strain and deadly. And it was strange that it hit the island at almost the same time the fire ravaged it. What a coincidence. But it did keep the villagers from dwelling on how the fire started, didn't it?"

"Yes, it did." Eve smiled faintly. "What a suspicious woman you are."

"Yes, I am. But I knew how many nasty bugs are stored in labs around the world. Maybe it was a step too far, but perhaps it wasn't. I'm used to investigating and putting things together with my work."

She met Eve's eyes. "And I might have picked up one or two things living with Joe. It would be hard not to."

"I can see that." She tilted her head. "You haven't gotten to Alon Hakali yet."

"I'm almost there. He's right there in the wings." She paused. "I was very angry and bewildered, and I felt as if I had to do something. All those deaths...I *hate* death. One of the reasons I became a doctor was that I really resented it, and once I started to practice, I regarded it as a personal affront. And if I was right, those bastards had used fire and then that flu to kill those people." She swore softly. "And I was almost as angry about the tri-roots. That was life, too. It was beautiful, and it led me to the bullet..."

"Then what did you do about it?"

"I had to have answers. Salkara Island was very primitive, and it wasn't as if I could prove anything. But something had happened there, and I had to know what it was so there was a chance whoever had done it would be punished. I thought about it and decided that the person most likely to have the answers was Alon Hakali. He was supposed to be the head of the family, and if anyone should have known what was going on, it would be him. He'd also been on the island the night of the fire and been injured. When he'd returned, he'd spent some time there before he'd left again." She shook her head. "He'd lost so much that night. If he was as brilliant as I'd heard, I couldn't believe he would have left Salkara before he knew why and who was responsible."

"I repeat," Eve said. "What did you do about it?"

"Exactly what you would have done," Diane said. "I went to find him..."

HAKALI ISLAND
TWO YEARS EARLIER

The man wearing white linen trousers and a cream-colored shirt standing on the pier watching as Diane guided the motorboat closer had to be Alon Hakali, she thought. He was a giant of a man, over six foot five, slim and muscular as a Greek statue, with a body that was totally magnificent. She had never seen a photo of him, but he was as powerful and as golden and beautiful as Lono had described. No, it had been Lono's daughter Malie who'd said that. But it was true. He was as close to being a perfect human being as she had ever seen, and his smile was just as warm and beautiful as he reached out to help her out of the boat. "Welcome, Diane. Did you have a good trip?"

"No, you made it as difficult as possible for me to get here," she said crossly. "Really? Parking this motorboat at that inlet in the Marquesas with only directions on how to get to your island? Could you have made it any harder?"

He smiled. "Oh, yes. However, I didn't want to discourage you since you'd worked so hard to find me. Lono had orders not to be found, but he told me that you'd tracked him like a bloodhound. Still, a little hardship always makes the triumph sweeter." He took her elbow and nudged her toward a house down the beach. "Come and have a glass of wine and we'll talk, and you can decide if all your work was worthwhile. Don't you think my island lovely?"

"Yes." It was gorgeous, with white beaches and flowering tropical trees. She could see several fishermen working with nets on the beach. "It's your island? It's not even on any regular map. I wouldn't have even known it was named Hakali Island if you hadn't scrawled it on my directions."

"Yes, it's mine. I purchased it several years ago when I was on one of my trips in this area. I did a favor for the man who owned it and he sold it to me for a song. It's not as if there was a great demand for property in

the Marquesas at the time. It can be one of the most remote places in the world. But as it happened, I was very glad to have a private place of my own after what happened on Salkara. Things became difficult for me and I traveled around and gathered all the Hakalis who'd deserted Salkara for more civilized places and brought them here. They're much happier on my island. I'll tell you about it over that wine."

"I don't want a glass of wine. I want information. That's why I came here. I told you on the phone that I thought the fire on Salkara might have been set and asked you if you knew anything."

"And I told you that I did. I couldn't have been more cooperative."

She gave a delicate snort. "Except you told me that you wouldn't discuss it unless it was in person. And this island is nowhere near Salkara. It's closer to Tahiti."

"But you agreed to come, and I found that encouraging. It showed how determined you were, and Lono said that you'd been good to the patients during the flu epidemic. All very good signs that you might be trusted."

"Then why didn't you just call me back and talk to me?" she said through set teeth. "Why am I here?"

"I needed time to reach out to and check you out further. Signs are all very well, but knowing a person's history is everything." He continued gently, "Two attempts to kill me have taken place lately. I wanted to make sure you weren't sent to make it three."

She stopped and stared at him in shock. "You thought I might kill you?"

"I hoped not. And now that I've met you, I don't believe it. You're positively brewing with turmoil and many things that are complex and interesting, but not evil." He added almost lightly, "It's a great relief to me."

Her hands closed into fists at her sides. "Are you crazy? Why would I want to kill you?"

"I only chose to be careful. You were searching for me with such determination. Though the reasons you gave were altruistic, I asked myself why you would care so much. My family was really nothing to you, and neither were

the other villagers on Salkara." He paused. "And then you described those four drums full of burnt plants that you called tri-roots you found in the cave with the gas cans, and I became very curious. I couldn't resist having you here even if you proved a threat."

"Why?" Her gaze was searching his face. "I barely mentioned those plants to you."

"But you did mention them, and you'd already named them." He shook his head. "Though I prefer the name I chose for them when I first realized what potential they had all those years ago."

"Potential?" She inhaled sharply. "What do you mean? What did you name them?"

"Kula. It's Hawaiian for 'golden.'" He grinned. "Golden promise. Golden horizon. You were entirely too practical describing them merely as roots."

"I don't know Hawaiian." She moistened her lips. "And I am practical. I usually call things as I see them."

"And you hadn't yet seen either the gold or the promise when you started working with them?" He tilted his head. "I find that sad. I believe it may be good that I decided to let you come here."

"How do you know I was working with the tri-roots?" Then she jumped to the next question before he could answer. "And how long ago was it that you discovered this 'potential'?"

"I always knew it was there. I just accepted it. I grew up eating the kula because it was family tradition." He grimaced. "It doesn't taste that good, by the way. That's why none of the other villagers ate it. But my mother was insistent, and I tolerated it because I loved her and wanted to make her happy. I suppose it was like you eating spinach because your mother told you it was good for you."

"Only I was too stubborn and refused to eat the spinach," she said absently. "And that's too glib an explanation. For a minute I thought you might be going to tell me the truth."

"That is the truth," he said quietly. "You want the exact moment when

I actually started to ask myself questions about it? Not for a long time. I was too busy living life and enjoying every second of it. I had the island and the rain forest as a playground. I had my younger brother, Kai, and we had other playmates from the village. It was a perfect childhood. I was a voracious reader and my mother saw that I was surrounded by books that taught, intrigued . . . and tempted me. I could see what lay beyond Salkara Island. I also had relatives, cousins, uncles, who had returned to the island to visit and told me stories. I was only fifteen when I said goodbye to my mother and sailed out into the world to have my own adventures. I visited wonderful cities like Shanghai and studied at universities in Australia. I discovered bad and good and all that lay between."

"Fifteen? Your mother let you leave home that young?"

"She wanted me to go. She was wise and knew I'd return. Love always draws you back. She wasn't alone. My father had died in a boating accident years ago, but she always had Kai. I came back many times over the years and tried to persuade her to go with me on one trip or another, but she never wanted to leave Kai or the island. She said he was so happy there."

"I'd think he'd want to go out on a few adventures of his own when you came home telling stories."

"He never wanted adventures. He had my mother, who adored him. He had the island." He paused. "Kai never really grew up. He suffered a head injury when he was out on the boat with my father the day he was killed, and he was never quite the same. Not that he appeared to care. He was the happiest person I've ever met. Every day he found some new delight."

Diane felt a sudden rush of pity for that youngster who had lost the life he loved in that fire. She made an effort not to think of him. She was getting too caught up with his stories of the Hakali family. "That's all very interesting, but it doesn't tell me what I asked you about the tri-roots."

"But it tells you who I am, and I believe that's only fair when I spent a good amount of time finding out who you were before I let you come here. Now you'll get your answer. It was on my last trip to Salkara that I began

making my plans for what I wanted to do with the kula. Over the years, I'd narrowed down the probability that this was the plant that explained both my family's seeming immunity to disease and our longevity. I was going to start in-depth research so that I could turn the information over to the United Nations World Health Organization. Though my mother wasn't pleased about the prospect of having strangers running around our island. She said she was hoping the research would take a long time."

"You think your mother knew the value of those tri-roots?"

"She might have had an inkling. She was very wise. Or she might have honestly believed it was just family tradition that had been passed down from generation to generation. She was always very serene and accepting if all was going well in her world. And we were all exceptionally happy and contented with our lives at Salkara." His smile faded. "I wondered later when I began to explore our physical and mental differences from the other villagers if that contentment was another effect of the kula."

"A narcotic?" She shook her head. "I guarantee there weren't any elements resembling a narcotic in them. I tested for everything."

"You're very certain." He was smiling again. "You must have done all the experimentation I intended to do when I realized what a wonderful gift we'd been given in that ugly little plant. I envy you. You must tell me about it."

"Why didn't you do it yourself?"

"I wasn't in a hurry. I knew life would change for my mother and Kai once I took that step, and she valued her peace. Kai had never been away from the island, and she was very protective of him. I wanted to share that gift with the rest of the world, but those plants had been there on Salkara Island since my great-grandparents were alive. I thought I had plenty of time." His expression darkened. "I did not."

"The fire?"

He nodded. "The house exploded like a bomb and there were flames everywhere. I could smell gas . . . It seemed as if the whole world were on fire.

The houses. The earth. The trees." His voice was hoarse. "Screams . . . I ran down the hall toward my mother's room, but she wasn't there. I ran outside and found her huddled on the ground near the path to the rain forest. Her eyes were wide open and staring up at me and I knew she was dead. She looked small and broken . . . It was all wrong. My mother was strong, and she would never be broken." He drew a deep breath. "And then my head seemed to explode, too, and I couldn't see her anymore. I woke up two weeks later and they told me my mother was dead and probably my brother, Kai, as well. They hadn't found his body, but they were guessing he was frightened by the fire and ran in the wrong direction deeper into the forest. The fire was so intense that it was reasonable that there might be nothing left but ashes."

"But you went back to the island to look for him?"

He nodded. "I knew he'd want to be buried with my mother. But I didn't find Kai's body." He paused, his expression hardening. "And I didn't find that cave, but I did find enough evidence to realize that the fire had been deliberately set. So I buried my mother and left Salkara Island and started to look for the people who had done it."

"And you found them?"

"I found them. I just followed the kula. But proving it will be difficult." He turned away. "I don't believe I'll tell you anything more until I have a glass of wine. It always hurts for me to talk about that night. So you can come along or go back to the pier, jump in your motorboat, and head for the far horizon."

She hesitated and then fell into step with him. "I'm sorry about your mother and your brother."

"So am I. Kai always had a childlike joy just being alive and reaching out to everyone. As for my mother, she was a singular woman and I miss her every day." He glanced thoughtfully at her. "But you may also be a singular woman. At least, you appear to have a conscience. Since you're here, we'll talk and perhaps we can find ways to learn from each other that will right some of the wrong."

She looked at him in bewilderment and exasperation. He was a strange combination of gentleness, bluntness, and keen intelligence and she didn't know quite what to think of him. Oh, well, he still had more to tell her. It wouldn't hurt to go along and have that drink and hear the rest of the story. After all, it probably wouldn't take more than another few hours to get all the information she'd come here for, and then she'd leave the island. "Perhaps we can. I have a little time . . ."

Eve gazed at Diane across the cafeteria table with narrowed eyes. "And when did you finally leave Hakali Island?"

"Almost two years later." She held up her hand. "I know. One thing led to another and it just worked out that way. It turned out that Alon had a small quantity of the tri-roots he'd brought to the island, and he let me compare the results I got with them with the serum that I'd just developed on my own. I had to—" She stopped. "But you want to know what Alon found out about who set the fire."

"Yes, I do," Eve said dryly. "If it leads me to why you showed up on my doorstep."

"I'll be as brief as I can," she said quickly. "When he found signs in the rain forest that the fire had been deliberately set, he went to the villagers and started asking questions. Visitors aren't that frequent on Salkara, and he found out that a few months or so before two boats had shown up on the south side of the island. There were seven or eight men on the boats. They told the villagers they were hunters on vacation and paid them for a map of the rain forest. No good descriptions, just a few Caucasians, two Chinese, and one Black. They didn't give names, and the villagers didn't ask. They were more interested in the money they were getting." She paused. "But one of them did remember that he'd seen one of the boats before. It was a rental that a company on the next island over sometimes rented out to tourists. Alon checked it out, got the contract information, and then tracked down the person who'd rented it."

"And that was?"

"Jeremy Franks, who's the head of a security at a public relations company. But the arrangements were made by text from Los Angeles, and when Alon followed up, he found that Franks had not left L.A. for the last six months. So he dug deeper and found Franks was in charge of worldwide personnel for Nalam Pharmaceuticals."

"Nalam," Eve repeated. "That's the name you mentioned before."

"It's the only name I had, but I couldn't prove he'd attacked Catherine. I couldn't prove anything. Neither could Alon when he was tracking down the person who had killed his mother and brother, but he tried. Nalam's base was in Santa Monica, and he was regarded as a model citizen as well as a mover and shaker in the political arena. He was not only a friend of the president, but also angling for a cabinet post that would increase his influence. Alon knew it would be difficult to touch him. He went to Nalam's office and started to ask questions. They threw him out, but that only made him more determined. He went to Nalam's home and then he started to follow him." She grimaced. "Alon wouldn't stop. You have no idea how determined he can be. Everywhere Nalam went, Alon found a way to be there and call attention to himself. Nalam didn't want a battle on his own turf, or to have awkward questions popping up that might tip his hand on the dirty hijinks he'd been up to. He did everything from calling the police and trying to get Alon thrown into jail, to having Franks attempt to bribe him to leave him alone. But then he must have gotten impatient because one night the brakes on Alon's rental car were cut and he ended up halfway down a canyon. If he hadn't been as strong as a horse, the accident could have killed him. Nalam must have been furious and frustrated as hell because he actually visited Alon in the hospital." She added bitterly, "And Alon finally got the answers he'd been fighting for. They weren't pleasant. No excuses or explanations why he'd ordered that atrocity at Salkara. Nalam had just decided to use another weapon to end what he considered an inconvenience. He told Alon that Kai was still alive. He'd been taken to a very private location to undergo tests that might tell Nalam's doctors if the attack on the island had been overkill or if the threat was very real. They had to know if they should be on the alert and set out to search for any other plants like the tri-roots that might pose a similar danger to his organization in the future. He told Alon that they would try to make the tests as painless as possible but it would depend on Alon's cooperation. Nalam would call him and let him talk to his brother once a month. He might even send him photos of Kai every now and then so that he could see that he was still alive. But only if Alon would cease bothering him and go away." Her lips tightened. "Alon said Nalam was positively oozing satisfaction when he got up to leave. Anything Alon did would hurt his brother."

"Bastard," Eve muttered. "What was he talking about... another threat to his organization?"

"Alon did research on Nalam's business practices after the asshole tied his hands when he told him about his brother. It was the only way he could think of to take him down. It seems Nalam is a complete megalomaniac as well as a sociopath. It's not enough for him to be a billionaire who controls companies all over the world. He wants to make sure that power only increases and that nothing causes even one bit of it to erode. His empire depends on people needing his very expensive pharmaceuticals. So whenever he runs across a doctor or company coming close to a breakthrough that might cut his profits, he eliminates the threat. Sometimes it's only behind-the-scenes manipulation in a lab so a researcher might not get funds from a grant to go forward." She waved her hand. "Poof. The research disappears into the mist. But Alon found other cases where there was actual interference in expeditions by researchers in the Amazon and the Congo. Nalam evidently regarded those doctors as far more dangerous because so many valuable drugs and medicines had been developed from those sources—lisinopril, penicillin, Taxol. Half of the top ten prescription drugs in the U.S. are of animal, plant, or microorganism origin. The more effective the miracle drug, the fewer additional medicines are needed to control the illness. At times it causes a complete cure, which probably cuts down his profits enormously." She added sarcastically: "It must have been a constant horror always with him. What if one of those researchers found a cure for cancer?"

"Or a silver bullet," Eve said softly.

"I don't think he suspected the tri-root was as powerful as it is. No research had even been done on it. Some of his people must have just run to him and told him it could contain some nutrients that might increase immunity and possibly increase the chances of longer life. That was enough of a danger to destroy it."

"Who told him about the tri-roots?" Eve asked. "You said that island was fairly out of the way."

"But the Hakali family traveled out to other places over the years. They were certainly magnificent enough looking to attract attention. I noticed Lono and his girls right away in that quarantine tent. Alon said it could be because they'd grown up on the island and might have been more trusting and guileless." She frowned. "Though I never found Alon all that trusting. Anyway, I'm sure if quizzed about their diet or anything else about their life they wouldn't see any reason not to answer."

"And it led Nalam's men to Salkara Island."

Diane nodded. "And what they did there eventually led me to

you." She said with sudden urgency, "I really need you to do that reconstruction, Eve. Look, I did something that I thought would help Alon, but it backfired. After hunting for over a year for any information about where his brother was being kept, Alon located the team who had attacked Salkara; they worked out of a Nalam warehouse in Manila. He managed to grab one of the team. After being 'persuaded,' the man said the team leader kept detailed records of all the jobs Nalam assigned them. One of those details had to be about Alon's brother and perhaps where he was being kept prisoner."

"And you went after it."

"If Alon had tried to go after it, he would have been recognized. For heaven's sake, he looks like a damn Greek god. If he wasn't killed, his brother probably would have been. I'm a woman and definitely not a Greek goddess, no one would connect me to the Hakali family. I stole the file and gave it to Alon."

"But you said everything went wrong. What happened?"

"I thought it was going to be okay. Alon tracked that file to an armed encampment in northwest Montana that had a stockade where he was almost sure Kai was being kept. He was planning on gathering a force to go after him." Her voice became agonized. "If he'd had just a little more *time*." She shook her head. "But Nalam was furious that anyone had the nerve to rob one of his facilities. He demanded to know what files were taken. I'd deliberately not taken the actual Kai file; I took photographs, and even grabbed an entire handful of other folders that night to distract him. But Nalam still focused on the Hakali file. A few months after I'd arrived in Hong Kong, Nalam called Alon in a terrible rage and told him that he knew he was behind the theft and he'd taken steps to punish him. He was tired of the game they'd been playing. He said Kai was only a whimpering boy and wasn't a good specimen to test anyway." She swallowed. "He texted him a photo of a horribly burnt man who was almost chopped into pieces. He was lying in an open grave. Nalam said it was Kai. Then he hung up."

"I'm so sorry," Eve whispered.

"That's the way I felt when Alon called me. Sorrow and guilt and a terrible anger," she said. "And then hope. Because Alon thought there might be a way out. He'd gotten a call later from one of Nalam's scumbags, Luis Belazo, who was a guard at the prison stockade where Alon thought Kai was being kept in Montana. Belazo had decided he was tired of being poor and taking crap. He said it wasn't Kai whom Nalam had ordered killed, and he could prove it. He said he knew where that body had been buried and he'd retrieve it and sell it to him for examination if the money was good enough. I guess I don't have to tell you that Alon made sure it would be. He made a deal with Hu Chang to lend him the money and transfer the initial deposit to Belazo's bank account. The next night Belazo called and said he'd kept his part of the deal and removed the body from the grave. He promised that as soon as the final payment was made, he'd deliver."

"Promises? No proof. That's pretty flimsy."

Diane nodded jerkily. "But Alon had to know if he still had a chance of freeing Kai. He said there hadn't been any change in the number of guards around that stockade. If Kai had been murdered, there should have been some change."

"It's a long shot. You said Nalam was furious."

"But I told you how vicious he was and how much he enjoyed tormenting Alon. Why get rid of him in one swoop? Why not torture him with the possibility and hold Kai to use again?"

"A long shot," Eve repeated.

"It's all we've got. Alon was going to attack that Montana camp regardless after that call from Belazo, but it was very well guarded; it would have been a suicide mission. I talked him into giving me a week to try to get proof that body in the grave wasn't Kai's. If he was going to take that big a risk, we had to make sure it was worth it. I know it's a long shot. We did everything we could to find some kind of proof that Belazo was telling the truth. We even grabbed at that photo he'd sent Alon of the grave. It had a mountain in the background. Mountains can be very distinctive, and that made it easier. It was logical that the Montana stockade might be close to the grave if it was Kai's. The farther away from it, the better our chance that the body wasn't Kai's. So Hu Chang and I got out our maps and photos and called in a couple of experts to help us determine the exact location of the grave." She drew a deep breath. "And we think we found it. It's in the Rockies in Nevada near the California border. Not that close to that encampment in Montana at all. So Belazo might be legitimate. You could have your body, Eve." She added with profound gratitude, "And that means Alon might be able to save his brother."

"I can see that." Eve's gaze was searching her face. "You appear to have developed an attachment for this Alon. You stayed with him for over a year?"

"Almost two years." She hesitated. "Attachment? You could say that. I started out just trying to learn from him about the plants, and then I realized that was only going to be the beginning. He became my friend. He's . . . rather incredible. I'd never had a friend like him." She was nibbling at her lower lip. "That's all. The entire truth. Does it change anything for you?"

"It might, I'll have to think about it. That's quite a story." She tilted her head. "You appear to be a wild mixture of unselfishness and complete bullheadedness. I'm torn between admiring you and wanting to help you accomplish something . . . wonderful, and the panicky desire to just turn and run for the hills."

"What does that mean?" Diane asked warily. "That's no answer."

"Tell me why you have to have me do that reconstruction. Why not analyze the DNA?"

"Belazo warned us that besides being burnt, the body was chopped up in pieces. That means the DNA could be denigrated; even if we could get enough to process, it might not give a true result—it could even give a false one. We have to know for sure before Alon risks everything." She moistened her lips. "And I know how good you are. It wouldn't matter if we couldn't get enough DNA or what condition it was in. When you were finished with the reconstruction, he'd know."

"DNA is always the final proof."

"And we'll try to get it. I want desperately to get two forms of proof for him. But I trust you," Diane said quietly. "And I'll make Alon trust you. So it's up to you, Eve. Will you do it?"

Eve didn't speak for a moment. "I believe in Catherine, and she believes in you. I'll seriously consider any reconstruction that you ask me to do." She repeated emphatically, "*Consider.* As long as I'm certain that it won't affect my family or involve me in anything illegal."

"I can't promise that," Diane said soberly. "What I did in saving those nine critically ill patients might be construed as a crime. Which might make anything you do for me the act of an accomplice." She shook her head wryly. "See how honest I'm being? I probably wouldn't have been if I hadn't almost gotten Catherine killed. When I came to see you before, I thought maybe Hu Chang was wrong and no one was after me. Alon said that Nalam hadn't mentioned me, and I wanted desperately to believe it. I needed your help. I decided as long as Catherine was with us and I was very careful, it would be safe enough if I took the chance and lied to you."

"But you're being extraordinarily honest now."

"It's about time, don't you think?"

"Yes, I definitely do," she said firmly. "Is there anything else I should know?"

Diane hesitated and then made a face. "I wish you hadn't asked me. It's not anything really bad, but I wasn't sure if you'd believe that lie I was going to tell you. I'm really terrible at lying, and that was a gigantic whopper. I asked Hu Chang to arrange to pad it a little so you'd be more likely to believe it."

"Pad it?"

"That email you got from Mexico when you first arrived. The request from Quantico to Joe's captain to request his services."

"That was you?" she asked blankly.

She shook her head. "Hu Chang."

"You," Eve repeated. She added dazedly, "Incredible."

"But it was only a little deception," Diane said quickly. "I promise I'll be honest with you from now on, no matter what it costs me." She paused. "And I told you before that I could give you and your family whatever price you wished if you'd help me. I couldn't spell it out for you then, but I'll still do it if you accept."

"It's quite an offer." She was suddenly smiling. "Does that mean eternal life for my Michael?"

"I don't know. We haven't had time to explore that far yet." She grinned. "But it could mean you might not have to worry if he gets a bad cold."

"That's a valuable gift in itself." Eve was gazing searchingly at her. "Providing everything you've said is true. I'm inclined to believe it is, but, as I said, I'll have to think about it."

"I knew you would." Diane leaned down and reached into the briefcase at her feet. She pulled out a file folder and offered it to Eve. "You'll have to take my word for it, and my credibility is definitely in question where you're concerned—so I brought along the files of those nine patients I treated and cured. I documented every step.

I signed the reports. You can imagine how damaging they would be to me if you handed them over to the authorities. I'd lose my license and probably end up in jail. Joe can verify these results with a few calls. Unfortunately, the treatment reports became 'lost' in bureaucratic foul-ups with One World's record department. What a shame. That file you're holding is the only record." She paused. "The fact that I signed it is the equivalent of a confession."

Eve looked down at the file. "You're taking an enormous chance." She drew a deep breath. "And you're forcing me to make a decision I don't want to make."

"You have to believe me," Diane said simply. "It's the only way I could think to earn your trust. Read the files. Have Joe check up on the patients."

"I will. I'll call Joe when I get in the car." Eve was silent again. "This must mean a great deal to you. I have to tell you that I believe in the law, and this doesn't make me more sympathetic toward you."

"I didn't think it would. But everyone knows you're honorable and fair, and there's always the bigger picture. There can't be a bigger picture than the one I'm showing you. I only hope that if you believe me, you'll weigh what I can offer in the balance and it might help me."

"And you've just made my decision even harder. I don't appreciate that, Diane." She pushed back her chair. "I'll let you know when I do make that decision. Now I'm going to go home and read these files. Later, I'll talk to Joe and see what he says." She got to her feet. "It's been an interesting afternoon. Until I make a decision, I'd appreciate it if you'd stay close to Catherine and within view of that officer Joe assigned you." She headed for the door. "I wouldn't want you to get killed, and waste all the time I'm going to spend worrying about what I'm going to do about you."

CHAPTER
7

9:40 P.M.

I've been waiting for you," Eve said as she watched Joe take the steps two at a time to the porch. "I was expecting you to call me back."

"I was checking and double-checking." Joe grimaced as he dropped down on the porch swing beside her. "I was hoping to find a lie or at least uncertainty among all those patients' relatives and doctors I was calling in three different countries."

"She was telling the truth?"

"I couldn't prove otherwise. Miracle cure. I heard that phrase over and over during every interview. If it's a scam, it's a very elaborate one and some very reputable physicians have been taken in by it. Something happened with those patients that was unusual and that's all I can determine with this shallow an investigation." He looked at the files on the swing between them. "What did you find in those records?"

"What she said I'd find. She tried to be clinical and they were very professional, but every now and then I could see through the science to the pain beneath. She *cared* about those patients. She made me care about them. I fought against it, but I felt the tragedy, and the worry, and the joy when those injections worked."

"She got you."

She nodded. "She got me. I was rooting for her through every one of those procedures." She paused. "And when I finished, I sat here and thought about the big picture that she'd shown me. It's one hell of an impressive picture, Joe."

"Eve, you know there's no way you should do this," Joe said quietly. "I told you that Diane has no right to ask anything of you. And that was before one of your best friends was attacked and almost killed. I can't believe you're even considering it."

"Yes, you can." She was gazing out over the lake. "Because you realize that what I told you about Diane and those damn plants changes everything. You're just fighting it because you're still feeling guilty you made that mistake all those years ago." She paused. "And in some twisted way you want to make certain it never happens again. Well, it won't, Joe. So we're right back at square one. Diane has turned into a remarkable woman who might just change the world if we give her a chance. I don't know how I feel about that. I think I resent it a little. She had enough going for her before she became a medical wonder woman." She reached out and took his hand. "But think about it," she whispered. "It's not as if it's just a cure for one deadly disease. It's the panacea. Think of the lives that she could save, that *we* could save if we can keep her safe."

"And if she's not spinning some tall tale." He hesitated. "You actually believe her?"

She didn't speak for a moment. "I was asking myself that as I drove myself home tonight. How do I know? As you say, it could be a tall tale." Her hand tightened on his. "But somehow I don't think it is. Hu Chang believed in her. Some monster believed enough in her to try to kill her. Catherine almost died to keep her alive." She added slowly,

"She took on tremendous risk handing these records to me. I think she was telling the truth. I can't vouch for whether that silver bullet actually exists. But if there's a chance that she's done it, then I can't ignore what she asked of me. After what the entire world has gone through lately, I don't have that right. I have to find a way to help her."

"And if you're wrong?"

"Then I have to find that out, too." She nestled her head on his shoulder. "Life is so precious. There's no telling what treasures we can discover if we don't have to worry all the time about what's waiting in the wings. Diane was joking when she said she couldn't promise Michael eternal life, but she might be able to keep him from having a bad cold. But you know, every mother and father in the world wants only the best for their children whatever that might be. Hope is a beautiful thing. And Diane only wants to give that gift to all the children out there."

He suddenly chuckled. "You talk as if she's Mother Teresa."

Eve lifted her head. "No way. Though I wouldn't mind her *looking* like Mother Teresa. She's entirely too gorgeous." She sat up straight on the swing. "Regardless, I'm not about to become one of her disciples. I'll just try to do my job and then make sure we get out alive." She looked him in the eye. "And I guess that means that I'm going to do that reconstruction."

"Duh." He smiled crookedly. "I'd have to be half-witted not to realize that when you started to talk about children and silver bullets. Diane hooked you and then reeled you in."

"Not true. My decision. It would be better if you could be more tolerant toward her."

"I'll work on it." He got to his feet. "But it may take a while before I get to that point. Right now, I'm just trying to accept that I lost the battle, if not the war. I don't *want* this. You'll forgive me if I don't pretend I do."

"You never pretend." But she could tell he was still upset. There was a hard edge, a recklessness, that she seldom saw in him. "I'm not certain exactly how I'll have to proceed, but I'll make every attempt not to be gone long." She hesitated. "And I'll understand if you decide to stay here."

"What the hell are you talking about?" He whirled around to face her. "That was never going to be an issue. Whatever you decide, we're going to be together. I just have to figure out how that's going to happen. Because thanks to Diane, I'm going to have to walk a tightrope with both my own precinct and Quantico so no one knows I'm trailing behind you. Then Diane has to tell me where she's supposed to connect with Belazo to get that body."

"I can take care of that. You don't have to be involved."

"The hell I don't. I'm going to be involved in this up to my eyebrows. Everything. So that I can get your ass back here as soon as possible." He was scowling. "And in the meantime, I'm going to find out who beat up Catherine. Any objections?"

"Knock yourself out. You appear to be on a roll."

"I do, don't I? Now, what about Michael? We're not taking him with us to Nevada."

"Absolutely not!"

"I thought we'd send him to Cara or Jane. Probably Cara."

It was a good idea. Cara Delaney had been a member of their family since before Michael was born, and he adored her. "Cara is on tour. I'll have to see if she can take him. But he just got back from staying with Jane in Scotland." She paused. "It would be more convenient if you would stay here with him."

"Forget it. I'll call Cara." He'd reached the steps and started down them. "You get in touch with Catherine and tell her that you're going to do what Diane's asking. You needn't add that I'm not at all pleased about it. That goes without saying."

She was frowning as she followed him to the steps. "Where are you going?"

"To the hotel to see Diane." His expression was grim as he glanced back over his shoulder. "We need to have a talk. She needs to know that just because she's talked you into this, it doesn't mean that there won't be rules to keep you safe."

"She appeared genuinely concerned. I don't think you need worry about her going rogue."

"I can only judge her by past experience."

"Why not try not judging her at all? There's such a thing as a clean sheet."

"I'll think about it. But don't hold your breath." He was heading for the jeep. "She's got to obey the rules, and that's something she was never good at."

RENAISSANCE HOTEL

"Hello, Joe." Diane answered the door and stood aside for him to enter. "Come in and sit down. One way or another, I imagine you have a lot to say to me." She went to the adjoining door across the room to shut it. "I don't believe Catherine needs to hear any of it. I can fill her in later." She sat down on the couch across the room. "She insisted on coming back here after she checked out of the hospital. I guess that policeman you assigned her let you know?"

"He called me on the way here and wanted to know what he should do about it." He shrugged. "She's amazingly loyal to you considering what you've put her through."

"Yes, she is. As well as incredibly professional in every way." She gazed at him. "And she believes me, Joe. I realize how lucky I am that she does. I'm very grateful."

"You appear to be entirely convincing." His expression was impassive. "Because Eve believes you, too." Then his expression was no longer without emotion as he added roughly, "I don't know how or why. Maybe it's just because she's such an idealist and she wants it so badly. But you've *got* her, dammit."

"Thank God." Diane closed her eyes for an instant. "I was so afraid." Her eyes flew open. "But not you, Joe? I suppose that would be too much to expect."

"You bet it would. Don't be greedy. You've got Eve, and whether all of this is a fairy tale or fraud or the real deal, don't expect me to trust you. The only reason I'm here is to make certain you understand that this must not damage Eve in any way."

"Then you've made that clear. Are you finished now?" Diane asked quietly. "I don't have to hear all the rules you're going to lay down. I'm not going to do anything that will jeopardize anyone and certainly not Eve." She got to her feet. "I'm not a fool. I know how lucky I am that you're going to permit her to help me."

"Permit?" He shook his head. "Permission has nothing to do with it. You must have forgotten that Eve runs her own show. She hasn't changed a bit since you first met her."

"I believe she has." She frowned thoughtfully. "She's a hell of a lot stronger. She was no pussycat when I came into your lives before, but now she's like a river that's grown deeper and more complicated with time and experience. But that doesn't change the fact that you could have made it more difficult for me if you'd chosen." She smiled crookedly. "You didn't choose and I'm grateful. It's obvious that you have no faith in me. How could you? We're strangers, and the only memories you have of me are bad ones. But you should know that these days I work very hard and I earn a good deal of respect for that work." She gestured to the door. "Now I'll let you get out of here and back to Eve." She added suddenly, "Do you think she'll change her mind about doing the reconstruction?"

"Not a chance."

"I don't think so, either. I had a lot going against me, but I hoped once she made up her mind . . . " She frowned. "But you're going to be involved in this, and you're not going to stay on the sidelines."

"No way."

"That will be awkward for me, but I guess I'll have to work with you. I'd better start cooperating." She picked up her phone and dialed. "I'll text you the info on our contact in Nevada who promised Alon he'd go dig up that body and have it ready to hand over to me whenever I show up. His name is Luis Belazo, and he's going to charge Hu Chang a pretty penny for the service. He's now hiding out in a house in the woods in the mountains near the California border. The closest airport is Reno, Nevada, so we'll have to rent a car as soon as we land." She ended the text. "That should be a place for you to start. I know you never used to really trust anyone's information but your own when we were living together."

"I still don't. But I never realized you noticed that about me." Joe heard the ping on his phone and glanced down at the info. "I'm heading for Nevada tomorrow. I'll follow up with Belazo as soon as I get there."

"We're leaving right away?" Diane asked eagerly. "That soon?"

"*I'm* leaving tomorrow. I'm not certain when it will be safe to bring Eve, Catherine, and you into the area. I'll have to make arrangements."

"Bullshit. I need to go now. And Eve isn't going to want to sit around and wait for 'arrangements.' I know that much about her."

So did Joe, but he had no intention of arguing with Diane right now. "Eve is always sensible when she has to be. Perhaps you wouldn't be aware that those arrangements are more difficult when a child is involved." Then something else occurred to him. "How did you get my number? Since I was pointedly left out of any notification of your arrival, I wouldn't have thought you'd have it at your fingertips."

"I'm much more prepared for any emergency these days," Diane said. "And you were always an emergency, Joe. Back then you pretty well ran my life. I knew when I decided I needed Eve that I'd also have to deal with you." Her smile was half bitter. "And here I am."

"Yes, you'll always have to deal with me. Eve and I are a matched set."

"I wish I'd known that a little sooner." She held up her hand. "Water under the bridge. I didn't come here to cause trouble. I'm not blaming anyone for anything. I've learned a lot since the days when I thought the world and everything in it belonged to me. I'll take whatever you can give me." She made a face. "Well, that sounded awkward. What I meant is that I'll be grateful for any help I get in finding a way to prove or disprove the value of those damn plants that are the bane of my existence."

"Really?" His lips indented at the corners. "But how can they be the bane of your existence if your body has become a glorious temple due to them?"

"Sarcasm?"

"I couldn't resist. I'm having problems with thinking of you as some kind of holy grail that will bring us all to never-never land."

"You think I'm not?" She made a rude sound. "All those tests and research were necessary, dammit. And I'll sock you if you say anything like that again."

He was silent. Then he chuckled. "Should I be intimidated? My, how you've changed, Diane."

"That's what I've been trying to tell you." She ran her fingers through her hair. "Give me a break, Joe."

"I'll work on it." His smile faded. "But not if you do anything that puts Eve in the least danger. Understand?"

She nodded jerkily. "No problem. I've already got a huge black mark for Catherine. I'm not going to add Eve to it."

"Okay." He stood looking at her. Eve had said she was gorgeous and maybe she was, but all he could see as he gazed at her was the weariness and almost childlike discouragement in her face at this moment. For an instant she reminded him of Michael.

There's darkness all around her, Michael said.

And Michael had wanted him to take that darkness away, and Joe had brushed him aside. He might be doing the same thing right now.

Diane was gazing at him curiously. "Why are you looking at me like that?"

"I was just remembering that you were targeted only a couple of days ago. I'm thinking that no matter what arrangements I make for Eve and Catherine, you shouldn't be included."

"The hell I won't!" She was staring at him, aghast. "What are you talking about? Of course I'm going."

He shook his head. "Whatever we run into there, your presence would only be a hindrance. If you were in danger here, you'd be twice the target out there in the mountains. I don't want to have to watch over you as well as Eve. I'll put you in a safe house here in Atlanta with adequate guards where you'll be absolutely secure. That's the only way to handle it."

"Oh, is it?" Her hands were slowly knotting into fists at her sides. "You're so sure about that, aren't you, Joe? Just lock me away and let you get on with your life the way you want it to go. Well, this time it's my life, and that's not what's going to happen." She walked slowly toward him. "Because I'm responsible if anything happens to Eve or Catherine or even you, Joe. But mostly Eve. It took me a long time to learn what responsibility means, but I've got it down pat now." She stopped before him and her eyes blazed up at him. "And you believe I'd let her go there without me? If I'm the target, then I'm the one who can save her if there's trouble. They wouldn't want her; they'd want *me* and what I know and what I could tell the world." She punched her index finger at the middle of his chest. "So suck it up, you're not her hero this time. You might be her bodyguard, but in the end I'm the one who will be your most valuable asset, if you'll use me." She whirled away from him. "That's all. Screw your safe house. The first thing I'd do if you locked me up there would be to break out and head for Nevada." She looked over her shoulder at him. "Now get out of here. I'm going to go tell Catherine I'll be ready to leave at six in the morning. So go home and make your damn arrangements, but don't you dare leave me out of them."

LAKE COTTAGE

"You were gone longer than I'd thought you'd be." Eve cuddled close as Joe slipped into bed. "Did she give you any arguments?"

"You could say that." He brushed her temple with his lips. "Did you talk to Catherine?"

"Catherine thought I was doing the right thing and said to call her when we're ready to head for Nevada. She mentioned that she'd checked back into the suite at the Renaissance to be with Diane. Did you see her there?"

"No, she was in her own room. Anyway, I was busy talking to Diane."

"I also called Cara," Eve said. "She *is* on tour, but she said she'd love to take Michael with her for the next few events." She paused. "You're stalling. What arguments did Diane give you?"

"The ones that had anything to do with me being in charge of what was going on. Though she did say she wanted to cooperate." He added dryly, "But cooperation for her might not be what anyone else would term it. She did give me the address of Belazo, who's supposed to deliver that body."

"Well, I'd call that mega cooperation. Anything to help me wrap the reconstruction up more quickly."

"I agreed. But she followed it with telling me to go to hell when I told her that she wasn't going with you when you did the reconstruction; I was sending her to a safe house for her protection."

Eve gave a low whistle. "I can see why she might have objected. But she must have known it was for her own good, Joe."

"She didn't give a damn. All she cared about was her blasted responsibility and getting her own way."

"And you gave in to her?"

"It was more like—I wasn't sure... Yeah, I guess I did. She kind of made sense."

"What?"

He was silent. "She said since she'd pulled you into this mess, she was responsible for you and she had to be there. I could understand that."

Yes, Joe was so responsible himself that Eve could see how he might bond with Diane on that issue. "I never would have thought that she'd feel that way about me. It's a bit bizarre. Did she mean it?"

Joe was silent again. "I think she did. She was very... passionate about it."

Passionate. The word sent a ripple of unease through Eve and reminded her of how she'd felt that first moment when she'd looked down from the porch and seen Joe and Michael with Diane. "'Passionate'?"

"Or whatever you want to call it," Joe said. "Driven? She

was different than I'd ever seen her...not the same person. She surprised me."

Eve tried to keep her tone light. "I told you that she might not be the woman you knew back then. Life changes people. Not a pleasant surprise?"

"Not unless you like dealing with hellcats," Joe said bluntly. "There's every chance she's going to be a royal pain in the ass when we get to Nevada. She informed me that she knew you wouldn't put up with being left behind while I scouted out the situation. She said she was going with us tomorrow."

Shock on top of shock. "She was right. Why would you think I'd let you go without me? It's *my* reconstruction."

"Because it's *safer*, dammit. I could but hope."

"No way." She drew a little away from him. "And what did you say when she told you that she was tagging along? I know when you make up your mind nothing gets in your way. If you'd decided to keep her in that safe house, you would have made it happen. But she's going with us, isn't she?"

He nodded. "I told you, she made sense." He frowned. "Are you upset about this?"

"A little. But not because I'm jealous." She grimaced. "Well, maybe I am, since we seem to be confronting an entirely new Diane. I don't know what to expect from one moment to the next. Why did she make such good sense to you?"

"Because she'll be a distraction and any attacks will be aimed first at her and not you," he said simply. "That's all that really matters. She said she'd break out of any safe house I put her in and she probably would. I'll do everything I can to keep her safe, but the choice was clear. The choice is always you, Eve."

She stared at him helplessly. How was she supposed to argue with a love this deep and unshakable? Hell, accept it and be grateful and try to be worthy of it. "It's not all that matters." She went back into his arms and said fiercely, "All life is precious, and I'm beginning to believe Diane might realize that more than anyone I've ever met." She held him more tightly and whispered, "And you're damn right we'll keep her safe."

Eve was on the phone with Catherine at five the next morning. "Sorry to not give you much notice, but it seems we're going to Nevada today. Diane gave Joe the address of Luis Belazo, who swears he's managed to find that body. Do you know anything about him?"

"What would I know? Neither Diane nor Hu Chang has been at all forthcoming to me until very recently. I'm glad that Joe's been able to get Diane to open up."

"It was actually purely voluntary. I'm hoping it's a sign of good things to come. At any rate, can you and Diane meet us at the airport this afternoon? Joe has rented a plane to take us to Reno, but we can't leave until two when Cara can arrange to come and pick up Michael."

"No problem." She paused. "I'll call Hu Chang and see if he'll be as generous with information now. I don't know how to approach this Belazo."

"Carefully. All Joe could find out from checking this morning is that he used to work for the Ramez cartel and he's demanding a lot of money from Hu Chang for his services. I'll see you at the airport." She cut the connection.

There was no question she'd handle Belazo carefully, Catherine thought grimly. If Hu Chang had been dealing with him, he was probably the real McCoy, but that didn't guarantee that he wasn't lethal. Not many of Hu Chang's contacts could claim that distinction.

"Who was on the phone?" Diane was standing in the open adjoining doorway. "Joe?"

"No, Eve." Catherine tossed her sheet to one side and got out of bed. "And it appears that you got your way. She wants us to meet her at the airport at two. Joe is renting a plane to take us to Nevada."

"Well, then I didn't quite get my way." Diane was grinning. "I told him to pick me up at six this morning. But at least I must have made an impression. Not bad. Considering how our relationship started out, I should be grateful for any weakness in his defenses."

"That's not what you said when you came storming into my room last night," she said dryly. "You were ready to go to war."

She nodded. "I was planning a massive assault if he didn't see reason by this morning. I might have even had to involve Eve and Michael." She turned to leave and added cheerfully, "But evidently that's not necessary now. I'm glad, I want Eve on my side and kids are out of bounds where I'm concerned."

"Good call," Catherine said as she headed for her bathroom. "But Joe never gives in easily. You must have managed to convince him that taking you made sense."

Diane nodded wryly. "Yes, I knew I could. I only had to appeal to his greatest weakness and then strike hard and deep."

"Eve." Catherine nodded. "So much for keeping her on your side. But right now, I'm interested that you mentioned Luis Belazo to him. What do you know about him?"

"Only what Hu Chang told me." Diane shrugged. "That Belazo is crooked, which isn't bad since he was more than willing to betray Nalam. All I have to do is authorize the transfer of the rest of the amount from Hu Chang's bank in Hong Kong to Belazo's Grand

Cayman account and he'll turn the body over to us." She paused. "And that I shouldn't trust him, but let you handle it."

"Which would have been fine if you'd told me about it." Catherine held up her hand. "Never mind. I'll call Hu Chang and get all the details. Just get packed so that we can be at the airport by Eve's two o'clock deadline."

GENERAL AVIATION RAMP
ATLANTA AIRPORT

"Do I have to go?" Michael looked away from Eve and out at the tarmac where Joe was examining the Learjet. "I don't want to leave you, Mom."

"I don't want to leave you, either." She slid her arm around him. "But sometimes it's necessary, and you'll enjoy being with Cara. You haven't seen your sister all year. You like going to her concerts."

"Yeah, it's cool seeing all those fans sucking up to her. They don't realize she's just an ordinary person. It's kind of funny."

"I don't believe using that term *sucking up* is cool at all." She shook her head. "And she's brilliant and deserves that they think she's not ordinary. You'll have a great time with her."

He nodded. "I know." He made a face. "I just don't want you to go off without me." He reached out and grabbed her hand. "It's . . . dark out there. You might need me."

"I'll want you. I won't need you," she said gently. "I've got your dad. We've got each other. I have to go, Michael. It's important."

He nodded jerkily. "I know it is. But it's dark, too."

"Your dad and I can handle it." She gave him a hug and was relieved to see Catherine and Diane coming toward them. Michael was being entirely too somber, and it was breaking her heart.

"Now go say goodbye to Diane and Catherine, and don't you dare be gloomy."

"Okay." He started to trot toward them and then looked over his shoulder, troubled. "But the darkness is all about Diane. You know that, Mom."

"No, I don't." She looked him in the eye. "I believe that often the brightness or darkness in life are what we make ourselves. Diane is trying to weave something bright and beautiful. So try to see only the brightness, Michael."

"It's hard." Then he forced himself to smile. "Okay, only the brightness, Mom." He ran toward Catherine and Diane and called, "It's about time you got here. Come on, Diane, Mom says you've never met my sister Cara. Well, she's not really my sister, she has another name, Cara Delaney. But Mom and Dad have been her guardians since she was my age so she might as well be my sister. She's out on the tarmac talking to Dad." He stopped before them. "You should have seen the big black limousine she arrived in, with a chauffeur and everything. Though he's really sort of a bodyguard. She said the musical director wanted to make sure she showed up for the concert down at Disney World tonight."

"Disney World?" Diane's brows rose. "She's a concert violinist, isn't she? I wouldn't think she'd play Disney World."

"Well, she's actually playing at some big auditorium a few miles from there, but Cara says everything in Orlando is connected with Disney World in some way or other. She says she's even playing the musical selections from a few of the Disney movies for this concert. She said she can't wait."

"Sounds great. I've never heard her play but I'm looking forward to it." Diane's gaze turned toward the tarmac, where Joe and Cara were still talking. "She's lovely and so young. She sort of shines... Catherine tells me she's on her way to being a big star."

"Oh, none of that stuff matters to Cara," Michael said impatiently. "It's only the music she cares about. But she does shine." He took Diane's hand and pulled her toward the door to the tarmac. "Come and meet her."

"It seems that's what I'm going to do." Diane glanced over her shoulder at Catherine as she reached the door. "Care to join us?"

Catherine shook her head. "You go on ahead. Evidently Michael wants to make sure you're brought properly into the family fold. I want to have a word with Eve before we leave anyway."

"By all means." She allowed Michael to pull her out onto the tarmac. "I'm sure I'll have plenty of time to talk to her on the flight. See you later..."

"And Diane probably will feel easier if she doesn't have to contend with Joe or me any sooner than necessary," Eve murmured as she came to stand beside Catherine. "Cara will make an excellent buffer. Isn't that the impression you received after that brouhaha between Joe and Diane last night?"

"I didn't hear anything until Diane came into my room later to tell me that we'd probably be leaving today. I'm certain you found out much more from Joe." Catherine smiled. "But I do believe we all have a better idea what we're going to have to contend with in Diane."

Eve nodded. "And from Joe." She looked at the tarmac, where Diane was now shaking hands with Cara while Michael stood leaning against his dad with a smile on his face. Joe was also smiling politely, but not at all warmly. "Joe's in protective mode. But that protection might be aimed at me and not Diane. You should know that, since you've told me enough times that your job is to guard Diane."

"I don't need to be reminded. Everyone knows where Joe's priority lies. But I'd still rather have him at my back than anyone else. And he'll be where he's needed no matter what he feels. He won't be able to do anything else. We both know that, don't we?"

Eve slowly nodded. "But he'll still think he can."

"Then that's your problem. I'll take care of mine."

"Which you appear to be doing. Joe said Diane gave him the Belazo address. By tonight we should be knocking on his door."

"Maybe." Catherine paused. "Unless Belazo changed his mind about his deal with us. I tried to make contact with him this morning after I spoke to Hu Chang and all I got was voicemail."

"Not good," Eve said. "Did you call Hu Chang back?"

Catherine nodded. "He said he'd spoken to him yesterday and the deal was still firm." She grimaced. "But he warned us to be cautious. There's no question we'll follow that advice." She was now gazing at Diane and Cara, who appeared to be getting along famously. "Diane is doing her best to give Michael what he wants and charm his big sister. Does it bother you?"

"No, Michael is Michael. If he's decided to adopt Diane, I'll have to accept it." She added dryly, "Particularly since I've had to adopt her, too."

"And how has Michael taken it that Cara has been called in to babysit him while you and Joe are gone? Will he resent her?"

She shook her head. "He adores her. If he resents anyone, it's me for not letting him come with us. He did everything he could to talk me out of it. I don't think he's happy, but at least at present he seems okay with it." She saw that Joe, Diane, Cara, and Michael were now turning away from the plane and starting back toward them. She sighed. "And now it's time to smile and pretend that it's okay with me, too."

"I should be with them, you know." Michael's hand tightened on Cara's as they watched Joe taxi the Learjet down the runway. "Mom is wrong. She shouldn't have called you." He was blinking hard to keep back the tears. "You shouldn't have come."

"You know better than that, Michael," Cara said quietly. "I'll always come when your mom calls me. We're family." She smiled. "Besides, I kind of like having an excuse to be with you. This being on tour most of the time can really be a drag. I practically never get a chance to see you guys anymore. It gets lonely."

"You have Jock Gavin. Mom says that he tries to visit you all the time when you're on tour."

"Yes, I have Jock." Her smile was suddenly luminous. "And I always will, but he has his own career and he keeps trying to stay out of my way so that I can become this great musical artist. Right now he's in New York negotiating some mega deal for Lord MacDuff. We're still trying to work things out."

"But you'll get there?"

"Absolutely," she said lightly. "He doesn't stand a chance against me. I can be very stubborn. You know that, Michael."

"Yeah, I know that," he said absently. "That's good. I really like Jock." His gaze was on the Learjet, which was now taking off. He shook his head. "But I can be stubborn, too, Cara. They wouldn't have left if you hadn't shown up to take care of me. I should be with them."

Cara had known this confrontation was coming. How was she going to handle it? She took one glance at his expression and then said, "Okay, we have to talk about this. Eve said it was very important she do that reconstruction in Nevada. She didn't give me all the details, only that it concerned Diane, that very nice lady you introduced me to. If she's in trouble, don't you think Mom and Dad should help her?"

Michael nodded jerkily. "But I should be there, too. They might need me. Diane is..." He stopped and then started again, "Mom thinks just because Diane's trying to do something good that it will be enough to stop the blood."

"Blood?"

"Blood and darkness. There was blood with Catherine but there will be more." His tongue moistened his lower lip. "I can see it. It won't stop, nothing will stop it. He doesn't want it to stop."

"Who doesn't want it to stop?" Her hands closed on his shoulders and she gently shook him. "Talk to me. The person who hurt Catherine?"

"No, the other one. The one who wants Diane to die. He was so angry with her..."

Her grip tightened on his shoulders. "Who, Michael?"

He stepped back away from her. "I don't know his name. But I'd know him if I saw him. That's why I should be there. I'd *know* him, Cara. I might not even have to see him. I might be able to sense that he was there."

"And you might not," she said curtly. "Hey, kid, I've been around since the moment you took your first breath and I realize that you're not like the rest of us. I was there in the mountains last year when you went after Dad when he was wounded. But I believe you're still experimenting with what you can and can't do. Isn't that true?"

He frowned and then nodded. "But I still think that—"

"But you're not sure, you're experimenting. Plus you're only ten years old. There's no way that Eve and Joe would voluntarily put you in a position where you'd be in danger. You don't have a chance of getting them to do that, whether I'm here or not. Right?"

Michael didn't speak.

"Michael?"

"I have to be there for them."

He'd spoken truly when he'd said how stubborn he could be, she thought in frustration. All she could do was appeal to his intelligence.

"Eve and Joe are two strong, smart people and they might not need you. How do you know you're going to *sense* anything? Isn't that true? Why don't you just come along with me and keep me company, maybe even hang out at that Star Wars amusement park for a day or so? By that time perhaps the reconstruction will be completed. If not, if you feel uncomfortable about it, we'll have another discussion."

"You're offering me Star Wars?" He stiffened. "Are you bribing me?"

"I wouldn't presume. Though you're just a kid and I admit I'm pulling out all the stops to get you to reconsider. For almost any other kid, Star Wars might be tempting. What else can I do to be sure you don't cause a ruckus and make me look bad?"

He was silent. "You're right, I can't do anything right now." He didn't speak again for another moment. "Okay, I'll go with you. But only if you'll promise to take me to Mom and Dad if something bad happens and I tell you I have to go."

Cara nodded. "That seems entirely reasonable." She hoped it was reasonable, and that the argument was temporarily over. But she knew she'd have to call Eve and Joe as soon as she got Michael settled. *Blood and darkness. He doesn't want it to stop.* She smothered a shiver as she remembered Michael's words. Forget it. She had been chosen to take care of Michael, and she would do it. No matter what the odds or difficulties. She gave him a quick hug. "Now let's jump into that limo and have the chauffeur take us to Orlando. Can I talk you into attending my concert at the auditorium tonight if I promise to throw a visit to the Harry Potter Universe into the mix for tomorrow?"

CHAPTER 8

SARCASA, NEVADA
8:40 P.M.

Luis Belazo's house was not what she expected, Catherine thought as she got out of the Mercedes rental car and stood beside it looking up at the two-story A-frame log cabin in these backwoods. He had referred to it as a hideout, but it looked more like an ultra-comfortable vacation getaway. Yet it was located in the foothills near Lake Tahoe practically on the California border, and the area appeared both isolated and... wild. Joe had parked some distance away from the house on the only flat plain on the property. It was shrouded by trees and bushes and wouldn't be visible from the house. From where she was standing, the log cabin itself seemed clean and well kept; she could see the cheerful glow of lights in the windows. There was a late-model beige Lexus in the driveway. "I don't know about this place," she murmured to Eve. "He said it was a hideout, but it's not exactly the setting I'd expect to house a criminal and a gory corpse. For that matter, these woods and all this natural beauty is a bit weird for a man with his shady past. I'd think a man with his cartel background would be more at home in Reno or Las Vegas."

"I imagine too many people would know Belazo in either of those places," Joe said. "He might consider it a risk he's not willing to take. A nice little shack in the backwoods that's close enough to the mountains for him to keep an eye on what's going on around him would probably suit him much better."

"And be much healthier," Diane said. "How do we make contact?"

"You don't." Joe started toward the house. "Catherine stays here in the car with you and Eve. I'll scout out the house and let Belazo know that we've come to line his pockets if he'll cooperate." He glanced at Catherine. "That okay with you?"

She didn't answer. She was still staring at the house. There was nothing threatening about it. Glowing lamplight shining from the windows. It even looked cozy...

She shivered. She wasn't feeling at all cozy. She didn't like this. It was too quiet. Was there anyone else here? If Belazo was hiding out, she didn't see any signs of it. And there was only that one beige Lexus in the driveway.

Belazo didn't call me back when I left that voicemail message.

"Catherine?" Joe was frowning impatiently.

"No." She emphatically shook her head. "It should be me. I'll do it. Hu Chang will have given him my name, and he'll be more ready to deal with me." She slammed the car door and started toward the line of trees bordering the house. "Joe, you watch out for Eve and Diane. I'll scout all around the property to make certain everything is all right. As soon as I make contact with Belazo, I'll call and tell you it's safe."

"Get back here, Catherine," Joe hissed. "I told you that I'd do this."

"You also told me that nothing must happen to Eve." She didn't look back. "You made that very clear both to Diane and to me. Well, it's your job this time. Belazo will deal with me because he'll be afraid Hu Chang will opt out of the deal if he doesn't." She ducked behind an evergreen and the next minute was out of Joe's view. She began to move toward the log cabin.

Joe did not call her again, but she could almost feel the anger that he was projecting ready to ignite. She knew she'd have to face that rage later, but right now it didn't matter. Because every instinct was telling her that something was terribly wrong.

It took her only fifteen minutes to make a tour around the house and grounds. She didn't turn on her flashlight. The night was clear and there was bright moonlight. She was moving quickly, her eyes scanning, her ears straining, listening.

She was close to the house again, and she slowed down as she reached steps leading to the back porch.

No sound.

No bright glare from a TV.

Check those windows.

Move slowly. Catlike. There must be no sound from her, either.

She was on the porch now.

Two more steps to the large window.

Looking into the kitchen, she could see the flicker of the flames in the fireplace in the adjoining living room. Cozy, again. Everything cozy and comfortable . . . and wrong.

Because she could sense someone, a presence, but not inside that room. There was only emptiness there.

The presence is here, on the porch, behind me!

With one lightning motion Catherine launched herself sideways over the porch railing! She landed in the dirt five feet below and rolled closer to the house so that she couldn't be seen from above. She pulled out her gun. "Belazo?"

"I'm afraid you've missed him, Ling." The man's low voice was mocking. "Permanently. What a shame." She heard his steps above her on the porch. "But you wouldn't have enjoyed him. I found him very boring after the first several hours when I attempted to persuade him to give me what I wanted without the fat fee he was looking for. He didn't understand he couldn't negotiate his way out of this. The fool wouldn't talk to me. And then he tried to escape, and I couldn't let him do that. It would have upset the asshole who pays me so well. But unfortunately, I broke Belazo's neck while I was trying to discourage him. Choke holds can be very tricky. Since you're CIA, you'd know that, Ling."

She recognized the voice, but she couldn't quite place from where. "Not if you know what you're doing." He was moving toward the porch steps and was probably going to try to come after her. Then she suddenly realized there was a slight limp in his gait. *Yes.* Now she knew him. She'd had trouble with the voice because before he'd been hoarse when he'd been cursing in that dark room. But she was the one who had given him that limp. "Evidently you screwed it up just as you did when you tried to kill Diane Connors. That was you?"

"I didn't screw it up. I did everything right." His voice had become ugly. "You interfered. I wasn't expecting you to come busting in from that other room. But I'm glad that I'm going to get a chance to take you out now. I knew you'd come. When Belazo called him and tried to make a better deal for himself, he was a dead man. That's why he sent me here instead of letting me finish you at the hospital. I was waiting for you after Belazo proved so boring."

"'He'?" She took a wild stab. "Nalam?"

He didn't answer for a moment. "Nalam. Why shouldn't I tell you? You're not going to be able to tell anyone."

"I don't agree." Probe. He was clearly in a mood to brag. See how much he knew. "Do you think I'd come here alone and walk into a trap?"

"Oh, I knew you'd show up with protection. But you did walk

into the trap, didn't you? I was watching and waiting for you. I knew where you parked that rental car and I know who's there in that car waiting for you. It's a good spot, decent view of the house, and cover if you didn't get a warm welcome. I thought you'd park down there, and I made some advance preparations. I'm just sorry you didn't bring Hakali. I would have gotten a bonus if I'd been able to take him out. You aren't really of any importance to Nalam, Ling." His voice lowered. "But you're important to me. Now I'll get my chance at you without anyone getting in my way. Though I do regret that Joe Quinn didn't come to the house with you. It would have made it much easier for me to get rid of Diane Connors if I'd taken him out first."

"And Diane is the target. All the rest of us are just collateral damage." He was starting down the stairs; the time for probing was over. Her hand tightened on her gun. "Except for me. I really pissed you off, didn't I? Come and get me. This time I'll put a bullet in your heart."

"No, you won't." His voice was mocking again. "You'll be too busy running back to your friends in that Mercedes, trying to save them. Because I seeded the entire area where you parked with IEDs, and I have the detonator in my left pocket." As he passed by the light from the kitchen window, she saw that he had a rifle cupped in his arm. He took another step and the light suddenly played across his face; Catherine saw the pure malice in his expression. Then he was in the shadow again, but his voice held the same malice. "I hold all the cards. Shall I set off the first explosion and see if it's close enough to get the gas tank? Maybe it will just frighten them enough so that they'll jump out of the car to get away. But then I'll be able to pick them off one by one."

"Stop." It could be a bluff, but it was one that scared her. "You don't want to do that."

"Maybe I won't. I'd much rather pick you off." She could see moonlight on the rifle barrel as he swung it directly toward her. "Go on. Save them. Run, little rabbit. You might be able to keep them alive. It's not likely, but neither was your chance of saving Connors in that hotel room." He added with soft menace, "But I promise you that your chances of coming out of this alive are very slim. Should I fire the first shot? Quinn will probably leap out of the car and come to your defense. But then I'd almost have to start setting off the explosives. What do you want me to do? Tell me, little rabbit. You know what I want."

He wanted her to run so that he could hunt her down.

And that might be their best chance if she could keep him occupied enough to distract him from setting off those explosives. She'd always been good with directions, and she'd paid attention when she'd done reconnaissance of the woods surrounding the property. Joe had trained in handling explosives when he was a SEAL, and his experience had grown over the years. Perhaps he could figure something out if she gave him the time to do it.

"I'm no scared little rabbit, and you'd probably end up screwing that up, too."

"No, I won't. But I'm getting bored. If you won't entertain me, I'll have to start some fireworks. Or you can toss out that gun I know you're pointing at me and we'll start the hunt."

He had that damn rifle. And she hadn't actually seen the detonator, but that was a hideous weapon aimed at people she cared about. She couldn't afford to take a chance that he was bluffing.

"What a coward. That sounds like a man who would sneak into a sleeping woman's room and try to kill her." She hurled her gun away; it landed in front of him on the step. The next moment she suddenly darted out from behind the shadow of the stairs toward the woods in the opposite direction from the rental car. "But let's see if you can bring me down."

"Oh, I'll bring you down, bitch." She heard him laugh as he ran down the rest of the stairs.

She was already in the woods and making no effort to be quiet. Let the bastard have something to hunt. She was running at top speed, but her fingers were already punching in Joe's number on her phone. She cut him off as he tried to speak: "Listen, it was a trap. There are explosives planted somewhere near where you are and a man with a rifle ready to pick you off. I'm trying to lead him away, but I can't be sure I'll be able to do it. You're on your own." She paused. "So am I. No matter what you hear, don't come after me. Take care of the others." She cut the connection.

Okay, she'd done the best she could. Now all that was left was to run like hell and keep the pace just fast enough not to discourage him. That might be difficult since she'd already wounded him once in the leg. And he was definitely motivated. She heard him crashing through the brush in the woods behind her.

Come on, Joe, what was all that SEAL training for? Get everyone away from that car before he can detonate those explosives.

A bullet splintered the bark on the tree next to Catherine!

Shit.

It was the first shot he'd fired at her since the hunt had begun several minutes ago. It probably meant that he was getting tired of the game. Not good. That might also mean he was ready to set off those explosives.

"Aren't you tired, little rabbit?" he called. "I am. It amused me at first but now it's beginning to annoy me. I think that I need to go and see if Quinn or your other friends would like to play with us."

No! That was the last thing she wanted.

Another shot. Closer.

Much closer.

Okay, change of plans. See if Joe had made any progress with those explosives. Maybe circle around and help him go on the attack. She paused an instant to get her bearings. Then she turned and headed in the general direction of the rental car.

"How obliging you are. You must be tired, too." His voice was suddenly harsh. "By all means, let's put an end to this."

She ran faster.

She was panting. Her lungs felt as if they were going to burst. But that bastard behind her must be in just as bad shape. She could hear his labored breathing and cursing as he tore through the brush trying to keep up with her. But he wasn't going to stop. That viciousness and hatred he'd shown her was too strong.

So she'd have to stop him.

She'd doubled back through the woods and must be near the rental car. If she waited until she was any closer, then he might either get impatient and set off the explosives or would be on top of her and there would be no chance of a surprise. There was a curve around the stand of trees just ahead...

She put on more speed.

She was around the curve. She could hear him only a little behind her. Two weapons. Plan the attack. He'd slipped the detonator into his left pocket, and that would be the most dangerous. He'd been carrying the rifle, but that was a difficult weapon to use at close quarters. So go for the detonator first.

She quickly stepped sidewise into the shrubbery to the left of the trail.

Come on, you son of a bitch.

The next moment he burst around the corner!

And the instant after that Catherine launched herself at his knees in a flying tackle. He grunted with pain as she brought him to the ground!

"Bitch!" He swung the butt of his rifle at her as he struggled to his knees. She ducked and grabbed the rifle, but he was too strong for her to wrest it away from him. She let the weapon go and brought the edge of her hand down on his neck in a karate chop. He was dazed but shook it off and then his fist plowed into her stomach.

Pain.

She couldn't breathe.

She didn't have time to recover before his fist landed on her right jaw.

The agony was dizzying. *Don't let him see it.*

He'd already seen it; his eyes were glittering with malicious satisfaction. "Nalam called me a weakling. But you're the one who's the weakling. Just a little weak woman who thought she could take me down." He reached for her throat. "I don't even need a rifle to rid myself of you."

She let his hands close on her neck. *Come on, bastard, see how weak I am. You're in my court now.* She permitted his hands to tighten for the fraction of a second. Then she reared back and struck directly, with absolute accuracy, at his carotid artery. "The *hell* you don't."

She saw his eyes start to glaze over as she pushed him away from her. Quick. She had to be quick. She figured she might have only a few minutes before he recovered. She started searching through his pockets. She found the detonator in the left pocket.

She shuddered. It hadn't been a bluff.

She also found a Luger pistol and a dagger in a holster on his left calf.

She was reaching for the rifle that was half buried under his body when his hand reached out and grasped her arm with bruising force and jerked her forward. His eyes were open and glaring fiercely up at her as his other hand searched wildly in his pocket. "You took it." He was gazing malevolently at her. "You think you've beaten me, Ling? You haven't, you know. I've been taught by experts that there's always more than one way to take down prey. I'll still kill you all." Then he was rolling to one side, grabbing his rifle, and jumping to his feet. Before she could raise the Luger to fire, he'd struck her forearm with numbing force with the butt of the rifle.

For an instant she thought he was going to turn the rifle on her. She struggled into a crouch to launch herself at him.

But he was shaking his head as if he was still dazed. Then he was gone, zigzagging into the trees.

And he still had that damn rifle!

There's always more than one way to take down prey.

She was on her feet, trying to hold the Luger steady in her bruised hand and arm as she streaked after him.

He couldn't be more than a few minutes from Joe, Eve, and Diane. She had to reach them first before—

"Stop, Catherine!"

She was tackled from behind and tumbled to the ground!

How had he gotten behind her? She was fighting furiously, striking out with all her strength as she tried to maneuver her body so that she could aim the Luger.

"Be still," he said harshly. "Don't fight me. You're going to make me hurt you, Catherine."

She froze. "Cameron?"

"At last." He let out the breath he'd been holding. "You can be very difficult." He got off her and pulled her into a sitting position. "Are you okay?"

"No." She was in a sudden panic. "You shouldn't have done

this." She scrambled to her knees. "I have to stop him. I have the detonator, but he's good, better than I thought. He still has a rifle. I have to help Joe. I don't know how much time I have."

"I do." He grasped her shoulders and shook her. "And you don't have to stop that asshole. You don't have to worry about the rifle. I sent Slade to run interference when I saw you still trying to go after him after he almost broke your arm." His lips tightened as he glanced down at her forearm, which was already turning purple. "Though it probably wasn't necessary after you grabbed the detonator."

She shook her head to clear it. "Slade?" Then she made the connection. "James Slade." She added sarcastically, "I'm glad you trust him, though I can't say I do." But she had to trust him. Three lives depended on him being as trustworthy as Cameron believed him to be. "Is he that good? You think they'll be safe?"

"What do you want me to say? He was good enough to spot Daniels earlier today, identify him, and then bring me here from Tahoe to help if needed."

"Daniels? That was his name? He admitted to me he was the man who tried to kill Diane, but I'd never even seen his face until tonight."

"Ralph Daniels. Slade took a photo of him and ran it through a face check. Then he called me and told me to come here right away. I jumped in my car and hit the road. But I only got here in time to see you disappearing into the woods with Daniels on your heels."

"And now we have a name. That's important. Slade might be as good as you say, Cameron."

He nodded. "He really is exceptional," he said gently. "Would I trust you to anyone who wasn't extraordinary?"

She felt a rush of warmth that she swiftly smothered. "But I'm not the one you assigned him to watch this time. I'm not fool enough to believe that you came here to search for anyone but Belazo."

"You're never a fool," he said quietly. "But sometimes you can be wrong. Hell, anyone can be wrong."

"How did you know about Belazo?" Her gaze flew to his face. "Dammit, did you have my phone tapped?"

He shook his head. "I've had a man monitoring Hu Chang since I became concerned about you. He's been very involved with Belazo over the past few days, which placed him on my list for a discussion."

"Hu Chang won't be pleased. He regards his communications network as invulnerable."

"Too bad. Ordinarily I would have been more cautious about offending him. But as soon as I knew that it was Diane Connors that you risked your life to save, my priorities changed. I've been pulling out all the stops, and I know a hell of a lot more than the last time I spoke to you. I couldn't walk away from this now even if you weren't involved."

She couldn't look away from him. She had seldom seen Cameron this intense, and that intensity was making her very nervous. "Really?" She moistened her lips. "And just what do you know?"

He suddenly smiled. "I know that this is no time for us to have a discussion. Not when you're still confused and worried about your friend Quinn and his party." He pulled her to her feet. "Let's go and make certain he managed to save the day, and that Slade proved to be just as exceptional at taking Daniels down as I told you he would be."

She pulled her arm away from him and was already starting to run through the woods again. He didn't have to tell her that was the first order of business. "Let's go. I haven't heard any shots from Daniels's rifle, but he said that he always had other weapons..." She pulled out her phone and started to punch in Joe's number.

Let him answer. Dear God, let him answer.

"Catherine." Joe's voice was rough. "Where the hell are you?"

"Heading right toward you." Her voice was shaking. "But someone else is on their way, too. If you're still in the car, get everyone out and be on watch."

"We're ahead of you," he said curtly. "I checked out the interior and exterior of the Mercedes and no explosives. I got Eve and Diane out of the vehicle and on the hood of the car while I scanned the area for IEDs. I only spotted two of them and they were easy enough to defuse and then get everyone into the woods. We'll wait for you here."

Catherine was now close enough to see them, and she breathed a sigh of relief. "Be careful. He's still out there. He has a rifle." She cut the connection and turned toward Cameron. "They seem to be safe. But I don't know where Daniels—"

But Cameron was no longer there.

Well, she couldn't worry about him. No one could take better care of himself than Cameron. She had to make sure that Eve and Diane were safe...

Joe was clearly still displeased with her. He only waited until she finished telling them what had happened with Daniels before he let her know. "You ever do that to me again, Catherine, and I might just choke you." His expression was just as grim as his voice. "Don't you dare interfere when I'm trying to do my job."

"Knock it off, Joe. I was also trying to do *my* job. It wasn't my fault that everything went crazy." She looked away from him to Diane. "You're not hurt?"

Diane shook her head. "But I wasn't the one who was being chased by that murderer. You?"

"I'm okay."

"But I gather that Hu Chang was right in telling you not to trust Belazo?"

"You've got that right. Though that will be difficult to follow up on since Daniels told me that he'd already killed him."

"Daniels?" Diane repeated. "Who the hell is Daniels?"

"The same acquaintance you crowned with a lamp in your bedroom. He was just as ugly tonight when I ran into him. All I found out was that his name is Ralph Daniels and he works for Nalam. So that confirms that Nalam's behind everything that's been happening since I got off that plane in Atlanta. Other than that, I have no other details regarding him."

Eve gave a low whistle. "You do manage to stir up a hornet's nest, don't you?" she asked. She glanced at Joe. "He wasn't amused that he had to contend with those IEDs after you ran out on us. I wouldn't advise you to do it again."

"I was right about being the one who should go," Catherine said. "I didn't go looking for trouble with Daniels. Belazo was my mission, and it's not my fault that Daniels got to him first."

Joe shook his head. "I've said what I had to say, Catherine." His gaze was searching the trees. "I need to have another look around. You said this Daniels is still on the loose?"

She nodded. "But it might be okay. Cameron sent one of his men, James Slade, to go after him, and he seemed to trust that he'd manage to take care of any threat."

"Cameron?" Eve's eyes were narrowed on Catherine's face. "Richard Cameron was involved in all this tonight? Interesting. Why didn't you mention it?"

"I was going to," Catherine said quickly. "It's not as if I've had the opportunity. And I had no idea Cameron would be here tonight. I told him when he checked on me at the hospital that I didn't want him involved in my business."

"I'm sure that impressed him," Eve said dryly. "I've only met him a few times, but it was clear he's not easily discouraged. And I don't remember you telling me that he visited you at the hospital."

"It wasn't important, a courtesy visit."

"Who is Richard Cameron?" Diane asked curiously.

"No one you need be concerned about," Catherine said quickly. "I'll tell you about him later." She turned to Joe. "But I'm sure you've heard enough about Cameron to realize that anyone he hired would be efficient enough to please even you."

"You mean all those wild rumors that are floating around about him?" Joe asked caustically. "I never listen to rumors, and nothing criminal has ever been proven. Besides, I also know you're too honest and smart to have anything to do with someone crooked." He paused. "But I'm still intrigued that he showed up here tonight, and you know I'll find out why."

Yes, Catherine knew that he would. Joe was too stubborn not to investigate everything connected to what had happened down to the last detail. She nodded. "I'm more interested in going back to Belazo's house and see what we can find out about what happened there. Daniels said that he'd killed Belazo when he couldn't coerce him into giving him information. But that doesn't mean we might not be able to find the body." She added with elaborate politeness, "With your permission, can we drive up there and search the damn place?"

"Not a bad idea. By all means, let's go." Joe turned and headed for the Mercedes.

Catherine felt herself tensing as Joe parked the Mercedes beside the beige Lexus in the driveway. The log house looked just as cozy from the front entrance as it had when she'd peered through the kitchen windows in the rear. A soft glow issued from the front window, and the wall lantern sconces on either side of the front door cast out an even more welcoming light. But now she knew what she was going to see in that house, and she'd never become accustomed to the death and violence that was an integral part of her job.

Just face it.

Yet after all the terror she'd gone through being chased through these woods tonight, she had to stifle the fear at being back here. "It might be easier to break in the kitchen door or windows than the front," she said as she jumped out of the backseat. "Lots of huge glass panes in that kitchen window. I was looking the place over before I approached Belazo directly." She was heading for the front door. "But it might not be necessary depending on the alarm system Belazo has here. I'm usually very good at picking locks."

"Really?" Cameron stepped out of the shadows beside the front door. "I didn't know that, Catherine. You're constantly surprising me."

She stiffened. "Good. You should have realized that you don't know everything about me, Cameron." She added curtly, "Would you like to tell me where you disappeared to when I was talking to Joe on the phone?"

"I had to deal with Slade and a few other matters. I thought I'd meet you here." He took a step toward Joe and held out his hand. "I'm Richard Cameron." He smiled. "I've only met your wife, Quinn, but I feel as if I know you. I've been studying your work and I admire it. I know that Catherine does."

Joe hesitated and then slowly shook his hand. "I can't say the same about you, Cameron. I've heard some wild stories about you from various sources that are probably fiction. You're something of a mystery man, and mysteries annoy me. My instinct is to solve them any way I can."

Cameron chuckled with genuine amusement. "Then good luck to

you. It should prove interesting." He looked back at the front door. "But in the meantime, perhaps we could band together to not waste time and make this bad situation more palatable. I've already taken the liberty of breaking into the house and taking a look around." He glanced at Catherine. "Just to save you the trouble. You've had a rough night and I knew you weren't going to rest until you searched the place." He smiled. "Am I wrong?"

He knew he wasn't wrong. "I'm fine. And I have to know if Daniels was telling me the truth about killing Belazo, and there might be evidence that would be valuable to us still on the property. So if you'll step aside..."

"Belazo is definitely dead," he said quietly. "I found him in the basement where Daniels had been torturing him. Broken neck. I did a perfunctory search to find out if there was anything in which you might be interested, but since I haven't been informed of what that might be, I'll leave any in-depth search to you." He turned back to Joe. "Or you, Quinn. I'm sure you're fully qualified to handle all facets of this investigation. It would probably be better if you'd take care of the ugly details."

"I'm glad I have your trust," Joe said dryly. "But you'll excuse me if I pay no attention to your suggestions until I know why you showed up here tonight. I want explanations, Cameron."

"And you'll get them. After we take care of accomplishing what you came here to do. I think that should be top priority. I'm waiting for a call from Slade that might cause us to depart here rather abruptly. Do you mind if I have a word with Eve?" He didn't wait for an answer but strode back the several feet to the Mercedes. He leaned into the passenger seat and turned on his flashlight. "Hello, Eve. Cameron. I'm sorry to meet you again under such upsetting circumstances but I don't have much time, and I'm going to need your help."

"Really?" Eve's brows lifted. "I imagine you don't ask that very often."

"As little as I can. Catherine is going to give me hell when I ask her to let you take her inside the house and examine all those bruises that she's been ignoring. And ordinarily I'd let her ignore them, but she's just out of the hospital and I watched part of the punishment Daniels handed out to her tonight."

Her gaze flew to Catherine. "Bad?"

"Not good. She held her own but he's a strong bastard. Pay attention to the left forearm. She wants to forget it and wear her CIA hat and help Quinn. He doesn't need her." He inclined his head mockingly. "He has me, and most people consider me adequate."

"Don't listen to him, Eve." Catherine couldn't believe he was doing this. "I'm fine."

"She always says that," Diane said from the backseat. "That's what she said before she passed out at the hotel. I chose not to believe her and called the ambulance." She paused. "And are you adequate, Cameron?"

"Ahh, you must be Diane Connors." He moved the light to her face. "I've been eager to meet you. I was being modest. I have references that say I'm much better than adequate. I can't wait to sit down and get to know you." The light shifted once more to Eve. "But you're the reason we're all here, and this is really your show. I promise I'll give Quinn my fullest cooperation if you'll persuade Catherine to be more reasonable. Will you help me?"

Her gaze was fixed thoughtfully on his face. Then she pushed the flashlight away from her and opened the car door. "We're wasting time. Stop talking and start performing, Cameron." She got out of the car and strode over to Catherine. "Don't argue. Evidently, he wants this very badly, and he might be right. Left forearm?" She gave a low whistle as she saw the swelling. "Nasty." She called over her shoulder to Diane: "Grab your medical bag and come inside. We might need you." She turned to Joe. "Catherine once told me that Cameron always kept his word. Do you think we can use him?"

"Possibly." He went to the front door and swung it open. "He appears to have certain skills."

Eve turned back to Catherine. "Then you're being officially replaced until Diane examines your arm."

"This is a total waste of time." She glared at Cameron, who was strolling back toward her. She couldn't believe that he had managed to get his way with only those few words of persuasion. She suddenly stiffened. What was she thinking? Cameron could always adjust any subject's thinking if he made the effort. It made her even more furious to think that he might have used that ability on Eve.

"No," he said softly as he stopped before her and met her eyes. "I wouldn't do that. I was tempted, but these are your friends. I'm building relationships." He followed Joe to the open door. "I'll check back with you later, Catherine. Eve, the dining room should be a good place to have Diane examine her. Do keep her away from the basement. Thank you." He disappeared into the house.

"I know you're frustrated, Catherine," Eve said gently. "But we'll get this over quickly and I think it's for the best. It makes sense."

"Cameron usually does," she said through set teeth. "But somehow the sense he makes turns into exactly what he wants to happen."

"Which is very intriguing." Eve took her elbow and nudged her toward the house. "You've always avoided telling me much about Cameron in the past. I think while Diane is patching you up, you should remedy that..."

CHAPTER 9

Everything okay?" Cameron asked Eve as he and Joe came into the dining room over an hour later. His gaze shifted to Catherine's bandaged arm. "No problem?"

"Just bad bruising," Diane said with a shrug. "And equally bad temper. But the short rest didn't hurt her."

"Did you find anything?" Catherine asked Joe impatiently. "Daniels said that Belazo never told him anything, and I'll believe that. But Belazo was expecting us, and he must have had some proof on hand to finalize the deal. Something else to negotiate for his payout."

Joe shook his head. "A thorough search and nothing."

"At least not here," Cameron added. "But that doesn't mean that he didn't dispose of it somewhere else." He paused. "Or that Daniels didn't find that proof when he tore the place apart after he'd killed Belazo."

Joe's eyes narrowed on his face. "What are you saying?"

"That Daniels stayed around for hours waiting for Catherine to show up here." He glanced at her. "I'd say he has something of an obsession where she's concerned. He had plenty of time to find any clues Belazo left behind, and he obviously wasn't worried about failing to do the job Nalam had given him. All he wanted was to take her out before he did it."

"What are you getting at, Cameron?" she asked.

"That I wonder if Daniels gave up too soon when he told you he was going after Quinn, Eve, and Diane. As soon as he found out that it wouldn't be easy—that Joe had managed to get them to the safety of the woods—Daniels gave up. It wasn't worth it to him. I think he'd played the game as far as he could safely go and decided to finish the original mission he'd been given."

"Guesswork?" Catherine said.

He nodded. "But you forget I had Slade following Daniels. He tends to clarify even the most complex guesswork. I gave him a call and he said that he was still in pursuit and that he'd call me later. He hasn't called me yet." He smiled. "So I suggest we wait and hear what he has to say. I'll go make a pot of coffee." He turned to Diane. "Would you care to help me?"

"No!" Catherine said.

"Yes," Diane said at the same time. She grinned at Catherine. "Back off. You put off telling me who he was before, and I let you get away with it. But I won't be tucked away in a corner until you get around to letting me know what's happening. Do I really seem as if I need your protection from him? He wants to get to know me. I think I should let him."

Diane was never shy about stating her rights and preferences in any situation. Catherine should have known this minor rebellion was on the horizon. She tried to return her smile as she waved a hand. "Have it your way. Though most people would need protection from Cameron. But that would only appeal to you."

Still, she wanted to jump up and run after them as she watched them head for the kitchen.

"Catherine?" Eve was studying her. "Are you worried about her?"

"I know she can usually take care of herself." She wrinkled her nose. "The question is whether she'll wish to do it. She told me herself she could be reckless. And Cameron can be very persuasive."

"But we have to count on the fact that she's not the same Diane she was before," Eve said. "She wouldn't be here if she was still that person."

"That's debatable," Joe said as he sat down at the table. "I'm more interested in why you're being antagonistic toward Cameron, Catherine. It's not like you. He knows what he's doing. In the short time I spent with him, I found him to be sharp, innovative, and very original. We got along fairly well."

"I'm sure you did, everybody does. And no one is more original."

"Then why are you having problems with him?" He leaned forward. "You don't trust Cameron. Why? Is it because he walked in here and suddenly dominated the situation? He was smooth and subtle, but you still wouldn't tolerate it. Talk to me."

She hesitated. She was always reluctant to discuss Cameron with anyone; after all they'd been through together, it seemed like a breach of trust. Add to that the fact that Joe was a detective, straight as an arrow, and Cameron was... Cameron. "He's very different. We just disagree on a few major issues."

"Eve told me that the two of you had several cases in the past few years that coincided. You never had trouble with him?"

Every minute of the time she'd spent with him had been both electric and explosive. "I wouldn't call it trouble. We worked well together."

"For heaven's sake, Catherine, stop tiptoeing around him," Eve said in disgust. "Tell him what he needs to know. You don't need to protect Cameron. It was evident tonight he can do that himself."

Joe glanced at Eve. "It appears that she hasn't been tiptoeing around you," he said dryly. "Or has she?"

"I met him briefly a few times when I was with Catherine. It was obvious she didn't want to talk about him, so I didn't invade her privacy. It didn't matter." Eve grimaced. "Until tonight. He's in our world now. So I got her to answer a few questions about him while Diane was cleaning her up and bandaging her arm."

"Taking advantage of the wounded?" he asked mockingly. "I'm surprised at you, Eve."

"No, you aren't. I have a reconstruction to do that's a huge risk for both of us. Plus, I wasn't sure if he might be a threat to Diane. Everything was crazy tonight, and he was right in the middle of it."

"So she gave me the third degree," Catherine said wryly. "I was helpless before her."

"Bullshit," Eve said. "I could hear you mentally picking and choosing every answer. But I believe I got enough to gain some confidence in Cameron. I realize why you're being cautious with Joe, but you'll just have to handle it."

"Yes, handle it, Catherine," he said silkily. "In great detail. Tell me about Cameron."

Cornered. There was no way he was going to let her get away without answering. "That's not easy to do," she said flatly. "He's very complicated, and so is his life. I don't believe anyone knows that much about him." She held up her hand as he opened his lips. "I'm getting there. You told Cameron that you'd heard some wild stories about him that were probably fiction. The most important thing you should know is that most of those stories were probably true. He belongs to an organization with worldwide membership. He and his group embrace the concept of forming a Shangri-La-type civilization to shelter the survivors who have to start over after the world blows itself up. When I first met him, he was Guardian of the organization—sort of a troubleshooter with extraordinary powers and influence. Now he's been given total powers and actually runs the entire organization. I met him in Tibet when he and his men were rescuing an award-winning journalist being held in the mountains. The odds were way against them, but he got her away and out of the country." She smiled wryly. "She was grateful and admired him enormously. For a while I thought she was going to disappear and join his merry band, but she chose another path. If she hadn't, then no one would have heard from her again. He's very careful to make sure anything he does, any scientist or teacher or technician that he coaxes to go underground, any action that might result in changing life as we know it, will remain secret." She could see Joe's expression and said quickly, "He's not a monster nor a criminal. The people he lures are volunteers who believe what he believes. He's a Pied Piper who is superbly clever and unbelievably persuasive, and he has the financial means and power to target anyone he chooses."

Joe's expression was impassive. "Anything else?"

"Only that I told him I believe he's wrong and that he should put all that effort he's using to create a super haven into trying to prevent Armageddon instead." She paused. "What might be more interesting to you is that he has contacts with corporations and governments all over the world. He's helped me a number of times when I needed information or assistance. He could be useful to you. He could be useful to *us*."

He was silent a moment. "You're trying to convince me that I should forget this man has probably committed criminal acts worldwide. I'm a detective and I could go after him myself. Or if I chose, I could reach out and cause him a great deal of trouble with my friends at Scotland Yard or MI5."

"Yes, you could." She grimaced. "But I'll bet they've already investigated him and come up empty. He would have been arrested a long time ago if anyone had been able to prove anything. I told you that he was clever."

He frowned. "You worked together, but you're still willing to betray him. Why?"

Betray. She flinched at the word. "I've never promised Cameron anything. Besides, there's nothing I could do that would betray him. I have no proof; all I can do is repeat the same rumors you were so scornful about. He's very careful not to leave any evidence behind."

Joe went back to the original question. "Why?"

She was silent. Finally she said, "Diane. Somehow, he found out about her. I'm sure he thinks she'd be the jewel in his crown if he could whisk her away and establish her in her own palace on some remote mountaintop while she finished her work. I don't want that to happen."

"You said it would be her decision."

"And it would." She added in frustration, "But he's *here* and right now he's in the kitchen making coffee with her."

"Are you asking me to find a way to get rid of him? You just said that my using my influence isn't going to work."

"That's not what she wants." Eve leaned forward. "Can't you see? She trusted you. Hell, she trusted *me*. She wants you to use Cameron's influence and contacts to help keep Diane safe from Daniels and Nalam until I'm able to do the reconstruction." She paused. "And then she wants you to find a way to keep Cameron from snatching Diane and sending her to that mountaintop."

"Really?" Joe glanced at Catherine. "Piece of cake. I'm surprised you don't want me to guarantee to go after Cameron."

She smiled faintly. "He'd enjoy that too much. He'd regard it as a challenge." Her smile faded. "I do want your help, but this is still my case. I'll fight Cameron and anyone else who gets in my way. This time it's too important. I'm not going to let him have Diane on a silver platter."

"I'd never do that to her," Cameron said from the doorway. He was carrying a tray with a coffee carafe. "I'm sure she'd be very uncomfortable, and the symbolism would offend her." He crossed to the table. "Or amuse her. I've discovered a surprising streak of sheer mischief in your friend, Catherine."

"Really? What else did you discover about her? And where is she?"

"She'll be here. Belazo was a lousy housekeeper and Diane decided to wash the cups. She hasn't quite finished, but I need to discuss something rather urgent." He met her eyes as he put the tray on the table. "Stop looking so guilt-stricken," he added quietly. "I expected it. I knew you'd tell Quinn and Eve what a wicked troublemaker I might turn out to be. I could see it coming."

She lifted her chin. "I don't feel guilty. I don't owe you anything, Cameron."

"No, you don't. What's between us has never had anything to do with debts." He looked at Joe. "I realize that our philosophies are probably very far apart, but I'm sure that Catherine has tempered her revelations with the fact that she knows I can be exceptionally useful on occasion. Perhaps we can discuss that at a later time?"

"Perhaps." He shrugged. "But you're right, I'm in complete agreement with Catherine's opinion regarding your bizarre notions. I'd be skeptical that any help you could offer would be worth paying attention to."

"What a challenge." Cameron paused. "Would it change your mind if I told you that I know where that body is located, and I can get it for Eve before the night is over?"

Joe stiffened. "It might. If I was certain you weren't in cahoots with Daniels."

"You know where it is?" Eve asked Cameron eagerly. "How? Were you lying to us?"

"No. We may not be on precisely the same side, but I wouldn't deal with Daniels. I got a call from Slade while I was in the kitchen. He told me that when Daniels gave up the chase for the three of you, he took off immediately into the woods again. He seemed... driven. Slade followed him into the hills behind this cabin. He was curious because there are only rough trails crisscrossing the area and Daniels had to go on foot and he definitely wasn't in any shape for hiking. But it seemed there are a couple of old played-out gold mines up there. Daniels seemed to be interested in a particular one. He had a map that he was following." His gaze shifted to Catherine. "And the reason he seemed driven was that he was frustrated that he hadn't been able to cut your pretty throat or kill anyone close to you. He wanted to be able to bring something to Nalam to prove that he'd at least gotten what he'd been sent to get from Belazo."

"How do you know?" she asked.

"Because Slade followed Daniels into that cave. He thought it was fairly safe, because after climbing the hill to find the mine Daniels was limping in pain and muttering curses. He wasn't paying attention to anything—just trying to find that grave. He found a heap of dirt that could have been what he was looking for thirty or forty yards from the mine entrance. He grabbed a shovel lying a few yards away and started digging. It didn't take long. He only had to go down a few feet to verify that it was what he thought it was." He smiled crookedly. "Daniels seemed very happy at what he'd found. Then he gave up digging and headed back toward the mine entrance. Slade said that he heard him punching a number into his phone as he left the cave. I'd bet that he was going out to call Nalam and tell him to send some of his men to help with the removal of the body."

"Then he'll have it." Eve's hands clenched. "He'll *destroy* it."

"Not if we get there first. Didn't I tell you that I could get it for you tonight?"

"Yes, you did," Joe said. "Your man Slade?"

Cameron nodded. "I told you he followed Daniels into the cave. Slade was examining the remains in that grave the minute Daniels left the cave. Which turned out to really be only a burlap bag with the skull plus a random collection of bones that were dumped into several other burlap bags and then thrown into the grave. He said he won't be able to manage to steal anything except the bag with the skull. He'll be on foot and he might have to dodge some of Nalam's men when he's coming down that hill. Will that skull do?"

Joe looked inquiringly at Eve.

She nodded slowly. "If the skull's in tolerable shape, it should give me what I need." She jumped to her feet. "Shouldn't we leave right away?"

Cameron shook his head. "None of you are invited. It will be safer if I go to meet him alone and run interference. Slade and I are used to working together, and I may have to make follow-up decisions on the spot." He glanced at Joe. "But I'll need all of you to be out of here right away before Nalam's men come streaming all over the property on their way up that hill. I'd suggest you hide out and wait on that approach road for us until we get down the hill with the skull. That's where I parked my car when I first got here. I'll keep in contact with you to advise if you'll have to change locations. I won't know until we find out how many of Nalam's goons Daniels invited to the party."

"You're turning me into a chauffeur?" Joe asked.

"With your permission. Any objections?"

He was silent. "Several. But I'll keep them to myself until I see if you know what you're doing." He glanced at Catherine. "Can I trust him not to screw this up?"

Cameron smiled mockingly at her. "Put the man's mind at ease. Can't you see he wants a recommendation?"

She ignored him and spoke directly to Joe. "He's never failed me.

He's brilliant, thoroughly professional, and always gets the job done." Her gaze shifted to Cameron. "It's only after the job is finished that you might have to be careful."

"As you are?" Cameron murmured. "So careful, Catherine... But I do like that you admit I never failed you. And I promise I never will."

She wanted to hit him. "Shut up, Cameron. I didn't want you here, and I don't want you near Diane. I'm wondering what you were saying to her in there." She got to her feet. "And how long would it take her to wash a few cups? Did you stuff her in the broom closet?"

He chuckled. "I was merely talking and getting to know her. It's all I'll ever do until she shows me she's ready. I told you once that I never use anything but ordinary persuasion on anyone I choose. It will have to be her choice. That hasn't changed." He tilted his head. "As for where she is? No broom closet. I imagine she followed me, caught a bit of the conversation, and was intrigued enough to want to hear the rest of it. I've discovered she's very curious. Now you can go find her and fill her in on anything she missed." He reached in his pocket and handed her a key. "My Tesla. It's possible we might require a quick getaway after we bolt down that hill. I'd appreciate any assistance." He turned toward the door. "Now I have to get the hell out of here." He glanced over his shoulder at them. "I'll be in touch. Be ready." The next moment he'd left the house.

Catherine followed him but he was already off the porch and starting to climb the hill. She stood watching him until he was lost from view. He would be all right, she told herself. He was always all right. And this time he had that "exceptional" Slade to back him. There was nothing to worry about.

"I like him."

Catherine looked over her shoulder to see Diane behind her

gazing up at the hill. "He can be very appealing," she answered. "That doesn't mean he's safe."

"Safe can be boring." Diane moved to stand beside her. "And from what I heard while I was eavesdropping, I'd say he's not ever going to be boring. But neither are you, Catherine." She paused. "Why didn't you want him to talk to me?"

"Why do you think?"

"The bullet. It's always about the bullet these days. Everyone looks at me and only sees the beautiful silver bullet. Are you afraid Cameron is going to try to steal it or use me in some way?"

"Not exactly. He'd never try to take anything away from you. But you've created something rather wonderful, and you should have total control of what you do with it. He might try to influence you."

She smiled. "He'd find that hard to do. I'm pretty tough these days."

"Not as hard as you'd believe. Not if he made the effort. He's already started." She turned to face her. "Look how he turned up here. Suddenly he's going to be deep in the reconstruction. He'll bring that skull down from the hill and be so helpful that Joe will let him stay until Eve is finished. Then he'll go on to the next step."

"Which will be?"

"I have no idea," she said wearily. "Only that I have to be there to run interference for you. So please don't be cocky and think Cameron is in any way ordinary."

"Not ordinary." She was silent a moment. "Or you wouldn't feel about him as you do. It's the ones who aren't ordinary that hold us and won't let us go. I've only known two men who fell into that category. Joe . . . and Alon."

"Alon?" Catherine hesitated before she asked, "Was he your lover, Diane?"

"Heavens, no. Everything else, but not that." Her lips twisted.

"But he is without doubt completely extraordinary, and I couldn't bear to have anything happen to him. So it won't, no matter what I have to do. I may not have your CIA training, but I know about running interference, too, Catherine."

"I found that out the minute you hit Daniels over the head with that lamp." Catherine lifted her shoulders in a half shrug. "I shouldn't have asked. It was none of my business." She turned to go back inside. "And it's time I went back inside and got my marching orders from Joe." She frowned thoughtfully. "I think maybe I should probably stake out the road and see how many men Daniels called on for help."

"You do that," Diane said dryly. "But I don't think Joe would regard that as getting your marching orders. It sounds a bit high-handed. I'd be a good deal more tactful after what happened earlier tonight. He was breathing fire." She followed her into the house. "But what do I know? No one could call me diplomatic."

Cameron used his phone to follow Slade's tracking beacon to his hilltop hiding spot. He crouched beside Slade and whispered, "Status?"

"The guy with the skull is near the bottom of the hill, near that big oak tree. He's carrying it in a burlap bag."

"You're sure the skull is in there?"

"Positive. He was looking at it and grinning like a hyena a few minutes ago."

"So what are they waiting for?"

"Us. They know we're near, and they're watching the cave entrances. I must have slipped up. I was probably spotted coming out of that cave over to the west."

"So we need to get ourselves down this hill, grab that skull, and meet Quinn on the road. He and the others are waiting with the car."

"You make it sound easy," Slade said. "Remember, there's at least five guys around here. Got any ideas?"

"A few," he murmured. "One that just occurred to me when I almost fell on my ass getting to you..."

"Any that you care to share with me?"

The corners of Cameron's lips indented. "You're not going to like it."

Slade rolled his eyes. "Ah, it's gonna be one of those?"

Cameron stood up straight to look down the hill. "How far away do you think they are? A hundred yards, one fifty?"

"Two hundred, easy."

"Good." Cameron reached into his jacket pocket. "Got any gum?"

Slade clicked his tongue. "You want chewing gum? Now?"

Cameron pulled out a bright blue package. "I have gum. I just wanted to know if I had to share mine with you."

"I don't chew gum, thanks."

Cameron tore off half a dozen pieces from a blister pack and handed them to him. "You do today. Chew this. All of it."

Slade gave him a wary look as he ripped the gum from the packaging and put the pieces into his mouth. "And I once told you that I respected you. I believe you've lost your mind."

Cameron smiled as he popped the remainder of the gum into his own mouth. "Trust me, I lost it a long time ago. It goes with the territory." He walked toward an expanse of black vinyl sheeting that was stretched between wooden stakes as a makeshift fence. He tore free some of the vinyl sheeting and ripped it into foot-long sections. He handed two sheets to Slade. "You ski, don't you?"

Slade looked warily at the vinyl sheets in his hand. "Not for a long time."

"It's like riding a bike. You never forget."

"People say that about a lot of things. It's almost never true."

"But I have faith in you." Cameron took out the chewed gum, pulled it apart, and affixed it to the vinyl. He stuck both sheets to the soles of his shoes, then steadied himself on the grassy hillside. He pulled out his two semiautomatics and checked the clips. "Remember, our objective is to grab that skull and get the hell out of there. Everything else is secondary."

Slade used the gum to secure the vinyl to his shoes. "And not break our necks or get shot in the process."

"Right. Keep low. The tall grass will give us some cover."

Slade pulled out his matching pair of Glocks. "You're definitely insane, you know that?"

"And . . . ?"

"And . . ." Slade suddenly smiled. "This could be fun."

Daniels gripped the burlap bag and strode toward two of Nalam's hired men, Galman and Bratt. They'd come highly recommended by Nalam, but so far Daniels wasn't impressed. "Anything?"

Galman, the team leader, shook his head. "Are you sure they're even still here?"

Daniels jerked his thumb toward the cave. "One of them was in there just a few minutes ago. You got here before he could get what he came for." He raised the burlap bag with the skull and bones. "I'm betting he didn't just go home with his tail between his legs. But to be sure, have one of your guys cover the road down below."

Galman nodded. "Already done. And we've got the other two stationed up on the hillside."

"Good." Daniels nodded grudgingly. Maybe these guys weren't quite the idiots he'd thought.

Galman suddenly cocked his head. "Do you hear that?"

"What?"

Ffft. Ffft. Ffft.

The sound was coming from uphill.

Ffft. Ffft.

Like wind blowing through the grass, but sharper, Daniels thought. More defined.

Ffft. Ffft.

Whatever it was, it was getting closer by the second. Galman, Bratt, and Daniels raised their handguns and aimed into the darkness.

Ffft. Ffft.

A scream followed by a volley of staccato whistles of gunshots fired through silencers.

A voice yelled from above. "Galman, they're headed your way! Watch out for the—"

The voice was cut off mid-sentence.

Galman touched his earpiece and whispered something. He turned to Daniels. "My guys aren't responding."

Ffft. Ffft. Ffft. That sound again. Louder now and closer.

Daniels raised his gun, trying to see what the hell was bearing down on them.

Ffft. Ffft.

A figure leaped into the air in front of them, silhouetted by the half-moon. What the hell kind of beast was this?

Its wings curled inward and flashes of light lit up the sky.

Daniels's lips curled. Get a grip. It was a man, not a beast. The "wings" were nothing more than the sleeves of a long jacket hanging from two outstretched arms. And the lights were silenced muzzle flashes from a pair of handguns.

"Shoot him!" Galman yelled.

The three men fired at the figure. BLAM-BLAM-BLAM-BLAM!

But he was too fast. The man hit the ground and rocketed past.

THWAP! Something knocked Daniels down.

What the hell—?

He pulled himself to his feet.

The bag! It was gone.

Dammit!

Daniels looked up just in time to see a second figure speeding away, gliding over the hillside with the burlap bag.

"Get him!" Daniels yelled. "He has the skull!"

He practically stumbled over Bratt, who was bleeding on the ground.

"Bratt's wounded," Galman said. "He needs help."

"Later."

"He may not make it."

"If you don't come with me, I'll put a bullet in his head right now," Daniels snarled. "I'm not losing that skull. Come on!"

Galman muttered a curse as he followed Daniels down the hill.

Joe's hands tightened in frustration on the steering wheel. "I should be out there. Shit. I hate this. I never should've let Cameron run the show."

"Shocker," Eve said. "How did I know that would be coming?"

"Some things really *don't* change, do they?" Diane asked softly.

Joe shot her a dagger glance as he peered down the dark road. "And where in the hell is Catherine? All she had to do was pick up Cameron's Tesla."

Eve checked her phone. "It hasn't been so long that— There she is!"

Catherine had emerged from the shadows driving the black Tesla and pulled in behind the Mercedes.

Eve leaned forward as Catherine got out of the car. "Did you see any sign of Cameron or Slade?"

"I couldn't see them, but I heard shots and yelling." She was frowning as she lifted her gaze to the hill. "*Something's* definitely going on up there."

Joe lifted his head as he turned to look up at the hillside. "Do you hear that?"

Ffft. Ffft. Ffft.

A dark-clad figure leaped over the base of the hill and landed in front of the car!

Joe and Catherine whirled around with their guns pointed.

Cameron quickly raised his hands. "Don't, it's me!"

Catherine lowered her handgun as she stared at him in shock. "What on earth are you doing? You were a nanosecond away from getting your head blown off."

"I was saving the day. Sometimes that requires weird and unusual methods. And you never would have forgiven yourself if you'd taken that shot. You would probably have been doomed to a lifetime of regret, bitterness, and alcohol abuse."

"I doubt that."

"This conversation's taken a nasty turn." Cameron quickly walked around to Eve's side of the car and handed her the burlap bag. "One skull and assorted bones."

Eve clutched the bag. "Hallelujah. I wasn't sure you could pull it off, Cameron."

"Don't encourage him," Joe said. "We're still not out of this. Where's Slade?"

As if on cue, Slade soared over the base of the hill and landed next to the car.

"What in the hell are you guys wearing on your feet?" Catherine asked.

Cameron tore off the vinyl sheets affixed to his shoes. "Makeshift skis. The grass on the hillside is the perfect height. And Slade here is ready for any black-diamond slope in the world. I might have to take him with me to Tibet next year."

"Not a chance," Slade said. "Can't stand the cold."

Cameron smiled at Catherine. "Then you'll have to go with me."

"Dream on." Her anxious gaze was lifting to the hill again. "Joe's right. I heard the shots. Did you two leave anybody alive and lethal up there?"

"At least two, probably more. We weren't in a position to concentrate on sharpshooting." Cameron was abruptly all business. "We lost them on the other side of the hill, but it won't take them long to find their way here." He wheeled and headed for the Tesla. "We should definitely leave. Slade, you ride with Quinn and guard that skull. Catherine and I will take my car and draw them away." He sprinted down the dark path toward the Tesla. "No time to argue. Come on, Catherine. You drive. I'll ride shotgun."

CHAPTER 10

Catherine heard shouts and a truck starting in the woods behind them before the Tesla had even reached the road.

"Where the hell are we going?" Catherine asked as she pressed on the accelerator. "That idiotic trick you pulled might have delayed them temporarily but they're right on our heels. How can we keep them away from Eve and that skull?"

"We only need a temporary diversion." Cameron was punching in Joe's number on his phone. "Quinn, turn left at the next road and go a couple miles. You'll see a 7-Eleven convenience store. Turn right there and you'll see an open field. A helicopter should already be there or will be in the next few minutes. Get out of here. We'll join you at Naponi. Trust Slade. You won't be sorry."

"Naponi." Joe was swearing beneath his breath. "I won't even ask. Take care of Catherine." He pressed DISCONNECT.

"Quinn is very protective of you," Cameron murmured. "I approve."

"A helicopter?" Catherine repeated. "When did you arrange for a helicopter?"

"Why do you think I stayed in Tahoe instead of coming up here with Slade? I had arrangements to make. Once I had them in place, all I had to do was place a couple of calls when I went up the hill to help Slade." He glanced at the rearview mirror. "Slow down. Daniels's men evidently got their shit together faster than I expected. They're behind us."

"Slow?" She shot him a glance. "You want them to follow us. A distraction? How long?"

"Not long. Ten, fifteen minutes, just enough time to let Quinn get them to the helicopter and take off."

"I'm surprised you don't have that down to the exact minute," she said dryly. "How inefficient of you, Cameron."

"I realize I'm a disappointment." He smiled. "But then I knew I'd have you to make up for all my weaknesses." He glanced up at the mirror again. "They're getting closer. The game is about to start. Would you like me to drive?"

"What?" she asked incredulously.

His lips were quirking. "Well, Quinn did tell me to take care of you." He leaned back in his seat. "Fifteen minutes will give them a nice safety net." He gave a mock yawn. "See if you can keep me awake."

"Damn you." She gave him a frustrated glance. "This is no game."

"Yes, it is. One we've played before, but this one is for higher stakes. It has you a bit upset." He smiled. "But I have your back, Catherine." His eyes were suddenly glittering. "Lose those bastards!"

She couldn't look away from him. She could feel the exhilaration zinging through her. "I'm not upset." She stomped on the accelerator. "And I promise I'll keep you awake!"

"Give it a few extra revs." Cameron took out his two automatic guns as he looked back toward the road. "We need to call attention to ourselves."

"Finally, something you're an expert at." Catherine gunned the engine.

Cameron stared into the darkness. "Again."

"Maybe you want me to tap-dance on the roof and sing show tunes?" She gunned the engine twice more.

Cameron studied the road a moment longer. "Sneaky bastards. They're in a Land Rover, rolling down the road with their lights off. They see us. Hit it!"

Catherine peeled out and sped down the road. A heartbeat later the black Land Rover roared to life and headed toward them.

She checked the rearview mirror. "It's working. They're on our tail."

"Good. Let's pull them as far away from the others as we can."

She skillfully negotiated the twisty, turning dirt road. It grew darker as trees blocked the moonlight and low-hanging branches scraped the roofline.

Cameron turned in his seat. "They're gaining on us."

"Only because I want them to."

"They're almost on top of us," he said quietly.

She smiled. "A little faith, please."

Catherine was staring at a large tree branch that had fallen into the roadway ahead. She cut the wheel hard right to avoid the obstruction, but the Land Rover was too close to make the turn in time.

SMASH!

The branch damaged the Land Rover's grille and left headlight, but the large vehicle managed to extricate itself and continue the pursuit.

Cameron raised his guns. "Plan B?"

She nodded. "Go for it. There's a curve ahead. I'll give you a good angle."

Catherine put on an extra burst of speed and went into the

curve. Cameron leaned out of the passenger-side window and took aim.

It was only then that Catherine saw the steep incline of a ravine on the other side of the road!

BLAM-BLAM-BLAM-BLAM-BLAM!

Cameron shredded three of the Land Rover's four tires. The vehicle lurched forward for a few seconds, then finally tottered on the edge of the road and toppled down the ravine.

Cameron holstered his guns as Catherine brought the Tesla to a halt. "We always did make a good team."

She was still staring at the car at the bottom of the ravine. "I guess maybe we did."

He raised an eyebrow. "Is that an admission?"

"A statement of fact. Nothing to get excited about."

His gaze suddenly narrowed on her face. "No, you're definitely not excited."

"What's next?" Catherine's heart was pounding as she gazed down at the Land Rover. She felt sick remembering the violence as that vehicle had barreled off the road and bounced down the ravine. Were they all dead? No. She hadn't thought anyone could survive that fall, but she could see that there were at least three men crawling out of the vehicle into the ditch. Maybe more. Was one of them Daniels? She couldn't tell because of the smoke from brush ignited by the engine. "I think we're safe. Even if there are survivors, they don't seem to be in any shape to come after us. But maybe we should get out of here." She shook her head. "Why am I asking you? I know that we should. Someone besides us might have seen them go down that bank into the ravine." She reversed and the tires screeched on concrete as she got back on the road. "Where are we going now?"

"Straight ahead," Cameron said quietly. "But pull off as soon as you get a chance."

"Why?"

"Just pull off."

Catherine's hands tightened on the steering wheel. She didn't want to question him right now. She was still shaking and trying to pretend that she was as cool and collected as he was. "Whatever you wish. Have it your way."

"I will," Cameron said. "Thank you for allowing me a few minor victories." He looked away from her. "You did a good job leading them away from the helicopter. Great driving." He paused. "But I was the one who shot out the tires, Catherine."

She stiffened. There was a layby just ahead and she pulled off into the side road. "What's that supposed to mean?"

"I just wanted to point out that it was my decision to put an end to the chase. My decision, my responsibility."

She put on the brakes and turned to look at him. "The hell it was. They were going to kill us. And if they'd found them, they would have killed Joe and everyone else. You had to do it." She had to stop shaking. "Do you think I don't know that was the only way to handle it? I'm a professional. It's not as if I haven't—"

"Hush." He unsnapped his seat belt and moved closer to her. "I know all that bullshit." His hands cradled her face in his two hands. "I know what you've been through in your life. I also know that if you have a choice, you do anything to avoid the kill. Even scum like Daniels who have put you through hell. I didn't give you that choice. That's why you're shaking and trying not to let me see it."

"Why should I care what you think?"

His lips gently brushed the tip of her nose. "You'll have to work that out for yourself. You're taking a long time about it, but you'll get there."

"Let me go, Cameron."

His hands dropped away from her face. "I'm not making any

moves. I'm just talking. There's a place for that tough CIA persona you've developed over the years. I've always admired it. I just wanted to let you know that I also admire the way you treasure life and want to preserve it. It's probably what's keeping you fighting for Diane Connors. Actually, I find it quite beautiful. Though in cases like Daniels I'm having trouble understanding it." He moved over into his own seat and fastened his seat belt. "But I'm always willing to take care of details like Daniels that might upset you. We can go now. I only wanted to give you a minute or two to catch your breath and get over the shock."

"I wasn't in shock." She started the car. He had been very close to the truth, though. She had to admit she was grateful to have the opportunity to gather herself. It annoyed her that she'd been so open and obvious to Cameron, but she wasn't surprised. And somehow his words had given her a feeling of comfort instead of resentment. "I'm not that sensitive."

"No?" His brows rose. "I must have read you wrong."

He never read anyone wrong, she thought crossly.

"Where are we going from here?" she asked.

"Straight north. Until we cross the Canadian border. Then east until we get to Naponi, where I've leased a place where Eve can work." He took out his phone. "I'll give Quinn a call and check on them. He'll want to know we're on our way. He wasn't sure I could be trusted to take care of you." He paused. "Suppose I take over the driving once we cross the border? That way you can cuddle down and take a nap, and I won't have to keep looking at those bruises."

She reached up and touched the bruise on her jaw. "They bother you?"

He nodded. "Yeah, they bother me. They're not going to go away soon enough, but I'll feel as if I'm doing something if I make you get a few hours' sleep and you don't look so haggard."

"I'm not haggard." She paused. "And I'll sleep. I want to be ready to function when I get to this Naponi. I'll have to keep an eye on Diane, and Eve might need me. Besides, that way I won't have to make conversation with you."

He smiled. "We've never had trouble with... conversation."

NAPONI
4:40 A.M.

"Hey, wake up." Cameron's fingers were gentle as he pushed her hair back away from her face. "You're missing the dawn. That shouldn't happen."

Catherine slowly opened her lids to see him gazing down at her. Such wonderful eyes, she thought drowsily. She'd always loved Cameron's eyes... "Dawn?" She yawned as she threw off the jacket he'd tucked around her and sat up. "It's still dark outside."

"It's coming." He opened his driver's door and got out. "I saw first light. Get out and stretch your legs. We're on a cliff right above Naponi. The ranch houses are just below us, and I want you to see the property as it should be seen."

"Naponi? Have you been driving all night?" She got out of the car. "The last thing I remember is crossing the border. How far did we travel?"

"I never said it was close. We're northwest of Calgary. But it's safe, and I have people nearby I can call on if we run into trouble."

"You always have 'people,'" she said dryly. "I take it you've used this place before?"

"A few times. It's very private, and I've had guests who have needed that privacy until I could get them settled." He smiled. "But

I've never had a forensic sculptor or anyone like Diane Connors to shelter here. It will be—"

Her hand grasped his arm, her eyes on the eastern sky. "It's magnificent," she breathed.

The night sky was now streaked with golden light, and pink and violet clouds were casting a shimmering glow on the lake below them. Beauty, color, and sheer drama were touching everything all around them. The snow on the peaks of the mountain range to the north was lit with the same glow.

"Told you so," Cameron said softly. "Now thank me for making sure you wouldn't miss it." He pulled her down to sit on the ridge overlooking the glittering lake below them. When she didn't answer, he took one look at her face and then shook his head. "Never mind. I've got what I wanted. No thanks required. Just drink it in and enjoy it. I'm not even noticing those bruises with that gold aura reflecting off them."

"Be quiet, Cameron." She leaned her head on his shoulder. "Just let me have this moment." All the pain and terror and ugliness seemed to be flowing out of her, lost in silence and beauty and healing. *Healing*, she thought. The idea of her being hurt had disturbed him, and he had been searching for a way to heal.

He had found it.

She didn't move for a long time. The brilliant colors were beginning to fade to blue-gray when she whispered, "You're a very wily man. I think I needed that. Thank you."

"My pleasure."

She lifted her head. "But it didn't change anything."

He looked down at her. "Sure it did. We're both changing all the time. The difference is I'm accepting it and you're still struggling."

"I can't let you take Diane."

"I might not. We'll have to see how it works out," he said quietly.

"I brought Eve here to protect her while she worked, but I would have found a reason to bring Diane here anyway. We're not sure what Nalam is up to at any given minute, and she's in far more danger. Right now she might be considered bait for Hakali, but that could change in a heartbeat." He stared her in the eye. "You should consider that she'd be safer with me. She's a prize that everyone is going to want. Even when we rid ourselves of Nalam, there will always be another dirtbag hunting her. Scientists are a precious commodity since the virus. In a changing, confused world, they clarify and sometimes offer salvation. They'll all want her. Politicians, mobsters—she might even become an international chess piece. The stakes are that high. She'll need an army to protect her."

"And you have an army?" she asked caustically.

"I can muster one if I need to do it." He smiled faintly. "But I probably wouldn't need to go that far. As you said, I can be very wily."

She shook her head. "No one is going to decide anything about Diane but her. I'll protect her and let her make her own choice. Go away, Cameron."

"As I said, we'll see how it works out. But I'm in this until the end. Resign yourself. You'll try to use me and that's okay with me. But I'm not taking a chance on this being fouled up. She's too important."

"Why are you being so stubborn?"

He was silent. "I lost several of my people to the virus a few years ago. That nightmare wouldn't have happened if they'd had the opportunity to be protected by Diane's bullet."

"Diane's bullet." She stiffened. "That's how Diane refers to the formula she developed. My bullet. I don't think you've had time yet to get her to confide in you, but you said you'd learned a lot more about Diane lately. How?"

He shrugged. "It's also how she referred to it when she was

talking to those eight doctors that Hu Chang had examine her in Hong Kong."

Her eyes widened. "You know about them?"

"I was only able to tap one of them, Professor Edward Judkal, but he was very voluble."

She muttered an oath. "But if he spoke to you, then he might tell someone else."

"No, he won't. I convinced him that would be very unwise. And I've assigned a man to keep an eye on that luxurious Canadian hotel where all of them are pretending to work." He shook his head. "Don't worry, it's okay for now. I repeat, *now*. But it does emphasize that I'm your safer bet."

"No, it doesn't. Not everyone could track Diane down. No one has sources like you do. Where else did they go?"

"Hu Chang's Hong Kong office. Nalam's warehouse in Manila. A place called Salkara Island. Right now I'm waiting for a report on the time Diane spent researching in the Amazon jungle. I still don't know everything, but I'm fairly close."

"Yes, you are," she said hoarsely. "And those busy-bee investigators of yours are probably gathering more info as we speak." She got to her feet. "I suppose as an agent I should compliment you, but I've heard a little too much for right now. All I want to do is go down to those ranch houses you mentioned and be with normal people who don't have spies peering behind every bush." She headed for the car. "Would you care to go with me?"

"Of course. I told you, I'm with you until the end." He was following her. "And you can trust me to guard you and Diane until that time comes. I'll watch your back, and it will be no different than when we've been together before." He got in the passenger seat. "In the meantime, I'll have my 'spies' see what they can find out from Nalam's camp that will keep us safe. Would that be all right?"

"Why not?" She had a sudden thought. "And while they're snooping, would you ask them what they can find out about Kai Hakali?"

"What do you want to know?"

"Anything. Everything." She paused. "If he's still alive."

"Ah, the man in the grave. Would you care to expand?"

"No." She started the car. "But I'm sure that Joe will tell you everything the next time he sees you. He'll think you earned it."

"And so I have. That's why I see no reason why you shouldn't tell me. It would mean more coming from you."

"Another minor victory. I'm really not in the mood to do that, Cameron. After all, you did say it was okay to use you."

"Absolutely. In every way. I'm at your disposal." His voice was sober, but he darted her a sly glance. "If you can only force yourself to do it..."

Naponi comprised two ranch houses and several outbuildings, one of which appeared to be a stable. The larger ranch house was a very good size and had several rocking chairs on the shallow front porch. The other was smaller; Catherine thought it was probably a bunk-house. Eve came out of the larger ranch house and stood waiting as Catherine drove up the driveway. "It took you long enough," she said as Catherine stopped and got out of the car. She gave her a quick hug. "Diane was worried, but I told her that you were probably just ducking the massive housecleaning job we had to do when we got here." She glanced at Cameron. "You get top marks for beauty and isolation, but there are no horses in that stable and your housekeeper sucks. This place was knee-deep in dust."

"Sorry." Cameron got out of the car. "I only have maintenance done once a year. Horses wouldn't be practical. The place is seldom used, and I don't want to draw attention to it when I do have visitors."

"Joe thought it might be something like that." She made a face. "But I wasn't in the mood for being reasonable when I wanted to get to work on the reconstruction. I knew I wouldn't be able to do it until I was able to set up a workplace free enough of grime so that I could see the damn skull."

"I imagine that you made sure that took place even if it meant putting Joe and everyone else to work on it," Catherine said. "And since you're up this early, my guess is that you're ready to get to work."

"You'd be wrong. I'm not quite that self-absorbed. We all needed a place to sleep, and we all pitched in on cleaning the bedrooms and bathrooms. After that Joe wouldn't even let me look at the skull; he made me go to bed. He said that I'd do a better job if I got a good night's sleep."

"Logical," Cameron said. "But I'm surprised that anyone, even Quinn, could make you do anything."

"I knew he was right." She shrugged. "But I figured that I'd take a short nap and then get up again after Joe went to sleep. It didn't work out that way. I must have been too tired. When I woke up about thirty minutes ago, Joe was already up and working on cleaning the library I'd chosen to make my studio."

"Then I'd better go help," Catherine said as she started up the porch steps. "Particularly since you called me a slacker."

"Just joking," Eve said. "Joe and I had almost finished when I heard your car and came out. From what Joe told me about what you went through on the road yesterday, I'd say you deserve a little rest." She turned to Cameron. "But I don't care if you rest or not. You have a few things to do that will make our lives easier while we're here." She drew a deep breath. "Slade."

He went still. "What's wrong? I gave him his orders. I can't imagine that he caused you any problems."

"He didn't cause *me* any problems. And Joe thinks he's fantastic, he seemed to be ahead of any order he gave him. It was Diane that was the difficulty."

"Diane?" Catherine repeated. "What did he do to her?"

"Nothing. But he was...shadowing her. From the moment we got off the helicopter, he wasn't more than ten steps away from her. Even when Joe gave him an order, he'd do it quickly and efficiently and then go back to her. I don't believe he said more than a few words to her, but whatever room she was cleaning, he was there and offering to help her. Joe said that when he got up this morning, Slade was in the chair outside her bedroom." She paused. "Diane can be very sharp. She didn't say anything, but she had to notice. I don't want her made uncomfortable."

"I see," Cameron said. "You want me to tell him to stay away from her?" His lips indented at the corners. "Yes, she's attractive, but I assure you that he doesn't have some kind of weird infatuation with her."

"He's shadowing her," Eve repeated firmly. "Tell him to knock it off."

Cameron shook his head. "I won't do that. He's obeying orders. Perhaps a little too enthusiastically, but it was brought home to him yesterday that the threat is getting closer. I'll let him know that he should be more subtle and discreet."

Eve glanced inquiringly at Catherine.

Catherine nodded slowly. "I can't see any looming threat here at Naponi, but I'm not going to object to having Slade keep an eye on Diane." She looked at Cameron. "But definitely more subtle and discreet surveillance is required, and I'll tell him myself. Where is he, Eve?"

"In the kitchen." Eve added dryly, "Which is only right down the hall from Diane's room."

"You're sure you don't want me to do it?" Cameron asked Catherine.

"You can reinforce. But I want him to realize that he should pay attention to someone besides you." She went into the house and found she was in the living room. It was open and pleasant enough with tall ceilings, a huge fireplace, and comfortable furniture. The scent of bacon was wafting toward her, and she followed it down the hall to the kitchen.

Slade was at the stove taking bacon out of a frying pan. He looked up as she came into the room. "Hello, Catherine. I'm glad to see you. Are you hungry? I'm making bacon and eggs."

He was towering over her and she instinctively straightened. He was much more imposing than she had thought. Cameron had shown her that photo of Slade on his phone, but other than that she had caught only that brief glimpse of him at the road when he had jumped into the Mercedes beside Joe at Cameron's order. He was very tall and lean yet clearly possessing wiry muscular strength. Craggy, high cheekbones in a tanned face, dark deep-set eyes that were cool and hard, framed by gray-white hair cut close with almost military precision. "The smell of bacon always makes me hungry. I'm glad to see you, too. Eve said that you've been very helpful since you arrived here."

"I think she appreciated the fact that I was able to hand that skull over to her more than my talent with a vacuum. She has her priorities straight." He smiled. "Particularly since I disturbed her a bit by hovering over Diane Connors. It appears Eve is very protective. I tried not to be too obvious, but it was difficult at such close quarters. I expected Eve to either confront me or go to Cameron as soon as he showed up. I didn't think she'd involve you." He pulled out a chair at the kitchen table. "Sit down. I'll get your eggs and bacon."

She didn't move. "And why were you hovering over Diane?"

He shrugged. "Cameron gave me my orders when you were in the hospital. I was not to let either you or Diane Connors be damaged. Since Cameron had clearly taken over guarding you for the time being, Diane Connors seemed my only responsibility. I wasn't going to let anything happen to her."

"And what were you supposed to be protecting her from? The ranch was deserted except for Eve and Joe."

"I didn't know that," he said quietly. "I hadn't had time to scout out the terrain after we arrived here yesterday. I was going to do that today." He paused. "And Cameron seemed to trust Joe Quinn and Eve, but I couldn't allow myself that luxury. I had no personal experience with them, and I couldn't take the chance."

She stared at him in exasperation. "For heaven's sake, do you trust any of us?"

"Cameron." He thought about it. "And you."

"Why me?"

"Because you almost got killed and ended up in the hospital." He smiled. "And later I saw you fighting with Daniels. That was genuine, no pretense. Blood or violence is usually proof enough."

"Usually," she said. "Well, evidently Eve isn't sure of your intentions toward Diane, either, and you're right, you weren't at all discreet. She asked that you not be quite so aggressive. She doesn't want Diane disturbed. I don't want it, either." She grimaced. "But Cameron said he wanted you to continue to keep an eye on her, and I don't have any real objection. Still, she's my responsibility, not yours, not Cameron's. Do you understand?"

"No," he said flatly. "My duty is to Cameron. But I'll try to not upset her. I don't believe I did. Diane impressed me as not being easily ruffled. The only one who appeared to be upset was Eve. She must have very close ties to her."

"You might say that," Catherine said dryly. "One way and another, Eve and Diane have been very close. But I'm glad that you're going to cooperate. Eve appears to have taken Diane under her wing, but she has enough on her mind with the reconstruction. I was just attempting to—"

"Leave him alone, Catherine." Diane was standing in the doorway behind her. She was yawning as she came forward. "Did Eve sic you on the poor guy?" She glanced at Slade. "It's not as if he was molesting me. I could have told him to back off at any time if I'd wanted him to do it. I still will, if I choose. But Cameron sent him with us, didn't he? That should make it all right. Besides, I was a little shaken up yesterday, and having him around was kind of comforting."

"I'm glad I could help," Slade said quietly.

"He bunked outside your door last night, Diane," Catherine said impatiently.

"Really?" Diane said thoughtfully. "But then so did you at the hotel, Catherine." She made a face. "That appears to be the way I have to live my life these days. I'm this precious commodity that everyone is afraid will be destroyed in the blink of an eye. Even Hu Chang had me watched while I was with him in Hong Kong. It pisses me off, but I'm not stupid and I'll go along with it." She met her eyes. "Because I *am* that precious commodity. I worked and studied to make my work that valuable, and somehow I ended up as part of the package. So I'll put up with it until I find a way to step away and let the work stand alone. That's not yet. I'm still in transition, and so is the bullet. It has to be absolutely perfect before I can release it." She added ruefully, "Though I never thought that Eve would be one of the people worried about protecting me. Funny how things work out." She turned to Slade. "I don't mind you trailing me . . . from a distance. But anything closer you get my permission. Do you understand?"

"I understand."

She gave him a shrewd glance. "But you'll still do what you want."

He nodded. "But from now on, most of the time you won't know about it." He paused. "And I promise you'll be safe no matter where you are." He smiled faintly. "You can bet on it."

She sighed. "Whatever." She added to Catherine, "You can fight it out between you. I'm not going to let it bother me. While I'm here I intend to spend most of my time either working or helping Eve on the reconstruction if she'll let me." She gestured to the jeans and plaid shirt she was wearing. "Which is why I yanked myself out of bed and got dressed this early. I thought I should show Eve I was willing and able to step up to the plate."

"What do you know about forensic reconstruction?" Slade asked.

"Nada. But I'm a doctor and I have a working knowledge of DNA. And I'm very good at keeping track of notes and developing cross associations that can sometimes lead to surprising breakthroughs. Besides, Hu Chang gave me a really cool gadget if I can get it to work. I could be useful to her." She closed her eyes and sniffed. "But the scent of that bacon is making me salivate. It practically lifted me out of bed and wafted me in here." Her eyes opened. "Since I'm being so reasonable, are you going to give me breakfast?"

"It's possible. Even probable." He pulled out another kitchen chair for her. "Catherine?"

Catherine hesitated and then dropped down in the chair next to Diane. "By all means. It doesn't appear that I'm going to get anything else of value from this conversation. Are you a good cook, Slade?"

"Excellent. I grew up on a farm in Iowa and when I wasn't working in the fields, my mother taught me that it was a skill that would take me far." He started dishing up the eggs and bacon. "Later I learned other skills that took me down other paths that weren't nearly so homey and wholesome. Of course, Cameron appreciates those talents much more, but this one never failed me." He handed Diane her plate and said quietly, "Because the ability to bring any kind of comfort in a harsh world is a wonderful gift, isn't it?"

"Maybe. It depends on how much you need it." She didn't look at him. "But you might be right..."

"You've almost finished, Joe." Eve's glance wandered around the library that had been turned into her temporary studio. "Sorry. I should have hurried back. I just wanted to check on how Catherine was doing."

"And politely tell Cameron he should call off Slade?" Joe poured a cup of coffee from the coffeemaker he'd set up on the cabinet in the corner. "How did he take it?"

"Not well." She took the cup he handed her. "But I had to let him know as subtly as possible not to make Diane feel uncomfortable. I think Catherine will tell him even if Cameron won't."

"I could have handled it." Joe dropped into a chair and stretched his legs out before him. "And you don't have to worry about Diane not being able to take care of it herself. She's never shy about speaking out."

Eve shrugged. "I just wanted to avoid any problems that might crop up. When I start work, I want to have a clear head and no interruptions."

"And that's what you'll have." He lifted his cup to his lips. "Stop trying to micromanage. All you have to worry about is doing that reconstruction so that we can get answers and then get the hell out of here."

"I'm not micromanaging. I'm just—"

"—trying to protect Diane," he finished for her. "That's not your job. She has Catherine. She has Cameron."

"Which could be an uncomfortable duo." She gazed down into the coffee in her cup. "And you?"

He shook his head. "Not unless you become involved in the situation. I intend to keep myself busy checking out the ranch and the grounds today. I may take Slade with me." He smiled crookedly. "That should please you."

"It does." She took another swallow of her coffee and then set it down on the worktable. "And it will keep you busy and worry-free while I start the reconstruction." She moved to the burlap sack she'd set in a corner of the room. "Which I should do right now. I tried to clean all the surface dirt from the skull last night before I went to bed but the deep cleaning is still to do. All before I can actually start to work." She carefully took the skull out of the sack and placed it on a stand on the worktable. She stood looking at it, fire-blackened and broken and monstrous. But *was* it monstrous? Or was it a victim? Had that face once reflected gentleness and wonder? She'd only be able to tell that once she finished. Right now those gaping dark holes where his eyes should be seemed to be glaring at her. She reached out tentatively and touched the cheekbone. It should have been cold, but it seemed... warm. Almost as if it were alive.

Imagination.

But she still found herself shivering.

"Eve." Joe was standing behind her. His hands gently cupped her shoulders. "It's okay if you put if off for a while. Why don't we go get some breakfast?"

She took a deep breath as she leaned back against him. He was hard and warm and *Joe*. The chill was suddenly gone. "Don't be silly. There's no reason to put it off. He's not very pretty, is he?"

"Ugly as sin," he said lightly. "But maybe he'll turn into a swan before you finish with him. Do you want me to stick around and watch the progress? What are you going to name him?"

"I have no idea." She always named the reconstructions, because she felt it gave her a more intimate connection with them. But at this moment she was shying away from that intimacy. "Maybe I'll wait a while until we get better acquainted."

"No matter what the outcome, we'll deal with it." Joe brushed his lips on her temple. "It just means we'll have to adjust."

"I know that," she said huskily. "But I don't like the idea of adjusting to the thought of it being a sweet kid like Kai Hakali who ended up like this. The description of him Diane gave me reminded me too much of Michael. I don't *want* this reconstruction to turn out a swan."

"But you'll accept it, if it is." His arms tightened around her. "I want to be with you when you get close to knowing. Okay?"

"Very much okay." She turned around and held him close. "Hey. It's not as if I can't take it, Joe. I've never even met this Kai."

"You can take anything. But this whole scenario is striking too deep if you're making comparisons with Michael."

"Maybe." She nestled her head on his chest. "Last night I started thinking about Kai. After that head injury, he never had a chance to really grow up. Then I started thinking about the bullet and wondering if it was really too late to help him. How many children out there could be helped? There are so many what-ifs connected to the bullet. And Nalam is trying to steal all of them and never let them be explored."

"Quite a few what-ifs and maybes."

She drew a shaky breath. "Yep, and I'm not getting anywhere

standing here and trying to make sense of it." She pushed away from him and stepped back. "I'll have to see if it all comes clear while I'm working on the reconstruction. Get out of here and let me get to work, Joe."

"Right." He kissed her. "I'll see you when I get back. I'll stop on the way out and ask Catherine to nag you into getting a bite of breakfast. Pay attention to her, hear?"

"I hear," she said absently as she turned back to the skull and rolled up her sleeves. "Bye, Joe."

She didn't hear him leave as she rifled in the worktable desk drawer for the cloth and cleaning agent to start the cleanup. She turned back to the skull. "Here we are together," she murmured. "Don't fight me. I only want to bring you home..."

CHAPTER
11

FOUR HOURS LATER

Diane didn't knock before she opened the library door. "I've brought you a sandwich," she announced from the doorway. "Catherine said she couldn't persuade you to eat any breakfast. I get that. When you're working hard, food just gets in the way. I'm the same. But this won't take you more than a minute or two and it will keep anyone else from bothering you for a little while." She moved across the room toward Eve. "So don't throw it at me. Okay?"

Eve pushed back her chair. "I'll consider it." She looked without enthusiasm at the ham sandwich and chips on the paper plate Diane set on the worktable. "It doesn't look very appetizing."

"I know. I'm not good in the kitchen. But I figured that I couldn't ruin a ham sandwich." She glanced at the skull Eve was working on. "Somebody gave that poor guy a rough time. But you seem to be doing a good job of cleaning him up. Though it appears impossible that you can put that face back together again. Alon gave me a photo of Kai, would you like to see it?"

"No, not until the reconstruction is done. It might influence me."

"I can see how that could happen." She picked up Eve's empty cup and took it over to the automatic coffeemaker on the cabinet. "I'll give you a refill. Black?"

"Yes." Eve picked up the half sandwich and bit into it. "He does look rough, but you don't seem to be having any problem with accepting him."

"I'm a doctor. I'd have a tough time if I did." She refilled the cup. "Besides, my favorite classes in medical school were the forensic labs."

"Why?"

"I got answers. Most of the other classes just posed questions." She brought the coffee back to Eve and set it on the desk beside her. "I like answers. Questions intrigue me but I like getting the opportunity to dig deep and have those answers leap out at me." She stood there looking at Eve. "May I get you anything else?"

Eve shook her head. "No, thanks." She finished the sandwich. "But you can tell me why you decided to come and do this nurturing. You're really awkward at it."

"I couldn't let you starve. I wanted to let you know that I appreciate you doing this." She hesitated. "And you wouldn't find me awkward if you let me help you with this reconstruction. Hu Chang gave me some DNA equipment that's pretty awesome if I can make it work. Besides, I can obey orders and I have a knowledge of DNA and the human body that you might find useful."

"That's the real reason you came?"

She nodded. "I know having to deal this closely with me must be driving you bananas." She smiled. "Hey, it might make it more comfortable for you if you can boss me around and see how meekly I take it."

"It wouldn't make me comfortable at all," Eve said dryly. "And I'd be suspicious as hell if you suddenly showed me a meek side."

Diane's smile widened. "Yeah, I can see that. Meek is hard for me, but I can be respectful if I know someone has more knowledge than I do. I'd show you that respect, Eve. Will you let me help you?"

Eve stared at her for a long minute. Diane was very appealing in that moment. She'd been honest and frank, and there had not been any bullshit in either her attitude or demeanor. "I don't believe I will," she said slowly. "I'm still a little uneasy with you, though it's not as bad as when you first came. If I made the effort I'm sure I'd be able to block it out entirely, but I don't want to have to concentrate on that when all I want is to get on with my work."

Diane nodded. "I'm uneasy with you, too. I was just going to consider it another challenge to overcome. I've got a lot of those on my agenda." She turned to leave. "If you change your mind . . . "

"Wait." Eve was silent. This was probably a mistake. She'd let Diane slip into too many corners of her life already; she didn't need to share her work, too. Or maybe she did, because she found herself saying, "Maybe when I get down to the last steps, I might consider it."

A brilliant smile lit Diane's face. "Cool. Just say the word and I'll be here. Count on me." The next moment the door had closed behind her.

Eve turned back to the skull. *Count on me.* Those words were echoing in her mind. When had she or Joe ever been able to count on Diane? She had only been a ghost who had drifted in and out of their lives, and now she was back and no longer a ghost. She had substance and was making her presence known in a dozen different ways.

Almost all of them disturbing and thought provoking and making her life extremely difficult. *Count on me.* But those words had given Eve an odd feeling of warmth and security. Diane was reckless and intense, and she shouldn't have been able to generate those feelings—but somehow she had.

Stop puzzling about her. Forget her.

She leaned forward and began working on the skull.

"No luck?" Catherine asked Diane as she came out on the porch. "I could have told you that she wasn't going to be bribed with a ham sandwich. She's used to working alone."

"I had to try. And I believe I made progress. She gave me a strong maybe for later." She sat down in a chair and opened her computer. "It's just as well. It will give me time to work on my notes. I had an idea how to develop the efficiency of the first injection so that it would cut down on the time needed to bring it to full potential. But I might have to go back to Madagascar to see if there's flora to—"

"Madagascar," Catherine repeated blankly. "I don't want to hear about it if you don't mind. I think we have enough on our plate without worrying about how to improve your beloved bullet."

"Sorry," Diane said. "I can't help but worry about it. I can't get it out of my head. It's been that way since the moment I finished synthesizing it. It has to be perfect, Catherine."

Catherine sighed. "Of course it does. And you should work on it. I'm being a bitch."

"A little." Diane looked up from her computer. "I think you're bored. All that adrenaline sparking and then nothing." She smiled slightly. "Maybe I could arrange to have Nalam do something to make things interesting for you."

"Forget it."

"Or you could go for a walk."

"Don't be ridiculous. I can't leave you."

"That's true. You'd regard it as a cardinal sin. Though I'm beginning to wish you would."

"Tough." She was suddenly grinning. "I saw a crossword puzzle book on the coffee table in the living room. I'll go get it and sit in that chair out of sight at the end of the porch. I'll work my puzzles and you can figure out how to save the world. Deal?"

Diane nodded solemnly. "Pressure. Pressure. But some people would argue I've already saved the world. I just have to refine and keep—" She stopped, her gaze on the bunkhouse next door. "Cameron." She watched him come toward them. "And he doesn't look very cheerful. Why don't you leave me alone and go see if he needs your help? It will save you from the crossword puzzles." She waved a dismissing hand. "I promise I won't move from this chair."

Catherine was no longer listening. She was on her feet and hurriedly crossing the yard toward Cameron. No, he didn't look cheerful and she didn't like it. His expression was usually impassive but now it was almost grim.

"What's wrong?" she asked when she reached him.

"Enough," he said. His gaze went to Diane, who was once more looking down at her computer. "More than enough to cause us big-time trouble. I told you I'd send people out to see what Nalam's up to. He's been very busy and he'll be motivated as hell now."

"Why?"

"One of the doctors attending the so-called medical conference at that hotel in Canada disappeared last night." He held up his hand as she started to speak. "No, it wasn't Judkal, the doctor who was so obliging about filling me in on the results of Diane's test in Hong Kong. It was Herbert Daltry, one of the other specialists. It was probably a random choice, just as mine had been with Judkal."

"Disappeared!" She reached out and grabbed his arm. "Why? He left the hotel? You said you'd have a man keeping an eye on the hotel. Where was he?"

"Doing his job. I'd told Corbett to watch Judkal in particular and to be aware of anything unusual to do with the conference itself. He was on guard all night in the hall outside Judkal's room. Before that he remembered seeing Daltry playing chess with one of the other doctors in the lounge, but he went to his room even before Judkal did. There was nothing that sent up any red flags. No one lurking or suspicious. This morning Daltry didn't answer the door when room service came with his usual breakfast order."

"And?"

"He wasn't in his room." He paused. "And there was blood on the floor of the bathroom. Quite a bit of blood. He didn't go willingly."

"Shit," she said hoarsely.

He nodded curtly. "His phone and his computer had been taken. The person who took him must have been very good. He not only was able to get into Daltry's room but managed to get him out without being seen. And depending on what time he was yanked, we have to assume that Nalam's man probably had all night to squeeze him for information." He paused before adding, "If he took Daltry with him, he was just trying to keep anyone from knowing that he was probably dead. I believe they'll find his body on the grounds if he wasn't tossed in the lake."

"Dead," she said numbly. "Then he would have told them everything he knew about Diane."

"That's my bet."

"He died because he knew the results of the tests." She had been so terrified about the consequences to Diane of the man's death that the significance hadn't sunk in. Daltry had been just an innocent man caught up in this nightmare. "Could he have gotten away? You said there was blood. Maybe he tried to resist..."

"Maybe he did," he said gently. "But Daltry was a doctor and not equipped to face the brand of thugs Nalam can afford. He wouldn't have had a chance."

"No." She was trying to think. "The choice of Daltry was obviously random, but the purpose wasn't. Information. How did they know they could get it from him? I can see how you might manage to track anyone down—you have practically an army at your disposal. But how did Nalam zero in on a supposed medical conference in Canada?"

"Hu Chang, again. That's how I traced it. Once he tracked Diane to Hu Chang, he'd want to know what she was doing with him. Hu Chang is a clever bastard and secretive as hell, but he was balancing eight physicians and an agenda that was very hot indeed. It doesn't surprise me that he couldn't keep it from leaking in a city like Hong Kong."

"It will surprise him. You're probably wrong. Hu Chang doesn't make mistakes like that."

"And you resent it." He smiled faintly. "Not so much the mistake but that I have the nerve to accuse your hero."

"He's not my hero, he's my friend," she said. "Hu Chang doesn't believe in heroes." She drew a deep breath. "Okay. We're not absolutely sure that it's Nalam, but it's likely."

"Very likely. And when Nalam knows, he'll realize that she's considerably more than a woman who stole from him and set herself up to be an accomplice to Alon Hakali. She'll be a prime target in her own right."

"Do you think I don't know that?"

"Then you should also know that he'll use every weapon to take her down. No holds barred. If he believes he's losing, he'll bring in powerful partners to help him who think the same way he does. He's got Wall Street tycoons, senators, maybe even the president in his pocket." He stared her in the eye. "I know how to play that game. I'll use every trick, every man and weapon at my command. I can protect her. I *will* protect her. Let her come to me and I promise she'll survive."

She looked at him in disbelief. "This is a hell of a time to pull this bullshit. We've gone over it before."

"Yes, we have. But the stakes are higher now. I thought I'd repeat the offer. I only want the best for her, Catherine."

"What you think is best."

"Are you afraid that she might think so, too?" He made an impatient gesture. "I'm not going to argue with you about it. The offer will always be there. I'm just giving you fair warning that things are going to change. Nalam has been hovering in the background like a spider weaving his web. His only real agenda was probably Alon Hakali and how he wanted to punish him for trying to get in his way. Even so, he was being careful not to take a wrong step that might spoil his image. Now he's going to stop worrying about the consequences and go for the jugular." He paused. "Diane's jugular. I swear I'm not going to let you be caught in the crossfire protecting her."

"Not your choice." She felt suddenly weary as she turned away. "And now I've got to go and tell Diane the bad news. She thought maybe she might have some measure of safety as long as Nalam didn't know she was involved with the tri-root research."

"She *is* the research," Cameron said. "No escaping it. He won't give a damn about Hakali if he can get his hands on her." He added softly, "But that won't happen if you let me keep her safe. Remember that when you're breaking the news to her that she might be either on the run for years or trapped and killed."

"I won't remember it," she said as she started across the yard. "Because you swore you wouldn't let me get hurt protecting Diane.

That means no matter what I do, you'll keep her alive. You always keep your word, Cameron."

There was silence and then he chuckled. "You'll remember it. I don't care that you'll remember it as a promise rather than a subtle threat. I rather like it."

She didn't answer. She'd reached the porch and she braced herself as Diane lifted her gaze from her computer and looked at her. Then she watched her frown and straighten in her chair. "Catherine?"

"Daltry," Diane repeated when Catherine had finished speaking. "I barely remember him. He examined me and asked me questions, but they all did. I just cooperated and hoped it would all end soon." She was silent. "It doesn't seem right that I don't remember him. I should remember someone who died because of me."

Catherine reached out and took her hand. "None of this is your fault."

"Of course it is. I started this and then followed through. It doesn't matter that I didn't mean for anyone to die. I knew that there might be people who had their own agendas and wouldn't want me to go on with the research."

"Only lamebrain sickos," Catherine said bluntly.

Diane smiled. "I like the way you think. That's what I thought, too. And who should pop up in my life but Nalam?"

"What are you going to do about it?"

"How the hell do I know? I'm scared. But I don't like the idea of cowering in a cave somewhere." She paused. "What Nalam did to Salkara and Alon's family was beastly. And now there's this poor doctor, whom I don't even remember, being killed because Nalam snapped his fingers. That's not right, either."

"Cameron said that Nalam will go on the attack and never stop."

Diane nodded. "He's right. I've seen how vicious Nalam can be. I was on Hakali Island while he was holding Kai prisoner and I heard some of the calls he made to Alon when he felt like twisting the knife. He bitterly resented that Alon had managed to hide out where he couldn't scoop him up as he had Kai." She shivered. "Once he took a whip to Kai and beat him while he was talking to Alon. Alon couldn't do anything about it. It was hideous. That poor kid, he didn't understand."

"And that's why you went after that file in Manila."

"I couldn't take it. It was the only way I could think that might give Alon an edge. But I was so scared. I really didn't know what the hell I was doing. I'm a doctor, not CIA like you. I had to play most of it by ear." She grimaced. "Just like I'm going to have to do now."

"You had a right to be scared. But you won't be going it alone. There are good people out there. And I'll be here for you." She looked away. Lord, she didn't want to do this. "And there's another possibility. You could use Cameron to run interference with Nalam. That would probably be safest for you. He probably has a bigger force at his disposal than Nalam. But it would mean he'd take you away somewhere safe until there wasn't a threat."

"Sounds too much like that cave I was talking about."

"It wouldn't be a cave. It would probably be a pleasant place for you to work. He'd just insist on you accepting someone to watch over you."

"I can see you don't like this idea," Diane said shrewdly. "Why not?"

Catherine glanced back at her. "He can be very persuasive. I guess I'm afraid that you won't want to come back. But it's your decision. I had to let you know all your options."

"And you did. As a good friend would. Thank you. You've made Cameron's hideout seem almost appealing." She released her hand.

"But even the most desirable caves make me nervous. I think I'll take a shot at fighting Nalam on his own ground. Look, I always knew that there would come a time when I'd need to fight all those bastards who would try to take the bullet, but I was so worried about Alon and Kai that I just didn't think about it. Now things have changed, so I have to change, too." She got to her feet and headed for the front door. "I'm only going inside. You don't have to follow me unless you want to help me move furniture."

"What?" Catherine scrambled to her feet and headed after her. She caught up with her as she threw open the door to Eve's workroom.

But Diane was striding toward Eve's desk. "I'm sorry to disturb you. I thought I should let you know I probably don't have time to be as polite and diplomatic as I was planning. I think I can help you, but I can't force you to let me do it. But I can remind you that I'm always here and available."

Eve was stiffening. "I don't know what you're talking about."

"I'm going to bring one of the chairs in from the living room and set it up outside in the hall. I can work just as well out there and I promise I won't bother you. You'll just know that I'm available." She turned on her heel and strode out of the room.

Catherine closed the door and ran after Diane, who was now heading for the living room. "That's no way to win friends and influence people," she told her dryly. "Eve doesn't like to be pushed."

"I didn't like pushing her. But I want her to finish that reconstruction ASAP. Like I told her, I don't know how much time I have. And I don't know how safe it is here. Nalam's man found Dr. Daltry at that hotel and killed him. He'll probably be after the other doctors, too. And how do I know that they won't find me here at the ranch?"

"Because Cameron set it up. I can't remember when he made a mistake."

"I don't want to be his first one." She pointed to a leather chair. "This will do. Are you going to help me?"

Catherine looked at her expression and then sighed. "It seems I am." She moved toward the chair. "I'll take the back."

"The bitch!" Nalam swore long and vehemently as he looked at the text on the computer screen. "It can't be true, dammit." But he knew it was true. Daltry had a sterling reputation, and so had those other doctors who had been brought to Hong Kong to examine Diane Connors. Nalam knew how to read the technical findings that they'd all agreed were absolutely genuine, and his rage was growing with every sentence, every figure.

"Bad?" Ed Galman came to stand behind him and looked down at the report on the screen. "It's what you said you wanted. That doctor didn't want to give up his computer. He fought me for it. Though it just looks like a bunch of numbers to me."

"It's *shit*," Nalam said through set teeth. "How could this happen? Everyone knows it shouldn't be possible." Panacea. His worst nightmare. It shouldn't even exist. He'd thought she was merely an accomplice of Hakali's who had stolen those files, someone to punish and set an example, or perhaps even be the key to finding that bastard Alon Hakali. But according to this report, it was much worse: She was on her way to developing a serum that could ruin him. He turned to Daniels, who was sitting in a chair across the room, and hissed, "I wouldn't have to worry about this nightmare if you'd done your job right. I should have relied on my regular crew and not brought in a so-called specialist. You let Ling derail you in Atlanta and then again in Nevada. When you called me from Belazo's, you said that you'd set enough explosives to blow Ling and

Diane Connors to hell and back. But it didn't happen. All I got was excuses. What good are you?"

"I don't have to take this crap." Daniels stood up. "None of this was my fault. How did I know Quinn would be able to disarm the explosives? I got rid of Belazo for you, didn't I? And I called Galman here to come and help with the skull. He's the one who let us be ambushed. Why blame me? The only reason I came here when you called me was to offer to find Connors and tidy up the job so that I could get my money."

"How kind of you," Nalam said sarcastically. "You're damn right you'll tidy up the job." He glanced down at the computer and started to swear again. "As for the money, you'll have to prove you can give me Connors. I'm tired of your blundering. After that, I have just one more special job for you and then I'll cut you loose." But that special job was too important for him to get rid of the man yet. He had to use someone no one had ever seen with him, whom he could safely dispose of later. He raised his head and glared at Daniels as he hissed, "When I called you to come here, I wasn't sure that you'd leave here alive. I don't accept incompetence, and you've shown me nothing else. I was going to tell Galman to be prepared to cut your throat. You were very eager to do that, weren't you, Galman? He wants to get back in my good graces after he let Belazo sneak out of camp and try to get a deal of his own."

Galman nodded. "Whatever you want."

Daniels tensed and for a moment appeared panicked. "I tell you, it wasn't my fault."

"Yes, it was, you're an arrogant son of a bitch who thought you could run the show. No one runs the show but me. But I'm going to let you wriggle out of this if you bring me Diane Connors. From this minute everyone will spend every waking hour looking for her and making sure I get hold of her." He turned to Galman. "You told me that you had a lead on that helicopter that picked up Quinn, Duncan, and Connors in that field. I don't want a lead; I want that pilot identified and tracked. And I want to talk to Connors. I might be able to make a deal... until I can set up a way to get rid of the bitch. Find a way for me to contact her. Go through Jeremy Franks. He'll be able to manage it and still keep me safe. He's the only one of you who has any brains."

He looked back at Daltry's report. The photo of Diane Connors was gazing boldly up at him from the first page. Blond and sleek with those eyes that seemed to burn with intensity. Fucking whore. When he'd first started to glance through the report, he'd felt a ripple of lust. Hell, he might have even considered finding a way to get her into bed. But then he'd continued to read, and the rage had begun to smolder. He felt absolutely nothing sexual about her now. He wanted only to hit and shatter and destroy. Who would have thought this bitch would be able to turn his life upside down?

She'd learn she couldn't do that to him.

She'd learn...

"Diane." Joe strode down the hall toward where Diane was sitting in the brown leather chair outside Eve's workroom. "What the hell do you think you're doing?"

"Annoying you." Diane held up her computer. "But that's your problem. I'm working. I'm not bothering Eve. I'm just showing my support and offering my services if needed."

"They're not needed. This is the second day you've been sitting out here. You'll just bother her." He hesitated, frowning. "Look, after what Catherine told me I can see why you might be upset right now. I can even see why you'd be frustrated and want to push things along. But you can't push Eve. That's not how it works."

She tilted her head, gazing at him thoughtfully. "Did Eve tell you to kick me out?"

"No. She said to leave you alone. She said that once she starts on the actual sculpting, she wouldn't even know you exist. It's just the right thing to do."

"Because you want her to be comfortable, and you're afraid I'll do something that will upset her. That's always what you've been worried about." She wearily shook her head. "You don't get it, Joe. I'm not the enemy. I told you before that when she agreed to do this reconstruction, it meant I'd do anything within my power to help her and keep her alive. Dammit, I'm *grateful*. Can't you get that into your head?"

He was silent. "I'm having problems doing it. Our situation was . . . complicated. I understand if you still have hard feelings and I don't mind being the bad guy." His lips tightened. "But I can't let any of it touch Eve."

"And it won't." She looked up at him and then said impulsively, "And I don't have hard feelings toward you about that disaster of a marriage. Not the marriage itself. That was on both of us. I had no compunction about reeling you in because I wanted my trust fund. I was a selfish bitch and vain enough to think that anyone would be lucky to have me around. I don't even know when it changed. All of a sudden there was bitterness and I wanted to strike out." She smiled sardonically, "And I did, and it was at Eve, so you sent me on my way. I guess I always knew that was how it would be, but like I said, I was vain." She slowly shook her head. "It took me a long time to get over that blow to my ego. I don't believe it actually happened until I ran into Alon Hakali."

"And why did that make a difference?"

"Alon is very wise. I learned a lot from him. He always made me look deep, even if it hurt. He said perhaps it wasn't ego." She held up her hand. "Don't panic. I'm not going to make any soppy confessions. I don't even know if I had the capacity for anything deeper than ego at the time. But you did mean something to me, and because you did, I began to open up and learn more about myself and everyone around me. You were . . . an enrichment, Joe." She made a face. "But that doesn't mean I won't have a few lingering flashes of bitterness now and then. Alon would tell you I can accept, but that doesn't mean I don't have trouble when I remember."

"I don't believe I've ever been called an enrichment before," Joe said dryly. "And I think I'd like to meet this Alon."

"You will." She met his eyes. "Because you know you aren't going to let Eve finish that reconstruction and then whisk her away. Whether that skull turns out to be Kai or not, you'd find a way to go after Nalam and punish him. You're a warrior, one of the good guys."

"You're wrong, I would whisk her away." He added, "And then I'd come back and see what I could do about exterminating a rodent that shouldn't be allowed to live. I don't like what I hear about Nalam." He paused. "I hope that reconstruction won't be Kai, Diane."

"I do, too. Alon does so much for everyone around him. He doesn't need to lose anyone else." She glanced at the workroom door. "How close is she?"

"Hard to tell. I'd say another day or so, but the final sculpting often goes very fast."

She closed her computer. "Then I think I'll go and get some air in case she needs me later tonight." She got to her feet. "Catherine was going to make some calls to Hu Chang and her immediate CIA superior. I'll be able to sneak out without her feeling like she needs to shadow me." She grinned. "And you can tell Eve you chased me off." She added with her best Schwarzenegger imitation, "But I'll be back."

"I'm sure you will." He started to turn away. "Be careful. Stay close to the property."

She sighed. "You, too?"

He glanced back at her. "Why should I be different?"

She watched him as he went into Eve's workroom. She had been very open; probably she shouldn't have been so frank. But she couldn't go on being cool and withdrawn any longer. It wasn't her nature and was too emotionally exhausting. She'd had to make the attempt to mend fences. Joe had been hesitant, but toward the end she had felt a subtle easing.

Oh, well, she'd done the best she could. Alon would have been proud of her.

Maybe. She could almost see his faintly skeptical smile, which always challenged her to go one step further.

She was outside on the porch now and drew a deep breath of the cool evening air. Beauty. Freedom. The sun had gone down but the sky was still a soft purple reflecting on the lake beside the ranch.

"Making a break for it?"

Slade. She turned and saw him sitting on one of the rocking chairs at the far end of the porch with his long legs outstretched before him. "Thinking about it. Would you try to stop me if I did?"

He shook his head. "Not my job. I'd just follow you and make certain you don't stumble either physically or figuratively." He smiled. "Besides, I'd judge you're not in the mood to bolt. You probably just wanted some time to yourself after being cooped up in that hallway making a statement. Do you want me to wander off and pretend I don't see you? Say the word."

"But it would only be a pretense, wouldn't it?" She strolled down the long porch toward him. "You don't impress me as being the type to loll around looking at sunsets. Who told you to keep an eye on me? Cameron? Joe?"

"Catherine. She wanted to make a few phone calls and thought that you were probably safely tucked away doing research. But she's very duty-oriented and decided to make use of me as a backup." He smiled mockingly. "I was flattered she trusted me to fill in for her. So it would be pretense. But I'm good at it, and I did promise you that you'd never know."

"Oh, for heaven's sake. Of course I'd know. I'd *feel* you out there." She plopped down in a chair a short distance from him and flipped open her computer. "Just be quiet and let me work for a minute. I want to finish checking something. Joe interrupted me and then I got involved trying to mend fences." Her fingers were flying over the keys. "Which I'm not at all good at, so I found myself running away."

"I can see you'd have trouble," he murmured. "I'll be quiet. Am I allowed to know what you're checking?"

"Madagascar," she said absently. "Hush."

"Right." He kept to his word, and she was able to close him out while she worked. She was vaguely aware that he got up once to turn on the porch lights for her. But it was fully dark before she finished and closed her computer.

"Did you get what you wanted?" he asked.

"I don't know. Probably not. I think I'll have to go there and explore for myself. I just wanted to check on any new medicinal plants that had shown up in Madagascar recently. I visited there once, and I was impressed by their high biodiversity and endemism, particularly in the Ambalabe region. Every now and then one of their local healers shows up with a plant that no one has ever seen before."

"And you thought that you might run across a tri-root variety?"

"You know about the tri-roots? Cameron?"

He nodded. "I do a good deal of his research for him. Cameron trusts me. He wouldn't leave me in the dark. Tri-roots?"

"It's doubtful. The local doctors and healers concentrate principally on antimalarial possibilities. And Salkara is in the South Pacific and nowhere close to Madagascar. But I wasn't expecting to find it on Salkara Island, either." She smiled. "And there it was. It would be great if I did find it again somewhere else."

"But you don't need it. You've already synthesized it."

"It's going to be a long time before I'll be satisfied enough to release it. I not only re-created it, I modified it. I have to be certain that it will do exactly what I need it to do. As I told Catherine, I won't do harm." She added eagerly, "But if I located another source of the tri-root in its natural form on Madagascar or someplace like that, it would be a simpler matter to test it and maybe get permission to release it much sooner."

"And what are your chances?"

"Don't ask me that. How should I know? But I know I won't have any chance at all if I don't start looking. That bastard will get away with all that ugliness." She frowned. "Heaven knows how many people he cheated when he burned all those plants in the rain forest on Salkara Island. And that might not even have been the first killings he ordered to steal other medicinal plants."

"You're angry."

"Yeah, I'm angry. Life is precious. I know what those tri-roots can do. It can be life or death or magic. I don't want Nalam to get away with stealing that from someone who needs it."

"Indeed? I do believe you're an idealist, Diane."

"I just don't believe in wasting my efforts." Then she made a face. "And there's nothing wrong with being an idealist. It's better than being a cynic. I can see why Catherine has problems with Cameron. You're cut from the same cloth." She looked him up and down. "And it's pure Kevlar and camo."

"I've no quarrel with idealism. Sometimes I'd like to go back there. But I've seen too much. So has Cameron. Still, it's nice when we can occasionally step into your world and make believe." He added simply, "I like it."

She stared at him. "Maybe not pure Kevlar?"

He shrugged. "I have my softer moments. It's a nice night, I've learned something about Madagascar, I've learned quite a bit about you. Those are all good things, Diane Connors."

She had learned quite a bit about him, too. Toughness, sensitivity, both very carefully balanced. Interesting. This seemed to be her night for—

Her phone was ringing.

She stiffened, then relaxed. It must be Hu Chang.

It was a blocked number, but it usually was with Hu Chang.

She punched access. "Hu Chang? What do you—"

"How are you, bitch?" The male voice was almost a snarl. "All smug and satisfied that you're going to beat me? No one beats me. Not you. Not Hakali. You're both dead, you just don't know it."

She fought through the shock to answer him. "Who is this?" Then she thought she knew, and the shock doubled. "Nalam?" she whispered.

Diane was vaguely aware of Slade's low curse as he rose to his feet with lightning swiftness and moved toward her. She motioned him away from her. "It is you, isn't it, Nalam? Well, I'm not dead yet. You're a monster, but I'll beat you. It's only a matter of time. You haven't been able to touch me yet."

"Because I'm surrounded by fools and I was being careful not to stir the waters. But I don't care any longer. I can't let you live. You should have known better than to meddle with those plants." His voice thickened with rage. "And you should never have let Hakali talk you into stealing from me."

"He had nothing to do with it." Slade was kneeling beside her tapping his ear. He wanted her to record. She pressed the RECORD and AUDIO buttons. She should have been doing that all along, she realized in frustration. "I just thought someone should stop a greedy bastard like you from causing any more blood and pain. Did you think that you could go on forever keeping anyone from discovering a miracle like the tri-roots and bringing it to light?" She laughed scornfully. "I bet you did. You're such an arrogant son of a bitch."

"I did stop it," he snarled. "I ordered every tri-root plant in that rain forest burned."

"And yet I still found a few plants to work with. Enough to get me started." Her voice lowered and became intense. "Enough to let me know what I'd found and what it could become. I synthesized it and made my own medicine better than you could dream."

"I know you did," he said hoarsely. "I read Daltry's report. It won't matter. After I kill you, I'll erase every trace of what you did. Everything will go back to the status quo. *My* status quo."

"The hell it will."

"That bothers you." His voice was malicious. "You're proud of what you did. I can use that. I was looking for a proper way to punish you. I think I've found it. You hate the idea that I'll be able to go on shaping my world to suit myself? What if I'd force you to use your fine discovery to make that go on indefinitely? You don't know how long you'll live after giving yourself those injections. I've no objection to waiting to kill you until after you've been forced to give me those same injections. It might be worth the wait to extend my life a long, long time. The idea is appealing for more than the obvious reasons." He was chuckling. "I was thinking about becoming the next president but maybe I need a position that would allow me to be dictator or emperor. I'd be a much better candidate than anyone else who will come knocking on your door if I let you live just that little bit longer. All that power I'd be able to gain with that extra time..."

Her hand tightened on the phone. "I'd never do it. I'd stab you in the heart with the hypodermic."

"You'd do it. If torture wouldn't work with you, I could always use it on someone you cared about to persuade you. Ling? Or Hakali? I'll have to choose. Lately I've found that method brings me a great deal of satisfaction."

"It will never happen. You don't think this call is being recorded?"

"I'm sure it is."

"So what's to keep this conversation from being used as exhibit one at your trial?"

"Besides the fact that my friends would never let it get to trial?" Nalam chuckled. "There will be no recording. I'm sure you've heard of Snapchat. Kids use it to send texts and photos back and forth to each other. The messages disappear after a certain amount of time to keep them from their parents' prying eyes."

"You're using Snapchat?" she asked incredulously.

"Oh, Diane. Something much more clever. These days all communications are digital. Ones and zeros. If you have a way of giving instructions to those ones and zeros, to scramble them up after a certain period of time, no recording is forever." He chuckled. "But I've given you an extra fifteen minutes so that you can run and have Hakali listen to it. I want him to know what's in store for you. After that, no more recording."

"You're bluffing."

"No, everything I've said, I intend to do to you. It's definitely going to give me something to look forward to until we can be together." His voice lowered. "And you'll think about it, too, won't you? That's good, I hope it gives you nightmares. But I promise I'll be your last nightmare. Do you think I'll let those people you have watching out for you stop me? I'll have them all killed. You left a trail, bitch. We're tracking you down and we're getting close. Look over your shoulder and I'll be there."

He cut the connection.

Slade immediately took the phone from her. "I doubt if we can trace." He was punching in a number. "But I'll try."

Diane jumped to her feet and walked to the edge of the porch. She had to stop shaking. He had wanted to upset her, and he had succeeded. That meant the bastard had won, and she wouldn't let him. She drew a deep breath. That was better. Now she was able to think and not just feel.

"Diane." Slade was behind her.

She didn't turn around. "Were you able to do it?"

"No, very high tech. It bounced off over a dozen sites around the world."

"I didn't think so. You can do so many things with phones these days. Before Hu Chang gave me my phone, he made sure it couldn't be traced, either."

He paused. "Are you okay?"

"No. But I will be soon. Nalam went to a lot of trouble to throw that load of ugliness at me, didn't he?" She was still shaking. She crossed her arms tightly over her chest to try to stop it. "He really wanted to hurt me. Catherine told me Cameron said that I'd be Nalam's prime target now. Maybe I should be flattered."

"He was in a rage. All those threats are bullshit. We're not going to let him touch you."

"I know you'll make every attempt to keep me safe." She tried to laugh. "Why wouldn't you? I'm such a prize. But he's not only going to try to kill me. Didn't you hear him? He's going after everyone who is helping me. I can't let that happen. I have to figure out a way to make certain it doesn't. I'm responsible for Eve being here, and Catherine wouldn't have—"

"Shut up." Slade muttered an oath and whirled her to face him. "Next you'll be telling me that you have to find a way to protect Cameron and me. That would be the height of insanity. You didn't ask us to invade the party. And none of us would be here if we hadn't decided we wanted to come. Look at us, Diane. Do you think Eve or Joe or Catherine could be coerced into doing something they didn't want to do? No. We made a choice. And that choice was you. Now remember that and pull yourself together."

She stared at him an instant before she pulled away. "I'll make the effort." She tried to lighten her tone. "It's just as well since all of you are probably better trained and equipped to deal with Nalam than I am." She suddenly frowned. "Except Eve. She's a sculptor, and Nalam will probably try to eat her for breakfast." She turned and headed down the porch toward the front door. "I'll have to let her know that Nalam might be closer than we thought." But she had to talk to Catherine first. "And I have to tell Catherine what Nalam said about what he intended to do to me. He was enjoying it too much. I think he meant it. I could never let that happen. I couldn't let him twist my work and make it as ugly as he is. She'd have to kill me before she let him do that to me." She looked at him over her shoulder. "I lost it for a minute. I'm sorry, Slade. Thanks for not treating me like the idiot I was being. It won't happen again."

"You might have had cause." His lips indented in a faint smile. "Nalam hit you where it hurt the most. Yet even now you're only planning on how you can get Catherine to kill you so that Nalam won't steal what's most important to you. That's either completely crazy or fantastically noble." He turned and headed for the bunkhouse. "Either way, I'm going to go talk to Cameron and see what we can do about eliminating the need to consider the option. I'll see you later."

CHAPTER 12

Nalam said she left a trail," Cameron said thoughtfully when Slade had finished. "He has to be talking about the helicopter. They think they're going to be able to trace the helicopter back to the pilot and persuade him to tell them where he took you after the pickup."

"That's what I thought," Slade said. "I didn't recognize the pilot. Was he one of ours?"

Cameron nodded. "Monteith. I couldn't take the chance of compromising the location with a strange pilot. But he works out of Calgary and they'll be able to track him."

"Should I call and warn him?"

Cameron was silent, considering. "Maybe. Let me think about it. Nalam was very eager, wasn't he? He smells blood."

Slade nodded. "And he wants Diane Connors. He's not going to stop until he gets her."

"Maybe we don't want him to stop yet. Maybe we should give him a little nudge." He reached for his phone. "And I think I'll call Monteith and see if he's noticed any surveillance since he got back to Calgary after he dropped you off..."

"Lord, I was afraid something would happen," Catherine said when Diane had finished telling her about the call. "Though I didn't think that nutcase Nalam would take it into his head to phone you. He must have been furious to spew out all that poison at you. I was just worried about the missing computer."

"I was worried about it, too. But all I could really think about was that I'd caused that doctor's death." Diane shook her head. "It seemed as if everything was roaring toward me at top speed. That's why I had to try to control what I could by setting up camp outside Eve's workroom." She grimaced. "Not that it did any good. She just ignored me. Followed by a lecture from Joe for bothering her."

"And then you were terrorized by Nalam. Not a good day, Diane."

She nodded. "Though it didn't turn monstrous until I got that call from Nalam." She shivered. "I can't let him get hold of me, Catherine."

"He won't. As soon as Eve finishes that reconstruction, we'll get out of here and send you somewhere safe. Until then, we'll make certain this place is tight as a drum. Don't you trust me?"

"I trust you." She moistened her lips. "I just wish I had a gun. I don't even like guns, but I feel . . . helpless. I don't like that feeling."

"Guns are dangerous if you don't know how to shoot one."

"You could show me. I probably know a little. Years ago Joe took me to a shooting range, but I was bored and didn't learn much."

"I'm not lending you mine, Diane."

She nodded. "Forget it. I bet Slade would be able to get me one."

"Slade?"

"I . . . like him. He reminds me a little of Alon."

"Really? He's no golden Greek god."

"But he's very deep and I think he's kind. He said that he was going to talk to Cameron and see what they could do about Nalam."

"I'd like to be in on that conversation," Catherine said grimly.

"Then go talk to them," Diane said wearily. "I want to clean up and then go check on Eve. You don't have to stay here and hold my hand. I'll see you when you get back."

Catherine hesitated. "You're sure?"

"I'm not nervous, Catherine. I'm just very cautious and I want to be able to protect myself instead of relying on everyone around me." She waved her hand, scooting Catherine out of the bedroom. "I thought I could take it, but it got old very quickly." She turned and headed for the connecting bathroom. "Talk to Cameron and find a way to move this along at light speed."

"I wish," Catherine said wistfully. She moved toward the door. "He's definitely into light speed, but that's asking a lot."

"Cameron!" Catherine knocked on the door of the bunkhouse. "May I come in?"

"By all means. I've been waiting for you."

"You might have been waiting a long time." Catherine opened the door. "I didn't know I was coming until a few minutes ago." She stood there looking at him. He was dressed in jeans and a black shirt with sleeves rolled up to the elbows, and he looked slim and tough and so damn hot that she felt a rush of very unwelcome heat. *Push it away.* That wasn't why she had come. "Diane said you and Slade were talking about what to do about Nalam. I need to know."

"I realize you do." He got to his feet and gestured to the two wineglasses on the rough-hewn table in front of him. He picked up the wine bottle sitting beside them. "But you've had a shock and probably a bad period comforting Diane. Slade said she was just trying to hold it together when she left him." He was pouring the wine. "Consider it therapy."

"I don't need therapy." She watched him walk toward her. "And neither does Diane. Slade was wrong. She's handling it fine. The only thing she asked of me was to get her a gun. She was disappointed that I didn't have one to give her. She said Slade would probably help her." But she took the goblet he was offering and took a sip. Why not? She should have known Cameron would sense how upset she'd be at Nalam's sudden attack on Diane. "Slade appears to be her new best buddy."

"That's good to know. It may come in handy." He took her elbow and nudged her toward a chair at the table. "I thought it was heading in that direction. Slade is one tough nut, but I got the distinct impression that he admired her spirit. He doesn't like many people, so that was fairly remarkable."

Her eyes narrowed. "Why would it come in handy? What are you up to, Cameron?"

"Nothing to alarm you." He dropped down in the chair across from her. "Just trying to lay out a scenario that you'd find comfortable."

"That would involve Diane and Slade? What kind of scenario?"

"Well, you asked me what I was talking to Slade about," he said. "It's all connected. Though I hadn't gotten that far with Slade yet."

"What's connected?"

"Nalam mentioned a trail. The only trail we could have left was the registration number on the helicopter. It will lead them to Paul Monteith, one of my pilots who operates out of Calgary. It won't be too difficult for Nalam's techs to locate Monteith and try to force him to tell him where he dropped his passengers off."

Her eyes widened in alarm. "Did you call and warn him?"

"I did call and question him. I'd just hung up when you knocked on my door."

"Question." She repeated the word. "Not 'warn.' Why not?"

"Because it might be more efficient *not* to avoid that move on their part. Even if I get Monteith safely out of Calgary, it would be reasonable for Nalam to order a search of the area around the city. I'm not really worried about them finding Naponi. It isn't that close, and I've been careful about making sure that all info about it has been erased. Still, with both Diane and Eve here I'd prefer to lead them in the complete opposite direction. We're not sure how long that reconstruction is going to take, and it could be a better idea to keep Nalam's people running around for a while thinking they're going to hit pay dirt any minute. If we're innovative, we'll be able to waste a good amount of their time leading them down the garden path. Possibly enough time to let Eve finish the reconstruction so that Quinn can start making arrangements to get her out of here." He tilted his head. "Providing you agree that would be a decent plan to go with?"

"You know it is." Her mind was whirring, trying to see where he was going. "You said 'we'll.' Are you talking about you and Slade?"

"He'd be very valuable." He took a sip of his wine. "But I believe you'd be a better choice. I'm leaving Slade here."

"What?" Her head lifted as she tried to hide the eagerness, then the instant disappointment. "I can't go. My job is to take care of Diane."

"But I'm afraid I need you too much in Calgary, so I've decided to have Slade take over your duties here."

She shook her head. "You don't need me in Calgary. You've told me what a wonder Slade is."

"But he lacks one asset that you possess." He went on softly, "Daniels hates your guts, almost has an obsession where you're concerned. He's certain to be there when they go after Monteith. Who would be better to lure Daniels to follow us? Not Slade. He has no personal animosity toward him. No, it has to be you, Catherine." He smiled cheerfully. "See, I've given you an excellent reason to do what you want. You have no excuse."

She was silent.

"We work well together," he said quietly. "I wouldn't have made that choice if we didn't. Everything I've said is true."

And it was damnably tempting. "I'll have to think about it."

He nodded. "Of course, but we should leave for Calgary right away. I've alerted Monteith and he hasn't seen any signs of surveillance yet, but we don't know how fast they'll move." He went on brusquely: "I'll leave Slade to watch over Diane, and there's no way Quinn would ever leave Eve. So we'll have two strong forces to protect Naponi that we can trust. I don't think you could fault either of them as your substitute." He set down his wineglass. "I have a few more preparations to make before we leave. When you make a decision, let me know."

"I'm dismissed?" she asked. "You've given your recruiting pitch and now you're sending me on my way? You've got to admit, using Daniels's sheer hatred of me to lure him is a weird strategy. No other reason?"

"I didn't say that." He leaned back in his chair, his lips tightening. "He hurt you. If you draw Daniels to you, there's a good chance I'll find a way to kill the son of a bitch."

She inhaled sharply.

"But that isn't the primary reason. I wouldn't be that undisciplined in these circumstances." He smiled. "So you can't use that as an excuse, either. Make your choice on the grounds I gave you."

"I will." She whirled and strode toward the door. "Because I did promise Hu Chang."

"The inimitable Hu Chang. But he's always willing to change strategy if the occasion demands. You know that, Catherine."

Actually, she knew it better than he did. But she had to make sure she wasn't letting the temptation of action on the horizon override cool reason. True, there was never anything cool about any decision she made where Cameron was involved—but this time it had to be different. She'd have to talk to Diane and maybe call Hu Chang. "I'll let you know."

She closed the door and headed for the ranch house.

Joe was coming out of Eve's workroom when Diane came down the hall. "I was just going to come looking for you. Slade told me about the call. Nasty business." He paused. "He said you handled yourself well."

"No, I didn't," she said bluntly. "I was scared, and I didn't know what to say. He didn't try to hide anything. Could we use it in court?"

He shook his head. "He was telling the truth. The recording disappeared within thirty minutes after he hung up."

"Slade said everything was high tech."

"He was right. But Nalam did give us warning so that we can keep watch."

"Not too close," she said wryly. "I don't want him near me."

"I don't blame you. Those threats were very brutal." He hesitated. "But here you are anyway."

"I have a job to do." She gazed beyond him to the workroom door. "Does she know?"

"Naturally. I don't keep anything from Eve."

"I know that. Not usually. I just wondered if you were trying to keep her from becoming upset while she was working."

"She wouldn't thank me," he said dryly. "She wants to talk to you. I told her I'd send you in if I saw you." He added, "And I knew I'd see you. It would be too much to hope that you wouldn't be camping out here."

"Yes, it would be. Nalam said he had a trail. That trail would lead to Eve, too. He'll have to take me to get to her. But he's now found out what a prize I am, which might make things safer for her. Or it might not." She shrugged. "I told you it might come down to that."

He nodded. "So you did. But I find, as time goes on, that I don't like the idea. I'm going to go see Cameron and see if he has any other plan." He jerked his thumb at the door. "Go talk to Eve."

"I heard you." She was already walking past him and knocking on the door.

"Come in," Eve said impatiently as she opened the door. "Why are you being so formal? Ever since you've been nesting out there, you've been creeping in to get me fresh coffee and then sneaking out again with nary a word."

"You summoned me. That's an entirely different kettle of fish." Diane entered the room. "I wasn't sure if you were angry that I'd brought Nalam down on you."

"I was angry. But I'd be stupid if I blamed you for Nalam's ugliness. I knew there would be problems after you told me what you were up against. I accepted it. I thought it worth it."

"So do I," Diane said. "But then it's my fight."

"It doesn't seem that way any longer." Eve rubbed her temple. "I don't like bullies, and Nalam qualifies big time in that category. It would be hard to find anyone else who's ready to make the entire world jump when he snaps his fingers. Joe doesn't like it, either."

"What a surprise. I'd think he'd appreciate anyone who would make me toe the line."

"He's coming around." She met her eyes. "And he doesn't like coercion. He won't let anything happen to you, Diane. You don't have to be afraid."

Diane felt a rush of warmth. "What will be, will be. The only thing I'm afraid of is that you won't get that reconstruction done before Nalam pounces. I can't let that happen." Her gaze shifted to the skull. "You've done a lot of work since I was in here last. I thought it would take you much longer, considering he looked like he'd been practically cremated. Now he's clean and you've done the repairs." Her gaze flew back to Eve. "You're ready for the sculpting?"

She nodded.

"How soon?"

"I'll start tonight, but I'll only be able to do the preliminary. I'll stop before morning and take a nap, and then I should be ready to begin the final."

"And that will tell the tale?"

"As far as I'm concerned, but it might not satisfy you." She looked back at the skull. "I can only tell you what my measurements and skill and instincts tell me. You said you had to be absolutely certain it wasn't Kai."

"It's life or death. I have to be able to tell Alon I'm positive." She looked at the reconstruction in despair. "And I can't tell anything from that skull yet. It's just a clay blur so far."

"I know." Eve reached over and took a small box off the counter and handed it to her. "But this might help. I found what could be a small bit of DNA content in a back molar. It might not even be large enough to analyze, and I can't be sure of the amount of denigration. His mouth was a complete mess."

Diane opened it eagerly and looked at the glass slide. She frowned. "You're right. It's tiny. Not much to work with. I don't know if..."

"It's all I can get for you," Eve said flatly. "What you see is what you get. What's your procedure? You said Hu Chang sent some kind of DNA kit with you. It's not good enough to process this?"

"I don't know. It might be. It's based roughly on a DNA machine that's used in police departments around the world. They call it the Magic Box. But Hu Chang's is more miniaturized and ultra-technical and connected to dozens of facial recognition programs around the world. He said that it should be able to give me a name and printout of at least one form of ID. I'll have to study this bit of DNA and determine whether I can get answers with it."

"Then we'd both better get to work and see what magic we can pull out of our hats." Eve nodded at a desk across the room. "You can set up there. It should give you enough room to work on the DNA machine. You said it was miniaturized?"

"Yes." She stiffened, gazing at her, stunned. "You want me to move in here?"

"Unless you'd prefer to set up outside in the hall. That wouldn't be efficient."

"No, it wouldn't." She moistened her lips. "You're sure?"

Eve turned to look at her. "You have the photo of Kai. You can verify if my reconstruction is of him. You have Hu Chang's DNA Magic Box and can perhaps tell me who he is if we get lucky and it's not Kai. That would be a final ID that would satisfy your friend Alon. Isn't that true?"

Diane nodded.

"Then, since you don't chatter and wouldn't disturb me, I think it's time that you get whatever gear you need and start to work." She smiled faintly. "Don't you?"

Diane's smile was brilliant. "It seems like a good idea to me. Like you said, efficient." She turned on her heel. "I'll be right back."

She hurried out of the workroom and ran down the hall toward her bedroom.

"Diane." Catherine had just come in the front door. "I need to talk to you."

"Then come with me to my room. I have to get my equipment and take it to Eve's workroom." She threw open the door, went to the closet, and pulled out her suitcase. "I have to get to work. Eve says that she'll probably be starting on the final sculpture tomorrow, and I want to be there to help. But that DNA sample is—"

Catherine had grabbed her shoulders. "Listen. Cameron says that I can help draw Nalam's men away from the Calgary area and point them in another direction. It might give Eve more time to finish and get out of here sooner. But that means I'd have to leave you. Slade would be here on guard. Would that be okay with you until I can get back here?"

Diane's smile faded. "Nalam... Would you be safe?" Her gaze was raking Catherine's face. "You're excited. You want to do this?"

"I think it needs to be done, and Cameron will make it as safe as it can be. We've worked together before, and he's exceptional. But I won't do it if you want me to stay."

Diane suddenly smiled again. "Why would I want that? You'd be terribly bored. I'm going to be in that workroom with Eve for the next couple of days and I guarantee *I'm* not going to be bored." She gave her a quick hug and grabbed her DNA kit out of the bottom of her suitcase. She looked back at Catherine as she went out the door. "But I won't forgive Cameron if he gets you hurt. Tell him I'll go after him."

"I'm sure that will terrify him."

"It should. I don't have that many friends. I can be relentless."

She ran out of the room and down the hall.

Cameron was driving up to the porch when Catherine came out the front door. "Ah, all is well with my world?"

"It depends on how you look at it." She threw her duffel in the back and climbed into the passenger seat. "You got your way. But Diane issued dire threats if you get me hurt or killed. She said she's relentless. I laughed, but perhaps I should have taken her seriously. Look at what lengths she's gone to help her friend Alon."

"Oh, I take her very seriously. All that fire and determination when focused can move mountains. I'll be careful to keep you in one healthy and extremely gorgeous piece."

"That may not make her happy enough." She took out her phone. "But I've just thought of something that might." She started to punch in a number.

"Who are you calling?"

"Slade. I'm going to tell him to take Diane under his wing." She smiled at him. "And to get her a gun."

Diane stared down at the Glock in her hand. "It's big... isn't it?"

"Not as large as some. The Glock 19 is very reliable and efficient. Sorry, I don't have any guns in my arsenal that would be in the derringer category. You wouldn't want one if I did. You don't want a toy; you need a gun that can take care of business."

And that business was taking life, she thought with a shiver. Slade was probably very skilled at that business. "How many guns do you have?"

"I usually travel with four, but one is enough if it's the right fit." He put his hand over hers and closed it over the gun. "Get the feel of it. It's not loaded. While you're working tonight, leave it out where you can see it. Every now and then reach out and touch it."

"I don't think I'd be comfortable doing that." She made a face. "And I'm not sure Eve would like it."

"I don't believe she'd object. She's married to Quinn and has probably needed a gun of her own on occasion. Stop making excuses. Catherine told me to give you a gun and teach you how to use it. That's what I'm going to do. Tonight you become accustomed to the weapon, and tomorrow morning I take you out for your first lesson. After that, I'll never give you an unloaded gun again, because you'll know everything about how to handle and use it." He took his hand away. "Agreed?"

"Agreed." She looked down at the gun. "It just makes me feel...strange. I've never liked guns. They've always represented death to me, and I've spent so many years trying to save lives."

"Yet you told Catherine you wanted me to get you one." His gaze was searching her face. "If you've changed your mind, we can forget it. I promised I'd keep you safe. No problem."

"Very big problem. This evidently is my life now. In the end I can't rely on anyone but myself to keep assholes like Nalam from attacking me." Her hand tightened on the Glock. "So I'll learn how to use this thing. It's what I should do. Right?"

"Right," he said solemnly. "I admit I like the idea of you being able to blow someone out of the water if I'm not around to do it for you. Tomorrow morning at nine then?"

There was that wry humor again. She grinned. "Nine." Her hand tightened on the gun as she turned to go into Eve's studio. "Thanks, Slade. By tomorrow this will be my new best friend."

"No, it won't. That will be too soon." He was walking away from her. "But there might come a time when you'll get to that point. I sincerely hope not."

WOLF FLATS, CALGARY
3:35 A.M.

"Monteith's place is right around the next bend," Cameron told Catherine. "It's a nice little airport that he's built into a thriving business. But I'm approaching from the rear so we can get a look around and see if he has any visitors in the area. Keep an eye out."

She already was, but it was pitch dark and she couldn't make out anything.

Except perhaps...

"There's a car parked in that stand of trees overlooking the plateau." She pressed the window lever down to get a better look. "Looks like a black Chevrolet Suburban. Someone's behind the wheel and in the passenger seat. I can't make out the backseat. But there shouldn't be anyone out here in the middle of the night."

"And that's what they'd think about us if they saw us." Cameron made the turn and drove past a concrete helicopter pad and up the driveway toward a one-story office building. "I'd say they're either waiting to make a move or waiting for reinforcements. So that's why we're going to tuck the car around the back of the airport office until we're ready to make *our* move." As he parked, he punched in a number on his phone. "We're here, Monteith. You have company. A black Suburban. Are you still okay?"

"No problem. I've been keeping my eye on the Suburban." The front door was opening to reveal a small, thin man with curly red hair dressed in jeans and a navy sweatshirt. "It looks like the usual stakeout. Except for sending out a man to make certain I'm still here, they've been leaving me alone." He stepped aside as he saw Catherine getting out of the car and coming toward him. He gave a low whistle. "Hello, pretty lady. I imagine they'll be much more interested in you than they were in me. I'm Paul Monteith. Who are you?"

"Catherine Ling," Cameron answered for her. "And we're hoping that she'll have that effect. She's definitely what you might call a magnetic personality." He shook Monteith's hand and then nudged Catherine into the house. "But right now I think she can use some coffee. We're probably going to have to be on the road again soon."

"I was expecting that." Monteith gestured to the pot of coffee on the cabinet. "Anything else?"

"You can keep her company while I do a little reconnoitering." He held out his hand. "You got the pack?"

Monteith reached into his pocket and pulled out a small black cylinder. He hesitated. "I can do it, sir. You shouldn't have to bother with this."

"It's no bother. I need to stretch my legs." He grinned as he took the cylinder. "Though I appreciate the deference. I don't get much of that commodity from my friend Catherine."

"No, you don't." Catherine's gaze was on the cylinder. "What is that?"

"Just a small protective device that might come in handy at some future date. I thought I'd install it on the rear fender of the Suburban."

"You're going to get that near to it? That's some reconnoiter. I'll go with you."

"No, you won't," he said quietly. "One-man job. My job, not yours. I'll see you later."

He was gone.

She muttered an oath and started after him.

"Please, no." Monteith stepped in front of her. "He said he wants to do it alone." He smiled. "Don't make me try to stop you."

"I guarantee it would only be an attempt. Get out of my way."

"I'm sure you're right. But I'd still have to try. He wants you here and I have orders to keep you safe," he said. "Let me get you a cup of coffee."

She didn't want this to disintegrate into a battle. The delay had already made it dangerous for her to run after Cameron and risk interfering with his play. This poor guy was only obeying Cameron's orders like all the rest of the people who followed him so devotedly. "I'll take it up with Cameron," she said curtly. "Get me that cup of coffee. Black."

Monteith gave a sigh of relief as he hurried toward the cabinet. "Thanks. Sit down. Cameron doesn't ask much of me, and I don't want to blow it when he does." He brought the coffee back to her. "I'm sure he didn't need your help."

"I'm sure he didn't, either." No one was more competent than Cameron. Yet she had wanted to help him and had felt shut out when he'd left her here. "But I didn't come here to sit and drink coffee." She took a sip. "Even though it's very good. And I'm sure you do more for Cameron than you say. It was you he chose to do the drop-off at Naponi the other day. That was important to him."

He shrugged. "Like I said, it's not enough. He helped me build this airport and run this charter business on my own, and all he asks is that I be available when he needs me. I know how you felt when he wouldn't let you go with him. I should have done it for him." He frowned. "I don't know why he didn't let me."

"I do." She took another drink of coffee. "He gets bored. There are so many jobs that he won't allow himself to do because he thinks it's not fair to take the risk." She smiled mockingly. "Heaven forbid the uproar that would echo through the world if something happened to the great Richard Cameron."

"He *is* great, you know," Monteith said quietly. "And it's natural that we want to keep him safe. There's no one like him. He can't be replaced." He smiled. "Why else did you try to run after him to watch his back?"

"That's a good question." She got to her feet and went over to the window. There was a faint glow in the eastern sky, but it was still dark enough to give Cameron safe cover... if anything could be considered safe when he was that excruciatingly close to those sons of bitches. She was feeling sick to her stomach at the thought. Why the hell hadn't he let her go with him? "Maybe because I drank the Kool-Aid and sometimes he convinces me he's everything you say he is." She added, "But only sometimes." This was definitely one of those times, however. All she could think about in this moment was the scent of him, the way he smiled, the way she felt when he touched her. She had no idea why she was suddenly being bombarded by all those memories. It made no sense. Maybe it was because getting into the car tonight had instantly taken her back to all the excitement, the breathless exhilaration, the adventure, the wonder, the sheer sexual delight she had known with him through the years. The feeling that whatever she did it would never be as good if it wasn't with him. She closed her eyes. Dear God, when had all that emotion slipped beneath the barriers she had erected against him? Probably when the fear and panic had torn them aside. And the panic was still there, keeping those memories alive, making her relive all those other experiences with him. Because life could be so damnably short and Cameron always lived on the edge.

Don't think about it. Nothing is going to happen to Cameron. She was silent a moment and then said to Monteith, "That car was only a few miles away. I've worked with Cameron before and he's very quick. He'll have to be very careful, but it shouldn't take him long. I'd say thirty, forty minutes tops, and he'll be back. What do you think?"

"That sounds right," Monteith said gently. "Maybe a little longer."

"Perhaps fifty minutes." She moistened her lips. "No more than that."

Fifty minutes...

It was an hour and thirty-five minutes later when she saw Cameron striding up the driveway.

Thank God.

She felt dizzy with relief as she threw open the front door. "You must have lost your touch, Cameron. You should have taken me up on it when I offered you help."

"My life is a morass of missed opportunities," he said mockingly. "That's just another one. I take it you missed me."

"Not at all." Then she couldn't lie to him. She was too grateful to see him. Those last thirty minutes had been excruciating. "Of course I did. You were too damn long." Her hands clenched. "And I should have been there. Don't you dare do that to me again. Do you hear me? I didn't come along to sit here and wait."

"I hear you loud and clear. You're really upset." His gaze was narrowed on her expression. "I'll definitely take that under serious advisement. Would it help if I told you I didn't want to chance Daniels catching a glimpse of you before we were ready for him? I want him to be very tense and impatient."

"Yes, I'm upset. You took forever. Did something go wrong?"

He shook his head. "I just wanted to make certain to check numbers and identify. I had to be careful. There were five of them and they were on edge. Very restless and not particularly pleased to be stuffed in the same car while they looked the situation over." He headed over to the cabinet and poured himself a cup of coffee. "At one point, Daniels got out of the car and went over to the bushes and took a leak. It was very tempting..."

"Daniels *was* in the car?"

"Backseat. But when he got out, he was just a few feet from

where I was standing. If we hadn't zeroed in on using him to lead the charge when he saw you, I would have taken him out." He paused. "But as I said, everyone in that car was edgy and wanting to make a move. I don't think it will be long before they decide to pay us a visit." He turned to Monteith. "Why don't you go and monitor the situation? There's a sentry about sixty yards west of the Suburban. Watch out for him. Otherwise just give us a call when they decide to make their move."

Monteith nodded, obviously eager to escape the tension he could sense in the room. "Will do." He left the cottage.

"I'm afraid I offended another one of your faithful fans." Catherine watched him stride hurriedly down the driveway. "Too bad, but then there are so many of them wandering around." Her gaze shifted to the woods. "Why wait? Maybe we should go after them now."

He shook his head. "I know you're eager, but our philosophy has to be hit and run. And we don't hit until we can lead them down the garden path. It's better if they come after us."

She'd known that, but when he'd said that Daniels was in that car, she'd wanted to forget everything but going after him. "Dammit, I'm afraid you're right."

"But you don't want to admit it."

"Too many people tell you that you're right about everything. I prefer to be in the minority."

"But that would mean you're wrong, and I hate the idea that anyone would believe that about you." His smile had a hint of mischief. "So you'd better join the majority."

"You're being utterly ridiculous." But, incredibly, she still found her anger and indignation slipping away. Had they only been another defense to keep back the panic and pain that were still with her? "And I'm having problems with your bizarre sense of humor at the moment."

"Are you?" His smile faded. "I can see how you wouldn't be amused. I think I'm trying to balance what I was feeling out there tonight. It was dark, very dark." His forefinger was tracing the line of her upper lip. "I was so close... only a few feet away from him." His finger was now on her throat and moving over the place where the bullet had seared across the skin. "I wanted him to hurt. But it wouldn't have stopped there." She couldn't look away from him. She couldn't breathe. Her pulse was beating hard beneath that finger stroking her skin. He nodded. "So I came back here and then I saw those bruises again and thought what a fool I'd been not to do it anyway. I could have found another way that wouldn't have required him alive." Both hands were on her throat now. "So a balance was definitely required." He tilted her head, his thumbs gently massaging her throat. His tongue moved to her lower lip and outlined it with exquisite tenderness before he lifted his head again. "And I made it." She inhaled sharply as the heat moved through her. She should move. This had come out of nowhere. *No, don't lie to yourself. It's always been there.* It had just been brought into the forefront again by her wrenching fear and tension as she'd waited for him. It always would be there, and she was so terribly weary of fighting it.

She didn't move. She stood there and let the heat flow over her. He felt so *good*. It had been too long.

"Much too long," he whispered.

"Are you reading me?"

"No, you're overflowing like a beautiful fountain, every emotion sparkling diamond-bright. I'd be a fool to close you out." He kissed her, hot, deep, sensuous. "When I'm so glad to have you here like this again. I try to be patient, but it was so hard not to push this time." He kissed her throat. "It was bad out there in the world without you. I needed you."

"You don't need anyone."

"Then why do I keep coming back to you when you push me away? There has to be a reason, Catherine."

"I'm a good lay?"

"Superb. Yes, that must be it." He kissed her again, this time with exquisite tenderness. "Why now? Why the surrender? You were angry and then you weren't. Tell me, so that next time I'll know what to do to make it come sooner."

"Perhaps I'm tired of fighting it right now," she said huskily. "I know I'm not being smart. I *was* doing the right thing. Maybe next time I'll make it."

"You could be more generous to me. I need it. We're going to have a rough time before this is over."

It was the second time he'd used the word *need*. There were many things she didn't know about him; perhaps this was one. She moved instinctively to give to him. "Then I'll repeat something Monteith said that will please your vanity. There's no one like you, Cameron." Her arms tightened around him and she whispered, "Not for me. And I'm afraid there never will be. Though I'll try very hard."

"I know you will. Thank you, anyway. And you don't have to tell me that once you gather all that cool practicality together, you'll say goodbye again. Today and tomorrow are good enough for me." He kissed her again. "I'm lying, but it will make you feel a little safer." He pushed her away. "But I can't touch you right now because I'll pull you down and make love to you. I refuse to do that when Daniels is such a bastard, I know he'd interrupt us." He slid his arm around her waist and led her toward the table. "So we'll sit down and have a cup of coffee together. I'll look at you and you'll tell me what you've been doing with your life these months since I saw you last. I'll take advantage of these minutes when all the barriers are down between us. Your memories will be my memories. It will make me feel more a part of you . . ."

CHAPTER 13

NAPONI

"You're ready, aren't you?" Diane murmured as Eve came back into the workroom the next morning. "You're going to go for the final?"

"Ready as I'll ever be." Eve sat down at her worktable and stared at the skull. "At least I was able to rest my eyes after laying those clay strips. I tried to nap, but that didn't work out. Maybe because he's ready, too."

"That sounds a little spooky."

"It depends on how you look at it . . . or what you believe in. I've always looked upon my work as trying to bring the lost home. The soul of anyone this savagely murdered must be truly lost. Perhaps he's looking desperately for his way."

Diane smiled faintly. "And not letting you sleep?"

"It's a thought. Or perhaps I'm just worrying who I'm going to see when I finish." She frowned. "I know you don't want it to be Kai. Neither do I. The idea of that young man who loved life so much ending up like this breaks my heart. But I have to do what I have to do."

"I can't be that philosophical." Diane's lips twisted. "Because it will break Alon's heart, too. I've got to pray that won't happen. I can't let myself care about anyone else but him." She cleared her throat. "What can I do to help?"

"Nothing." Eve looked back at the reconstruction. "It's between the two of us now. You have the Kai photo?"

Diane nodded at her briefcase on the desk where she'd been working all night. "You said you didn't want to see it."

"But I will when I've finished. I'll have to be sure." She reached out and touched the cheekbone of the reconstruction. "Did you get that DNA gadget Hu Chang gave you to work?"

"I don't know. I have a little bit more to do. I did the best I could. We'll have to see." She went still. "Unless you want to forget about doing the final reconstruction and let me keep on trying for the DNA? I know how much work you've already done on it."

Eve's brows lifted in surprise. "After you told me how important it was to give Alon both proofs to convince him? How noble. Why this change of heart?"

"It *is* important." Diane looked at the reconstruction. "I think I'm feeling guilty. I've made you go through so much already."

"And if I agreed?"

"I'd probably beg you not to pay any attention to me and just finish the reconstruction. Because I'd also feel guilty if you didn't do it."

Eve shook her head. "Impossible." She smiled. "So the best thing to do is for me to do whatever I want to do? Which I intend to do anyway."

Diane nodded. "That would be a big help to me."

"There's no way I could stop now." She nodded at the reconstruction. "He wouldn't let me."

Diane breathed a sigh of relief. "Then you do your part. I'll do mine." She went over to her desk and sat down. "I'll be here if you need me. Anything. Everything." She leaned back in the chair. "Did I tell you how much this means to me?"

"You might have mentioned it a time or two," Eve said absently. "Now be quiet, Diane."

She closed her out, her gaze and attention focused entirely on the skull.

Here we are. I've done all the measuring so I'm not going to make a stupid mistake. But there are other kinds of mistakes that come from me not knowing who you are inside. I'm going to do my best, but you've got to help, too. There are things that only you can tell me.

She reached out and touched the curve of his cheek. *We'll start here . . .*

She carefully smoothed the clay.

Cool to the touch.

Every movement sensitive.

Don't be in a hurry to start out. That will come later.

But it didn't matter what she told herself. Her hands were moving faster anyway.

Her fingers were warmer now as they molded the clay.

Don't think. Just feel.

Help me.

Go to the ears. They had to be generic. She had no idea if they stuck out or had long lobes. Just feel.

The nose. Ordinary length and width.

Though if it was Kai, it probably would be long and well shaped as Diane had described the classic Hakali features.

Don't think of that. Go with her first instinct.

On to the mouth. Generic again. She knew the width but not the shape. No smile. Yet Diane said according to Alon, Kai was always smiling. Don't let that make a difference. Make the lips without expression.

Don't touch the orbital cavity of the eyes yet. She always did the eyes last.

Go back to the cheeks.

Smooth.

Mold.

Fill.

She was moving faster now; her hands were hot. The clay also seemed hot, almost as if it were coming to life.

Slow down. She was getting too excited. She was beginning to visualize. This was also a science.

Check the measurements.

Nose width, 32mm. Okay.

Nose projection, 19mm. Okay.

Lip height, 13mm. Wrong. It should be 12. Bring the top lip down, it's usually thinner than the bottom lip.

Build up more around that mouth, there's a major muscle under there.

Do one more check and then she'd allow herself to let go.

She could feel the excitement building. Her pulse was pounding. We're not there yet, but we're on our way.

Now help me, dammit!

WOLF FLATS, CALGARY

It was barely getting light when Cameron's phone rang.

"That's Monteith." Cameron accessed the call while he jumped to his feet. "It's a go?" He got his answer and jerked his head at Catherine as he strode toward the door. "Come on. They're on the move. They'll be here any minute."

Catherine was already past him and throwing open the door. "You bring the car. I'll wait for you outside."

"The hell you will."

"That's why I'm here. Daniels has to see me. Isn't that what you said? Go get the car."

Cameron muttered a curse. Then he was gone.

Catherine ran outside. Bright sunlight. Good. *Get a good view, Daniels. Here I am.*

And there they were. The black Chevrolet Suburban was roaring down from the plateau toward her. She heard a shout from the vehicle. Daniels? She wasn't about to wait around to find out. She ran across the road as Cameron came around the corner.

"Go!" She jumped in the passenger side. She was hurled back against the seat before she could put on her seat belt as Cameron took off. "I think he saw me."

"No doubt about it," he said grimly. "You made sure of it." He stomped on the accelerator as he glanced in the rearview mirror. "Hold on. It may be a wild ride."

"Do you want me to drive? If Daniels can see that I'm driving it might make him—"

"I don't want you to drive. Suddenly the idea of using you as bait doesn't appeal to me anymore."

"It was a good idea. It's still a good idea. You know it, Cameron." She looked back over her shoulder. "They didn't stop at the helicopter pad. Monteith is going to be able to get it out with no problem. What do we do now?"

"I did a little advance planning before we left Naponi. Get the folded map out of the glove box."

A minute later she was unfolding the map and gazing at the multitude of marks drawn on it. She gave a low whistle. "And we're supposed to do all this? It's going to take up most of the day."

"Isn't that the point?"

"Yeah. I just didn't realize it was going to be a marathon." She gazed over her shoulder and frowned. "But I think they're gaining on us. Are you doing that on purpose?"

"Of course. Why else would I have gone to the bother?" He

looked at the mirror. "Time to speed up a little. Let's make them work for it."

Cameron gunned the engine and turned left onto an off-road path. The wheels spun and kicked mud as they traveled along a slight incline.

Catherine glanced back. "They just left the road."

"Good. They'll be able to follow us, but it'll take them longer. It'll give us the time we need."

Catherine held up the map. "For this?"

"Exactly."

Cameron followed the trail as it sloped around the long hillside, out of view of their pursuers. He abruptly stopped. "Okay, we're getting out."

"Here?"

He threw open his car door. "Yes, we're heading out on foot. Run toward those rock formations on the left. We need to be on the other side of those by the time they make it up here. Stay on the pine straw and don't make tracks."

Catherine jumped out of the car and followed him toward the rock formations. "They'll be here in less than two minutes. Everything else on that map doesn't work if they follow us up there."

"They won't follow us."

"How can you be so sure?"

"Watch and be amazed."

She shook her head. "Arrogant prick."

They crawled over the rock formations and hugged the ground, positioning themselves so that they could watch their abandoned vehicle from behind the rocks. After another minute, the Suburban came into view.

It stopped about twenty yards from their car. The occupants were clearly sizing up the situation before making their move. After another minute, all four doors flew open and Daniels and three other men jumped out and circled the vehicle. Satisfied that no one was inside, they began to look around the surrounding area.

Daniels crouched beside the path, taking the squat assumed by master trackers in nature documentaries.

"Seriously?" Catherine whispered.

Daniels stood and pointed off to the east, away from the rock formations. The men held up their assault rifles and followed him into a clump of trees and brush.

Catherine turned to face Cameron. "What just happened?"

He smiled. "I told you I had to lay the groundwork. I know this countryside. I gave Monteith exact instructions on what to do on this stretch. He flattened the tall grass near the trail and walked out far enough to leave a path for them to follow. I even had him snag a couple of fresh threads on the branches out there."

She nodded. "Okay, I admit it. I am impressed."

"Wow. I believe that was a compliment."

"Maybe. It depends on how much time all this convoluted planning got us."

"About ninety minutes. They'll reach a plateau that'll give them a view for miles. That's where the great white hunter will realize he's been had and will double back to look for us. But by then we'll have already engaged our next alternate mode of transportation."

Catherine patted the folded-up map. "The next stop on our tour?"

He grinned. "You know it. Let's roll."

NAPONI

Smooth.

Mold.

Fill.

She was on fire, Eve realized. Her fingers were flying over the clay. Only it didn't seem to be clay any longer. It was changing, almost taking on a life of its own.

She was almost there.

Small changes. Sun lines around the eye cavities. No, not deep enough. Deeper. Almost fanlike.

More shaping in the nostrils.

Smooth.

Mold.

Fill in.

The nostrils weren't right. A slight flare.

Now a little creasing on either side. How deep?

It didn't matter. Only a little.

Smooth.

Mold.

Deep lines on either side of the mouth.

Almost there.

She was working with feverish intensity.

Smooth.

Mold.

Fill in.

She drew a deep breath.

Done.

No, not quite. It was time for the eyes.

She reached in the drawer and got out her eye case and flipped it open. Blue, green, gray, hazel, brown eyeballs glittered up at her. Brown eyes were the most common. She hesitated, her fingers hovering over the lighter selections. No, go for what was the most common. She carefully inserted the brown eyes in the orbital cavities.

Now she was done.

Her eyes were stinging, and she closed them. She was totally exhausted. In another moment she'd push back the chair and look at him, but she had to give herself that time.

"Eve." Diane was standing behind her. "You're finished?" She was looking at the reconstruction and tears were running down her cheeks. "Tell me you're finished."

Tears. That could only mean one thing. Eve nodded. "I'm sorry. I did what I had to do. I didn't want it to be him."

"Didn't you?" She dropped to her knees beside Eve's chair and put her arm around her. Her voice was shaking. "Then it's a good thing it isn't Kai. Look at him, Eve." She handed her the photo of Kai. "I was standing behind you watching you finish, and I couldn't believe it. But, oh, how I wanted to believe it."

Eve looked down at the photo of a young man with long tawny hair, green eyes, and a gentle smile that lit his face with joy. He might have been in his early twenties, but there was a boyish wonder about him that made him appear younger. Then she lifted her gaze to the reconstruction she had just completed. This man had been a good twenty years older than Kai. The creases and sun lines she'd sculpted made his face appear weathered. The flared nostrils gave him a Slavic aura vastly different from Kai's gentle good looks. "The photo is really Kai?"

Diane nodded. "Alon gave it to me."

"Then who is this?" She was looking back at the reconstruction. He had a bold, hard face, not particularly good looking, but she knew every line in that face.

"It doesn't matter," Diane said. "As long as it isn't Kai."

"It matters," Eve said grimly. "Because I didn't want him to be Kai. In the beginning of the reconstruction I had to stop myself from slanting the sculpting in that direction. I was sure I'd made the correction, but what if I didn't? What if I sculpted what I wanted to see in this reconstruction?"

"You wouldn't do that."

"I don't think I would, either, but I have to be sure." She looked at Diane. "And so do you. You have to know the truth, too. Isn't that why you brought that Magic Box?"

"Yes, but now you've scared me. It was just supposed to be a final verification."

"And that's what it is."

Diane suddenly nodded. "And that's all it is." She got brusquely to her feet. "You're too good to make a mistake. So let's get this DNA hoopla out of the way so I can call Alon." She moved quickly around to her own desk where she'd set up the DNA decoder. "I've got it adjusted and ready to go." She checked the power source. "The only thing that might hold us back is if that sliver is too small to be read. But Hu Chang said the machine is incredibly sensitive." She drew a deep breath. "Here we go." Then she pressed the lever.

Nothing happened.

"Shit."

"I agree," Eve said. "It seems Hu Chang is wrong."

Then the machine started to whir!

"Thank heavens," Diane said, relieved. "I thought I did something wrong."

"God forbid you blame Hu Chang." Eve got up and came to look down at the machine. "How long is this supposed to take?"

"I'm not sure. It's supposed to be super quick, but the ID process might have to access several different lists worldwide. We'll just have to wait and see."

"Well, there's no way I'm going to stand here staring down at this machine with fingers crossed." Eve turned away. "You monitor the darn thing. I'm going to go find Joe."

"You do that," Diane said, absently looking at the numbers on the machine's dial. "I'll let you know." Then she raised her gaze to Eve's face. "And you didn't make a mistake. You're not listening to me, but Joe will tell you. He'll make it right."

"I'm not looking for reassurance. I just want to *see* him."

Diane nodded slowly. "And share whatever there is to share."

"Right." Eve was already hurrying out of the workroom.

She found Joe on the porch and walked straight into his arms. "Hi, I was looking for you."

His arms tightened around her. "Finished?"

"My part." She nestled her cheek against his chest. "It wasn't Kai. Diane is checking on the DNA. I might have screwed up."

"You didn't." He smiled down at her. "You don't do things like that."

"Diane said you'd say that. She said you'd make it right."

"Really? What a statement of confidence. She's been surprising me lately. And am I?"

"You're making me feel better now that I have you here with me. That's a given. If I did screw up, I'm the only one who can make that right. I just wish that DNA genius-machine would put on some speed. I want this over."

"You told me it was supposed to be far superior to the one we use at the precinct. If that's true, it will be done quickly and be completely accurate." He pushed her back and cupped her face in his two hands. "And then you'll know what an idiot you were not to believe in yourself." He kissed the tip of her nose. "You saw the photo?"

"Of course." She pulled out the photo she'd stuffed in her pocket and showed it to him. "Such a sweet expression, full of joy. I'm glad I didn't see it before. I had enough trouble keeping the thought of him from interfering. It reminded me of Michael."

"Yes, it does. That same boundless enthusiasm for life." He stared down at the photo. "I gave Michael a call while I was waiting for the great unveiling. He's still disapproving, but he's doing as well as can be expected with Cara. He wanted to talk to you."

She nodded. "I'll call him. At least I can tell him that we're making progress."

"Speak for yourself." He grimaced. "I'm twiddling my thumbs and guarding the gates." He looked back down at the photo again. "And developing a thorough detestation of Joshua Nalam. I believe that something has to be done about that son of a bitch very soon. I'm glad that you've wrapped up the reconstruction."

"Maybe," Eve said.

"Positively," Diane said from behind her.

Eve whirled to face her. "You got it?"

"It came in right after you left." She was beaming. "I told you that you hadn't made a mistake. Generally I hate I-told-you-sos, but this is an exception. I bet Joe told you the same thing."

"Except he called me an idiot." She took a step toward her. "Stop congratulating yourself and tell me who that man was that I've spent days working on."

"Very rude, Joe. I wouldn't have dared to insult her like that." Diane held up her hand as Eve took another step toward her. "Okay. Okay. I did tell you what was most important. According to his DNA, the man on whom you did the reconstruction was Willem Tesar, born in Austria. When the machine pulled up a very scanty ID report, it stated his age as fifty-two, gave a Los Angeles driver's license, and referred other questions to Interpol. I printed out the driver's license." She handed Eve the sheet of paper. "You did a much better job than the photographer at the license bureau, but it's definitely him."

"Yes." Eve took one glance at the photo and then ran toward the workroom. She skidded to a stop in front of the reconstruction and held up the photo. She drew a relieved breath. She'd clearly created a sculpture of Willem Tesar.

"Satisfied?" Diane had followed her into the workroom. "You did good, Eve."

"Yes, I did." She was still staring at Tesar's reconstruction. "But that DNA report could have told us more about him."

"It pointed us in the right direction. Interpol. Evidently Tesar was one of Nalam's crooked cohorts who displeased him. Get Joe to check him out if you want more info."

"I'll follow up on it," Joe said as he came into the workroom. "But I don't think there's any great hurry. Nalam obviously just used his death as a convenience to taunt Alon Hakali."

"Fine," Diane said. "Anything you like." She was heading for the door. "Since that's settled, I've got to go and tell Alon that Kai is alive." She made a face. "Even though that's probably going to cause more trouble trying to figure out how we can keep him that way..."

Eve turned immediately to Joe. "There is a hurry about Tesar," she said quietly. "I did that reconstruction. In a way, that makes him my responsibility. I don't care if he was crooked or not. He was murdered by Nalam, and he deserves to be brought home as soon as possible. Find out if he had family, Joe."

"Of course," he said gently as he took out his phone. "But there are a couple more urgent calls I need to make before I call Interpol. We should let Catherine and Cameron know that you've completed the reconstruction. They can stop trying to stall Nalam's men and keep them from searching in our direction." He was punching in Catherine's number. "And we should tell them to get the hell back here so that we can make some decisions." He listened and then suddenly frowned. "Catherine's call just went to voicemail."

"They're getting closer," Catherine yelled as she and Cameron crossed a brook and ran toward an open field. They'd followed Cameron's map precisely for most of the day, leading Daniels and the others on a bewildering cat-and-mouse chase through the entire area. But the chase was ending, and they were timing their movements so that they could be spotted by Nalam's men after they'd returned to the Suburban. The vehicle was now gaining on them.

"All part of the plan." Cameron looked over his shoulder. "Every minute they're out here buys Eve more time to finish that skull. But it's almost time to stage the misdirection."

"Good." Catherine was looking up at the clear sky. "There was a helicopter drawn on your map. Where in the hell is it?"

"Patience."

"I have plenty of patience. I'm not sure about those guys with the assault weapons."

Cameron paused. "Hear that?"

"Hear what?"

Before he could reply a helicopter rose from behind the hillside!

It swung closer to them and Catherine could see Monteith at the controls. The helicopter touched down.

BLAM! BLAM! BLAM!

Gunfire erupted from the car behind them.

Cameron fought the wind of the helicopter blades and managed to get the door open. He lifted Catherine and threw her into the aircraft. "Get out of here," he yelled at Monteith as he dove into the helicopter. "They're right on top of us."

Another bullet hit the door as Monteith lifted off and headed south.

Another shot!

Catherine pulled herself up and was looking out the window at Nalam's men below. They were all out of the Suburban and shooting at them. She could see Daniels aiming his rifle carefully at the helicopter. *Shit.* He'd had a rifle at Belazo's place, too, she remembered. He probably knew what he was doing with the weapon. "He'll aim at the gas tank," she shouted to Monteith. "Dip south!"

Monteith dipped down as a bullet hit the underside of the helicopter. He veered left and then took on altitude. Within minutes they were out of range.

"Which direction?" Monteith asked.

"Straight east," Cameron said. "Keep low enough so that they see we're definitely heading east. Then when we're out of sight, make a turn and go west to Naponi."

It was over.

Catherine could no longer see Daniels, but she could still visualize him standing there aiming that damn rifle. Her heart was beating hard, and her adrenaline was still running high from those last minutes in the field. She turned to Cameron and grinned. "Nalam is going to be disappointed. What a pity."

He smiled back at her. "You enjoyed yourself. I'm glad I could show you a good time."

"You usually do. But I'd be even happier if I could see Nalam raking Daniels over the coals."

"That might be arranged, but this isn't the right time. We have to get back to Naponi."

Naponi. Catherine was jerked back to reality and instinctively looked down at her phone. "I have a voicemail." She started to access the message. "Somehow I missed the call."

"Now, I wonder how that happened?" Cameron murmured. "Do you think they'll understand when you explain?"

NAPONI

"You can't do it, Alon," Diane said desperately. "Not yet. You've got to give me time to work this out."

"I can't *not* do it," Alon said. "And time is running out. You know that, Diane. You told me that Kai is still alive, and I'm grateful to you and Eve Duncan for giving me that gift. It brought me hope. But how long will he stay alive now? Nalam is full of rage and he hates me. He may have kept Kai alive to use him to torture and hurt me, but now he's been frustrated and that torture will increase." His voice hoarsened with pain. "I can't *bear* it. And I don't know how much Kai can bear. He doesn't understand any of it; no one has ever treated him like this. He may just want to escape it, and then he'll die even if Nalam doesn't intend to kill him at that particular moment. I have to get him out."

Diane hesitated. She didn't want to do this. "You know that just because the skull wasn't Kai, it doesn't mean he's still alive."

"But there's a chance. Why else would Nalam go to that much trouble to try to fool me?"

She wasn't going to be able to persuade him. "How? Are you still on the island? What are you planning?"

"What I've been planning all along. I'm going to attack that encampment in Montana as soon as possible. I'm on the island and I've been talking to my people here and they want to help. Kai is our family and everyone loves him. It won't be enough, but I've been contacting other friends I've made over the years who are more trained in what's necessary. They're on their way here. I'll pull together a plan and we'll go get him."

"You make it sound simple," she said in despair. "It's not going to be simple, Alon. Those men Nalam has on his payroll are criminals, and they know what he expects of them."

"And I know what he expects, too. No, it won't be simple. I won't go into this blindly. I have family and friends to protect. But I spent days watching that camp and I know it like I do the back of my hand. I know the times the sentries go on duty. I know the time the prisoners are fed. That will be an advantage." He paused and then said gently, "Don't worry, Diane. Look, we're not trained thugs like Nalam's men in that camp, but most of us grew up on the island and we're strong and smart and we'll give everything we have. The plan will come together. I'll get Kai back."

"I know how smart you are. Hell, I realize how much you've taught me. But this might take something more. Take a little time and let me help and we'll—"

"Hush," he interrupted softly. "I told you that time's almost up. I can't thank you enough for what you've done for me. But now you have to let me go so that I can do my part."

"The hell I do."

"Diane."

She knew that tone. He wasn't going to be moved by anything she could say. "Don't leave me like this. Promise you'll let me know before you leave the island."

"It will only upset you." He sighed when she didn't answer. "How stubborn you are. I promise I will think about it. Goodbye, my friend."

He cut the connection.

"Damn. Damn. Damn." She took a deep breath and wiped the tears from her cheeks as she turned away and started to run back into the house. She almost collided with Slade, who was leaning against the doorjamb. "Sorry. I didn't see you." She took the handkerchief he handed her and dabbed at her damp cheeks. "As a matter of fact, I don't remember seeing you since yesterday. Where have you been?"

"Around." He smiled slightly. "I assure you, I've made certain I've been seeing you. You were clearly busy and I didn't want to disturb you. I promised you that you wouldn't know I was here."

"Well, you kept your word. Why are you here now?" She held up his handkerchief. "To supply a need?"

"And ask if I can help. Though I was debating whether to offer the handkerchief. I thought you might resent it. But Quinn said that everything had worked out well with the reconstruction, so I thought that I might be able to help straighten out what else had gone wrong." He paused. "Your friend Alon? He wasn't happy?"

"He was ecstatic. For about three minutes. Then he started to think about what he needed to do to keep Nalam from killing Kai and how he was going to get him away from that camp."

"I can see that. It's the obvious next step. How?"

"He hasn't a clue yet," she said in frustration. "He said he knows the camp and the sentry schedules, and he has his family and friends to help him. He said a plan would come together eventually."

"Sometimes that happens."

"I know that. And Alon is brilliant and intuitive and brave and has a hundred other qualities that might make it happen." She added desperately, "But the odds are against him and he's not going to let me help. He said I'd done my part and I should let him do his."

"Did you mention Nalam's call to you?"

"No, why would I do that? It would just have upset him more."

"It's a mistake to try to protect him from the truth. I know I'd like to be filled in on every move of Nalam's."

"Not if it would make him even more stubborn. How could I do that? You don't know how special he is. I *have* to help him."

"Like you had to go get the file at that warehouse in Manila."

"Which I screwed up. All the more reason for me to help him now."

"I believe your reasoning is a little faulty. But you'd probably be looking for an excuse anyway. I hope you appreciate what a good sounding board I made." He tilted his head and studied her. "No more tears. I suppose you've decided that they don't do any good and you're ready to start thinking." He gave a low whistle. "Heaven help us."

"That's not funny."

"I rather think it's amusing." He smiled and his expression was suddenly lit with mischief. "It's very interesting to watch you and guess what's going to be next on your agenda. But evidently, I can't help at the moment, so I'll fade into the background again. If you come up with anything that you need to talk about, I'm always at your disposal." He stepped aside as she went past him through the doorway. "And so is my handkerchief."

"I won't need either. And I'll return the handkerchief." She went down the hall toward her bedroom. She needed to wash her face and then just have a few minutes to herself. That short time with Slade had been strange; she couldn't decide if he had been sympathetic or merely curious. Either way, it had been good for her to get out all that frustration and stored-up terror. Now with a clear head she could concentrate on whatever she must do.

But perhaps that had been his intention...

Diane saw the blue lights of Monteith's helicopter two hours later and she walked out to greet them as they set down. She gave Catherine a hug as Cameron took Monteith to the bunkhouse. "Joe said Cameron thought everything went well. How do you feel about it?"

"Good. We definitely bought the time we needed. And we don't have to worry about Nalam knocking on our front door. Since Eve's finished the reconstruction, we should be able to get both of you safely out of here. That will be a relief."

"I can see how you'd feel like that." Her gaze was following Cameron, who had paused at the bunkhouse door to talk to Monteith. "You got along well working with Cameron?"

"Yes." She was suddenly smiling. "I told you that we never had trouble working together. We just sometimes have differences of opinion later."

"Not this time." Diane's gaze was narrowed on her face. "You have a . . . glow. I'd bet you were of the same opinion most of the time."

"Maybe." Catherine's smile faded. "But that doesn't change anything as far as my job is concerned. I'm back now, and you're my only responsibility. I take it Slade took good care of you."

"Absolutely. Just the way I prefer it. I didn't even know he was around until he showed up tonight after all the hoopla was over. But he assured me that he hadn't forgotten me."

"And where's Eve?"

"I hope she's asleep. Joe whisked her off to bed right after we finished the reconstruction. She was totally exhausted."

"From what Joe told me on the phone, I imagine both of you were."

"She had the roughest part. It was tearing her apart. I don't know how she keeps doing it."

"How do you keep working? Your work is a passion to you, too. It's the same process."

Diane shook her head. "The work and total dedication maybe. But hers goes above and beyond. There are all kinds of nuances I never dreamed existed."

Catherine was silent. "I've always realized that. I didn't know you had."

"I finally got there. No one can say I'm a slow learner." She grimaced. "Except when my emotions get in the way." She paused. "You've got to take care of her. While I was waiting for you, I came out here on the porch and I was thinking. Nalam is going to want to punish everyone connected with this. He's so full of venom that he's going to spew it in all directions. I'm betting he's made a list and is checking it twice. He knows that Eve was the key to exploding that lie he told Alon about Kai and spoiled his plan to cause maximum pain. That makes her high on the enemy list."

"Not as high as you," Catherine said grimly. "You were pretty high before because he knew you were in Alon's corner. But the minute he found out about the panacea, you were promoted to the stratosphere. I'm going to have my hands full taking care of you. She has Joe, and he's more than enough."

"Situations change." They had reached the porch, and she stopped. "I just want to make sure she's going to be taken care of. I brought her into this and she's my responsibility. All of this is my responsibility. So will you be sure to keep her safe?"

"Of course I will," she said impatiently. "She's my best friend, almost family. You don't have to ask me that."

"I thought I did. Right now everything in my world has to be very cut-and-dried."

"Well, you must be as tired as Eve if you can't understand something as basic as friendship. Why don't you come in and go to bed?"

Diane shook her head and dropped down on one of the chairs. "You go ahead. I think I'll stay outside for a while."

Catherine frowned. "Why?"

Diane hesitated. "I'm waiting."

"Waiting for what?"

Another pause. "Nalam is going to call me."

Catherine froze. "What? How do you know?"

"I've been thinking about him. Going over everything I've learned about him. He's not going to be able to resist striking out at me personally after you made Daniels and his other men look weak and ineffectual. I'm the target now, and he won't be able to rest until he does something that hurts me. Even if it's only hurling insults and threats."

"Shit."

"No, that may be a good thing. It may take the heat off Kai and Alon." She frowned. "Or it might not. It's difficult to know which way he'll jump. Maybe I'll be able to judge when I'm talking to him. Or maybe it won't be difficult at all, and he'll tell me what particular punishment he has in mind for me."

"You already know," she said roughly. "He told you and scared you so badly you made me have Slade get you a gun."

"And he taught me how to use it. I'm not bad. He said I'd get better with practice." She wearily leaned her head on the back of the chair. "Maybe that's the way I should go."

"Don't even think of it."

"I can't think of anything else. Alon isn't going to let me help him if he has his way." Her lips tightened. "So he can't have his way. I just have to figure a way to handle this."

"Maybe Nalam isn't as focused on you as you believe."

"Oh, he's focused. He'll probably be calling me soon."

"Then I'll sit here with you and we'll see if he does."

"No, you won't. You'll go to bed and let me handle Nalam on my own. I can't always run to you or Slade. Nalam shook me the last time. I'm not accustomed to dealing with assholes like him. I've got to learn how to take everything he throws at me and not let it hurt me."

"I can't leave you alone."

"I won't be alone. Slade is always somewhere around; he just keeps out of my way."

"I probably won't sleep anyway."

"Then you'll be awake when I come to your room and tell you how well I was dealing with him."

"Diane."

"Good night, Catherine."

Catherine gave a sigh of resignation.

Then Diane heard the door shut behind her. She tried to relax her tense muscles. It could be that Catherine had been right and Nalam wouldn't call tonight. But every instinct was telling her that he would, and if she didn't take the call and say the right things then something terrible might happen. But how could you say the right things to a monster?

Take deep breaths and sit here and don't think of anything but the fact that they'd beaten him today when Eve had finished that reconstruction. He'd lost again when Catherine and Cameron had led his men on that wild chase. Think of the victories and not the challenges of facing that son of a bitch.

Because her phone was ringing now and when she picked up the call that monster challenge would be there.

"Hello, Nalam. I hear you didn't have a good day?"

"Don't mock me, bitch." His voice was a savage snarl. "You'll pay for every spiteful word you say to me. I'll remember every one of them. Alon Hakali has learned that lesson and so will you."

"He didn't learn anything other than that you're a coward. You sneak around and hire those goons to do your dirty business and then hide behind them. Like you did when you sent Daniels after me. Like you did when you burned down Salkara Island and killed Alon's mother."

"You fool, don't you know that's always the privilege of power? A few rule and others do their bidding. It's been that way since the beginning of civilization. Why should I run any risk if I can hire others to do it for me?" He paused. "And some fight that privilege and end up as you will, Diane. You didn't know what you did when you went up against me. Those friends of yours might have won a minor battle today, but I'm already starting to punish them for it. First, that nice little airport Monteith owned? I ordered it blown up. I was just waiting to call you before I told Daniels to press the button.

Ah, there it is. *Kaboom.* Very satisfying. Did you hear it? Too bad you can't be here to see it. The flames are such a pretty sight."

A ripple of shock went through her. She *had* heard it, and the violence of the action had shaken her. "I imagine you usually find pain and destruction to your taste."

"That's very perceptive of you. For instance, I'm beginning to anticipate all the many ways I can make you hurt before I actually attack you physically. I did some research on you after I discovered what a horror you were going to be to me. For a scientist, you appear to be both very emotional and ridiculously sentimental to devote yourself to healing as well as medical research. It's a weakness I can take advantage of. No one you care about is safe from me. I prefer to use torture, but a sniper bullet is always a second option. I knew you must have a relationship with Alon Hakali if he could talk you into stealing that file for him. But who would have thought that you'd also maintain an attachment to an ex-husband and his wife that was so strong you could persuade them to do a dangerous thing like getting in my way? Naturally, they'll pay for that foolishness. And Daniels can't wait to get his hands on Catherine Ling. I'm going to let him take a long time with her. I'm very annoyed about her luring the idiot on that chase today. Who else? Oh, Daniels said that there was a little boy at the hospital that night. Duncan's child? Yes, I must include him. Children can be very entertaining, and their torture would have such an agonizing effect on a woman like you."

"Are you finished?" She was trying to smother the anger and fear. "I'm not impressed by your threats."

"Oh, then I'll get down to a threat that will impress you. You've probably had time for Duncan to have finished that reconstruction, and you know that Kai Hakali is still alive. I was going to keep Alon Hakali dangling for a little while longer until I found just the right moment to kill him—the one that would give me the ultimate pleasure."

She couldn't breathe. She swallowed hard. "And has that time come?"

"Actually, I believe it has. But not in the way I thought it would. I'm going to offer him his brother's life if he'll trade you for him."

"What?"

Nalam chuckled. "But can't you see? It's truly the ultimate solution for me. I get rid of that simple-minded boy who has been boring me lately. Alon Hakali truly loves his brother but he's going to writhe in an agony of guilt that he has to give up his lover to get him back."

"We're not lovers."

"Of course you are. Why else would you risk your life to rob me? And when I saw your photo, I was considering fucking you until I realized what an abomination you are. Sex is the only answer."

It probably was for him, she thought. "It doesn't matter what you think. You'll have to find a better way to bargain with Alon."

"But there is no better way," he said softly. "You're what I want and need. Power is everything, and once I've persuaded you to give me those shots that power will last indefinitely. I've even been planning on how I can use it to open another, even more profitable door. You'll be a much better toy than Kai has been, and at the end when I kill you, I'll be removing a threat that could ruin me. It's absolutely perfect."

"Except that Alon is an honorable man, and even if he could, he'd never strike a bargain like that. You're insane to think he would."

"There's a chance he'd do it. Though I'd never make the trade, I could tell by how upset he'd get when I was punishing Kai that he really cares about him. If he didn't do it, I'd still win. Because if he's as honorable as you say, he'd be tortured that he'd killed his brother because he didn't want to give up his whore."

"I'm not his—"

"But there's still another way I could win." His voice took on even more malice. "You could strike the deal with me yourself. I'm sure you're such a noble, caring person that you'd be willing to sacrifice yourself to save him. Alon would always have such good memories of you. But if he knows you refused, I doubt if he'd ever be able to look at you again."

"You're completely crazy."

"No, I've just come up with a plan that would splinter out in all the directions that would hurt the most." He laughed. "It's brilliant. I'll give you a few days to talk to Alon and think about it. Then I'll send you both a Skype that will be the last you'll see of Kai. He'll be in tremendous pain and you won't enjoy it." His voice was suddenly harsh. "But that's only if I haven't tracked you down before that time. I've told my men they'll get a million-dollar bonus if they bring you to me, and they didn't like the other alternative I gave them. They're very eager to please." He paused. "So you can see that you didn't win anything today. You only gave me more motivation, bitch."

He cut the connection.

She couldn't move for a moment. She felt as if she'd been physically beaten. All the ugliness that he'd been hurling had been stunning. It had been worse than that first call. He had been raving and yet there had been a clear, cold, almost logical malice that had cut like a knife. That logic had been purely from his twisted viewpoint and was as evil as the mind that had created it. She had to absorb what he'd said, all the threats, anything that might be of value, but it was difficult. Her mind was whirling... She'd be all right, she told herself. Just a little more time...

CHAPTER 14

It was another ten minutes before Diane felt she was back to some semblance of normalcy and had analyzed and tried to make sense out of that nightmare call.

Then she straightened in her chair and punched in Catherine's phone number. "I got the call."

A moment of silence. "Come and talk to me. Are you okay?"

"I'm fine now." It was almost true. "But I can't come to you right now. I've got to go to the bunkhouse and talk to Monteith."

"Monteith?"

"He has to know. If you want to talk, that's where I'll be."

She ended the call and started for the bunkhouse. She was only halfway there when Cameron swung open the door and stood there waiting. His shirt was half unbuttoned, his hair mussed, and he was holding a bottle of beer. "Catherine just called and said you'd be paying us a visit," he said quietly. "Monteith and I are playing cards. I take it you don't want to sit in?"

She shook her head. "I have to talk to him." She went past him into the bunkhouse.

Monteith was still sitting at the table, but he jumped to his feet. "Is something wrong, Dr. Connors? Is there anything I can do?"

"No, I just had to tell you that I talked to Nalam and he told me that he'd had Daniels blow up your airport."

Monteith flinched. He tried to smile. "He could have been lying."

She shook her head. "I heard the explosion. He wanted me to hear it." She said jerkily, "I'm sorry, Monteith. It's my fault."

He shook his head. "It's Nalam's fault. And it's just the luck of the draw. Naturally, I'm disappointed that I put in all that hard work building it into a great business only to have him tear it all down around me." He turned to Cameron. "But it looks like I'll have plenty of time if you need to use me somewhere else other than here in Canada."

Cameron shook his head. "Our arrangement was just fine with me. I like you right where you were. We'll just have to do a little cleanup and then build it back, bigger and better." He smiled. "I hope that will be okay with you. I never believe in going backward."

"That will be great." He grinned. "Thanks, Cameron."

"There's nothing great about it," Diane said bitterly. "It only means that you're absorbing a loss that Nalam meant for me. And that I should be apologizing to you, too."

"I've suffered a lot of losses in my time," Cameron said. "And I've always found apologies boring and useless. Unless you can make them fresh and productive, I'd prefer you skip them. I'd rather you tell me what—"

"I'm here." Catherine threw open the door and strode into the bunkhouse. "And I'm not pleased you left me to throw on my clothes and run after you like a puppy after a bone, Diane." She glanced over her shoulder at Slade, who had come in behind her. "And I saw him lurking by the corral and told him he might as well come, too."

"I don't lurk," Slade said. "I thought I'd receive an invitation when Diane got around to it." He looked at Diane. "Did you decide to stir up a little trouble?"

"No, I'm trying to make apologies and sort everything out so that I can see where I need to go." She took her phone out of her pocket. "But since I seem to have a captive audience, I'll let you listen and make your own conclusions. This recording should still be within Nalam's time limit." She turned on the recording, put the phone on the table, and spun on her heel. "I don't have any ideas myself at the moment. I'm hoping something will come to me. That appears to be what Alon is counting on, but I'm much more cynical than he is. He always said it was one of my faults. I'll talk to you all later." She walked out of the bunkhouse and headed toward the front porch of the ranch house. As she passed the helicopter, she noticed the bullet holes in the door. She hadn't seen them before, but they were only another example of the violence she'd brought down on Catherine. Had it been Daniels?

Stop wondering. Catherine would tell her later. Now she would just sit and rock and wait until they digested the ugly few minutes of disturbing dialogue that she'd thrown at them.

It was twenty minutes later that Catherine and Cameron came out of the bunkhouse and walked toward her. Diane braced herself and sat up straighter in her chair. "You heard that Nalam ticked off a long list of all the people he wants to punish for helping me," she said as they reached the porch. "He missed you and Slade, Cameron. I'm sure he'll rectify that when he does more thorough research."

"I can hardly wait," Cameron said dryly. "No one has put a million-dollar bounty on my head this week. I was getting quite envious."

"Well, he didn't leave out Michael," Catherine said grimly. "Eve and Joe are going to be furious and start circling the wagons. What slimeball targets kids?"

"One who wants to hurt me and has no conception of decency or humanity," Diane said. "And who believes I'm so self-centered that I'd allow it to happen." Her lips twisted. "Maybe he's right. I've lied and spun webs and drawn good people into danger because I thought what I was doing was worth the risk. But it wasn't only my risk. Monteith not only put his life on the line but lost that airport he worked so hard to build. Dr. Daltry was tortured and killed, and so was Belazo." She reached out and took Catherine's hand. "I almost got *you* killed. Eve, Joe . . . the list keeps growing." She let go of her hand. "It's got to stop."

"Are you finished?" Catherine asked. "I've never heard such maudlin hogwash. You really let that asshole get to you." She leaned down and grasped Diane's shoulders. "Do you think any of us have been helplessly drawn into that so-called web of yours? You flatter yourself. No way. We're all intelligent people who would have told you to go to hell if we hadn't decided that what you were doing was worth that risk." She straightened and jerked her thumb at Cameron. "And I asked Hu Chang at the beginning of all this if the reason Cameron was nosing closer was that he thought you were worth it, and he said it was. Cameron is too busy to waste his time."

"Nosing closer," Cameron repeated. "I don't believe I like that description. But I'm glad you realize how valuable my time is."

She ignored him. "Diane, the truth is that you were right, and the bullet is worth any risk. We all know it; we've just got to negotiate a way to overcome that risk."

Diane shook her head. "I only asked you to help me with that reconstruction. It's done now. You're under no obligation to do anything else. It's up to Alon and me to get Kai away from that bastard."

"From what Slade said, you're having trouble getting through to Alon on that score," Cameron said.

"I'll find a way. It's my responsibility."

Catherine made a rude sound. "I'm getting tired of all this. Let's get this clear. I don't care what you think is your responsibility. Like it or not, we're not going to let that son of a bitch get hold of you or your research. It would be the worst thing possible for you, us, and the rest of the world. So you can just forget about it."

"You don't understand. It's the right thing—" She suddenly stopped. Then she smiled ruefully. "And just when I was feeling so noble. I don't have many moments like this and you've ruined it."

"Thank heavens." Catherine breathed a sigh of relief. "I was getting scared. Is it safe to stop being tough and say that you've more value to me than what's stored in that convoluted brain of yours?"

"Maybe. But it doesn't change what I said about Kai and Alon."

"And that means that Kai's one of those hurdles we have to overcome. I thought we'd end with it being a package deal." She turned to Cameron. "Yes?"

"Oh, am I to have some input?" He tilted his head. "I was wondering if I'd be allowed to toss in an idea or two."

"Of course you are. This is your area of expertise. You can probably handle it with your eyes closed."

"That wouldn't be efficient. But it sounds like an interesting problem."

Catherine frowned. "I want you to know I'm not taking you for granted. I didn't mean to do that."

"I'm glad that you respect my free will," he said solemnly. "But we're on the same page as far as this is concerned."

"Good." She turned back to Diane. "How about you? Are we on the same page?"

"I'd be an idiot not to take help when it's offered." She shook her head. "But we have to get Eve and Joe back to Michael. Nalam threatened him." She paused. "I might have to deal with Nalam by myself."

"I thought that might be where this was going. No deals." Catherine grimaced. "We've got to keep that bastard away from you. He's zeroing in and making points with every call."

"That might be the wrong thing to do. I've no intention of being stupid enough to sacrifice myself, but there might be some way..." She shrugged. "I don't know. I just don't think we should close any doors." She got to her feet. "And I do have to talk to Eve and Joe and get them on their way. But not tonight. I'll let them sleep." She was heading for the front door. "And I'll try to sleep myself. I just might do it." She looked over her shoulder at them. "You've made me hope. I didn't start out that way and I probably shouldn't listen to you, but I think I'm going to grab it and hold on tight. I hope you don't regret it." She disappeared inside the ranch house.

"I don't understand what that last remark was supposed to mean," Catherine said wryly as she turned to Cameron. "Maybe she's afraid we're going to end up dead. Nalam scared her."

"And you weren't particularly gentle with her. No words of comfort. Not your usual demeanor when you run across someone in the midst of that kind of upset." His gaze was narrowed on her face. "I was curious why."

"You think I was too rough on her?"

"I wouldn't presume. I'm only curious."

She was silent a moment. "That Nalam message sent a chill through me. It was deliberately crafted to ignite guilt and fear and make Diane feel helpless. He wanted to push her to fall apart. I could see she was close to that point. Everything had been going badly for her, and she was feeling very much alone. I've found that Diane is essentially a fighter and she would have recovered, but I didn't want Nalam to have even a temporary victory." She shrugged. "So I appealed to her reason and not her emotions and got rid of the guilt. Then I made it a team project so she wouldn't be alone. It was all I could do on short notice, but it was a start."

"Yes, it was." He reached out and gently touched her hair. "A very good start. I believe you've gotten to know her very well. You're very convincing. You might give me serious problems after we rid Diane of Nalam and move to a more competitive position."

She felt a ripple of shock. Their day together had been full of action and excitement and finally intense satisfaction. For a little while she'd forgotten who he was and why he'd come here. She'd *wanted* to forget. Those moments at Monteith's had awakened the familiar heat and hunger. She was still feeling it now. But those words had jarred her out of that haze she'd felt and brought her back to reality.

And he'd meant to do it. Cameron always knew what he was doing and never blundered. He'd meant to remind her that no matter what happened, the conflict was still looming in the future. She instinctively moved back away from his touch. "I have every intention of causing you problems, and it's not a competition to me. I'm protecting Diane."

He shook his head. "You're wrong, but we won't discuss it. I just wanted to let you know how much I admire both your skill and your ethics. I value both."

"No, that's not all you wanted. You were trying to tell me something and I'm not reading all the nuances." She shook her head. "Or maybe I didn't want to read them. You can get me pretty dizzy sometimes, and maybe this was one of them. Why did you do it?"

"Because I knew you were vulnerable today and I had to make sure that I wasn't exploiting that vulnerability." He added with sudden harshness, "You were *ready* for me. It was what I'd been waiting for and there it was. I really didn't know why, but it was going to happen. Then I started to think and that's when disaster struck. What a mistake. I had to be fair. I wouldn't have been able to forgive myself if everything wasn't clear between us. What would have been worse is that you wouldn't have been able to forgive me." He paused. "Diane is important, and I have to keep trying. I told you I was her best option and that was the truth."

"You said that we weren't going to discuss it."

"I've blown it anyway. I had to get it out. There were moments today when I was talking myself into just going with the flow. We could have gone to bed and had a fantastic time as long as we didn't talk about Diane. I was tempted. I was so tempted." He took a step closer and said urgently, "Don't you see? We have everything against us, but we still gravitate back to each other. There has to be a reason."

"Your fault."

"Guilty. But I'm not in this alone, Catherine. So admit that you want me as much as I want you and nothing else matters when we come together."

"Other things do matter. They have to matter."

"Not at the time." His voice lowered to a whisper. "Then all I can think about is moving in and out of you, the rhythm, the way you put your legs around me and pull me closer, harder, the way you clench until I—"

"Shut up, Cameron," she said hoarsely. She could see it all. She could *feel* it all.

"I will. But I knew I'd lose ground when I had to remind you about Diane. I have to take it back any way I can by also reminding you of something much more pleasant." He shook his head. "Though going with the flow would have been much easier for me. I hope you appreciate that and will think kindly of me because I took the hard path tonight."

"I don't want to think about you at all tonight. It was probably good that you reminded me how far apart we are. I just want you to go."

"I'm going. I thought I'd be tossed out." He paused. "But I did the right thing, Catherine. When you get over being angry, you'll realize how difficult that was for me. The right thing is boring and sanctimonious and no fun at all. It's also a step back for me. I know you'll expect me to go back to square one, and I'll do it because we have to wrap this up. But I can't promise I'll be patient and wait until lightning strikes again." He turned and went down the steps. "I'll go back and talk to Slade, and we'll start going over plans. Maybe we can find a way of bringing Alon Hakali into them. He's got to have information we can use. If you think of anything else, jot it down. I'll see you in the morning, Catherine."

She watched him walk toward the bunkhouse. Of course she didn't want to call him back, she told herself. It was just that her emotions were in a turmoil. She didn't know what she was feeling, but it had to do with a wild multitude of physical and mental sensations generated by bewilderment, anger, lust, regret, and disappointment.

Yes, definitely disappointment.

EVE'S WORKROOM
7:40 A.M.

"You're in here early, Eve," Catherine said as she came into the workroom. "I heard you and Joe talking in the hall. I thought you were done with the reconstruction. Any problems?"

"Not with the reconstruction," Eve said dryly. "I'm just boxing him up and getting ready to send him back to the local police. I'll tell them where they can find the rest of the corpse so they can notify family. Tesar had a criminal background and Joe couldn't find any close relatives, but almost everyone has someone." She wrinkled her nose. "That could be a little awkward. It might be a better idea to wait until we can hand them Nalam along with the skull."

"Not unless you have proof, and that could take a long time. Nalam is sure his many connections mean he can do anything and not be prosecuted." She paused and then asked hesitantly, "Has Diane been in to see you yet?"

"No, but Cameron was knocking on our door at six." Her lips tightened. "He said that Diane wanted to give us a decent night, but he thought he should issue a warning ASAP. He filled us in on that damn call and then left." She added grimly, "Needless to say, we weren't able to doze off again. I got up and took a shower and tried to do some work to lower my blood pressure. Joe threw on his clothes and followed Cameron out to the bunkhouse to talk."

"That's why Diane wanted to give you a night's sleep before she saddled you with that horror story." She paused again. "What are you going to do?"

"I don't know." Eve's half smile was weary. "I'm waiting until I'm sure Michael is up and then I'll talk to him. That will be a start."

"You don't know what you're going to say?"

"How could I? I'll play it by ear." She moistened her lips. "I just want to hear his voice."

"He'll know something's wrong."

"I don't give a damn. I'll handle that when I talk to him. Maybe he won't. Joe said when he talked to him yesterday that he wanted to talk to me."

"Eve."

"I'll handle it then," she repeated. "Did you hear what that bastard said he wanted to do to him? He thought torturing him would be entertaining. For God's sake, he's ten years old!" Her voice was low and fierce. "I want to *kill* him."

"I thought you'd feel like that," Catherine said. "I do, too. He was just picking out the things that would most hurt Diane and serving them up to her. She realized how much this would hurt you. She said she knows you and Joe will want to get back to Michael as soon as you can."

"You bet I do. And I want to build a bomb shelter at the cottage and set up housekeeping for us down there. Anything to keep him safe."

"You told her?" Diane was standing in the doorway. "I wanted to tell you myself, Eve. I can't tell you how sorry I am that he might target Michael. I'll do anything I can to make sure that doesn't happen." She came into the workroom. "I know it's my fault. You have a right to be furious with me."

"I would be if I hadn't made the decision. And maybe I will once I get over the first shock. I haven't had a chance to recover yet." She added impatiently, "And Catherine didn't break it to me. Cameron decided that Joe and I shouldn't be the only ones who escaped feeling Nalam's wrath. Maybe he was trying to protect you. My first reaction was pretty explosive."

"I deserved it," Diane said soberly. "I'm the cause of all this. You should be angry with me."

'I'll work on it. But I don't have enough energy right now." She made a shooing motion. "Go away. I want to call my son. Then I'll have to talk to Joe if I can pry him away from Cameron. Catherine, go get her some breakfast."

"I can get my own breakfast," Diane said. "Maybe I should get something for you."

"Later." Eve sat down at her desk and took out her phone. "And stop looking so gloomy. Nothing's going to happen to Michael. We won't let it. If Nalam even tried, we'd feed him to the grizzly bears I've seen wandering in the woods up here."

"That sounds like a suitable end for him," Diane said. "But he'd probably give the bears indigestion. I'm really sorry that—"

"No more." Eve pointed at the door. "Out." She watched as Catherine took Diane firmly by the arm and pushed her out the door. Then she punched in Michael's number. He answered on the third ring. "Hi, Mom. You're finished with the reconstruction? Dad said you were almost done."

"All done." It was good to hear his voice. But she wanted to visualize everything about him. "Are you at one of the Disney hotels?"

"Yeah, it's really cool. And it's only a train ride from the park. Cara got me a guest pass and we go whenever she has some time."

"No Star Wars?"

"Not yet. I didn't feel like going." He was silent. "I thought maybe when you came here to pick me up that we'd go together and then—" He stopped and then said, "But you're not going to come here, are you?"

"What are you talking about? I've just finished the reconstruction and was thinking about when I could come."

"You finished the reconstruction, but it's still not good. You *can't* come. So many bad things..." He was silent again. "And why are you scared about me? I'm okay, Mom."

"I know you are." She'd hoped he might not sense her fear, but it had taken him only a few minutes. "And Cara is taking good care of you. I just don't like us to be apart."

"Neither do I. It's wrong. So I should come to you."

"No!"

"Yes." His words were tumbling one after the other at a frantic pace. "Bad things have already happened. Terrible things. And it's not going to stop. I should be there." His voice was suddenly panic-stricken. "I *have* to be there. You're going to need me."

"Shh. I always need you. I'll come to you and we'll be together."

"That's not the way it has to be. That's not where the darkness is. I have to come to you."

Her hand clenched on the phone. "No, Michael."

"Mom..." His voice was shaking. "Listen, I did what you wanted me to do. But now I can't stay here any longer. I need to come to where you are. Where Diane is. Everything is going to go wrong if I don't."

"What's going to go wrong?"

"He might die. You might not find him."

"Who?"

"I don't know. I just have to be there."

"That's not enough for me, Michael."

"It has to be enough," he whispered. "Because I can't do what you want, Mom. I can't stay here any longer. I'm going to come to you and I'm going to leave right away."

The whole situation was throwing her into a panic. What the hell was she supposed to do? Michael couldn't be more serious. Yet he was asking her to accept a course of action that terrified her even when it wasn't clear to him. But she had seen him like this before, and he had not been wrong. She had almost lost him once when she hadn't listened to him. "No, stay right where you are. Give me a little time to talk to your dad. It's not that I don't believe you, Michael. It's just that the situation is... difficult. You'd be safer with Cara."

"No, I wouldn't. I'd be safer there with you and Dad."

She felt a chill. How could she be sure that he was safe there at Disney World or anywhere else? Hadn't there been something in Diane's call about a sniper? "Let me talk to your dad," she said again. "I'll call you back, Michael." She hung up the call and sat there a moment trying to pull herself together. Then she called Joe. "I need to talk to you. Come back here."

"He shouldn't come here," Joe said. "No way. You should go to him."

"You're speaking in the singular," Eve said. "Which probably means you've decided not to go with me if I decide to leave. I don't like the direction this conversation is heading."

"It's heading toward the fact that you and Michael would be in a civilized place surrounded by law and order. That's a very safe direction."

"As long as everything goes the way you want it to," she said. "Which it most probably will not. He believes he can help if he comes here. I told you that he's determined. I couldn't talk him out of it."

"Convince him."

"Bullshit. When he makes up his mind, it's cast in stone. I remember the time he ran away from the Lake Cottage and took off after you into the mountains of West Virginia when you'd been wounded. He made it all the way there before I caught up with him. You might have been too ill then to realize what a traumatic time that was, but I recall every second of it."

He was silent. "Then I'll go with you."

"That's not going to cut it. He said that he had to be with us here. I've no idea what kind of voodoo mumbo jumbo is calling those shots to him, but I know that we don't have much time before he takes off on his own to try to get to us. He's very smart and more than likely he'll be able to do it. He had no problem with West Virginia."

Joe muttered a curse. "He'll really do it?"

"You know he will. He said that bad things are going to happen, and he has to be here." She looked him in the eye. "And you think he's right about those bad things, don't you? That's why you were trying to send me to Michael by myself. You were going to stay here. What were you talking about with Cameron?"

"You mean besides that extremely poisonous call that threatened everyone Diane had ever reached out to? Cameron has been researching Nalam very extensively and he's come up with a profile that's fairly hideous. A narcissist with no conscience, who has been clever enough to enlist some of the most powerful political, legal, and financial figures in the world to protect his empire. There's literally nothing that can be done to him in the courts even if he does what he threatens to Diane. It would simply be 'erased.'"

"That's truly terrifying," Eve said.

"I agree. And I have a definite dislike of anyone who believes he can run the world to suit himself." His jaw tightened. "This time he's decided to steal something from the world that we can't allow him to take."

"And your solution?"

"We erase him. I told Cameron that I was at his disposal." He frowned. "But how the hell to do it and keep Michael safe."

Bad things are going to happen.

Michael was right, she thought. Bad things were bound to happen, and Joe was probably going to be right in the middle of it. The idiot was going to save the world. It was clear that the world was going to need saving from that son of a bitch, but she still wanted to reach out and shake him. "It seems evident that if you erase Nalam, then you erase the threat to Michael," she said curtly. "And it's obvious you're going to be too occupied to worry about keeping him safe."

"I'm never too worried for that," Joe said quietly. "You're not being fair. Why are you this angry?"

"I don't feel like being fair. I'm worried and I'm frustrated, and I know I'm not going to be able to talk Michael out of showing up here. I also know that I'm going to have to watch him like a hawk and make sure that I know what he's thinking in case he tries to save the world, too." She got to her feet. "So I'd just as soon you go away and talk to Cameron again and make very good plans for how to end Nalam as soon as possible. I'll call Michael and Cara back and tell her to arrange to fly him to Calgary. I'll pick him up there. From now on Michael is my responsibility, and I'll be the one to take care of him and keep him safe."

"Can we talk about this?" Joe asked.

"Not until I get over being pissed off," she said. "I realize exactly where you're at, and part of me admires and wants to cheer you on. But that's only part. The other part is a mother who doesn't give a damn about anything but her son and wants you to find a miracle to solve my problem."

"Miracles aren't on my résumé, but I could work at it."

"Not good enough." She was punching in Michael's number. "Talk to me later. Go away."

7:10 P.M.

"Eve!"

Eve turned as she was heading for Monteith's helicopter to see Diane running toward her. "I can't stop to talk. I'm on my way to pick up Michael."

"I know. I'll only be a minute. I haven't gotten a chance to talk to you since you called Michael." She watched Slade open the helicopter door for Eve. "I don't think you should bring Michael here. I'll do anything I can to help you, but you should consider going back to the Lake Cottage with him."

Eve looked at her. "Should I?" she asked sarcastically. "Why didn't I think of that? This isn't your concern, Diane."

"I'm just worried about him."

Eve sighed. "Sorry. I didn't mean to snap. Just accept that this is the only option for Michael at present. I'm worried about him, too."

Diane glanced at Slade. "At least you have someone with you who will take good care of him."

Slade nodded. "Or face Quinn's wrath. Monteith's going to pick up his son across the border from Calgary in Montana. Cameron arranged to have him flown there from Orlando by two of his men. Quinn wasn't going to take a chance on anything happening to him before he was delivered to Eve."

"Just what I'd expect of Joe," Diane said. "I can't imagine him doing anything else, can you, Eve?"

The faintest smile touched Eve's lips. "No, and this time I'm sure he was especially careful."

"He thought there might be trouble?"

"Not specifically." She got into the helicopter. "Let's just say he was a bit wary about any upsets I might encounter along the way."

"That lake is cool, Mom." Michael jumped out of the helicopter and stood looking at the reflection of the moon on the water. "Not as nice as our lake at home, but I bet it has fish."

"I couldn't tell you. We've been a little too busy for fishing." She waved goodbye to Slade and Monteith and headed for the ranch house. "But you can check it out in the morning."

"I'll ask Dad if we can go." His pace quickened. "Is he at the house?"

"Probably not. He's been spending most of his time in the bunkhouse. He's been doing some research with Cameron."

"Bunkhouse? A real bunkhouse?" Michael's eyes lit up. "How neat can you get?" He wheeled and started running toward the bunkhouse. "I'll go see him and say hi."

"Michael. He might be—" She stopped. *Let him go.* There was no way Joe wouldn't want to stop anything he was doing to see Michael.

By the time she caught up with him, Joe had come out of the bunkhouse and grabbed Michael up in a bear hug. He swung him around in a circle. "Good flight?" Then he set him down and turned to Eve. "No problems?"

"Not one."

"You didn't tell me there was a lake here, Dad," Michael said. "Can we go fishing tomorrow?"

"Maybe, if it's early enough. You'll have to ask your mom." He looked at Eve. "She's in sole charge of you while you're here."

Michael frowned. "Okay. Whatever you say. Mom?"

"I don't see why not. I might hang out and keep an eye on the two of you."

"That would be great." He gave Joe another hug. "I'll see you later at the ranch house, okay? Mom says Catherine and Diane are here and I want to say hi." He was running toward the house.

Joe was gazing quizzically at Eve. "Am I out of hot water yet?"

"You're getting there. I'll let you know when it's a done thing." She looked past him at the other men gathered around a map on the table. "Progress?"

"I'll let you see for yourself. I wanted to show Diane the map anyway and ask a few questions." He paused. "How was Michael on the trip here?"

"Normal. Maybe a little quiet and hesitant until he saw the lake. He definitely knows that he upset me."

"That goes for both of us," he said ruefully. "You made it very clear."

"Because I'm scared. I don't like being scared." She shook her head. "And you weren't scared. You were being all tough and macho and just looking for solutions. It infuriated me."

"Macho?" he repeated. "You were looking for solutions, too."

"But then I had to look for solutions that could save both of you. Because I knew if anything happened to either one of you, it would be my fault." She held up her hand as he started to speak. "I was the one who made the decision that put us on Nalam's radar. I was the one who wanted to help Diane with her damn bullet. You tried to talk me out of it. I should have known that you'd get caught up and end up being Superman. It's ingrained in your DNA, and you—"

"My turn." His fingers were over her lips. "I like Superman better than macho but admit that neither term is really accurate. I'm just a guy who does his utmost to have the best possible outcome to bad situations. You were the one who wanted to save the world, and it was the right thing to do. My main interest is always just to keep you alive because you *are* my world." He took his fingers away. "Now am I out of hot water?"

"Close. Very, very close." She had to clear her throat. "But you still haven't come up with any miracles."

He jerked his head back toward the map on the table. "We're working on it."

"Then keep on doing it." She turned and started toward the ranch house. "But remember Michael will be waiting up for you."

"And will you?"

"What do you think?" she said over her shoulder. "I still believe you have Superman potential. I might want to test it again..."

She was still smiling when she walked in the front door and found Michael sitting on the living room couch with Diane showing her a game on his computer.

Diane immediately got to her feet. "I was just keeping him company. Catherine's in the kitchen seeing what she could find for supper. I'll go help her."

"You told me once that you couldn't cook," Eve said. "We're probably all better off with you in here playing with Michael's computer. You both looked like you were having a good time. I'll go see what I can scavenge."

"If that's all right with you." She sat back down on the couch. "Call if you need me."

Eve gazed at her thoughtfully for an instant. Then she turned to Michael. "On second thought, why don't you go help her? I can trust you in the kitchen. Then I can tell Diane all about our trip."

"Right. I'll show you the game later, Diane." Michael jumped off the couch and ran out of the room.

Diane stiffened. "Is something wrong?"

"Yes, but it's not something you did. I thought I'd get everything clear with us so that you wouldn't be jumping up every other minute because you thought you'd offended me. In circumstances like this, it could get old very quickly."

Diane tried to smile. "Not every other minute."

"Every five minutes would still annoy me. So let's go down the list. I don't mind you spending time with Michael if you want. He's good company and he likes you." She paused. "If he's a little pushy, it's because he's worried about you and wants to help. I think you can guess why. I'm not worried about you stealing his affections. He's got plenty to spread around, and I've got the inside track."

"Anyone can see that," Diane said. "I didn't want to intrude. I've pushed my way back into your life and I'm trying to make it bearable for you." She added wearily, "I didn't want you to bring Michael here. I thought you'd all be safe if you got away from me so that Nalam wouldn't target you."

"Too late. I had the same thought. It might have worked if you'd been dealing with different people. But Michael decided that's not how this should go down, and Joe thought the same thing for different reasons. It seems he believes Nalam is a horror story that can't be allowed to keep existing. I tend to agree. So that means we're going to have to keep working together until we get to the end of the road. My job is to take care of Michael and make sure he doesn't do anything that would break my heart. If I succeed in doing that, I have to work on being a bitch to Joe because I'll want to treat him as if he's made of glass. There's nothing in the world he'd hate worse."

Diane smiled slightly. "I remember that."

"And *your* job is to not remember any personal details like that too clearly. Or if you do, don't comment on them. I'm trying not to dwell on your time with Joe."

"You have to know you have nothing to worry about," Diane said quickly.

"On one side of my brain. It's the other side that gives me trouble." Eve added, "And another duty you have is to keep an eye on Michael if I'm not around. That should be easy because I'll be paranoid about being certain he's safe. But sometimes things go wrong if you get too cocky. I refuse to be too cocky."

"I'll be glad to watch out for him. He's a great kid."

Eve nodded. "Yes, he is. And that great kid will probably be watching out for you at the same time. He's already started. He's been worried about you from the first day he met you."

"And yet I'm the one who heaped all my problems on you," she said bitterly. "I didn't mean to do it. Well, yes I did. I thought it was worth it. But I didn't think it would get this bad."

"You were obviously wrong. But if it makes you feel any better, I think it will be worth it to me, too, as long as we keep my son and Joe alive." She added brusquely, "Which we will do." She turned. "Now let's go and see about getting something to eat. We understand each other?"

"We understand each other," Diane said quietly. "I promise you that nothing will happen to either of them. Nor to you, Eve." She fell into step with her as she started down the hall. "Though I may not be here all the time. I might have to go to Hakali Island. Alon wasn't listening to me before, but maybe if we're face-to-face."

"Or maybe not. Joe said he needed to talk to you about a map. I don't think it was Hakali Island. Did he talk to you at all about that encampment in Montana?"

"A little." She grasped Eve's arm. "Is Joe that close to finding Nalam's prison camp?"

"Baby steps. We're going to need Alon's help for the actual location, and you're going to have to persuade him he can trust us. Cameron has been on it since he and Catherine got back to the ranch house the other night, and his contacts are amazing. But put Cameron and Joe together and we get something very interesting."

"I'll talk him into it. Though it won't be easy," Diane said grimly. "He's got a chance of getting Kai back, and he'll want to do it himself." She added, "But it had better be damn soon."

Michael was already in bed and asleep when Joe finally got back to the ranch house.

"Sorry," he murmured to Eve as he came into the living room where she, Catherine, and Diane were sitting. "I'll make it up to him tomorrow. I was busy with—"

"I know you will," Eve said as she took from him the rolled map he was carrying and unfurled it. "This is all that's important right now." She turned to Diane. "Do you recognize any of this terrain from the map Alon showed you?"

"Maybe here." Diane pointed at a hill near the Canadian border. "Or here." She indicated another place farther south. "I only got a glimpse of the area on Skype. I need to get Alon to send the map to me."

"We all agree on that," Catherine said. "But will this help at all, Joe?"

"It might. Cameron will send teams to both areas to take a look around. We need to know where to deploy all around the exterior of the encampment." He paused and looked at Diane. "But we need to know everything about that camp and the stockade before we launch an offensive. We'll send those teams out tonight, but we'll need you to persuade Hakali to give us what we need by tomorrow."

"I'll call him tonight," she said. "I'll do everything I can." She got to her feet. "I'll let you know, Joe."

He nodded as he turned to Eve. "Where's Michael bedding down? I thought I'd peek in and see him."

"I set him up on the couch in my workroom. It's close to us but gives him his privacy." She smiled. "Though he did ask if he could sleep in the bunkhouse with the other guys. I told him that there was a lot going on over there right now and I didn't think he'd sleep. He was disappointed."

"But it was the right decision," Joe said. "Cameron made a call, and there will be fifteen or twenty more men arriving here before morning. It might be fun for Michael, but it could get crowded."

"Why did he make that call? I'd think they'd be heading for Montana."

"There will be a bigger force going down there. Things are moving fast. I wanted more guards here at Naponi. We don't need any slipups when Nalam is showing his fangs." He shrugged. "We might need Slade and Monteith in Montana." He glanced at Catherine. "If you don't mind a little additional help keeping an eye on Diane?"

Catherine shook her head. "Not as long as Cameron vouches for the men he's bringing here. They'll probably take orders from me much better than Slade." She hesitated. "Are they all still working over at the bunkhouse?"

He nodded. "Probably most of the night. I opted out because I'd promised to see Michael. I'll catch up tomorrow."

"Then I think I'll go over and get filled in on any tentative plans in the works." She moved toward the door. "Everything seems to be getting along okay here."

"I believe I can handle any difficulties," Joe said solemnly.

She made a face at him. "See that you do." The door closed behind her.

Diane was already heading for her room. "I'll make that call to Alon. If you don't need me for anything, Eve."

Eve glanced over her shoulder as she followed Joe toward her workroom. "Didn't we discuss this?"

"Just checking."

"What's that all about?" Joe asked.

She put her finger to her lips as she silently opened the door. The light was off, but the hall light fell on Michael huddled under a blanket on the leather couch. He was asleep.

She closed the door again. "Out of luck," she silently mouthed.

"Damn," Joe whispered as he moved back down the hall toward their bedroom. "I hate breaking my word."

"You didn't." She followed. "He did. He was the one who fell asleep."

"I don't think it counts when you're ten." He glanced at Diane's room down the hall. "What was that interplay before?"

"Nothing. We just had a discussion about duties and comfort levels. She was having a few guilt issues." She smiled wryly. "And since I'd been having more than a few myself, I thought I was the right person to confront them. It went pretty well until we got down to the more serious problems. Then she was very stubborn about what she owed me and her duty to me. She started to make promises."

"About?"

"She promised me that she'd never let anything happen to either Michael or you."

He chuckled. "That's bizarre coming from her. Did you laugh?"

"No, she meant it. I didn't want to hurt her feelings." She suddenly grinned. "And Slade did give her that Glock. She has the equipment."

Joe's smile faded. "And am I out of hot water?"

"How can I say no?" She came into his arms. "We've just been talking about how understanding and helpful your ex-wife is being. I wouldn't want her to put me in the shade. We both know I was being a bitch."

"You had a right."

"No, but I had a reason. Let's leave it at that." She began to unbutton her shirt. "But I think I might be able to make you believe that the new wife is much more talented than the old one."

CHAPTER 15

I told you to stay out of it, Diane." Alon's voice was impatient. "I'll take care of it from now on. I don't need help from your friends. I'm glad you phoned to tell me about Nalam's calls. You should have told me before. But it only means I have to move faster and I have to trust the people I'm dealing with. I trust my own friends and I have my family. They will be enough."

"You might not be able to move fast enough," she said desperately. "Nalam could be making a move at any time. Look, I'm certain your people are strong and skilled, but they're no match for Nalam's men."

"And Quinn and Cameron are?" he asked skeptically. "Where did you find such sterling choices?"

"I've told you about Joe Quinn, and Cameron sort of found me." Her voice was urgent. "I realize that I'm no expert, but Catherine is, and you can call Hu Chang. He trusts them." She went on quickly, "And Cameron can bring in a special forces team that's trained to take down men like the ones you'd be facing. That could help you." She paused. "Then you wouldn't have to use your family against Nalam's men. I know you've been worried about doing that."

Silence. Then he said, "Yes. They want to help Kai, but I'd rather handle it alone."

"And you can't do it. It would be suicide." She added persuasively, "It may still be suicide if you don't have really competent people with you. Let me help. Let *them* help."

"So that Nalam can get his hands on you?" he asked harshly. "He'd destroy you. Didn't those calls tell you anything? It's what I've been trying to avoid since the first day you came to my island. He's got Kai, I won't have him take you, too."

"What those calls told all of us is that he's the one who has to be destroyed, Alon. We can't let him keep on taking and torturing." She paused. "If you want to keep him away from me, pick the sure thing."

He was silent again.

He was wavering, but she wasn't sure he was convinced. "Look, you don't trust my judgment? Well, talk to Quinn and Cameron yourself. I'll have them set up a Skype call with you for tomorrow. They'll convince you."

"It's not that I don't trust your judgment. But you can be emotional and sometimes reckless and that . . . interferes."

He knew her too well. "It didn't interfere this time. You'll see." She went on brusquely, "But you can trust me enough to send me a copy of the map of that encampment tonight, complete with as many details as you remember. I need it right away."

"You can't use it until I give permission," he said warily.

"Of course not." She had a sudden thought. "Where are you?"

"Honolulu."

"You left your island?"

"I told you I might. I'm on my way to Vancouver." He added, "I've arranged to meet people there tomorrow."

She might have caught him just in time. "Well, don't get on that plane until you get the Skype. Okay?"

"Evidently it has to be since you've decreed it." He added softly, "It might not work out, Diane. I don't want to disappoint you."

"You won't. Because this is the way that's best for everyone. You'll see. Good night, Alon." She ended the call.

She gave a sigh of relief. She had done it!

Now all she needed to do was sit back and wait for the text.

Catherine stood outside the bunkhouse, hesitating. It was going to be okay. It wasn't as if she was here to see Cameron. She had an entirely different purpose. She raised her hand and knocked firmly on the door.

"Welcome." Cameron threw open the door at Catherine's knock. "You don't really need to knock, you know. We're very informal here."

"Of course I do. It's only courteous." She looked beyond him to Slade and Monteith. "Hi, we missed you in the kitchen tonight, Slade. But I did my best. They sent Michael to help me."

"I told you it was my one skill that was always appreciated," Slade said. "I'm afraid that you can't count on me for a while. Can I offer you beer or a glass of wine?"

"Wine." She turned to Cameron. "Joe said that you were making plans. What are you doing? How can I help?"

"Not much. We need the location and any pertinent info Diane can get from Alon Hakali. After that, we'll be in better shape."

She took the wine Slade handed her. "Thanks."

He smiled as he turned back to Monteith. "My pleasure."

She took a sip as she looked back at Cameron. "But you already have the basics. You're going after Kai Hakali."

He nodded. "And any other prisoners in that stockade. We'll have to get all of them out before the action starts."

"An attack on the stockade?"

"Possibly. I was considering using a drone to eliminate the stockade, Nalam, and any nearby guards. It would be much more efficient, providing the area is far enough from innocent civilians to make it safe."

"A drone..." She was thinking about it. "A bomb's not your usual weapon of choice."

"I'm generally old-fashioned and prefer to go after psychos like Nalam in the conventional fashion, but I'm trying to modernize my techniques." His lips tightened. "I've been getting more research on Nalam lately, and I don't want to risk not sending him to hell when I get the chance. Kai isn't the only victim that Nalam's ordered taken for 'experimentation.' The investigations uncovered another camp deep in the Amazon where the local police found twelve dead bodies that were later identified as a local doctor and his research team, who had disappeared several years before. As far as they could tell, they'd been tortured before they were murdered."

She shivered. "Nalam?"

He shrugged. "No proof. And he's so powerful, the Brazilian government wasn't about to ask him any questions. It's the same situation here. We either stop him or he'll slide out from under any investigation."

"That's what Joe said." She shook her head. "And there's no telling how many times he's done that before. How many places in the world does he have 'stockades'? He told Diane on that call how much he enjoyed torture."

"And he regards anyone who threatens his empire as the enemy," he said quietly. "At present, Diane heads that list. So I believe a bomb will be an excellent choice that will forever remove him and also any trace of evidence that might be uncomfortable for us. I hope you agree?"

She didn't answer.

"No? Of course, I wouldn't expect you to have anything to do with the act itself."

"I didn't say no. I was just thinking. You persist in trying to protect me from the consequences of being an agent. I don't appreciate that, Cameron."

"My apologies." He inclined his head mockingly. "May I ask what you were thinking about?"

"I was thinking that I'd worked with drones when I was in Pakistan, and I was very good. But they weren't weaponized, and I was wondering if I could still help with setting up the trajectory?"

He chuckled. "Another thing I didn't know about you." His smile faded. "You're sure you'd want to?"

"I'm very sure. Stop trying to protect me. Nalam is not only a monster, he's going to try to kill Diane. I won't have any trouble helping rid the world of him." She frowned thoughtfully. "I could also determine the exact location of the prisoners by adjusting the thermal imaging scope. That was my main skill. When will you get the drones so I can check them out?"

"I'll call tonight. Probably late tomorrow."

She nodded. "Call me when you receive them and I'll be over." She finished her wine and set the glass on the table. "There's nothing else I can do here?"

Cameron shook his head. "Though it appears you're going to do quite a bit tomorrow." He opened the door for her. "I'll walk you back to the ranch house."

"Not necessary." But he was falling into step with her, and she glanced at him. "Do you think I need an escort? You're definitely in protective mode."

"I wouldn't dare suggest that you couldn't take care of yourself. I just wanted to know why we were honored by your presence tonight."

"I told you, I wanted to know what was happening. I wanted to help."

"And?"

She made a face. "I was bored. Being a bodyguard may be a worthy occupation, but not for me. It involves too much sitting around and not enough action. I'm used to being busy. Hu Chang definitely owes me."

"I could have told you that when I visited you in the hospital. But the pressure should be off. By tomorrow, Naponi will have sentries galore to keep watch."

She shook her head. "Pressure won't be off. She's my responsibility."

"Unless you're working on the drones. Shouldn't that fall into the category of saving Diane?"

"Maybe. If I have a suitable substitute."

"I'll work on it." They had reached the porch steps. He was silent a moment. "Whatever the reason, I was happy when I opened that door tonight. I was glad that you came to me. I don't expect anything anymore, but I wanted you to know."

She gazed at him standing there in the moonlight and was suddenly filled with sadness. Of course she had come to him. All the years of passion, laughter, adventure, and tragedy had woven a bond that couldn't be broken. "It's good that you don't expect anything more. I can't handle the seesaw that I'm on with you. But you were honest with me and you tried to remind me that the seesaw always goes down." Then the sadness was abruptly gone. She took a step toward him and said fiercely, "But why does it have to go down? Why can't you realize that the Shangri-La you've been trying to build for the time when some idiot destroys civilization just doesn't compute? After what the world has gone through with the virus, depression, and the deaths that left us all crippled inside, we should have been destroyed. You said you'd lost some of your own people to the virus. We weren't destroyed and we're fighting back. Did you ever consider that might have been the big bang you were waiting for?"

"Actually, I did." He reached out and gently touched her cheek. "During that hellish period, I was too busy trying to help people to survive to worry about what might come later. And then I saw the spirit and the dawning in the people around me and I thought it was beautiful. Everyone was going to get a new start, and all the poison was going to be gone."

She had never seen him like this. He looked younger and filled with that dawning he'd spoken about. "*Yes.*"

"But it didn't happen, Catherine," he said quietly. "Monsters like Nalam survived and used all the tragedies around them to gain more power. They made alliances with other ambitious bastards to protect themselves. They found dirty politicians who could be seduced even deeper into the dark side, and the poison is starting to build again."

"It has to be only a minority now."

He shook his head. "I wish you were right. I'm starting to see it all over the world. That's why I can't stop." He paused. "That's why I can't let them get hold of Diane. Even when we get rid of Nalam, I'll bet there will be someone else waiting in the wings to pounce."

"Then we'll knock him down and stomp on him."

"And the next?"

"I'll worry about that when the time comes." She shook her head as she stared at him. She wanted that other Cameron back, the one who had touched her, the one who'd wanted to believe in a spiritual awakening. "And I refuse to let you frighten me with all those dire predictions. I think you had me half convinced before, and that was why I was scared and a little desperate. But I believe we all do have a new start now, and I'm not going to stand on the sidelines and worry about what comes next. I'll take one fight at a time."

He smiled. “Exactly what I’d expect. I’m very proud of you.”

“Don’t be patronizing.” She lifted her chin. “I’m very proud of you, too. Even though I still believe you’re wrong, you’re the best kind of wrong. And it’s not as if I can’t handle it. It’s all a question of taking what I need and not letting the fact that you’re wrong upset me. I’ll just blank it out unless it gets in my way.”

“Interesting philosophy.”

“I should have discovered it sooner.” She took a step back. “I’ll see you tomorrow, Cameron. Let me know about the drones.” She started to turn around and then suddenly whirled and kissed him, quick and hard. Then she was heading for the front door. “I needed that. Good night, Cameron.”

She didn’t wait for an answer but slammed the door behind her. She stood there in the dark, shaking. It was all very well to be bold and definitive when she was with him, but it was different when she was alone. The “interesting philosophy” was shattering, and she had to fight to keep it intact. It was the right way to go, she told herself. She didn’t know how long it would last but she would hold on as long as possible. After all, they had both made strides tonight. He had been willing to show her a vulnerability she hadn’t realized was there.

And she had realized that she was going to fight with all her strength for what they had together.

RANCH HOUSE
7:25 A.M.

“Oh, you’re up?” Diane looked up at Eve from the kitchen table on which she had packets of papers spread in neat piles. “Do you want coffee? I just made it, but I’m afraid there’s nowhere to drink it.”

"I can see that. I'll get my own cup." She went to the cabinet and took down a cup. "What are all those papers?"

"Alon texted me the plans of Nalam's encampment and stockade. I printed them out and divided them into ten piles. I wanted to get them over to Cameron as soon as possible. I saw Joe earlier and gave him his copy. He was taking Michael fishing."

"I know. He left me a note." Eve sat down in a chair, cradling her cup between her hands. "I was going to go with them, but I decided they needed guy time. Joe might not be able to see much of him for the next few days. I hope they won't be disappointed. I don't know if there are any fish in that lake."

"Slade said he saw bass. He was considering them for dinner one night."

"I don't believe Michael actually wants to catch them. He just likes to watch them jump in the water." She was watching Diane gather up the piles of papers. "May I help you?"

Diane shook her head. "I want to keep busy. And I want to get them distributed before ten. I set up a Skype call for Alon with Joe and Cameron, and I want them to have the maps and info while they're talking to him." She moistened her lips. "It's *got* to go well, Eve. Alon has to trust them. He doesn't want to risk his family and friends, and that probably means he'll try to do most of the rescue himself. Nalam would love to get his hands on him."

"I don't think there will be a problem. Cameron can be very persuasive, and Joe is . . . Joe. Who wouldn't trust him?"

"That's what I'm counting on." She was loading the packets into her briefcase. "But Nalam could make his move anytime. And his move would probably be on Kai." She was heading down the hall toward the front door. "I don't think Alon could bear it."

Eve wasn't sure that Diane could bear it. "Don't borrow trouble." She followed her down the hall. "Everyone is moving as fast as—"

"The troops have arrived," Diane interrupted. She'd thrown open the front door and was looking toward the bunkhouse. "It looks like a SWAT team."

Eve was standing behind her and gazing at the trucks and other vehicles parked in front of the bunkhouse. Dozens of men in jeans and dark plaid flannel shirts were pouring out of the trucks and lifting out boxes and weapons. "More like a bunch of lumberjacks. Much less noticeable considering the locale. But those are supposed to be the sentries? A little overkill?"

"Joe probably doesn't think so," Diane said. "You're here. Michael is here." She was going out on the porch. "He might not think there's enough."

Eve watched as Diane started to cross the yard toward the bunkhouse.

"She's in a big hurry," Catherine said as she came to stand beside Eve. "And she stayed up half the night going over that map and Alon's notes about that encampment so that it would be crystal-clear for Joe and Cameron. I wasn't sleeping so I asked if I could help her, but she turned me down."

"Me, too," Eve said. "But at least she didn't bring up that responsibility thing this time." She glanced at her. "Why weren't you sleeping?"

She shrugged. "Who knows? It might be because I was curious about those notes Alon had sent her about his observations when he was at that camp in Montana. One of them worried me."

"Why?"

"It was about the frequency of Nalam's visits to the encampment. He didn't visit Montana very often. Maybe once a week, maybe every other week. That's not good. We need Nalam to be at that camp, visiting the stockade."

"You couldn't rescue Kai if he's not there?"

"Not with any degree of satisfaction," Catherine said grimly. "Cameron wants to drop a bomb on his head. If we just stage a rescue of Kai and go on the run, his men might hunt us down. We need to be able to make certain he never bothers us again. Alon said that Nalam liked his comfort; he usually stayed in his mansion in Santa Monica until he got a yen to go up north and play the big boss man. He'd torture one or two of the prisoners for a couple of days, and when he'd had enough, he'd go back to civilization."

"Then you have to make it worth his while to leave his happy home," Eve said quietly. "Are you going to tell me why you're finding it necessary to take care of this yourself?"

"I had some experience with drones when I was assigned to prisoner extractions in Pakistan," she said. "I should be the one to make certain it's done correctly." She added, "And Diane is going to be involved in Kai's rescue no matter what I do. I have to make sure she comes out of this alive."

"Because you promised Hu Chang."

Catherine smiled faintly. "We both know that we've gone beyond our initial reasons for diving into this. Now we've just got to finish the job." She tilted her head. "Correction. *I* have. You've already finished what you came here to do."

"So I thought," Eve said dryly. "Michael seems to have a different idea." She suddenly stiffened. "And there he is, down at the bunkhouse in the middle of all that hoopla. Where's Joe?"

"Easy. I see him. He's climbing in the back of that truck." Catherine was outside on the porch, her gaze on the truck. "Because I think he's examining a drone the guys brought with them." She was running down the steps. "Which I should be doing. Don't worry, Eve, I'll send Michael to you..."

Eve watched her run toward the bunkhouse, which had become a magnet. She was feeling suddenly alone. First Diane. Now Catherine.

Both busy and involved and doing something to bring an end to this nightmare. While she was standing here, twiddling her thumbs.

"Hey, Mom, did you see what's going on?" Michael was running toward her. "All those guys and I saw a drone. But it's bigger than the one Dad and I play with at home. Do you think I could get him to let me play with this one?"

She looked at him and then leaned down to give him a hug. He was so full of excitement and wonder and joy and was the very essence of life and all it meant to her. Caring and protecting him should be enough for her right now. She grinned at him. "No, I don't think you have a chance. That's going to be Catherine's drone, and she already has plans on how she's going to play with it."

Diane received the call she'd been waiting for from Alon at one forty that afternoon. "I've been waiting," she said as soon as she jumped on. "Why didn't you call me sooner?"

He chuckled. "Why did I know those would be the first words out of your mouth?"

"Because you know how anxious I've been and worried that you'd be stupid. How did the Skype call go?"

"How did Quinn and Cameron say it went?"

"I haven't been able to talk to them yet. Cameron has been on the phone all morning and all I got was a nod from Joe Quinn in between his trips setting up the sentries."

He chuckled. "A nod tells its own story. You should have been able to interpret it."

"Alon."

"It went well, Diane," he said gently. "You chose superbly and I was very impressed. They outlined their plans and their resources and I couldn't ask for more. I'm just grateful that they've agreed to help. You must have been very persuasive."

She almost collapsed with relief. "Then why the hell didn't you call me earlier?"

"Our call went on for a long time. I had to give them a good deal of information. Then I had to catch my plane to Vancouver right after I hung up. I'm calling you from the plane now."

"Vancouver? You still took that flight?"

"And am meeting a few of my friends there. Those plans still survived intact. We'll be going to Montana and rendezvousing with one of Cameron's teams near the encampment. I hope that meets with your approval?"

"You know it does."

"Then will you kindly step away from the action now? You've done more than enough for me."

"Don't be silly. I can't step away. Nalam wouldn't let me if I wanted to. We just have to determine how best to use me."

"Diane, I don't want—" He stopped. "Why am I even trying? I know it's futile. I'll speak to Quinn. He seems to be a reasonable man who would honestly care whether you live or die."

"I might have argued that point when all this began but I think you might be right." She added quickly: "However, you're not to talk to him. I'll do as I wish, Alon."

"Don't you always?"

"Whenever possible, and you should be grateful those wishes often coincide with yours."

"Oh, I am. I only wish to stretch that status into perpetuity. Goodbye, Diane." He ended the call.

Done! She jumped to her feet and slipped her phone into her pocket. She was almost dizzy with triumph and relief. It wasn't an unqualified success, but it was as close as she'd come to date. Alon had a better chance to save Kai now than he'd had before, and it would be with enormously less risk.

But that didn't mean the risk wouldn't be there. Nalam still held Kai, a trump hand that might stop them in their tracks. Okay, then treat him like a complication in one of her experiments. Think. Verify. Find a way around it. Catherine had mentioned something when they'd been talking last night... Diane left her room and went to look for her. She found her on the porch reading a manual and plopped down in the chair next to her. "The drone? I thought you'd be at the bunkhouse taking it apart."

"We're not using the bunkhouse for the drone launches. It's too small. Cameron has the new team cleaning out the stable. I'm not ready to do an internal examination of the drone yet. That's time consuming, and I can learn a lot by reading the updates and explanations listed in the manual. These models are more advanced than I'm accustomed to." She looked up from the manual. "Besides, I can keep an eye on you while I'm doing it."

"Sound distribution of time," she said absently. "I was interested in that thermal imaging process you were telling me about last night. I was wondering if you can tell which prisoner in that stockade is Kai through the body measurements indicated by the thermal imaging?"

"Possibly. But it depends on how close the prisoners are to each other in height and bone structure. There's no real way of telling unless you're in the same room with him." Her lips twisted bitterly. "And you definitely can't use weight or body mass as a clue. After months in prison they usually end up as skeletal as one of Eve's reconstructions."

"But it's possible?"

"That's what I said." Her eyes were narrowed on Diane's face. "Why?"

"I need to know everything I can about those prisoners. I want to rule out the possibility that Nalam has already killed Kai. We only have Belazo's word that Nalam didn't do so. Just because Nalam lied about the body in that grave doesn't mean he couldn't have killed Kai anytime afterward on a whim. We can't be sure of anything with that psycho bastard. Time's running out, Catherine. If Kai is imprisoned in that stockade, I want to know where."

"So do I," Catherine said. "We'll find out. I had every intention of doing that. Cameron said we had to clear the stockade before we sent in that second weaponized drone."

"But we might have to move Kai before we get the others out. It could come down to that. When are you going to be able to send this drone out?"

"Tonight. As soon as Cameron gets the stockade location and details from Alon."

"He's already got it. He should have everything he needs now."

"Then I should have the thermal imaging info by midnight." She smiled mockingly. "Providing you let me finish reading this manual."

"Absolutely." She got to her feet. "I'll even hold your screwdriver while you're examining the drone."

"They don't require ordinary screwdrivers."

"Whatever." She moved toward the door. "Just so you get it done."

Catherine's lips were twitching. "Yes, ma'am." She went back to her manual.

Another hurdle taken, Diane thought. Though she had no idea what was on the other side.

"You're scared."

Diane looked up and saw Michael standing in the hallway ahead of her. His face was pale, and his hands were clenched at his sides. She instinctively stiffened but didn't take the easy way out as she would with any other child. "We're all scared sometimes. But then we just have to fight it off."

He nodded. "But sometimes when you can't do that, you have to go ahead and do something. That's why I came here even though Mom didn't want me to, Diane." He came toward her and took her hand. "And that's what you're going to do, isn't it?" he whispered. "That's why you're scared. You should be scared. Though it might be okay."

She forced a smile. "Not encouraging, Michael. I *will* be okay, whatever I choose to do." She added, "And we won't discuss this with your mother. I've caused her enough worry."

He nodded. "Dad says we should never worry Mom if we don't have to." He paused. "I'm sorry. I don't think she's going to be able to help you, Diane."

"Then it's good I'm excellent at helping myself." Her hand tightened on his. "Now I need a tall cup of strong coffee. Let's go find your mom and see if I can persuade her to have one with me."

NAPONI STABLE
10:05 P.M.

"You're nervous." Cameron's gaze was narrowed on Catherine's expression. "Is something wrong with the drone?"

She shook her head. "I don't think so. It appears to be operating with maximum efficiency. It should be back here at Naponi in another five minutes." Her gaze shifted to the computer whirring and spitting out information across the stable. "And its camera is still reporting even though I only set it up for the stockade and encampment. It's a very sophisticated piece of equipment."

"I'm glad you're pleased with my selection," Cameron said lightly. "I always like to keep my techs happy. Now, are you going to tell me why you're nervous?"

"I'm not nervous. I did everything right. I'm just worried that those computers aren't going to give me the answers Diane is hoping for. I promised I'd call and let her know as soon as I got a final report. But I'm not going to be able to tell Diane that Kai is there if the imaging says he's not."

"She'll understand."

"We're talking about Diane. She's very stubborn. She's fully capable of asking me to do another run if the result isn't what she wants."

"Will you do it?"

"I'd think about it. You said you were having Nalam shadowed? Did your man say Nalam was at the encampment?"

"No, he's still in Santa Monica."

"I don't know whether that's bad or good."

"He's been involved with hosting a presidential fundraiser for his pal Adam Madlock tonight, so I'd say that's good. He hasn't had the time to think about harassing Diane."

"But it's probably over now."

"I'll be told when he decides to head for Montana, Catherine," he said quietly. "With any luck he'll get drunk with his political cronies and end up in a hot tub with an equally hot hooker."

"Fingers crossed." She looked down at her watch. "The drone should be landing outside on the tarmac. Slade will call me after he checks it out and makes sure the cameras and scope are in perfect shape. I have to know that before I check the imaging reports."

"And call Diane."

She nodded. "I want to get at that computer. I hate waiting." Her gaze wandered restlessly around the stable. "Your guys did a good job cleaning this place. I was afraid that the dust or straw might get in the computer and interfere with the transmission. But it's spotless."

"I know a little bit about the care and maintenance of drones," he said solemnly. "And I knew you'd be very demanding."

"As if you wouldn't be." She grinned at him. "You had everything ready to operate on greased wheels when I got here tonight. All I had to do was enter the codes and make the necessary adjustments. I think you were afraid I'd screw this up."

"Perish the thought. But since this was my first gift to you, I didn't want to give you an inferior product."

"The drone and computer were gifts to me?"

"Certainly. And since they might eventually bring you Nalam, I decided that they might be worthy. Was I wrong?"

She was smiling. "No, you weren't wrong. It's a marvelous gift, a spectacular gift. Just what I've always wanted. Thank you."

"You're welcome." He leaned back as her phone rang. "Let's see if it's what Diane wanted."

She snatched up the phone. "It's okay, Slade?" She got the affirmative and cut the connection. The next moment she was across the stable and going through the info the computer was spitting out.

"Would you like any help?" Cameron asked.

She shook her head. "I need to concentrate. You'd get in my way."

"Heaven forbid. Tell me when you're ready."

She didn't answer as she went through the thermal images transmitted by the drone.

Good.

Good.

Maybe.

No.

What?

She paused and then went back and checked the image again.

She couldn't figure it out. It didn't have the same thermal energy as the others.

A mistake by the drone camera or scope?

But it would have shown up on the other images.

And then she realized what it was that she was looking at.

She inhaled sharply.

Shit.

Then she reached for her phone and called Diane.

She picked up on the first ring. "It's done?"

"Yes, come over to the stable." She hung up and just stood there a minute looking down at the report.

"Catherine?" Cameron was behind her.

She whirled and went into his arms. "Just hold me, okay? Don't say anything, just hold me." Her arms tightened around him. He was warm and strong and alive. She wasn't going to let him go. "I wasn't expecting it. Maybe I should have expected it, but I didn't. Please hold me."

"Easy. If I was holding you any tighter, I'd be behind you." He was rocking her back and forth. "And that's fine with me. But I need to know what hurt you, so I can fix it."

Then she heard Diane outside talking to Slade. Catherine couldn't let her see her this upset. She pushed Cameron away. "I'm all right. You can go now."

"The hell you are," he murmured. "But I'll cover for you." He moved a few yards away and leaned back against the stable wall. "I'm not going anywhere, though."

"Catherine." Diane was in the stable. "This is quite a production. That's a really cool drone outside." Her gaze flew to the computer. "That's the thermal imagery thing?" She was striding over to it. "Show me how it works."

Thank heavens Diane was so absorbed with getting the info she wanted that she wasn't noticing anything else. She followed her to the computer. "It's fairly simple. The equipment does most of the work." She pulled out the sheet. "I indicated the cells in the stockade to the drone, and it showed me the thermal energy in each one. There were only three possibilities that it sent back. Evidently the stockade is almost empty." She pointed to the first cell on the second floor. "This red streak is the energy source and it matches Kai's approximate height and bone structure. He's tall and powerful like all of the Hakalis. That's your best bet." She pointed to another cell at the opposite end of the stockade. "This streak is considerably shorter." She pointed to the third cell, which was next door. "Shorter still."

"So Kai should be on the second floor, first cell?" Diane asked.

Catherine was silent an instant. "That's what I'd guess."

"You hesitated." Diane's eyes were suddenly narrowed on Catherine's face. "Why? Are there other cells you haven't shown me?"

"Not a cell." She pushed the paper up. "The basement. And there aren't any thermal indications down there, but there's something else." *Go on, tell her.* "There are . . . objects. More than a dozen, but there's no life." She swallowed. "It seems Nalam didn't get around to burying all of his victims' bodies like he did Willem Tesar after he got finished playing with them."

Diane's gaze was focused helplessly on the basement area. "You're saying that Kai could be down there?"

"No, I'm not saying that. I don't want it to be the truth. That prisoner on the second floor could be Kai. The physical dimensions are correct. But I had to tell you what I'd found."

"It's a morgue," she said numbly. "No wonder you didn't find many prisoners. I was so full of hope after Eve did that reconstruction."

"Then don't lose it. Don't let that bastard take it away. Kai could be alive."

Diane lifted her chin. "Yes, he could." Her eyes were glittering fiercely in her taut face. "I won't believe anything else." She pushed the computer papers aside. "And I'm not afraid of morgues, or that sick son of a bitch who decided he wanted one of his own to add to his horror collection. All I want to do is arrange for him to join them." She turned on her heel and strode out of the stable.

"I believe she handled that better than you thought she would," Cameron said.

"I know she did," Catherine said blankly. She felt almost dazed that those last minutes had completely reversed what she'd thought would happen. "Like I said, I wasn't expecting that morgue even after you told me about those murders in the Amazon. I didn't know how I was going to tell her. I should have remembered that she told Eve once that forensics was her favorite class in medical school."

"She did?" He grinned. "Then I'm beginning to understand." He straightened away from the wall. "I gather I'm not going to have to comfort and soothe any longer? How do you feel? Not horror-stricken or unable to cope?"

"I'm never unable to cope. Sometimes it just takes me a little while. And I was horror-stricken at the idea of Nalam doing something that hideous. Life is precious." She shivered. "And I knew Diane felt that way. So I lost it a little. I suppose I should apologize."

"Are you?"

"No." She walked toward him. "Because I needed what you were giving me. All I could feel was death all around me, and you were *alive*. I wanted to feel *you*." She put her palm on his chest. "All of you."

He went still. "That wasn't the impression I got."

"I hadn't gotten there yet. We were interrupted." She was unbuttoning her shirt. "Do we have to worry about Slade or anyone else coming in here?"

"I doubt it. They have work to do with that drone." She could see the muscles of his belly tauten as he watched her bra drop to the floor. "Would you care?"

Her breasts were swelling; she was clenching. "Not enough to matter. I *want* this." Her hand slipped inside his shirt and she was rubbing his chest, her nails lightly scoring his nipples. "I always want this. And I'm going to take it." His shirt was open now, and she was rubbing her mouth back and forth on his chest. "With your permission. I wouldn't want to force you."

"After all I've gone through to get you this far?" His lips were on her breast and he was biting, licking. "By all means force me."

"But let me help you do it." He was pulling her down to the floor and tearing off the rest of her clothes and then his own.

Then he drove deep inside her!

She smothered a scream as her nails bit into his shoulders.

Heat.

Electricity.

He was lifting her with every thrust.

Deep. So deep.

Not enough. She slid her legs around his hips to take more of him.

He rolled her over and then was lifting her, walking across the stable, his hips still moving piston-like. Deeper, the rhythm filling her more with every step. But it was too much, *he* was too much.

"What . . ." She was clutching desperately at his shoulders. "I can't take—"

"Yes, you can." They were inside one of the stalls and he was lowering her. She felt wood and straw beneath her bare buttocks before he was spreading her legs. "We'll just slow it a little." She gasped as his fingers plunged inside her. "You can take every bit of me. You've done it before. It was only different because I wanted to get you into one of the stalls and I didn't want to leave you."

"I said—it didn't—matter."

"It mattered to me. I didn't want anyone else seeing you." She bit her lip as he added another finger and started moving. "My call. After all, I was the one being forced. Tell me when you're ready for me again." He held her body still, his fingers plunging, twisting, while his lips went to her breast and began sucking.

She cried out and arched upward.

He didn't stop. "I think that's a yes?"

"Yes, dammit. Come into me."

He was already pushing her legs wider. "I thought you'd never ask. I'll be very gentle."

"Don't you dare." She reached up and brought him into her. "Now move!"

"Oh, delighted." He plunged deep.

Heat.

Darkness.

No breath.

Tingling.

Deeper.

His mouth on her breasts, biting, pulling, pumping.

Deeper. Deeper. Deeper.

His fingers clenching on her buttocks, not letting her escape as he brought her up to every thrust.

Deeper. Deeper. Deeper.

Her head was tossing from side to side as she frantically tried to take more of him.

Deeper.

No, there was no deeper.

"Catherine?"

She couldn't answer. She cried out as she lunged upward and took him and took him. She could feel the force and the hardness and the madness. Yet there was also the gentleness she'd told him not to show her. It didn't matter, that was good too now that he'd given her what she'd needed.

Her eyes were closed and she was panting as he collapsed on

top of her. She held him tightly. Don't let him go. Don't let *this* go.

But he was moving. She could feel his lips brush her cheek as he left her. "I'll be right back," he whispered.

He was true to his word. She hadn't been able to gather herself together enough to do anything more than open her eyes and begin to fight off that delicious lethargy before he was kneeling beside her again. He'd already thrown on his own clothes and was carrying hers, which he tossed down on the floor. In his other hand, he had a bucket of water and a couple of towels. He set them down beside her. "It's cold water. I should let you go back to the house and shower, but I don't want to lose you yet." He dipped one end of the towel in the water and began rinsing her upper body. "This isn't such a good idea," he said thickly. "The cold water is making your nipples stand up and—"

"I know it is." She took the towel away from him and sketchily finished and then did the same with her lower body. Then she tossed the towel down. "I appreciate the thought, but the hot shower would have been better for both of us. You'll probably want to get out to the drone with Slade. I'll slip on my clothes and I'll—"

"Be quiet." He was wrapping a long strand of her dark hair around her breast. "What a beautiful frame." Then he bent down, his mouth enveloping her nipple. "I just want another minute or two."

She inhaled sharply as she felt his tongue. "Which is going to lead to considerably more than that. I was the one who started this, and I'm the one who has to end it. I was aggressive. It was a completely inappropriate time to try to—"

"Seduce me?" he finished. "I agree the timing surprised me, but I'll never find your aggressiveness inappropriate." His teeth nipped gently. "I'll only celebrate it."

"I got that impression." She had to move away from him. Lord, she didn't want to do it. He was everything that was beautifully sensual, every move graceful and catlike, yet that almost barbaric passion he had shown her was still there on the horizon coming closer every second. "Thank you very much. But I still shouldn't have inserted sex into a scene that was all about something more serious. I had no intention of doing that tonight. I was caught off guard and I obeyed impulse instead of good sense." She pushed him aside and started to dress. "Now I'll get out of here."

"Pity." He was watching as she pulled her shirt over her breasts and started to button it. "And that's filling me with profound self-pity."

"Cameron." She sighed wryly. "I don't believe you're going to have to worry about that. I knew it was only a question of time before I ended up in bed with you. I was just hoping that I'd be a bit more professional about it."

"So did I." He shook his head as her eyes widened. "Because you caught me off guard, too. If you'd been a little more wary, I might have talked myself out of being so damn eager." Then he shook his head. "Nah, that wasn't going to happen."

She finished putting on her clothes and slipped on her shoes. "Thank God."

"Everything is different with you." His eyes were narrowed on her face. "Why?"

"I just realized that I wasn't going to waste time cheating myself out of something I've wanted for a long time. Whatever else goes wrong, this is always right. We may fight on any number of issues, but so be it. We may even go to battle if we can't work it out, and that's okay, too. But we'll do it together." She looked him in the eye. "I was going to break it to you gently, but you'll have to come to terms with it. If you get tired of me, if I'm not worth it to you, then you'll have to be the one to leave. Do you understand?"

He nodded. "I've listened and understand." His eyes were twinkling. "As a reward, will you take your clothes off and let me make love to you again?"

She headed for the stable door. "I'm going back to the house. I'm serious, Cameron."

"And so am I." His smile faded. "Oh, very serious. I'm just being cautious. You know how obsessed I am with you. This means too much to me. I'm wondering if that declaration is a little too good to be true. It's been such a long time coming."

She glanced at him over her shoulder. "You'll have to decide that for yourself. And how do I know that you aren't only drawn by the excitement of the chase? I've put myself as far out on a limb as I'm willing to go." She added, "Let me know when you hear Nalam's on his way. Diane's going to want to know."

CHAPTER 16

Diane met Catherine in the hall when she came back to the ranch house. "I'm glad you're here at last. I didn't mean to stalk out of that stable spitting fury. I was pretty upset. I didn't know what to say."

"Neither did I. It was a shock. Cameron and I agreed you did very well considering." She frowned as she gazed at her expression. "Or maybe you didn't? What can I do to help?"

"You can tell me what's going to happen now that we know where Kai is in that stockade."

"We can't be sure, Diane."

"You said I had to believe. Well, that's what I'm going to do. It's what I have to do," she said. "Tell me."

"We'll send a couple more exploratory drones out to verify the results of the initial one that you looked at tonight. If they come back high-confidence, then Cameron will advise the team we already have near the encampment to make plans to get the prisoners out of the stockade."

"Make plans," Diane repeated. "They'd better already have them. There's not much time left."

"Cameron's men are very competent." She smiled. "And Alon Hakali arrived at their camp just before we sent out that exploratory drone. I know you trust him. Monteith will be flying Joe Quinn down to join them in a few hours to head the team. They'll try to coordinate the rescue right before Nalam shows up at the stockade." She paused. "He's been busy sucking up to the president and arranging a fundraiser. He hasn't left Santa Monica yet, and that may mean we have more time than you think."

"They grab Kai, release any other prisoners. What next?"

Catherine hesitated and then said, "Next, the weaponized drone should be overhead to blow Nalam and his thugs to kingdom come."

"Good," Diane said. "I wasn't sure if you were going to depend on law and order to take care of him or not. I feel much safer now." She turned. "And I have to go call Alon and tell him that Joe Quinn is coming to help with the rescue. He was impressed by Joe and Cameron."

"And you're relieved, too."

"What can I say?" She shrugged. "In one way or another, Joe's been impressing me for most of my adult life. Why change now?"

Catherine watched Diane go down the hall toward her room. It was all very well for Diane to be relieved and happy that Joe was going to help that team at Nalam's encampment. It was an intelligent move for one of their best assets to work that rescue.

But she wasn't at all sure how Eve was going to feel when she found out.

2:15 A.M.

"I hate this, you know." Eve's voice was shaking as she turned away from watching Monteith climb into the helicopter. She stepped closer to Joe. "I *hate* it."

"I'll be fine. We've talked about this before. We've got to get that kid out of the stockade." His arms slid around her. "Can I talk you into going back inside? That's a chilly wind blowing, love."

"Yes, it is. And it will be colder in those mountains in Montana." She burrowed her face in his chest. "'*We've* got to get that kid'? You mean you've got to do it. It's always you. Superman would never share the load with anyone else."

"Hey, I'm sharing this one." He kissed her. "I'm sharing it with those guys at the camp and I'm sharing it with you. And you might say Cameron is going to help a bit with that drone before it's over. I believe he'd give you an argument."

Her arms tightened around him. "But he's not playing Superman, is he? You've got to promise me that you're not going to be idiotic and get yourself killed. I won't have it. Michael won't have it. You just do something incredibly smart, snatch that poor kid, and get yourself out of there. Do you hear me?"

"Loud and clear." He kissed her again. "It will be fine, and I won't be idiotic. I have to go, Eve."

"We'd have a debate on that if I could just forget the photo of that boy." She grudgingly released him and stepped back. "How soon will you call me?"

"It's a two-hour flight." He got in the passenger seat of the helicopter. "As soon as I get on the ground. Tell Michael I'll call him later and explain."

"You probably won't have to explain. He'll know, but he'll want to hear your voice." She stepped off the tarmac as Monteith started the engine and the rotors began whirring. "And so will I."

She wasn't sure if he could hear her now, but he was smiling at her. She didn't feel like smiling, but she did anyway. You didn't send Superman out to save the world with a sour face. She kept smiling until the helicopter lifted off and turned south. Then she turned and started back to the house, the tears stinging her eyes. "*Damn. Damn. Damn.*"

Monteith set the helicopter down in the foothills ten miles north of the encampment and turned to Joe. "You'll have to go on foot from here to where Cameron's team has set up their camp. But there should be someone here in a minute to lead you to it. Put on your jacket—the temperature is plummeting. There's supposed to be snow later."

"That's all I need, a walk through the snow." He raised his brows. "You're not bundling up. I take it you're not coming with me?"

Monteith shook his head. "My orders are to lift off and find a convenient place to land, settle, and wait for someone to call if they need me." He was peering out the window. "But I think that's your escort now." He pointed his flashlight at ten or twelve figures in heavy winter gear and hats coming toward them. "The first guy is Mark Fallon, but I don't recognize the others."

"I do." Joe was jumping out of the helicopter. "At least, one of them. He sent me a photo on Skype, but it pales before the reality. He didn't mention he was a giant." He took five steps forward and held out his hand. "Hakali? Joe Quinn. I'm glad to meet you."

Alon Hakali's brilliant smile lit his face as he shook Joe's hand. "I feel I already know you. I wanted to come and greet you and tell you how much it means to me that you're going to help me get my brother back." He gestured to the man next to him. "Mark Fallon. He's learned more about this encampment in two days than I did camping out here for over a week."

Fallon nodded at Joe. "And one of the things I know is that Nalam's crew are scared enough of him that they do a decent job of reconnaissance and that we'd better get out of here in case they heard that helicopter and get curious. Are you ready?"

"No, the *hell* he's not ready." Monteith was swearing. Joe whirled to look back at the helicopter to see him struggling with someone who appeared to be trying to exit from the passenger seat. "I had nothing to do with it, Quinn," he yelled. "She hid out in the cargo compartment. Do something about this. You tell Cameron I didn't know she was here."

Diane!

Joe started to swear to himself as Diane gave a final lunge, rolled out of the helicopter, and fell to the ground.

But Mark Fallon was running over to her, flipping her on her back and raising his hand to give her a karate chop.

"No!" Alan Hakali was there, jerking Fallon off her and tossing him out of the way as if he were a child. "You don't hurt her. She sometimes lacks reason and can be exasperating but she means well." He pulled Diane to a sitting position. "Though I must apologize for her in this case, Quinn. Really, Diane? A stowaway? She's been under a lot of stress lately."

"Be quiet, Alon." She was dusting herself off. "I merely found the easiest way to accomplish what I needed to do. It avoided arguments and refusals and got me where I wanted to be. Everyone is trying to protect me these days, even you, who should know better." She turned to Joe. "So I'm a fait accompli, and what are you going to do about it?"

"Send you back with Monteith."

"But he's not going back. He told you he had other orders. I'm here, you'd do better to let me come along in case I'm needed." She got to her feet. "I told you once that the time might come when I would have to deflect harm from Eve—that I was a weapon you could use. Thank God that didn't become necessary. But Nalam is still out there, and he's still torturing and killing, and I'm still the bullet that might get rid of him for you if anything goes wrong with your plans." Her lips twisted. "So consider me insurance and take me with you. There's no question that I'll keep up. My body will adjust to protect me from the cold or snow. I have more cellular endurance built into me than any of you, even Alon, and he spent his life being fed those tri-roots."

"What's going on here?" Fallon was picking himself up and turning to Joe. "Who the hell is she?"

"A pain in my ass. I'll handle it."

Fallon muttered a curse. "Then it had better be soon."

"Diane." Alon shook his head. "Don't do this."

"I'm not doing anything yet. I'm only insurance. But you're not going to lose your brother. You've lost too much already." Diane lifted her chin as she took a step toward Joe. "Going soft, Joe? I'm not as expendable as you thought? Then do the right thing and let's get out of here before those sentries show up."

"You're not expendable. You've never been expendable," he said through set teeth. "But you're just as difficult as you've been all your life. I'll take you with us, but you'll obey orders and as soon as I get the chance, I'll send you back with Monteith." He turned to Fallon. "I'll be responsible for her. Let's get to your camp and get to work on freeing those prisoners. If there's a snowstorm coming, it may give us an edge."

NAPONI

"I can't believe it, Joe." Eve's hand tightened on the phone. "I thought Diane was safely tucked in bed."

"Well, you would have gotten a shock in the morning, wouldn't you? She's worried about Kai and Alon, and she says she's our insurance policy. I wasn't sure if anyone was aware she was gone, so I had to let you know. I'll get her back to Naponi as soon as I can."

"Insurance policy," Eve repeated. She was feeling a chill. "I don't like the sound of that."

"Neither do I. But I can't interpret everything she says and does. I have a job to do. We're almost at Fallon's camp now. Diane hasn't caused any trouble since we got on the trail. She was right about her stamina and keeping up with us. She even checked the weather report before she pulled this stunt and she's dressed for the cold. I couldn't believe it."

"That's what I said, but that part doesn't surprise me. She's a scientist and very detail-oriented. I found that out when we were working together." She paused. "I know you have to go, but is Diane nearby? Can I talk to her?"

"Be my guest. Try to talk her into staying in camp. Otherwise I might have to hog-tie her."

The next moment Diane came on the line. "Hi, Eve. How angry are you with me? It's not as bad as it sounds. I just realized I had to take things into my own hands, and it was easier to handle it this way."

"I thought that might be why you did it." She paused. "But you are *not* to consider yourself insurance. Did you think that I wouldn't remember all that Nalam raving? I know I can't convince you to do anything except what you want to do. Just don't be stupid, because then Joe would think he has to rescue you. It's in his genes."

"I realize that. I won't trigger anything that would upset you." She lowered her voice. "And I'll keep my promise. I'll keep Joe alive."

"Yes, you will, or I'll come after you. Goodbye, Diane." She cut the connection.

It was crazy, and scary, and bizarre, Eve thought as she put her phone on the nightstand. And it was just like Diane to make her own decisions, then try to mold everyone to her way of thinking. Yet some of those decisions were meant to save, and the molding was—

"Can I come in, Mom?" Michael was standing in the doorway, his eyes big in his thin face. "I can't sleep."

That probably wasn't all that was bothering him. "Sure." She threw back her blanket and held out her arms. "I'm having trouble, too."

He flew across the room in a flash and was in the bed. "I thought you might... Dad being gone." He cuddled closer. "He always makes you feel safer. Me, too. Nothing can go wrong when Dad's around."

So much for her having to break the news that Joe had left, she thought ruefully. "He'll be back soon. He wouldn't have left if it hadn't been important."

He nodded. "It's just that it might get bad." His voice was low. "It's starting, Mom."

She inhaled sharply, her arms instinctively tightening around him. "Your dad will be able to handle it. Is there anything you'd like to tell me?"

He shook his head. "I can't see it. But maybe I will when it gets closer. It's scary, Mom."

"I knew it was, or you wouldn't have been so determined to come here." She gently smoothed his hair. "But we always come out on top even when it does get scary, don't we?"

"So far." He was starting to yawn. "But Diane isn't sure and that worries me. She's trying not to let anyone see it, but Alon knows..." He asked drowsily, "Do you think we should tell Catherine that Diane is there with Dad? She's always watching out for her."

"I think we should let her sleep. She can't do anything, and your dad is watching out for her."

"That's right. Like he watches out for everybody. He just handed her a blanket because it's started to snow and it's getting colder..."

He was asleep.

But Eve didn't sleep until almost dawn.

"I don't need your help, Diane," Alon said quietly. "Why won't you believe me?" He dropped down before the campfire beside her. "I've never had a closer friend and your generosity is beyond belief, but I can't take any more from you."

She grinned at him. "Am I embarrassing you? I can see how my not only chasing you down but practically falling from a helicopter at your feet would be awkward for you."

He grinned back. "But it wasn't at my feet, it was at Quinn's. I was only the one who had to rescue you. You gave Quinn a very bad time, Diane. I thought we'd talked through your problem with him."

"We did, but a few things popped up once I had to actually deal with Joe and Eve again. Still, I worked through them just as you told me to do." She tapped her chest. "So here I am, almost totally free of all that baggage and ready to start life as it should be lived." She grimaced. "There's only one thing missing. I can't do without you. You're my friend and my therapist and all those other dozens of things that you've managed to incorporate into what we are together." She tilted her head. "Except my lover. Catherine asked me if you were my lover, and I told her everything else, but not that. Why aren't you my lover?"

"Have you felt cheated that I wasn't?"

"No, never."

He smiled at her. "And that's why we're not lovers. The minute you felt cheated, we would have had to do something about it. But your life is full and rich enough without it. It would have just gotten in your way."

"And yours?"

His smile deepened. "And mine." He looked back at Joe Quinn. "And was one of the things that popped up when you encountered Eve and Joe a lingering memory of what he'd meant to you?"

"Perhaps. But it was gone in a heartbeat and there were only the problems." She added slowly, "I think I . . . like him. It's a great relief."

He laughed. "Only you, Diane. But you tried very hard tonight to make certain he wouldn't like you."

"That doesn't matter. I'm here, aren't I?"

"And that's where I don't want you to be."

"You can lecture me once we get Kai out of that place and on his way to the island." She looked him in the eye. "I'm not going to pay any attention until then, so you can save your breath. Now, what were you talking to Joe about that I wasn't permitted to hear? When do we go for Kai?"

"Not until just before Nalam gets here. And he doesn't seem to be eager to move his ass from Santa Monica. I suppose that means we twiddle our thumbs and warm ourselves before this fire until he does."

"That doesn't sound like Joe. He's always been impatient and looking ahead to find a plan that he can move forward at top speed." Her gaze shifted back to Joe, who was now on the phone. "I'd bet he's doing that now. Who is he talking to?"

"He seemed concerned about the weather. He was going to check the forecast . . ."

"Diane's gone," Catherine said as she strode into the stable. "Did you have anything to do with it, Cameron?"

"Not guilty. The first I heard about it was a few hours ago from Monteith. He wasn't pleased. He said Quinn wasn't, either."

"That's what Eve said, but I had to be sure."

"Of course you did. When I'd made it plain that my intentions toward Diane hadn't changed." He smiled. "No, it was entirely her own idea. I don't believe you'd have a chance of changing her mind even if you followed her to that encampment."

"Neither do I. But I'm still responsible for her." Her lips tightened. "I could *shake* her. What am I supposed to do?"

"Wait for Quinn to find a way to send her back?" He paused and then said softly, "Or stay with Slade and me and help get the weaponized drone ready to do its magnificent best to blow Nalam to bits?"

He knew what she wanted to do, dammit. In this moment Cameron was mischievous, teasing, and as sensually alluring as she'd ever seen him. Oh, what the hell. "What a hard decision. Have we heard if Nalam has left Santa Monica yet?"

He shook his head.

"Then I think we should have a welcoming present for him when he does finally get to that stockade." She started to roll up her sleeves. "Do I get to program it?"

SANTA MONICA
8:15 A.M.

"What do you mean he's gone?" Nalam bit out. "He wasn't supposed to leave before this evening, Daniels."

"Adam Madlock is the president of the United States. It's not as if he asked me if he could change his itinerary," Daniels said sarcastically. "But I still made adjustments, and I already had my own plans in place. Complete with that Barbie-doll hooker you introduced him to at the fundraiser last night and the special-quality fentanyl that I sent to her to keep him happy."

"It went off okay?"

"Perfect. You said he liked the young ones. That Secret Service agent I bribed said Madlock had a very young woman aboard Air Force One when he took off for Washington." He stared Nalam in the eye. "So what else do you want me to do? You took me away from the Connors search to do your political dirty work. Everyone else had a chance at that fat bounty you offered, but not me. Now I've done the job you wanted and Madlock should be dead within a week. I think I deserve a bonus."

"Within a week?"

"You wouldn't want it any earlier. The poison you gave me might be undetectable, but you'll still need time to establish a foolproof alibi. He *is* the president."

"No, a week is fine," Nalam said absently. "I just have to make arrangements for what comes next on the agenda."

"My bonus," Daniels repeated.

"You'll get it." But it was important to get rid of Daniels as soon as possible, he thought. He'd made sure that no one in Santa Monica had seen them together during the few days they'd both been here, but the quicker he got the man out of town, the better. "You'll get a bonus for this job and I'll give you the chance at that bounty, too. Galman says they haven't been able to track down Ling or Connors yet." He smiled. "I thought you'd be interested in trying your luck again. You wouldn't want to have that kind of failure on your excellent record."

Daniels stiffened and then leaned forward eagerly. "No, I wouldn't. When are we going to leave?"

"Soon. Ling isn't the prime target here, but I'll give you a bonus for her if you can get me Connors."

"And I'd still get the bounty for Connors?"

Nalam nodded. "And I'll even help with a setup that will bring her running to us. Could I be more generous?"

"A little too generous," Daniels said warily. "Why?"

"I'm grateful to you for disposing of Madlock for me. Lately I've realized just how much I want all that power he wields. Thanks to you, I'll be in an excellent position to act the grieving best friend who will try to continue the president's good works until I'm pressed to run for the office myself. And Connors was going to be a difficulty I didn't want to face. I can afford to be generous." He paused. "If you want the deal?"

"I want it," Daniels said curtly. "You didn't tell me when we're going to leave. We're going back to Calgary?"

"We leave this afternoon." He turned away. "And we're not going to Calgary. We're going to a cozy little camp in Montana. It's one of my favorite places, but I don't believe it will be one of Connors's. However, I guarantee you'll find it interesting." He was starting up the grand staircase. "But you're leaving sunny California behind, so dress warmly. I hear there may be snow..."

"Nalam's left California with our friend Daniels. His plane is heading north toward Montana." Cameron smiled as he hung up and turned to Catherine. "It's starting."

"Don't tell me, tell Joe," she said curtly. "He's the one who has to get those prisoners out of the stockade before we send out that drone."

"That's what I'm doing," he said soothingly as he started to punch in Joe's number. "I just wanted to assure you that everything is going our way..."

"Quinn has called a meeting," Alon told Diane as he got to his feet. "That must mean we're going to be moving out soon."

"But you're trying to tell me politely that I'm not invited?" She nodded ruefully. "I understand. He was pretty pissed off. I know I was lucky just to get him to let me stay." She motioned for him to go. "Besides, you'll tell me what's going on when you get back."

She watched him cross the campground toward the group of men surrounding Joe. She was glad that everything seemed to be moving forward. It didn't matter whether or not she was allowed to be part of any planning. After all, she really knew nothing about—

Her phone was ringing.

She stiffened. Blocked.

Coincidence that a call would come right after they'd gotten word that Nalam was on the move? Not likely.

Stop hesitating. This is why you came here. Face the bastard.

She pressed the access. "Nalam?"

"Did you think I'd forgotten about you, bitch? I was delayed on important business, but even my old buddy the president couldn't keep me from you for long. And you can be sure he won't interfere between us ever again." He laughed. "Or anyone else for that matter. Have you discussed my offer with Alon Hakali? I do hope so. I can't stop thinking about the boundless possibilities you're going to offer me. I'm finding it very exciting."

"Are you insane? Why would I speak to him about it? Alon would never agree to a trade like that. It would only hurt him more. And you've already taken too much from him."

"And you cared enough for him to risk everything to try to find where I'd hidden his brother. But you're only a woman and you blundered, didn't you? Those doctors who tested you in Hong Kong believed you were so intelligent, but they were wrong. I'm going to be able to crush you and everything you stand for with no problem."

Don't answer back. Give him the response he wants.

"I admit that I made a mistake at that warehouse in Manila. You're right, I've no experience and I blundered."

"And you and your friends have gotten in my way several times since then when I wanted to punish Hakali. Do you know how angry that made me?" His rage was clearly escalating. "Is it any wonder that I want to make him pay? Make *you* pay?"

"No, but it really isn't him that you want to punish right now, is it? I'm the one who's most in your way. I'm the one who can hurt you and turn your world upside down. Alon can't offer you what I can." She took a deep breath. "So I thought we might make a deal. I'll go along with the trade you offered. You'll get me the minute you turn Kai over to Alon."

He laughed. "You do care for that son of a bitch. I was wondering if you could be that soft. I knew you must be a stupid do-gooder to waste your career developing that panacea. Though I thought I was going to have to offer you a small incentive to step into my parlor. I might anyway, just to make sure that you don't try to trick me."

She went still. "Incentive?"

"I've been very angry with you and Alon. I might not have chopped Kai into pieces as I told Alon I did that day, but I did need some release."

"Release? What are you talking about?"

"I spent a full day with Kai that I enjoyed very much. And when I left to go back to Santa Monica, I left orders with his jailer to continue with my excellent work."

"What are you talking about?" she asked hoarsely.

"Talk is cheap. A photo is so much better. I'm going to send you one of Kai, and you'll realize that you really don't want to trick me or do anything but come meekly to the place I designate. Because anyone as soft as you appear to be wouldn't be able to stand what would follow. Poor Kai. He's had such a bad time. I concentrated on the whip but his jailer, Bart, preferred to use his fists and sometimes put him in ice baths all night. He's developed a fever. Have you gotten the photo yet?"

She had just received it and she slowly opened the file. She flinched. Dear God.

That sweet golden young man who had been Kai Hakali was barely recognizable. He was chained to a wall and his half-naked body was covered with bruises and whip marks. His face was also swollen and terribly bruised, and his eyes looked glazed and feverish. She felt sick looking at him. "You have to be a monster."

"I was angry." His voice was completely devoid of feeling. "He was available."

"So you did . . . that?"

"As I said, it was enjoyable, but as it happens, it will also be a lesson if you plan on doing anything foolish. I will give you Kai, though you'll probably have to use a stretcher to take him from his cell. You can see he's not well."

"Anyone can see that," she said harshly. "He should probably be in a hospital."

"Well, Alon will have to attend to that because you'll be otherwise engaged, won't you? I might decide to play with you a bit before we get down to those injections that you're going to give me. You'd be much more satisfying than Hakali's younger brother. He's been a total failure. Though Bart did have a bit of fun with him." His voice lowered with malice. "And will continue to do so if you change your mind about our arrangement. He's with him day and night and I have trouble keeping him under control. Bart's rather sadistic and I don't believe Kai will last too much longer."

"I'm not going to change my mind," she said. "But I'm going to try to change yours. I don't want to die. You'd be stupid to kill me when I can be of such value to you. I don't believe you've thought it through."

"I've thought it through. I've always been attracted to the easy way, and getting rid of you is definitely the easy way." He chuckled. "But I might keep you around and let you try to convince me."

"You'd be a fool not to be convinced. You want power? I can get you power."

"We'll see," Nalam said. "I'll be in touch very soon and tell you where and when. I can hardly wait for us to be together."

He cut the connection.

Diane sat there, staring down at the photo Nalam had sent her. Kai had taken so much punishment. All the joy of life robbed from him. Wrong. Wrong. Wrong.

And his situation was even more dangerous than she had thought it was going to be. Joe's plan for getting Kai away was probably going to be lethal and clever, but she didn't see how it could work.

She got to her feet and headed over to where Joe was having his meeting. She pushed through the crowd toward Joe.

"We'll use the snow." Joe was using a stick to point at the square he'd drawn on the ground to indicate the stockade. "The forecast says there will be blizzard conditions for the next ten hours, and that should discourage any sentries from being too active. They'll be huddling in their tents." He turned to Fallon. "You said you have a team ready to blow the gates of the stockade?"

Fallon nodded. "Explosives set. And the storm will permit me to smuggle a man into the stockade to check out prisoner placement if that's necessary. Just give the word and we'll—"

"I need to talk to you, Joe," Diane said. "Right now. There's something you should know."

"I'm busy, Diane."

"Right *now*. I'm not that spoiled kid you knew all those years ago. I wouldn't interrupt like this if it wasn't important." She turned and made her way back through the crowd. She didn't look to see if he was following until she was back at the fire and whirling to face him. "Good. I wasn't sure if you'd believe me. You have trouble separating past from present."

"I'm trying. You seemed dead serious."

"Not dead. Not yet. But it could happen anytime. That poor kid." She ran her hand through her hair. "You're expecting to whisk Kai out of that cell and get him away in a cloud of gunfire and explosives. Good plan. Except that he's chained to the wall in that cell with a jailer who will shoot him rather than let him escape. And there will be no whisking because he won't be able to walk, and I don't know how much other damage they've done to him." Her hand was shaking as she handed him her phone. "You want to know what we've got to work with? Look at his photo."

Joe muttered a curse as he stared at Kai. "Who did this?"

"Nalam and one of his favorite goons. I think he called him Bart. Nalam was angry and Kai was 'available.'"

Joe was swearing again and then he stopped. "Where did you get this photo? Talk to me."

"You know where I got it. He wanted to make certain I was intimidated enough to do whatever he wanted." She nodded at her phone again. "Listen to him." She turned away and dropped down in front of the fire. "But don't start yelling until you finish. I can't take it right now."

Joe didn't yell at all. He just listened to the call and then sat down beside her, staring into the fire. "Insurance, hell," he said gruffly. "You never meant to do anything but take him up on that trade."

"Not true. I don't want to die. I thought there might be a chance it might go your way. But I couldn't take the chance of not being prepared." She shivered. "He's an evil, evil man, Joe. You saw what he did to Kai. If he ever got his hands on Alon, it would be worse. I might be the only one who would have a chance with him. I have the bullet, and he hates it, but he's into power. There was a slim possibility I could twist that to give me enough time to get away."

"Slim possibility," he repeated. "You're an idiot, Diane."

"I took that probability under consideration." She grimaced. "But there was also the chance that if I was inside the stockade, you might be able to think of something that would save my ass and still allow Cameron's drone to rid the world of that bastard."

"Pressure."

"You always did your best work under pressure. But you'd better think fast, because Nalam's not going to give me much time. I'm getting to know him, and there was a kind of... euphoria about him when I was talking to him this time. Everything is going his way and he can't wait for it all to fall into his lap." She had a sudden thought. "That remark he made about the president was... interesting. That might be one of the reasons Nalam was like that. I'll have to think about it." She made a dismissive motion with her hand. "But not right now. What's important at the moment is getting Kai out of that stockade alive and keeping him that way. I wouldn't put it past Nalam to try to double-cross me. He wants it all. Have a doctor ready to treat Kai when Nalam releases him and then get him away."

Joe's brows rose. "Any other orders?"

"Don't tell Alon about the trade. Maybe put him in charge of getting Kai to a hospital. That should distract him."

"It might not work. He impresses me as being very intelligent."

"Brilliant. But he's always loved his family and he's been obsessed with freeing Kai. Keep him busy. Make it work."

He was silent for a long moment. Then he said harshly, "You know I could end this insanity by putting you under guard and confiscating this phone. What about your work?"

"Eve has my notes on those nine cases. If she finds the right scientist, they might find enough clues to start putting my formula together."

"Or not. Eve wouldn't think that was a good alternative to keeping you alive."

"I don't think so, either, but it was the only solution I could think of." She paused. "But she'd understand that a life is precious and worth almost anything to save."

Joe was muttering another curse.

"I agree." Diane forced a smile. "My sentiments exactly. So you'd better stop swearing and go away and start thinking. I'm counting on you."

Nalam's next call came four hours later. "I'm going to text you directions to my stockade in Montana where I'm keeping Kai Hakali. You come alone and no weapons. No telephone calls. No outside communication. I want you here in two hours. If you're still in Canada, I'm sure that will work for you. However, I don't really care if it does or not. I'll just have Bart start working on the boy again until you get here."

"I'll see that I get there within your time frame." She paused. "And here are my requirements. I'm not about to trust that you'll keep any bargain you make with me. I'm willing to take a risk, but I'm not going to give something for nothing. You *will* free Kai. So I'll send Joe Quinn to look over this stockade and the grounds and make sure that you don't have any of your men waiting in the wings to take Kai back. If he says it's okay, then I'll call and tell you to send Kai outside that place on a stretcher for Joe to pick up and take to safety. I'll be with them when they pick Kai up, and then I'll come directly into the stockade."

Nalam was cursing. "I don't like it."

"That's all you'll get. I won't be cheated."

Silence. She held her breath.

"What the hell," he finally said. "It won't make any difference in the long run. Just don't be late, or it's Kai who'll pay." He hung up.

Diane looked at Joe. "Well, he's heading this way. I was half afraid that he'd decide to take Kai somewhere else for the trade." Her smile was bitter. "I guess he's become too attached to that jail cell where they've been torturing Kai to abandon it. Now it's up to you, Joe."

"Not quite," he said grimly. "You've still got to figure a way to keep Nalam from killing you until I can get you out of there. That's not going to be easy."

"All I can do is appeal to his greed. I've had a long time to weigh the pros and cons of the bullet. The pros can be pretty spectacular if it falls into the hands of a power-hungry bastard like Nalam." She wearily shook her head. "If I talk fast enough, I might be able to stall him until I can get to that gun Fallon said he planted on the second-floor upper hall."

"You don't have to do this. We can go back to the plan I was working on," Joe said roughly. "I can just try to up the timing."

"And get Kai killed. You know we can't risk that." Her gaze flew to his face. "You didn't tell Alon why we had to change the plans?"

He shook his head. "But he might suspect something. He knows you very well, Diane."

"Too well. That's why I've been dodging him. It's good you've been keeping all the men so busy." She looked at her watch. "Two hours. It's going to be nerve racking trying to wait until it's time to show up on Nalam's doorstep. Particularly since it's right over that hill. What are you going to be doing?"

"You mean besides checking to see that Nalam's men are moving out and making sure that when Nalam flies in, he doesn't see any sign of our activity? And then there's getting a team launch ready in case we need to go and rescue you?"

"Point taken," she said wryly. She had another thought. "But while you're sitting around doing nothing, will you get in touch with Madlock's Secret Service team and have them check and see if everything's okay with the president? I keep thinking about that remark Nalam made."

"What should they be checking?"

"I don't know. Maybe nothing. But it sounded . . . fatal. A sniper?" She was frowning. "Or poison? That would be more subtle. I have no idea. Just put them on the alert. You could tell them you heard a leak. They'd believe you, Joe. You always know someone in law enforcement."

"I don't know anyone in Madlock's Secret Service team," he said dryly. "Maybe I'll make it an anonymous tip."

"That might work, too. Whatever you think best."

"Thank you for your confidence."

She watched him walk away. His last sentence had been sarcastic, but she did have confidence in Joe. She always had and she always would. She knew he would have even tried to make it safer for her if she'd said the word.

Her head lifted in alarm. Was that a plane overhead? Joe had been worried that they not be spotted by Nalam when he flew in. It could be him arriving at the stockade. That two-hour deadline had been for her.

It would probably be okay. Their tents were tucked under the cover of the cliff and, if there was a problem, Joe would take care of it.

Whatever nightmare waited for her today, she could trust Joe.

CHAPTER 17

NAPONI

Screaming!

Eve jerked upright in bed!

Michael!

She was out of bed and running down the hall toward the office. She saw him standing in the doorway, tears running down his cheeks, and then he was flying into her arms.

"It's okay. It's okay." She was on her knees, holding him tightly, pressing his face into her shoulder. "Whatever it is, we'll fix it, Michael."

"Blood. There's too much blood." He was sobbing. "You're here and you can't fix it. But maybe Diane can. She didn't want to take it with her. She thought it wasn't safe. But she has to have it, Mom. There's too much blood."

Terror was icing through her. She had wanted to soothe him. But this wasn't the first time he had spoken about the blood, and she had a horrible feeling that she must not ignore it.

"Whose blood?" She pushed him away from her and her hands grasped his shoulders. "I'm listening, Michael. *Talk* to me."

Forty-five minutes later Eve walked across the ranch yard and entered the stable.

Cameron looked up, startled. "Eve. What the hell are you doing here? Is something wrong?"

"Maybe. I don't know. Michael is very upset, and I just managed to get him back to bed before I ran down here. He thinks something is different in Montana and may be going wrong. I tried to reach Joe, but he doesn't answer. Why would he do that? So I decided to come and ask you." She stared him in the eye. "Should I be worried? Was Michael right?" She looked at the drone on the landing pad. "Is something different going on?"

"There's been a change, a delay. But Quinn can handle it." He said quietly, "You should know that better than I do."

"Of course I do. Stop trying to soothe me. I just got finished doing that with Michael." She moistened her lips. "You've told me what I need to know except for one thing. How quickly can you get me to that camp in Montana?"

"I can't let you go there, Eve."

"You can't stop me. Where's Monteith?"

"Running equipment and personnel back and forth from Calgary to the camp."

"Then I'll be right on his way. Call him and tell him to pick me up." She turned to leave. "While I go back and say goodbye to Michael and then ask Catherine to take care of him for me."

He called after her, "Quinn might murder me, you know."

"You're not worried. You didn't even fight me." She glanced back at him. "Why not?"

"I didn't fight you because I knew it wouldn't do any good." He added, "But I'm very, very worried, Eve."

THE BULLET

1:40 A.M.

Monteith's helicopter had landed and he glumly shook his head as he saw Eve hurrying toward him. "Quinn's not going to like this. But at least you're not hijacking a ride. I hope he knows you're coming."

"He would if he'd answer his phone." She threw her duffel in the backseat and climbed into the passenger seat. She waved at Cameron standing in the doorway of the stable and buckled her seat belt. "Tell him that when you talk to him, Cameron."

"I hope we'll be discussing more important things," he said dryly. "And that you'll be in a better humor when— Oh, shit." His gaze was on Catherine who was moving quickly toward the helicopter. "I thought you said she was going to take care of your son, Eve."

"That's what she told me." Eve was frowning down at Catherine as she reached the helicopter. "Didn't you, Catherine? What are you doing here?"

"Don't worry, Michael's not alone." Catherine opened the helicopter door and got in the backseat. "I called Slade and told him to take over. Michael will like being one of the guys. I decided I'd be of more value going with you."

"I'd rather you be with Michael."

"And I was perfectly willing to do it." She met Eve's gaze. "Until I had time to think and remember that Diane is in Montana and whatever is going wrong there might be attributed to that fact. And if it is, since she's my responsibility, I'll have to fix it." She leaned forward and yelled to Cameron over the sound of the engine, "The drone is programmed and ready to go. I was really hoping I'd be able to set it off from here. But Montana might do just as well. I'll call you . . ."

"It's okay." Joe was walking toward the spot where Diane stood beneath the snow-covered trees at the beginning of the forest line. "Nalam's men's tents are still there, but they're gone and so are the vehicles. Nalam's plane is on the tarmac next to the stockade, no vehicles there, either."

"So I'm safe?"

"Hell, no. But whatever you're going to have to deal with is in that stockade and not outside. Make the call."

She still hesitated. The stockade wasn't large, but it looked like the prison it was and loomed over the wide stony approach that was the size of two football fields and equally intimidating.

Shake it off, she told herself.

She punched in the number Nalam had given her. "We're on our way," she said when Nalam answered. "Put Kai and the stretcher outside. When we see him, we'll start toward the stockade."

"Welcome," Nalam said. "I can't tell you how pleased I am to see you. I'm certain Kai has been waiting eagerly for you. Though it's hard to tell in his present condition." The double doors opened, and a stretcher was rolled out onto the concrete by a short, powerful dark-haired man. "That's Bart Jessup who's pushing his friend out there. He's very sad to see him go. You'll have to come back in now, Bart. But I might have more work for you later today." He paused and then said softly, "Your move, Diane. Don't be shy. Bring your friend Joe Quinn for me to meet."

"You can still stop this, Diane," Joe said quietly.

"No, I can't." She ended the call and continued to walk toward the stockade. "Come on, Joe. The man wants to meet you."

"But he'd much prefer to meet me, Diane," Alon said quietly from behind her. "Don't be insulted, Quinn."

She whirled to stare at him in shock. "What the hell are you doing here? You're supposed to wait in the forest for Joe to bring Kai. Go away, Alon."

"I can't do it. He's my brother. It's my job. You never understood that." He smiled. "Just as you persist in never understanding that you can't deceive me. We know each other too well. Of course I know what you're up to with Quinn." He turned to Joe. "You'll excuse me for interfering, but I can't let her do this alone." He looked at Nalam, who was frowning and had taken a step toward them. "And we'd better finish this and let you get my brother the help he needs or Nalam will interfere." His pace quickened as he started toward the stockade. "Oh, he's recognizing me. There's no way he'll interfere now."

"What can we do, Joe?" Diane whispered as she hurried to catch up. "Nalam *hates* him."

"Choices," Joe murmured. "Kai is in bad shape. And you're not going to get rid of Alon. I'll take Kai back to Fallon to care for and then work at getting you both out. It's all we can do. I'll call Fallon on the way back with Kai and tell him to be ready." His voice lowered. "Remember, the gun Fallon's man slipped into the stockade is fastened beneath the oak table on the second floor."

Alon glanced over his shoulder at Diane. "Don't be afraid. We'll get through it. It's just another thing that we have to learn to do together."

Then they were standing only yards from Nalam. Diane tensed as she saw the almost hungry look on Nalam's face as he stared at Alon. "This is such a pleasant surprise," he said. "She didn't mention that she was going to invite you." He glanced at Diane. "But was it a surprise to her, too? I believe it might have been. She only mentioned Quinn." He turned to Joe. "I didn't mean to be rude. I've heard amazing things about you, but Alon and I have been so close. I can hardly believe we've been reunited. Have you missed me, Alon?"

"No, but I'm sure you missed me, so I thought I'd let Quinn take Kai back to see a doctor while I keep Diane company." He raised his brows. "If that's acceptable?"

"More than acceptable. I've had fantasies about having you here with me. I've even told Bart about a few of them."

Alon was no longer paying attention to him. He'd seen the stretcher and was staring down at Kai. "My God, what did you do to him?"

"Another surprise? She didn't show you the photo? I suppose she wanted to spare you. I'm rather glad that I got the benefit of your first glimpse of my handiwork."

Alon closed his eyes with agony. Then they were open again. "You did *nothing*," he said fiercely. "You took nothing. I'll get him back again. He'll be the same."

Nalam shrugged. "Nothing is permanently damaged. We were only toying with him. I had to keep him alive to lure you here."

Joe quickly stepped forward. "Let me get him out of here." He pulled up the blanket on Kai's terribly bruised body. "I'll take care of him, Alon." He glanced at Nalam and asked harshly, "Are you finished, Nalam?"

"No, but it's enough for now." He waved for him to go. "You don't seem to want to join our party, Quinn. But you've brought me Alon so I'll forgive you. Do be careful on this rocky ground. We wouldn't want Kai to be hurt any more than he is."

"He won't be hurt any more," Joe said coldly. "I'll see to that, Nalam." He started to swiftly wheel the stretcher away from the stockade toward the forest.

"A tad upset. He doesn't like having me in charge." Nalam opened the door wider. "Neither will you." He picked up an automatic weapon from the table beside the door and pointed it at Diane. "Both of you come in. Bart is waiting to do a weapon search." He leaned back against the wall, his gaze shifting to Alon as Bart's hands moved roughly over Diane's body. "I think we'll wait until we have you chained and a bit more helpless before we search you, Alon. I'd almost forgotten how intimidating you could be during those first days when you were being such a pain in my ass in Santa Monica. I can't tell you how often I wanted to have you at my disposal here at the stockade."

"Because you were a coward," Alon said. "You prefer to pick on the helpless."

"That's not cowardice, that's intelligence. The minute you knew I had your brother, you were helpless." He turned to Diane. "And now you're even more helpless since she brought you running to save her. What a lovely weapon you've given me." He took three steps forward and his fist lashed out and struck Diane in the stomach.

Pain.

She had no breath.

Her knees gave way as she fell to the floor.

He kicked her.

More pain.

She caught a fleeting glimpse of the anger on Alon's face.

No, that's what he wants. Don't let him see it.

She had her breath back now and she looked up at Nalam. "You think it bothers him to see me in pain? I'm nothing to him compared with Kai, and you've lost Kai. You made a bad trade, Nalam."

He glanced at Alon, but Alon's expression was now totally impassive.

He muttered a curse as he kicked her again. He grabbed her by the hair and jerked her head back to look into her face. "I didn't lose him," he said harshly. "Do you think I'd let them go that easily? I set Daniels to stalk Kai and Quinn. It's only a matter of time."

Fear jarred through her. "You're lying."

He laughed. "You know I'm not. But I'm not interested in Kai right now." He pointed his gun at her. "Bart, take Alon upstairs and chain him to the same wall where you had Kai. We'll make it a family affair. He won't give you any trouble—will you, Alon? Not as long as I have Diane here to punish."

Alon shrugged. "Why should I? It would be a waste of time. But she might be able to take more than you think. I guess we'll see." He moved toward the stairs. "Show me this wall you're bragging about it. I'll want to remember it, and what you did to Kai. Bring her along if you like."

Alon was taunting him, she realized suddenly. He was also positioning her, getting her ready to make the move he wasn't going to be able to do himself.

"I have your permission, you son of a bitch?" Nalam jerked Diane to her feet and shoved her up the steps. "I have every intention of doing that. She's not as hard as you. It will hurt her to see you suffer."

Diane deliberately stumbled and fell to her knees as they reached the second floor so that she could get her bearings.

It's fastened underneath the oak table.

The oak table was pushed against the far wall several yards from the cell into which Bart was pushing Alon. Nalam jerked Diane to her feet and shoved her toward that same cell.

She almost gagged at the foul smell of urine, sweat, and blood that pervaded the place. There were also streaks of blood on the gray walls to which Alon was being chained.

"That's Kai's blood. Will you remember this wall?" Nalam asked mockingly. "Tighten those chains a little, Bart." He released Diane and pushed her to the floor as he strode forward to strip Alon of his jacket and shirt. "Yes, now we have it. Hand me the whip, Bart." He looked at Diane. "Pay attention. I'm very good at this."

He struck Alon's bare chest with the whip!

She inhaled sharply. She could feel that pain herself. But it wasn't stopping. He began to stroke the whip across Alon's chest with his whole strength. Stinging, cutting the flesh. Over and over and over. Alon flinched but didn't scream.

"So strong. Do you know how I hate that strength?" Nalam said hoarsely. "But I'll break you. You'll scream. You'll beg me."

Alon was looking at Diane. He nodded imperceptibly.

Yes, it was time. Thank heavens. She didn't know how much more of this she could have taken.

She started to sob and got to her knees. "No, please. Don't do it. I can't take it anymore." All very true. "You're hurting him." And that was agonizingly true.

Nalam was laughing as he renewed the strokes. "This is better than I thought. I told you she was soft."

She covered her eyes with her hands. She was shrinking back toward the door. Make it hysterical. Let them think they had a hysterical woman on their hands, not an escapee. "Stop it! I can't watch it any longer." Then she jumped to her feet, jerked open the door, and ran!

"Get her, Bart!"

But she was halfway down the hall. Four more steps and she'd reached the oak table and was running her hand underneath. She grabbed the pistol as Bart's hand on her shoulder jerked her around to face him.

His eyes widened when he saw the gun in her hand. No time to think. She jabbed the muzzle of the gun into his stomach. "The keys to those chains."

He hesitated and then slowly handed her the key ring. She pointed to the floor. "Down."

He knelt but she could see that he was stiffening, getting ready to move on her. If he did, she'd be no match for him.

End it.

She lifted the gun and brought the butt down hard on his head!

He grunted and slid down to the floor.

Then she was moving back toward the cell. She no longer heard the sound of the whip. He must be coming to check to see if Bart had caught her. She moved to the side of the door and waited.

Nalam was coming through the door. "Bart, where the hell—"

She was standing in front of him. Her gun was pointed directly at his heart. "Don't move." She jerked his gun out of his hand. "I've been wanting to hurt you ever since I saw that photo of Kai. Watching what you did to Alon..." She shook her head. "Don't think I won't press this trigger."

"You can't do this to me, bitch," he hissed.

"It seems that I can." She kept the gun pointed at him as she nudged him back into the cell toward Alon.

"And exceptionally well," Alon said as she unlocked one of his chains and then handed him the key ring to unlock the other one. "Very good, Diane."

"Nothing was good about it. I didn't know what I was doing. I just did whatever I had to do to keep that bastard from whipping you. It was *killing* me."

"But your instincts always lead you in the right direction. I've told you that many times."

"Don't stand there bleeding and lecture me. Are you okay?"

"I'm more than okay. This is nothing. What's important is that we stopped him, Diane."

"You didn't stop me," Nalam snarled. "You only postponed it. No one stops me from doing what I want to do. I give the orders and it's done. Daniels will be back soon and he'll—"

"Daniels." She shoved Nalam's gun at Alon. "Do something with him. I've got to go warn Joe."

"I'll be right behind you. I'll just have to stop a minute on the way to release those other two prisoners on the third floor." Alon lifted Nalam's left arm and chained it to the wall. "I don't have time for you now, but you and Bart enjoy this stinking cell so much that I think you should share it. Where's Bart, Diane?"

"In the hall." She was heading down the stairs and looked back to see Alon dragging Bart into the cell and begin fastening him to the wall beside a cursing and screaming Nalam.

Justice, she thought. Alon had always had a gift for poetic justice. It was only a start, but it would have to do for now.

But she couldn't wait for him to finish. She was reaching for her phone to call Joe as she ran out of the stockade.

"I'll have to land here, Eve," Monteith said as he got off the phone after talking to Fallon. "The situation is very iffy down there. Fallon said Quinn didn't want anyone to tip his hand with Nalam while he was trying to get Kai out of the bastard's hands."

"Then take us down. The last thing I want to do is cause a misstep," Eve said. "I can see the stockade from here anyway. We can stay in the forest until it's safe for us to get closer. I just want to *see* him."

Catherine shook her head as she looked down at the forest. That wasn't all that Eve wanted. Catherine had never seen her more on edge, or she would never have left Michael to fly here. She leaned forward and put her hand on Eve's shoulder. "Have you tried to call him since we left Naponi?"

Eve shook her head. "And disturb him when he's in the middle of something? You heard Monteith. It's very iffy down there. But then I knew that. Michael couldn't have been more clear." Her teeth bit into her lower lip. "No, that's not true. He wasn't clear at all. That's what scared me. He kept saying he couldn't see it. It wasn't what it should be."

"But you've told me before that Michael isn't always sure about what he's seeing."

"Not like this. He knew, it just wasn't what it should be." She gestured impatiently. "Don't ask me. It was just wrong. And I have to get down there and see Joe."

And Catherine's interrogating Eve wasn't helping. *Just keep quiet and be there to support or help.* The helicopter was landing, and she waited until Eve got out before she jumped to the ground. They were at the foot of a good-size hill, and in the distance she could see what might be the tents where Monteith had first told them he wanted to land. She gazed around at the snow-covered ground and the steep pitch of the hill before she started after Monteith and Eve.

Monteith was talking on the phone and he turned to Eve. "Fallon said one of his sentries has spotted Joe. He's just entered the forest. He has the stretcher."

"Stretcher?" Eve asked.

Monteith hesitated. "Fallon said things hadn't gone according to plan."

"And my son said things are 'different,'" Eve said. "Same song, different chorus. May I go see Joe now?"

Monteith nodded. "No sign of pursuit. And they checked out the forest before." He was leading them quickly down a path. "Just do me a favor and let me control the moves?" He glanced at Catherine over his shoulder. "I got a call from Cameron just after we took off, and he's definitely not pleased about you being here."

"Tough," Catherine said curtly. "I'm not pleased that I haven't been able to get in touch with Diane or Joe, and that everyone appears to be walking on eggs about telling us what's going on."

"Drop it," Eve told her impatiently. "None of that matters. We'll find out as soon as I talk to Joe." She stopped, her gaze on the trail ahead. "And that will be soon. I see him up ahead..."

So did Catherine, and at first she was relieved. Joe appeared fine; he was standing in the middle of the trail talking on the phone to someone. A few yards away there was that mobile stretcher Monteith had mentioned. What the hell was that about?

Then the relief vanished in a heartbeat!

Joe dropped the phone, his body tense as his gaze flew around the path and the trees of the forest! "No!" He was suddenly electrified as he ran toward the stretcher. He dove forward and gave it a shove as a rifle bullet struck the stretcher's framework! Then Joe threw himself on top of the man on the stretcher, covering him with his body.

"Joe!" Eve was streaking down the path toward him even as two bullets tore into Joe's body. Monteith muttered a curse as he ran after her. "Eve, stay down!"

Catherine was jarred out of the horror. Eve wasn't going to do anything but run to Joe where that bullet had struck him down and try to save him. She just hoped Monteith was close enough behind her to keep her out of the line of fire. But Joe already had two bullets in his body, and that shooter was still out there.

She tried to focus on where Joe had been looking when he'd made that dive toward the stretcher.

The hill. He'd been looking up at the hill and caught a glimpse of something. Not something. Someone. She was already running toward the hill, her gaze searching the trees on the slope. Then she caught sight of the shooter. She recognized that rifle, she realized bitterly. Daniels's weapon of choice, and even as she watched, he was aiming it again. Two shots hadn't been enough? She'd reached the hill and was running up the back slope to try to get close enough to fire her gun.

Don't shoot. Don't you dare shoot him again, you bastard.

But Catherine heard the whistle of that rifle bullet only seconds later, and then Eve's cry of agony as that third bullet struck Joe.

Daniels was laughing, Catherine realized. There was a good chance his first two shots had killed Joe, and he should have been trying to get away. But he was enjoying this power trip too much to let it go. Even as she watched him reloading the rifle.

But she was close enough now. There was no hesitance, no regret, about taking this life. He was never going to fire that rifle again.

"Daniels."

He whirled to see Catherine standing there in the trees pointing her automatic weapon at him. His eyes widened in panic and he jerked his rifle up to aim it. He didn't have time.

"I wanted you to see it coming," Catherine said coldly.

She pressed the trigger and shot him in the head.

Then she was turning and running back down the hill toward the crowd now gathered around Joe's body lying on the ground. Eve was on her knees beside him trying desperately to stop the bleeding. Catherine fought her way through the crowd to fall to her knees beside Eve. "How is he?"

"I can't stop the bleeding," Eve said desperately. "And he has three rifle bullets in his upper body. How do you think he is?" She was putting pressure on the blood welling up from the wound above his heart. "Michael kept saying it. He kept talking about the blood. But he didn't know whose blood."

"Because it wasn't supposed to be Joe." Diane was running toward them. "It was supposed to be Alon who was going to be the one taking his brother to meet the emergency response plane. He insisted on switching places with Joe." She reached out and touched Joe's chest. "Oh, God. Joe..."

"What are you doing just sitting there moaning?" Eve said harshly. "You're a doctor, do something." She turned to Monteith. "You men get him inside one of those tents back there out of the weather." She ran along beside them, still putting pressure on Joe's wound. "Diane, grab my duffel and get in that tent with him. You've got work to do."

"I'm coming," Diane said as she grabbed the duffel and ran after her. "Keep up that pressure."

Catherine started after them and then stopped in shock beside the stretcher as she saw Kai's bruised and beaten body. A giant of a man who must be Alon was kneeling beside him, his face haggard with pain. "Is he all right?" she asked.

"No. But he will be. The plane with the medical team should be arriving here any minute." His hand was infinitely tender as he touched Kai's cheek. "Nalam did this to him. I should have killed him myself." He gathered Kai in his arms and carried him as if he were a child toward one of the tents.

Nalam, she thought. He'd been talking about Nalam and the monstrous things he'd done to the boy. The monstrous things he'd done to everyone. She called after Alon, "Is Nalam still in the stockade?"

He stopped at the tent and looked back at her. "Yes."

"Are all the prisoners out?"

He nodded and then smiled as he saw her expression. "Yes." He ducked into the tent with his brother.

Catherine took out her phone and dialed Cameron. "Blow it!"

"*Yes*," Cameron bit back. "On the way!"

Catherine turned and quickly hurried to the tent where they'd taken Joe.

They'd already stripped off Joe's clothes, and Diane was examining him. Eve was kneeling motionless, one hand clasping Joe's, the other knotted into a fist. He was so still, Catherine thought. Pale and still, and there was a trickle of blood coming out of that wound.

"Is there anything I can do?" she whispered.

Diane didn't look up. "Kai."

"Alon is taking care of him."

Kaboom!

The explosion shook the earth beneath their feet.

"And I took care of that other problem you left undone," Catherine said.

"Good." Diane braced herself and then turned to Eve. "But that's the only thing that's good. I can't be sure of anything without X-rays, but he's lost a hell of a lot of blood and there has to be organ damage. I don't know how much time he has left, Eve."

Eve's gaze never left Joe's face. "He's not going to die," she said fiercely. "I won't let him. *You* won't let him." Her gaze shifted to Diane's face. "Don't give me excuses. I didn't come here for you to tell me that. Michael kept saying over and over that you couldn't do anything because you didn't have your bag, that you'd been afraid to take it here because you couldn't let Nalam get his hands on it. There must have been a reason for him to tell me that." She threw her hand out in the direction of her duffel. "So I brought it, dammit. Now *do* something. Because Joe's *not* going to die."

Diane stiffened, her gaze flying to Eve's duffel. "You brought it?" She crawled over and unzipped it. "You brought it! Thank God." She pulled out her medical bag and turned to Eve. "You want me to do something? Well, maybe you don't. Because I wouldn't have time to do the same kind of painstaking procedures that I performed on those nine patients I managed to save. All I can do is give him the same type of injection that I took when I was experimenting on myself. It might repair damage, it might make it worse, or it might only buy me time so that I can go in and work on those wounds. I don't even know what the response down the line might be because I can't judge how much damage he's suffered." She paused. "I could kill him, Eve."

"But you keep talking about time," Eve said. "He's going to die if you don't do something. Isn't that right?"

"Unless there's a miracle."

Eve didn't speak for a moment. "I believe in miracles. Joe and I have had quite a few of those in our marriage." She was silent again. "But maybe that bullet of yours is a miracle, too. I believed it was when we first started out. And Michael must have felt it was, or he wouldn't have kept talking about you and that damn bag." She turned back to Joe and took his hand again. "Give him the injection. I'd rather blame you than God anyway."

Diane nodded jerkily. "Feel free. I accepted that responsibility when I started down this road." She opened her bag and said over her shoulder to Catherine, "Go talk to Monteith and tell him to get me a portable X-ray machine. I'm not going to be able to move Joe until he's stabilized, and I want to see what the hell I'm doing to him."

TWELVE HOURS LATER

Catherine crept into the tent and tapped Eve on the shoulder. "Coffee," she whispered as she handed her the cup. "Why am I whispering? He's not conscious yet, is he?"

Eve shook her head. "But I think he stirred the last time Diane changed his bandages." She sipped the coffee. "And she gave him another injection after she removed that bullet in his hip." She looked at Diane, curled up beside Joe's cot. "That's where I want to be. I want to be close to him in case he—" She stopped. "But that's not going to happen. We haven't lost him yet. We're not going to lose him. And it's better if Diane is there beside him. She has to monitor him all the time. I *want* her there."

"I tried to give Diane a cup of coffee the last time I came in, but she wouldn't take it." Catherine sat down on the floor beside Eve. "She's doing a great job, isn't she, Eve?"

"A fantastic job. He's *alive.* I just have to be patient and I'll have him back." She closed her eyes for a moment and repeated as if it was a mantra, "I just have to be patient. It's so *hard*, Catherine."

"I know." She paused. "I called Michael like you asked me to do and told him that you were busy with Joe and would call him later. He said he knew; that he could feel you here."

"That's why I wanted you to call him—I thought I could feel him here, too. I wanted to make sure he knew I was thinking about him." She tensed as she saw Diane suddenly get to her feet and bend over Joe's cot. Was something wrong?

Then Diane was motioning Eve to come, and she flew across the tent. "What's wrong?"

Diane shook her head. "I think he's trying to open his eyes, and I know it isn't me he wants to see." She gave Eve a gentle push. "Your turn. I could only do so much."

Joe's lids were blinking, trying to open. Eve bent over him, her lips brushing his cheek.

"Eve?" His voice was hoarse, but his eyes were now open. "I missed . . . you. Where . . . have . . . you been?"

"I've been right here. You're the one who was off saving the planet, Superman."

"It . . . didn't feel . . . like that." He was drifting off. "You were . . . gone. I . . . was . . . lonely. Don't do . . . it again . . ."

"You won't be able to get rid of me." But she could see that he was asleep again. She still stayed there for an instant more. *Thank you, God.*

Then she jumped to her feet, turned to Diane, and gave her a tremendous hug. "And thank you, Diane." She whirled her in a circle. "He's going to be okay, isn't he? You saved him!"

"I hope so." Diane was smiling. "But we don't know quite what I did to him. We'll have to see. He'll have to go through zillions of tests."

"And he'll hate it. But I'll save you from him."

"Will you?" she asked dryly. "That's very good of you, considering."

"Considering what a patchy history we have?" Eve's voice was suddenly husky. "Or considering that you saved the man I love and I'll be grateful to you for the rest of my life? The one erases the other, so we'll have to start building a new relationship." She gave her another hug. "Think about it. I'm a little too giddy right now to do it myself." She whirled back to Joe and knelt beside the bed. "All I want to do is think about Joe and be here for him."

"I can see that." For an instant Diane sounded a little wistful; then she said brusquely, "By all means, concentrate on cementing your relationship with Joe. When the testing begins, I'm going to need all the help I can get."

"You're wonderful. Congratulations!" Catherine was suddenly beside Diane. "We're all grateful to you. Joe means a lot to us." She took her arm and gently pulled her toward the tent door. "Now that he's over the first hurdle, why don't you come to the mess tent and get something to eat? Eve will take care of him."

Diane glanced back at Eve and Joe for only an instant. Then she stared straight ahead. "That sounds good. I'm hungry." She walked out of the tent and didn't look back. "Yes, I can always count on Eve taking care of him."

TWO DAYS LATER

"Diane says you're being difficult." Eve sailed into the tent and stooped to give Joe a kiss before she tossed the bag she was carrying on the bottom of his cot. "Stop it. She's been magnificent and doesn't deserve you being this crabby."

"She's had an easy job of it," he growled. "I'm feeling fine. But every time I wake up and try to ask her questions, she either starts giving me one of those tests or gives me a shot to put me back to sleep. I'm not going to put up with this, Eve."

"Yes, you are." She dragged a camp chair close to his cot. "Though she says tomorrow she's transferring you to a hospital in Boise until she's ready to release you. You'll be more comfortable there. She needs more sophisticated equipment for the final tests, and she's thinking of bringing in one of the doctors who examined her in Hong Kong for a consultation."

"No," he said flatly. "I've had enough."

"Actually, the question is if you've had more than enough." She sat down in the camp chair. "And that's what we're trying to find out. Okay, I know you must be frustrated. I'm glad to see it. It means you're even better than I hoped. Two days ago you were almost dead, Joe."

He shook his head. "I'm fine. I don't need all these drugs she's giving me."

She made an impatient gesture. "I'll get to that. Part of your frustration is that you wanted your questions answered? Cameron blew the stockade on the day that Daniels shot you. For the past couple of days he's had cleanup crews up here removing any evidence that the stockade, Nalam, and Kai's jailer, Bart, ever existed. The rest of Nalam's crew appears to have vanished to the four winds."

"Kai?" Joe asked. "He was in bad shape."

She nodded. "Alon had a doctor go over him that first day, and his condition wasn't life threatening. Alon thought he'd be better off with him at Hakali Island."

"And Adam Madlock, our presidential commander in chief?" Joe asked caustically. "Any news about him?"

"He's still out garnering campaign publicity and photo ops. So Diane might have been wrong about him. Or maybe he was Daniels's next target." She tilted her head. "Any other questions? Satisfied?"

"No. Back to square one. Why can't I get out of here and go home?"

She hesitated. "I told you after you woke up that second time that Diane had to give you several shots of the tri-root liquid that she'd synthesized. It was the only way she could keep you alive."

"And she did it. Good for her. I still want to go home."

"Stubborn..." She shook her head. "You can't do it yet. It appears there are some changes manifesting in your body, and we have to identify them and make sure we know what's happening."

"Happening?" he repeated warily.

She took a deep breath. "Principally cellular, but also muscular and physical. She said the same thing is happening in your body that happened in hers after those experiments."

"And that is?"

"You're not only healing at an unusually fast rate, but there appears to be cell renewal, and you're getting physically stronger."

He thought about it. "I don't see a downside here." His smile was suddenly mischievous. "Particularly if it applies to sexual performance. Does it?"

"Joe." She threw back her head and laughed. "I have no idea. We'll have to experiment."

"That's a given." He took her hand and brought it to his lips. "Now I really want to go home."

"You're not taking this seriously."

"I'll leave that up to Diane. She's altogether too serious about all these tests and their ramifications. All I want to do is live my life as if every minute will be my last."

"Wonderful philosophy," Diane said dryly as she came into the tent. "But I always like a forewarning when my patients might draw their last breath. Since I gave you a new lease on life, I intend to make sure you're going to stick around for a long, long time. The tests continue, Joe."

"You're getting very bossy." He was suddenly serious. "But I might put up with it for a little longer. I'm damn grateful to you. I wouldn't want you to look bad if you decide to write me up in one of your scientific papers. I'll give you another two days."

"You'll give me a lot longer than that," Diane said. "I've gotten very tired of you giving both me and Eve a hard time. I've brought in reinforcements."

Eve suddenly chuckled.

"What are you laughing about, Eve?" Joe glanced back at Diane. "Reinforcements?"

"I sent Catherine back to Naponi to pick up Michael. He's very grateful to me, too. I explained my problem and he's very eager *and* determined to make sure that you have a full recovery. He can keep you company while I'm doing the testing." She went back to the door and called, "We're ready for you, Michael. Your dad can't wait to see you!"

EPILOGUE

BOISE GENERAL HOSPITAL
THREE WEEKS LATER

It's the president!" Catherine burst into Joe's hospital room, where Diane was checking Joe's chart. "The arrogant bastard is down in the lobby making one of his public appearances that's supposed to endear him to the masses. There are Secret Service agents all over the hospital trying to interrogate the doctors about Joe . . . and you, Diane. Lots of questions about his attending physician."

"Then I think it's time Joe was discharged, don't you?" Diane grinned at Joe. "I know you think it's past time. You've been very patient."

"You bet I have." He scowled. "I know you said you had to have all this hospital apparatus to check me out, but I should have been out of here days ago. What's the good of you finding out if I'm strong as Hercules if I have to lie in bed all day?"

"Hush." Eve was helping him into his bathrobe and grabbing his slippers and clothes from the closet. "I wanted her to do it. I didn't want any surprises popping up in a month or two." She was pulling him toward the adjoining hospital room. "Now be quiet and get dressed so I can smuggle you out of this place." She glanced at Diane. "Still the same plan?"

Diane nodded. "Catherine's made all the arrangements to get the three of you out of town and back to Naponi. She'll let you know when it's safe to go back to the Lake Cottage." She glanced at Catherine. "You have Michael in the car?"

She nodded. "He's with Slade. He thinks all this commotion is cool. Slade will pick us up at the delivery dock entrance." She hesitated. "Are you sure you don't want to come with us? I don't trust Adam Madlock any farther than I can throw him. Everyone knows he cheated during the last election. He's almost as much a slimeball as Nalam was."

"And he was asking for Joe's attending physician." Diane nodded thoughtfully. "Madlock may be a crooked politician, but no one can say he's stupid. I want to talk to him and see how much of a threat he is." She smiled as she saw Catherine's frown. "Stop worrying. I've learned how to cover my tracks." She tore off the info on Joe's chart and gave it to Catherine. "No one is going to find any records in this hospital that will cause me or Joe problems. Now get them out of here. I'll let you know if I need a rescue." She sat back down in her chair. "Go!"

Catherine was still frowning as she ran out the door. "I'll check back with you later..."

Of course she would, Diane thought. Because that was Catherine. She would always be there if needed.

"Dr. Connors? Delightful to meet you!" Adam Madlock's booming voice preceded him into the room, and so did two discreetly dressed Secret Service agents. Then he made his appearance and his famous smile lit up his equally famous regular features. He gestured for the agents to leave them, then crossed the room and took her hand. "I was so glad that you've been taking care of a hero like Detective Joe

Quinn. I understand that he tracked down some information that might have saved my life. I've been a bit ill myself lately, but once I recovered, I felt I had to come and thank him. You wouldn't know how he stumbled on that information, would you?"

"How could I, Mr. President?" She dropped his hand as soon as she could. "I'm a doctor, not a detective or a politician."

"Yes, I know. Actually, I heard about you recently from an old friend of mine, Joshua Nalam, who recently passed on. What a pity. He was excited and was telling me quite interesting things about you. He was drunk at the time and he was raving about what a threat you were to both of us."

"*Both* of you?"

"We did a few deals together, but naturally I never considered that we were partners." He chuckled. "And he lacked imagination, particularly when he mentioned you. He considered you a threat, but I thought if what he said was true, you'd be an asset."

"He didn't impress me as being a particularly truthful person. You did well to take what he said with a grain of salt."

"But it was such a fascinating concept. I was just about to explore what he'd told me when I became distracted by a charming new toy he tossed at me." He threw up his hand dramatically. "And then my good friend disappeared and is now presumed dead. One never knows, does one? I thought about bringing all my presidential powers to bear on discovering what happened to him, but I decided sometimes it's better to just leave things alone. I really don't want our relationship to be thought anything but a close friendship. Everyone is telling me how well I'm holding up during this mourning period. My aides say it will show how empathetic I am during the next election campaign." He smiled. "But I did want to stop in and tell Quinn how grateful I am that he let my Secret Service know about that spot of indigestion I was about to have. We have a few questions to ask him." He glanced around the room. "But I see I've missed him. Another time?"

"I'm sure it was a leak and he knows nothing else about it. I'd forget it if I were you."

"I never forget anything unless it suits me." He smiled. "And you can be sure I won't forget you, Dr. Connors. I'll make sure we'll meet again." He turned and strode toward the door. "Do give Detective Quinn my thanks if you happen to see him."

"I won't see him." But she didn't know if he heard her through the bustle of his departure down the hall with his entourage.

She didn't move for a moment as she allowed the words he'd spoken to sink in. Not good. There was a chance that Madlock might become an even greater threat than Nalam had been. She'd told Joe they had to try to save the president, but she was beginning to believe she might regret that gesture.

She leaned back, her mind going over anything and everything she could do to keep this new development from turning out to be a disaster.

Then she slowly reached out for her phone to make a call.

HAKALI ISLAND
SIX MONTHS LATER

"No!" Catherine jumped out of the motorboat and strode down the pier toward Cameron, who was waiting for her. "Hell, no! I'm not letting this happen. You're not going to get away with it. Where's your free-choice philosophy now, Cameron? Diane got cornered and you just scooped her up and snatched her away. Where is she? I need to talk to her."

"And she needs to talk to you." He smiled. "She's at the office Alon set up for her at the big house. I told her I'd bring you to her as soon as I got a chance to have my say. I figured that after all my extensive efforts on her behalf, she owed me that much."

"You practically kidnapped her. It's been *six* months. After I left her at the hospital, she just disappeared with only that note telling us not to trust Madlock and that she'd be in touch."

"And she *is* in touch," he said quietly. "She just had to let me handle it. It would have been dangerous if she'd left any clues. You're right, she disappeared, and I'm an expert at doing that successfully. But I didn't 'snatch' her. She called me and asked a favor. She said she had to fall off the face of the earth and would I make it happen?" He shrugged. "But she also said that it was only until she finished her work and I could arrange a safe way for her to negotiate any traps set by Madlock while she gradually released the tri-root results. Not an easy agenda."

She went still. "But you agreed to it?"

He nodded. "I told you that she was a special case. But she's been very demanding. She not only wanted me to meet all her specifications, but she chose where I was to hide her." He gestured to the beauty of the island surrounding them. "Paradise. She was worried about Kai and wanted a chance to work with him. It's a good thing that Alon's island is so completely remote from civilization."

"How is Kai?"

"Better. Not entirely well; he still has an occasional nightmare. But he smiles and sometimes jokes, and he likes being with Alon." He tilted his head and was smiling again himself. Those beautifully shaped lips, the warmth, the sexuality... "So do you believe that I've done as well as I could for Diane?"

He knew she did. He must sense her relief that she wasn't going to have to fight him on this. Fighting was the last thing she wanted to do with him. It had been far too long since she had seen him. She nodded. "But it depends what you do next. It would be very hard for anyone to leave paradise. Are you going to be tempted to persuade her to stay?"

He shook his head ruefully. "You're very tough, Catherine. What do I have to do to please you?"

"Well, I'm certainly not going to let you have sole jurisdiction here. After she finishes the bullet, it's still going to be difficult getting rid of Madlock. I don't know if I can trust you to do it alone."

"I realize it's difficult for you to trust me," he said solemnly. "It might take me a long time to earn it."

"That's what I was thinking." She frowned, as if considering. "I should probably come and check on you periodically."

"What a wonderful idea."

"And as far as pleasing me is concerned, you have no problem there, Cameron. Not now. Not ever." She smiled as she started walking toward him. "And paradise isn't a bad place to start."

NAPONI
FOUR MONTHS LATER

"Michael asked if he could have a horse," Eve said as she cuddled closer to Joe on the porch swing. "He said we already had a stable, so he'd have a comfortable house to live in. Actually, I was expecting it before this." Her gaze shifted to Michael, who was sitting on the bank of the lake, staring up at the mountains. The sun was going down and the peaks were ablaze with scarlet and gold color. "He's settled in beautifully, but he might be a little lonely without his friends. What do you think?"

"I think he's putting out probes to see what response he'll get," Joe said quietly. "Just like his mom." His lips brushed her temple. "And I think that it's time you stopped watching me and started asking questions."

"Okay." She looked up at him. "We've been happy here, but it's not really home. Though you did everything you could to make it resemble it. You even built this porch swing for me. You've kept yourself busy every minute of the day with repairs and spending time with Michael."

"And?"

"I *have* been watching you. At first, it was because I didn't want you to overdo it since you were just out of the hospital. But then I stopped worrying about that because I realized you weren't trying to be a world-class handyman." She paused. "You were testing yourself."

"You didn't say anything."

"I was waiting for you to talk to me. You didn't do it."

"I had some thinking to do." He made a face. "And I didn't want to worry you. I should have known."

"Yes, you should." She sat up and moved a little away from him. "And now I'm asking you those questions. I suppose you were seeing what effect Diane's bullet had on you as time passed?"

He nodded. "I began to feel better and better. I felt more energy than I've ever experienced, and it's not as if I ever lacked energy."

"That's for sure," she said dryly. "I've barely been able to keep up with you and Michael when you're normal. Increased energy. What else?"

"The strength factor almost doubled. My body adjusts perfectly to heat and cold without any problem and maintains it. Vision seems much sharper, and so does my hearing. Then there's always the possibility of increase in longevity, but all I can tell right now is that I feel like I did when I was in my twenties. That's about it, so far."

"That's a hell of a lot." She was trying to smile. "But you left out sexual stamina. I've been appreciating that since the second month we got up here."

He grinned. "So have I." He leaned forward and kissed her. "But that's always been perfect anyway."

She nodded. "Who am I to argue with Superman?"

His smile faded. "Argue all you please. That's what this is all about. What are you holding back?"

She looked away from him. "You've called Diane several times since you've been here. Why?"

"I wanted to make sure my progress was entirely normal." He paused. "And if I should expect anything else? The answer to the first was yes. The answer to the second wasn't as satisfactory. She doesn't know. She said we're breaking new ground, and our bodies are changing, perfecting themselves. But she didn't know what that really meant."

"She couldn't even tell you if you're going to fly, Superman?"

"No way. You're joking, but it's really not funny. I like my life just the way it is. Even with all the turmoil and chaos, it's damn near perfect." He hesitated again. "But not entirely. The longer I lived with all these changes, the more I could see possible problems emerging. That's why I didn't talk to you right away about it. Like I said, I wanted to think about it. And I had another question I had to ask Diane first."

"What question?" she asked warily.

"I asked her if there was any way she could reverse the work she did on me."

"What?" She stared at him in shock. "Why on earth would you want to do that? You'd be crazy even to think about it."

"Easy." His hand was caressing her cheek. "It was just a question. I think I already knew the answer. She said the process was so radical that it might kill me if I tried to undo her work. That someday in the future she might be able to figure out a way to do it, but it was doubtful."

"And I bet she probably called you an idiot," Eve said. "Didn't she?"

"Words to that effect." He nodded wryly. "She was insulted that I'd dare to mess with her handiwork. I had to explain to her, too."

"You haven't explained anything to me yet."

"I'm about to. Give me a chance." He added quietly, "I know that I should be grateful for what I've been given, and I am. But I didn't have a choice whether to accept or refuse. The two of you were determined to save my life, and you did. The panacea was just a fantastic prize thrown in for good measure."

"You're saying you wouldn't have accepted it?" she asked blankly.

"Of course I would. But I didn't have the choice," he said gently. "And I don't want to live into the next century if I have to do it without you. I'd just as soon have the same life span as everyone else. As for the rest, I got along just fine without all the bells and whistles. That would be my choice, if I couldn't have you."

"Oh, for God's sake, Joe." For an instant she could only stare at him. Then she threw herself into his arms and held on to him with all her strength. She could feel the tears running down her cheeks. "That's quite a gesture. I'm sure Diane was impressed."

"I don't think so. She was swearing at me and calling me a melodramatic fool who couldn't see the simplest solution to the problem." He pushed her away and looked down into her eyes. "But it's not that simple. She's right—it's new territory. What if something goes wrong with her bullet? Or what if the future isn't what you'd want it to be? These last years haven't been all that great for any of us. We don't know what's ahead. I didn't have a choice. But you do, Eve. You have to be sure when taking a step like that."

So protective he was even trying to save her from herself? She couldn't believe it. Yes, she could, and how she loved him for it. She went back into his arms. "Diane is right, you are a fool," she said brokenly. "When did you decide I might be afraid to face anything that the world could throw at me if we were together? I knew the night she gave you that panacea that she was actually giving it to both of us. It was only a matter of time before I would have gone to her and told her to make her promise good. We talked about miracles that night, and I told her I believed her panacea could be a miracle for you. And it was." She held him tighter and whispered, "It *was*, Joe. But we don't need any silver bullet to get us through any tough times ahead. We'll make our own way just as we always do, and it will be good because we have love and family and friends. It might be here, or at the Lake Cottage, or Hakali Island, or even Cameron's Shangri-La. It won't matter, Joe. None of it will matter."

"No, it won't." His eyes were glittering moistly as he stroked her cheek with a feather-light touch. He kissed her and then suddenly chuckled. "But what might matter is that Diane was very annoyed, and she told me that she was coming here to straighten me out."

"What?" Eve was taken aback in surprise. "When?"

"When did she say it? Or when was she coming? I talked to her two evenings ago." He looked at his watch. "And I expect that Monteith will be bringing her anytime now."

"Today?"

He nodded, and his eyes were twinkling. "I was fully intending to be noble, but I was hoping I wouldn't have to be."

"You knew what I'd say. But it's not like you to drag her from that island where she's safe just to convince you what an idiot you were."

"I didn't drag her, she was ready. I think she's regarding this trip as a chance to tie up loose ends before she gets too busy." He added quietly, "She finished the final formula on the bullet last week. It doesn't mean that she's not going to have to go back to the island and hide out. But it does mean that she'll have to start the process of getting the bullet approved and into the right hands for production. Which also means that she'll have to be traveling back and forth to do it."

Eve frowned. "I don't like it. President Madlock is probably still waiting to pounce."

"Cameron hasn't been standing still. I'm sure he has plans to rid her of that particular threat." When he saw she was still frowning, he said, "Stop worrying. When Slade isn't with her, Alon Hakali will be. And I can't imagine Catherine not being somewhere in the mix."

Neither could Eve, and she was beginning to feel better. "And you too, Superman?"

"You never can tell. You have to admit we've both been a little bored since we've been here." His gaze shifted to Michael down at the lake. "But at least I didn't ask you to get me a horse as Michael did."

"We'll have to tell him that Diane is coming." Eve got to her feet and headed toward the lake. "He'll be excited. He was talking about her the other—" She whirled to face Joe, who had followed her. "Michael!"

He nodded. "We can't make his choice for him, either."

"I know that. But if Diane's in a mood to tie up loose ends, she might decide that she should make it for him. She was obviously pretty upset with you."

"We won't let her."

"Maybe we should explain it to him ourselves so that she can't influence him."

"Explain it to him?" He was looking beyond her at Michael, who had just gotten to his feet and was staring up at the sky. "How can you be sure he doesn't know already?"

She turned and saw Michael running toward them. "The helicopter is coming, Mom!" he was shouting. "It's right over the ridge. Diane's almost here and she wants to see all of us. Why didn't you tell me she was coming?"

"Your dad forgot to mention it. I told him you'd be excited." She took his hand and looked down at his face. He was flushed and his eyes were shining with vitality, joy, and eagerness. "And you are," she said softly. "Is this going to be a good visit, Michael?"

"Sure. Why wouldn't it be?" Then he looked into her eyes and all the joy was still there, but there was also that strange knowing that was always with him, as he tried to answer the other question she hadn't asked. "It's going to be fine. We're together, aren't we?"

Eve's other hand tightened on Joe's. Michael's words almost echoed what she had told Joe a little while ago. Life was zooming toward them at full force again. All the peace and serenity of these months would be gone soon. Adventure, danger, difficulties, and excitement were right there on the horizon, and she must reach out to them because they were all part of life. She looked up at the helicopter that had just come over the ridge and was bringing that life to all of them. She raised her chin with a touch of defiance. *Come at me. I'm ready for you. We'll make the best of anything you throw at us.* "You're absolutely right, Michael." She smiled down at him. "That makes all the difference. We're together, and everything will be fine."

ABOUT THE AUTHOR

Iris Johansen is the #1 *New York Times* bestselling author of more than 30 consecutive bestsellers. Her series featuring forensic sculptor Eve Duncan has sold over 20 million copies and counting and was the subject of the acclaimed Lifetime movie *The Killing Game*. Along with her son Roy, Iris has also co-authored the *New York Times* bestselling series featuring investigator Kendra Michaels. Johansen lives near Atlanta, Georgia. Learn more at:

IrisJohansen.com
Twitter @Iris_Johansen
Facebook.com/OfficialIrisJohansen